Hi Deena, I just met your wonderful mother who has filled me in on your progress! Two children ad in Florida! How wonderful. I can still see your beautiful eyes! Take care dear one. Love to all me when you come home! Carolyn

The Green Drake

a novel by C. B. Johnson

To a person with a fly rod, no hatch is more revered than that of the Green Drake. Voices of American trout fishermen take on a tone of awe when they recount past experiences when they had caught the hatch 'just right.'

If the hatch is a strong one, the most wily of trout will come up to take their fill, and the experienced dry-fly fisherman is guaranteed something to brag about in his creel.

Indeed, the green drake hatch is so special that many trips are planned in an attempt to 'hit it this year.'

Erin McCort and Ted Weaver are just as special, just as rare!

W9-CZV-784

***The Green Drake* is a work of fiction.**

The author is not a medical expert and intends that no individual act on fictional medical technique found in the text.

All characters are purely fictional. The author neither has known nor knows of any individual who was the basis for their development.

The towns are real, as are some locations; however, all are used fictitiously. The Pine Creek Gorge is famous among fishermen. Sadly there is no Sally Ann's; every town should have one.

The actions and histories of all characters existed only in the author's imagination regardless of whether they were engaged in historic or fictional events.

* * *

Copyright 2006 by C. B. Johnson
TXu1-311-036
Cover photo and line drawing of green drake by R. N. Johnson

All rights are reserved and held by the author and Sigurd Press.
This book, or parts thereof, may not be reproduced in any form, for any purpose, whether for profit or not for profit, without written permission of the author.

* * *

First paperback edition 2007 by Johnson's SIGURD PRESS
12652 Maysville-Williams Rd.; Logan, Ohio 43138
Printed in the United States of America by Morris Publishing
ISBN numbers 978-0-9795635-0-8 & 0-9795635-0-x
Library of Congress Control Number: 2007904399

* * *

An order form is on the last page.

Dedicated
To:
Ellsworth and Ann (Bill) Biggs
and
Sigurd and Lucy Johnson
who, like Emma and Rowdy, gave us the best of themselves.

To:
Robert N. Johnson for introducing me to the art of fly-fishing and for his
unwavering support for this project

To:
Martha Serio, who wouldn't let me give up when I hit a wall.

To:
My former students who contributed much more to my life than
they will ever know.

No day spent in nature is ever wasted!

**A fly rod, a good dog,
and quiet time without outside influence
invite peace.**

People heal on the water!

1

Friday, June 7, 2002

The white Land Rover pulled in beside their slightly dusty black Suburban.

Max automatically glanced over to see if he recognized anyone. He didn't, so his eyes returned to Ted who had a royal coachman on the line just now.

The line glistened in the late afternoon sun as Ted expertly moved it forward and rearward in a false cast.

With one minor adjustment, Ted directed the line to the spot where he had noted the last rise. A straight flash of yellow cut gently down to the water-darkened stream bed; the coachman barely had time to kiss the surface of the water as the trout rose, mouth open, to suck it in.

Max turned back and, frankly, stared at the little girl and the woman as they got out and walked toward a picnic table.

It was the little girl who most interested him.

Something wasn't right. They didn't laugh or wave to anyone in the stream. They didn't even talk between themselves. And the way the little girl moved was all wrong: not skipping ahead or holding the woman's hand while pulling off in some counter direction, yet she wasn't on crutches or anything.

She moved, not in a forced march exactly, but surely dutifully. There was no limp or stumble, but almost the movement of a very tired older man.

Max's brow furrowed in thought. *How old would she be? Seven or eight; thin, with porcelain skin and dark red hair controlled in two tightly-braided pigtails.*

The little girl went to a picnic table. She sat facing the stream with the afternoon sunlight on her back, just sat, breathing deeply for a while. She had carried a small, clear satchel containing a coloring book and crayons, but she did not remove them.

Max frowned. *Is she blind? ... Could she actually be*

identifying the stream by its smell?

All streams have an identifying odor to them if one has a good nose.

After a glance from the woman, the little girl opened her coloring book and the box of crayons, but she did not begin to color. Instead she just stared blankly towards the stream, stared with that half-dazed, faraway look one has when recalling a scene from the past rather than recording the present one.

She didn't appear to notice the mixture of wildflowers and weeds that grew along the bank. She did, however, look up and smile when a jay took offense at an intruder.

She can hear.

She began to chew her lip and took a deep breath.

The blond woman, also thin and pale where the makeup didn't cover, glanced at the little girl and forced a long breath. She fumbled in her purse for a pack of cigarettes. She selected one, inhaled deeply on her first draw, and moved her attention back to the little girl.

I knew better than to make this stupid trip. I need to trust my own instincts.

Suddenly there was life in the little girl's voice, excitement, a trace of happiness; all hesitation was gone: "Look, mommy, a green drake!"

Max looked around the scene too. The sun, at the cusp of its descent, was casting long, warm shadows on the now glistening surface of Pine Creek, and, sure enough, a hatch was beginning. *She can see.*

Ted gathered his line slowly then turned toward the picnic table, a broad smile on his face and a twinkle in his intensely blue eyes. He stepped up onto the bank and looked, through the rays of the sun, directly at the little girl. "How did a young princess like you learn to name the hatch?"

He was walking toward them, the smile still on his face, the sun in his eyes, so he did not see what Max noted: the quiver of the little chin and the single tear which began to make its way down her cheek as she looked toward her toes and quietly replied, "My Daddy taught me."

Ted also failed to notice the change in tone. He glanced

at the Land Rover and then at the thin blond sharing the picnic table as he continued toward them. *Dad must be sorting gear.* He smiled to himself. *It'll get good in a little while. He has great timing.*

"Then your daddy must be an old streamwalker like me." Again he checked for a wave from the rear of the Rover.

"He was . . . until he died. . . . My Daddy is dead; he was killed," she whispered coarsely.

Ted was close enough this time. He heard the ache in the tiny, empty voice, and his quick eyes caught the moisture on her cheek. The friendly twinkle in his eyes was replaced with concern. He quickened his pace toward the two.

After four strides he was on one knee five feet from the child. "I'm . . . I'm so sorry; . . . I . . . I feel ashamed that I didn't know." He turned to make eye contact with the thin blond woman. "I am so very sorry."

She looked toward Erin. *Why in the world can't people just leave us alone? How can we be strong when everyone wants to dish out pity like it's ice cream readying to melt in front of us? . . . Sorry! Stupid bastards, that's what they all are, just clods trying to make themselves feel better or, worse still, trying to make themselves somehow useful!*

She dropped the cigarette and ground it under her foot, wishing she were grinding the damn do-gooders of the world.

When the cigarette was thoroughly pulverized, she glanced at Ted. *Oh, well, why make a scene? It isn't worth the energy; he'd never understand anyway.*

She drew a long breath. "There was no way for you to know."

The woman made a distinctly cold, somehow distant, eye contact with Ted. "Erin wanted to come, and the all-knowing psychologist thought it might help."

Ted rose and extended his hand; a warm smile sat on his face. "I'm Ted Weaver. I, . . . ah, . . . I teach English and coach baseball at the local high school. Summer vacations I freelance as a fishing guide here in the gorge and the streams around her. I am truly sorry that I misspoke."

The smile sat there on his handsome, tanned face; the

sincere eyes fought for meaningful contact.

Silence reigned.

Ted could almost feel a coolness enter the air space between them. *What the hell?*

Finally the woman looked directly at him. "Laura Barnsworth McCort."

She glanced toward the girl, "My daughter Erin."

Ted, feeling the dismissal, allowed his hand to drop.

But Erin, who had been looking at Max sitting in the rear of the Suburban, turned toward Ted and extended her tiny hand along with a smile. "Hello, Mr. Weaver. Is that your dog?"

Ted took her hand in his, careful not to apply much pressure, "He sure is, Erin. Would you like to meet him?"

"Oh, yes! My grandpa had a dog. I loved him!" Erin began twisting around on the seat of the picnic table.

"Well, come on. I'm sure Max would like to meet you."

Ted allowed his right hand to fall to his side as they started toward the Suburban and was pleasantly surprised when the little hand encircled his two outside fingers.

Then, just as quickly as it had joined, it disjoined, and Erin said quietly, "Sorry."

As they paused beside the Suburban, Ted quieted the questions bombarding his brain. He kept an easy smile on his face and opened the side door.

Only two parts of Max's body moved, his head and his tail. His brown eyes danced as his mouth opened in a smile, and his tail moved side to side on the seat.

"At ease, Max. Come on out and meet Miss Erin McCort."

Max stepped down, tail wagging, eyes dancing with love. He went to Ted's left side and sat at heel. The still-wagging tail swept the sandy soil of the angler's park.

"At ease, Max."

Max and Erin met halfway, each doing his best to show delight in the meeting. Max sat as Erin reached for his chest and then rubbed behind his jowls.

Both Ted and Max were surprised at her care. *This little girl has been around a dog before.*

The fact that she did not bong Max on top of his head earned her three quick Labbie kisses: two on the arm, the last on her cheek which earned Max a full-fledged giggle and a hug. "Oh, mommy! Isn't he great? He's just like Rowdy."

"Erin!" The voice was shrill and harsh. "All Labrador Retrievers remind you of Rowdy. I have told you a thousand times to stay away from dogs you don't know. I will not have you bitten! You never know. Now get back over here. You were lucky this time."

Ted looked at the woman. *What kind of woman would believe that a man would invite a child to meet an untrustworthy dog, especially when the man worked with kids?*

Erin chose not to hear her mother and concentrated on Max. "Does he like the water, Mr. Weaver?"

"Max loves the water, Erin, but he knows he might spook a fish here close to the hole."

Ted glanced at Laura, "If your mother feels like stretching her legs a bit, we could walk down to the boat launch, and I can show you." He nodded toward a spot a hundred yards downstream where there were four more picnic tables encircled by a gravel driveway which allowed floaters stream access.

Erin looked questioningly at her mother.

Laura drew a long breath and looked squarely at Ted. "Erin knows she can not go near the water. I can't swim. . . . Water can be dangerous."

Laura lit another cigarette.

Seeing the little girl's distress, Ted nodded. "Your mother is right about that, Erin. Water can be your best friend or your worst enemy. A person has to read it carefully and respect its power."

He smiled toward this intense woman who obviously carried so much weariness, so much anger and pain, yet, at the same time, fiercely protected the little girl.

He studied the little girl somehow too old and weary too, but committed to trying to claw her way through something, *hopelessness?*

Erin, for a moment there, had shown a spark of joy, the sense of adventure that a healthy child has. *What the hell?*

Right is right!

Ted's smile was gone; the look he directed toward Laura was open. "There's good footing, and the water is quiet at the boat launch. . . . We won't be in the water; Max will."

He continued to hold eye contact during his pause. "I'm a strong swimmer and a licensed guide."

He had tried to present these facts delicately, but he glanced back toward Erin and Max, then made eye contact with Laura again.

Laura turned to look at Erin whose face glowed with happiness and the late afternoon sun. "If you're absolutely certain she will be safe, I guess a walk would feel good." She ground another cigarette under her foot as she stood.

Ted walked to the Suburban and pulled a blue net containing three objects from under the rear seat.

Max immediately stood up. His entire body began to wiggle.

Ted handed the net to Max who eagerly took the handle in his mouth.

The four of them started down the shaded fisherman's path between the parking lot and the boat launch. At an open spot, the rays of the setting sun cut through the leaves whose shadow made a delicate pattern on a nearby rock.

Laura, noticing the pattern, paused for a moment to admire it.

Crows that had been feeding on the sumac berries flew a short distance, landed, and scolded while waiting to return to their dinner.

Laura stopped, "Wait here; I want to get my camera."

"Have you seen a Labrador Retriever work, Erin?"

"No, Mr. Weaver."

He turned and once again half-knelt in front of the little girl. He waited until her mother had returned from the Land Rover then looked into the little girl's eyes. *Turquoise?* "I would like you to call me Ted, Erin. What would you like me to call you?"

"I am just Erin."

Ted nodded, "Then I am just Ted, okay?"

He extended his hand again; she shook it with a grip which told him she had not always been quite so frail, not always so without hope.

"How about you, Laura? Do you know retrievers?"

"My father purchased a Labrador when he moved up here from Philadelphia. He and the dog lived and hunted together until the dog died a couple of years ago."

Erin, who had decided to help Max carry the net bag, gently ran her free hand behind Max's ears and then from above his eyes over his head down to his withers. "It was almost three years ago. 'Cause he wasn't here the year my Daddy got me my rod for Christmas."

Rod, not pole.

"Or the next year when Daddy got me my waders." She smiled in Ted's direction. "His name was Rowdy, and he was the best dog that ever lived."

Erin's eyes took on that dazed look again as though she was looking backward through time; her eyes misted; her voice lost its happiness, "Grandpa Sam is dead now too."

Suddenly the pieces fell into place in Ted's brain. He looked, again, at Laura. . . . *Barnsworth!*

"I knew a Sam Barnsworth. He had a black Labrador named Rowdy." Ted took a deep breath, remembering. "Great retriever; he worked pheasant and grouse, too. We lost Sam this spring during our school's Easter vacation. I had my baseball team in Cooperstown and missed the funeral."

Laura nodded as Ted went on fitting the pieces, talking now almost to himself. "I could never get Sam to fish; he was strictly a gun man, but he always said he had a son-in-law who loved to fly-fish." Ted continued quietly as he closed his eyes and lowered his head against the thought. "Worked in New York City as a stockbroker."

He exhaled, then glanced sideways at Laura. "He had taken Sam up to his office once to show him the city from," . . . Ted's voice took on a harshness; his hand made an involuntary pass over his mouth and chin; his eyes clouded as they met Laura's. The words came almost as a whisper, "the Towers."

Laura turned away.

It was Erin who had the courage to break the strained silence. She nodded her little head. "Everybody's dead: first Rowdy, then my Daddy, then Grandpa Sam. . . . Now it's just mommy and me." She paused. "Oh, and Maria."

Fighting to control her emotion, Erin shook her head sideways, "And I." She looked at Ted, "I have trouble with that one."

She walked over and took her mother's hand. "But we made it. Didn't we, mommy?"

The words started to tumble out of her now. "We went back to school the first of October just like my Daddy would have wanted us to. And the firemen hunted for my Daddy. . . . And we came to Grandpa Sam's like we always did at Christmas. And Grandpa said I could teach him to fish with me this summer. . . . And then we came back at Easter 'cause Grandpa Sam had died and gone to heaven to be with my Daddy. . . . I guess my Daddy will teach him to fish up there."

Erin paced in a little circle around Max. "After the funeral I told Mommy that I wanted to take some of the flowers to Rowdy's grave, but we didn't know where it was."

Erin stopped and looked first at the ground, then at Ted. "We don't even know where Rowdy is buried. And that is not right 'cause he was a good dog and deserves for us to visit him and tell him about my Daddy and Grandpa 'cause he would want to know."

A single gut-wretching sob escaped, but Erin squared her shoulders, sniffed a little, and went on. "And I told mommy I would have to fish by myself now. And she said, 'No! That I was too little. And she couldn't swim.'"

Erin turned and looked almost defiantly at Ted, "But I can. . . . I can swim because my Daddy taught me."

Ted cleared his throat and met Erin's gaze as his hand went automatically to her little shoulder. "I'll bet he taught you a lot."

She nodded, "He was a wonderful Daddy. And now we don't know where Daddy is buried either. . . . Daddy and Rowdy, . . . just lost. . .forever. . . . And it is not right!"

Suddenly the little girl looked spent as tears started

down her cheeks. She seemed to shrink before his eyes.

Ted couldn't think of a single thing to say. . .or to do. His mind searched for something she might grab on to, something that wouldn't let her fall completely apart right in front of him.

Max had watched the pathos play out and sensed that Ted, for once, was lost and needed his help.

Max reviewed the rules: *Never grab. Never run ahead without a command or an "at ease." Never bark. . . . Well, extreme conditions call for extreme measures!*

Max grabbed up the net with the dummies and ran to the bank where he stood and barked and wagged his tail.

It worked! Ted, Erin, and even Laura seemed glad to have someone else to focus on.

Ted went to the black dog and patted his ribs, "Well done, Max. You ready to work some? Huh, boy?"

Ted pulled a training dummy from the net. "Max, mark!"

It was easy to see one reason Ted was the baseball coach. He seemed to toss the dummy effortlessly a good thirty yards upstream into the water.

The Labrador's eyes never left the dummy as it sailed toward the glistening ripples. The muscles of his body tensed. He was on full alert, ready to spring at the right word.

"Max, fetch!"

Oh, how he loved this part! Max sprang from the bank into an arc that carried him to the water.

Erin gave a hoot. "Mommy, look at him go! Oh, mommy, just look at him."

When you had been bred for it and you lived to do it, it was easy.

As soon as he shook the water out, Max's eyes locked on the dummy which was drifting downstream.

Max adjusted his diagonal approach so he would intersect the drift line of the dummy, then he would turn in the water and actually take the dummy from the far side. *The job is a lot easier when I don't have to do a one eighty in the water with my mouth full of bird or dummy.*

The retrieve was picture perfect: clean, swift, graceful. Max had made the considerable challenge look easy.

He came up the bank like the hero he was, full of himself: head level, legs doing a slight strut, eyes dancing with excitement as his tail was wagging.

He paused to shake off the water, then trotted directly to Ted and stood quietly waiting for Ted to kneel, extend his hand, and ask Max to drop the dummy.

Of course, Max did not drop the dummy; he laid it quietly in the center of Ted's outstretched hand and took a step back, instantly alert in case Ted allowed it to fall off to the side to imitate the action of a live bird flopping out of his hand. *Fat chance!*

"Good boy, Max!" Ted was down in front of him rubbing his chest and rib cage.

Erin couldn't contain herself. She went to the big dog. "Oh, Maxie, you are such a good boy!" She rubbed him too and was rewarded with a quick kiss. It had to be quick because Ted still held Max's attention.

"Max, at ease."

Max made a little victory circle around the three of them and came in for some more praise.

Ted looked at the little girl for whom everything seemed to be out of control, everything but herself. She was in a constant struggle to remain calm.

Ted laid the dummy down and backed up twenty feet. *She would have to get it that far out for Max to have time.* "Hey, Erin, could you toss me that dummy?"

Erin bent, picked up the dummy, and started to bring it to him.

"No, honey, just toss it here. Take hold of one end, hold your arm out to the side a little, and show me what you've got."

It wobbled, but it made it.

"Good arm, Erin; when you get a little older, I could sure use you on my baseball team."

She grinned, and he walked toward her. He knelt down, lowered his voice slightly and spoke conspiratorially, "You know, I've been trying to get Max so he'll work for someone else. He appears to like you. Would you try to work him once for me?"

"You mean me tell him and throw it and everything?"

"I'd sure appreciate it."

Her head nodded exuberantly, pigtails flying.

"Want me to go through the commands with you?"

Erin's expression became thoughtful. "I think I remember. First say his name; then say, 'mark;' then throw. Say, 'fetch;' then put out your hand; then say, 'drop.'"

Ted wondered what her IQ must be. "You've got it, Erin. Give me your hand. Let me pass him to you."

Hand-in-hand they walked to Max. "Max, sit. Max, Erin." Ted placed her little hand on Max's collar then looked at Erin. "When you want to take him to the bank, say his name, then say 'heel,' and walk off like you're going somewhere. You know the rest. Here's your dummy."

"Max, heel!"

Max would have walked through fire for the little girl; somehow he knew he was doing this to help her. He stayed an inch away from her left leg and adjusted his steps to the shortest stride he had known. They stopped at the bank where Ted had stood.

"Max, mark!"

She heaved the dummy with all of her strength. A smile crossed her face as the dummy landed in the water.

"Max, fetch!"

There was a black flash in the fading sunlight, some splash on the little girl, a giggle, a few mighty strokes, turn, make contact, eyes dancing, powerful strokes to the bank, then up it, pause, shake. No hesitation, go directly to the little girl and wait for the outstretched hand.

"Max, drop!"

Placement was as soft as a feather, back one step; *stay alert; it really might slide off her hand.*

"Good boy, Max! Max, at ease." Then, "Oh, Maxie, you did it! You did it for me."

Her thin arms encircled his wet chest. "Oh, Maxie, I love you! You are the best dog ever, the best dog in the whole world. I will never forget you, Maxie!"

Max might not have known all of the words, but he sure got the message. Kisses were exchanged. He delicately took her right hand in his big mouth and looked at her with pure adoration. He finished two victory laps before Ted called him in.

"Thank you, Erin. You were a big help to me. You did just great. I think he'll get the idea now."

Ted turned toward his vehicle. "Time to head home, Max. We have a gentleman to guide early tomorrow morning. Better shake the cobwebs off things a little."

By now they were near the cars. "Ladies, I am proud to have met you both. Like Max here, you both come from good stock; I knew Sam Barnsworth well. We taught together for a few years, remained close friends and took a lot of hunts together."

He shook Laura's hand. "Your father was quite a man, Laura."

Ted took a card from his vest pocket and handed it to Laura. "I knew Sam well. If I can help you with anything, don't be too proud to phone."

He turned to the little girl. "Thanks again for the help, Erin." He extracted another card and squatted to hand it to her. "Same goes for you. If you get in a pinch of some kind, dial this number."

He and Max walked to the Suburban.

Max stood while he was dried.

Once Max was loaded into his seat in the SUV, Ted closed the rear door, climbed in the driver's seat, and pulled out to the main road.

As he started to turn onto the blacktop, Ted paused to look in the rearview mirror and check.

Their lights were on.

They were moving.

They'd be okay.

He swung towards home.

2

Wellsboro was a somewhat isolated small town the center of which consisted of some magnificently restored old homes. Some had been put to use as bed and breakfasts and some turned into law offices and such. The wonderful old PennWells Hotel still held pride of place among the usual businesses.

Laura parked across the street from the Diner. *Maybe the novelty of the place will do something for Erin's appetite.*

They found an empty booth. Laura returned the smile of the waitress. "I'd like vegetable soup, a bacon sandwich on whole wheat toast, and orange juice for my daughter. I just need a black coffee and a bacon sandwich."

Erin was bubbling. "Oh, mommy, wasn't that Max just the smartest dog? Mr. Weaver was really nice, too, and he had known grandpa Sam. . . . I never thought he'd let me work Max."

Laura concentrated on encouraging her to talk and was amazed when Erin actually ate all of the order and asked for a dish of vanilla ice cream. *Maybe Jamie was right after all. Maybe the trip wasn't a bad idea; we'll have to come here anyway to close up the house.*

They had not gone to Sam's house on this trip.

Jamie had said that the first trip to Wellsboro after the funeral would be crucial in Erin's state. "Keep it light, Laura. Just take her down there and try to make it be as normal as possible. Don't dredge up any bad memories. She is very fragile right now. Make it pleasant and relaxing."

After eating part of her ice cream, Erin began sliding back into her old self, so Laura paid the check, and they walked back across the street to their car to drive to the Whitfield Bed and Breakfast.

Grace Whitfield met them at the door. "Hello, Laura. Did you and Erin have a pleasant afternoon?"

"Yes, under the circumstances, it did turn out to be pleasant."

"We met a nice man with a wonderful black Labrador Retriever, Mrs. Whitfield, and he let me give the commands," Erin added.

A knowing smile came over Grace Whitfield's face. "Oh, sounds like you met Ted Weaver and Max."

"Do you know them too?" Erin still found it hard to believe there were places where people knew their neighbors well and knew most everyone in town by sight.

"Oh, my yes, Erin. Ted teaches at the high school with my husband. He's a wonderful baseball coach. His team won the state championship this spring. The whole town knows Ted. And when you know Ted, you usually meet Max."

Grace motioned to the dining room where a selection of snacks was set out on the old cherry buffet. "Help yourself to something to nibble on and something to drink."

Grace stopped and turned on her way to tidy the kitchen. "What time will you want your breakfast tomorrow, Laura?"

"Erin and I have to beg off on breakfast, Mrs. Whitfield. We'll get an early start for the City tomorrow. In fact, I would like to settle up with you folks tonight if that is convenient."

"I'll buzz Walter, Laura; he's in the library with the Rossers. The first coffee pot is ready at 4:30 in the morning, and there's juice and milk in the refrigerator. Cereal, fresh fruit, bagels, and fixins will be put on the buffet after I remove the snacks later this evening. Please take some food when you leave."

Grace gave Erin a warm smile and focused on Laura. "You be careful driving back, now. We hope to see you folks again real soon."

"I'm sure we'll be back. I'm not exactly sure when we'll begin getting dad's house ready to sell. His will hasn't been read yet."

Grace 's eyes lost their twinkle. "Yes, of course. We all loved Sam, Laura. I sure miss him and Rowdy. Their morning ritual brought them right past the front of our porch most mornings." Grace smiled. "Rowdy's tale was always going, and Sam always brought his smile."

Walter appeared. They made short work of the bill.

3

Erin awakened crying.

The nightmare always began the same way.

The little freckle-faced girl was dressed in sky blue corduroy overalls that ended just above her knees. The bright orange/green/yellow/blue crazy-striped top and matching knee-highs completed her primary outfit. She wore navy Birkenstocks and a navy backpack.

There was no smile on her face, no giggle in her voice, no lilt in her step as she hurried across the large neatly-maintained lawn, up the steps, and into the foyer.

The minute she was inside, her control broke. "Mommy," she screamed. "Mommy!"

The mommy, still in the curry-colored linen suit, walked into the living room doorway. Her makeup was tear-streaked. Her eyes bloodshot.

The mommy drew a heavy breath, gathering her strength.

"Is it true, mommy?" . . . The little girl stamped her foot. "Mommy! Is it true?" Her lower lip covering the upper one, her chin quivering, eyes filling with tears, her expression pleading to be told one word: *no.*

The mommy placed her hand on the frame of the door. "Yes."

"My Daddy, my Daddy! Did my Daddy come home yet?"

"No."

The little girl looked at her feet which had never moved. Her normally erect, shoulder-square posture deserted her. Shoulders dropped; the little girl began to slump forward. She took a deep breath and raised her eyes to her mother's face. In a coarse whisper, she asked, "Has my Daddy called?"

"No.

"The little girl ran to the mother, flung her arms around the hips that had given her birth, and buried her face against her mother's taunt stomach, "No, mommy. No! Oh, mommy, no!"

The mommy knelt and put her hands on the little girl's shoulders. She shook her a bit. "Erin," she said sharply. "Now, Erin. Listen to me. . . . This is no time for hysterics."

The woman took a deep breath "Life. . . life. . . life just happens." There was a long pause followed by another deep breath. "And so does death. There is no rhyme, no reason to our existence. It's all just lies."

"No, no, no!" First there were sobs, then fists were pounding her mother.

"Yes, Erin! No one controls this mess; it just happens. The rest is just a fairy tale."

"But my Daddy is okay! . . . He just hasn't been able to get the phones to work. . . . My Daddy will come home tonight. I know he will!"

"No!"

The mommy had her hands on the little girl's shoulder. "No! I won't have it! Now listen to me, Erin. The second plane hit five hours ago. There will be no false hope in this house."

The woman straightened her spine and looked down at the little girl. "Your daddy is not going to come home. If he were alive, Nick would have contacted us by now."

"No!" The little girl's hands went up and covered her ears.

The mommy reached out and shook her daughter again. "That is the truth, and you might as well know it."

"No, no, no! You are lying, and that is bad. You are lying to me."

The little girl pulled backward, away from the hands on her shoulders. She squared herself and looked directly at the woman. "My Daddy will come home! . . . He will come home because I love him even if you don't."

The woman stepped forward and lightly smacked the little girl across the face. "Erin! Come to your senses right now. . . . I loved Nick. . . just as much as you did."

The little girl shook her head. "Do, mommy. Do! I *do* love my Daddy."

The woman turned and walked to the giant-screened

television. She turned it on. The footage of the planes hitting the towers was rolling at the time.

The little girl turned away and once again put her hands over her ears.

The woman, hands on the little girl's shoulders, forcibly turned her to face the screen. "There. Do you see that?"

The picture changed to the present scene: fire, twilight at mid afternoon, the sun's rays opaqued by the smoke and the silt in the air.

The lady reporter was stopping firemen, policemen, anybody who would say anything to her as sheets of paper blew in the street and fragments resembling gray snowflakes fell through the air.

The talk was always of people still trapped. Shots of disoriented people who wandered aimlessly shared shots of people hurrying away from the mess.

The lady reporter was told to move: what was left of the towers might collapse.

The station cut back to the picture of one of the planes moving in slow motion toward the Tower.

"No, no, no," Erin screamed as she grabbed for the remote in the mommy's hand. "Turn it off, mommy. Please, please make it go away. Turn it off!"

"No! You will watch this, Erin. You must learn to accept the facts. You cannot live in a fantasy world where this did not happen. It did happen right here in America in New York City!"

. . .

The dream usually ends for the little girl with the woman's coming to her, awakening the sobbing Erin, and, finally, comforting her as best she can.

For the woman, the dream normally ends when she awakens herself calling out, "Nick, Nick, I didn't mean it. You know I didn't mean it." Her only comfort comes from the decanter which she now keeps on the stand next to her bed.

Oh, Erin, Erin, baby, how I failed you that night. Oh, dear Lord, if You exist, help my baby; help her please. . . . I can 't. . . . I didn't.

. . .

On that first night, by now, the mother was talking to no one.

The little girl had spun from the woman's grasp and had run toward her room. Once inside her doorway, she had stopped and looked back at her mother, hoping, praying for an indication that some comfort was there waiting for her. What she had seen was the woman pouring vodka from the decanter into a glass.

The little girl had squared her shoulders again. "My Daddy said you shouldn't drink 'til after you eat your dinner," she said as tears glistened in her eyes.

The woman had drunk deeply from the glass. "Your father is dead, Erin. No reasonable being would think someone could live through that."

"But people did! . . . People did live! The lady reporter talked to them. I saw her."

Another gulp had gone down the woman's throat. "Those people worked on the lower floors. Your father worked near the top, and you know it. Your father is gone. Nick is dead!"

The little girl had turned away, dropped her head, and walked far enough into her room to close the door. Then she had run to her bed, thrown herself on it, and sobbed into her pillow.

. . .

In truth, Laura, had come to Erin's bedroom later that first evening. She had knocked lightly and then had opened the door. She had found Erin sitting cross-legged on the floor. Scattered around her were her fishing vest, her rain jacket, her waders, and her rod case: physical links to her father.

As she had stood studying her daughter, Laura had recalled the heated discussion she and Nick had had about Erin's gear years ago when Nick had announced that he had measured Erin and intended sending the orders off the next morning.

Laura had protested that she did not want her daughter near the water, "She could drown. I want her safe."

Nick had insisted that his daughter would have the opportunity to learn to love the outdoors as he did. "Laura, safe also means healthy. I want her to exercise. I would never try to force her to like or dislike anything; I want her always to be herself. . . . She will have a chance to see and taste all that is good as long as I live."

"I don't want you turning her into a fisherman! I want her to love art, and museums, and fine food." Laura had slammed herself into a chair.

"But, Laura, I don't intend that either of us turn Erin into anything. You see, dear, all I want is for Erin to be herself, just herself: not you and not me; just herself. I trust her to live her life. We only get one, you know. She should be allowed to live hers, not ours. I want her to see and feel and taste and smell everything and anything that won't immediately hurt her, and I want her to decide who she is and whom she will grow into."

Laura had changed tactics. "Erin will too quickly out-grow these expensive custom-made things. You should buy off the shelf until she is grown and we can see whether she is really interested in this stuff. By then, if she is interested, she will know how to properly care for things. If you must drag her off into the woods, at least buy inexpensively. The money, at present, would be better put in Erin's college fund."

Nick had taken a step backward in order to study Laura. "Laura, have I ever denied you anything?"

"No. Of course not."

"Do we live very well?"

"Certainly better than most." That said, she had started to rise to leave.

"No, now stay here for a minute. Please. We need to set this straight once and for all. I am the youngest senior manager at my firm. I make an embarrassingly substantial salary. Erin, at five years of age, has a fully-funded college account. You have annuity accounts which would kick in and keep you just as you live now, or maybe better, should anything happen to me. Erin takes far better care of anything she owns: her books, her clothing, anything, than either of us does."

He shrugged and smiled at Laura. "Fly-fishing requires a certain grace of movement. Erin is athletic, but she can't be graceful when trying to use a rod which is too big for her."

Nick had paused for a moment of thought. "And I'm not even sure I could find the proper clothing her size. Although she swims like a little fish, I want her vest to do double duty: as an accommodating fishing vest and as a life vest in the water should she lose her footing. I want her waders to have a seal at the top so they can't fill with water if she goes down."

"See, I was right! This is too dangerous. I won't have it."

"Laura, Laura, oh, my darling, Laura. How can I make you understand?" He had smiled warmly at the wife he so loved. "You and she are the light of my life, Laura. I don't want her hurt."

He had stood and extended his hand to allow Laura to easily rise from her chair and come to his arms. "Now, my love, I will buy Erin what she needs. I will show her how to care for it. I will replace it as she grows."

He had held Laura tight, inhaled her scent, and rocked her gently from side to side. "And I think we have much better ways of spending our energies with each other than by talking about this subject again." He had given her earlobe a playful nibble. "Okay?"

"Yes, of course, if that is what you really want."

"How about better-spending some energy right now?"

They had, and he had purchased the vest, jacket, and waders from Simms in Bozeman, Montana. They had been custom made. The green rod case had arrived holding a rod custom- sized for a child. Orvis, in Vermont, had produced it.

. . .

On the afternoon of that dreadful day, Laura had wiped the memory and the tender tears from her eyes, squared her shoulders, and taken a deep breath, forcing herself into the present. *Well, there will be no more of those. That seemed to be Nick's solution to all of our disagreements.*

"Erin, what are you doing with that stuff strewn all over the floor? Surely you aren't getting ready for a fishing trip. There will be no more fishing. Now put that stuff away."

Erin had just looked at Laura. She had not said a word. She had heaved a little sigh and focused her attention on her fishing net.

"You are not going fishing. Not now, not ever again. And listen to me, young lady." Laura had Erin by the shoulders now, and her nails were biting into the thin shoulder blades. "You are absolutely forbidden to go near that damn lake. Do you hear me?"

Laura's eyes were biting into Erin's just as her nails had bitten into Erin's shoulder blades. "Nick is dead. Fishing is over. Never, never go near that lake unless I am with you. Do you hear me?"

"Yes, mommy. Mommy, you're hurting me!"

"Promise me!"

"I promise, mommy."

Erin, who had been looking up at her mother through tear-filled eyes, allowed her eyes to drop to her fishing net. She rubbed her little hands over the handle, grasped it, and lifted it to inspect the net itself.

"I said put this stuff away now."

"But, mommy, you don't understand. I like looking at my gear. I want it out here where I can see it, mommy. I want to think. . . . I want to remember when my Daddy brought it home for me, and how he taught me to put it on."

She continued, trying to explain. "I like remembering how he took me to the park and taught me to cast and how he taught me to clean my gear when we came home and how to put it away. I like remembering when we went fishing." . . .

"I like to remember each and every time: where we went, what we caught, how we laughed when he fell and showed me how to get back up using my walking stick."

"I want to think and remember."

Tears started their trip down through the freckles to the chin. No sobs. Just gentle tears moving rather slowly down the little face.

"I want to remember my Daddy. I want to remember it all."

"That will just make it worse. Believe me, I know. You should put that stuff away and forget it." Laura turned from Erin and decided. "I'll have the cleaners clear all of these things out when they come next Monday."

Erin was on her feet, hands on hips. A defiant look took control of her face, even her posture. "You will not have them take my gear or my Daddy's fishing gear. I will go get my

Daddy's fishing things right now and move them to my closet!"

Erin began walking toward her parents' bedroom, then paused. "And, mommy, if one thing is missing, ever, I will do something awful, so awful that. . . .Well, you'll wish for the rest of your life that you had left our things alone."

. . .

On that night, she had gone to her father's huge walk-in closet just off the bedroom which he had shared with Laura and had begun carrying, pulling, dragging all of his fishing gear into her room and putting it in her own big walk-in. Once that was accomplished, she had moved all of her gear to the left side of her closet. Then she carefully placed her father's gear directly behind her own.

When placing her father's gear, she had discovered a bonus. Two of his wool fishing shirts and three wool fishing sweaters had not been cleaned recently: they still held his scent.

She had brought one of the sweaters out of her closet and put it under her pillow. Then she locked her closet with the key that she had always kept in her desk drawer.

Key still in hand, Erin had looked around her room. Where should she keep the key now?

Under the mattress was no good. Maria would find it when she changed the linen.

The desk drawer, with Laura's threat, was no longer of use.

It had to be someplace where she could get to it, since she would have to use the key every day of her life. After several perfect places were discarded as too obvious, Erin's eyes had fallen on her house slippers. She laid the key in the sole near the toes. She slipped her foot in.

A grim half smile surfaced briefly.

Erin walked to the closet, unlocked it, took out her little Swiss army knife and made a clean slit in the inner sole of her left slipper. She slipped the key inside the lining; it fit! She replaced the army knife and closed the closet door as she went into her bedroom. She walked over and locked her bedroom door.

Of course, mommy and her Daddy had always had a key to her bedroom door, but her Daddy had given her the only key to her closet on her fifth birthday.

Then, with her bedroom safely locked, she had taken her closet key from the sole of her slipper, locked her closet, replaced the key in her slipper, and had gone to her bathroom for her shower.

Erin had put on her nightie and knelt beside her bed as her Daddy had taught her.

She had said her prayers asking God to take care of Daddy and to bless the other poor souls and their families.

She had climbed into bed, and gone to sleep with the light scent from her Daddy's sweater calming her mind and bringing sweet memory-dreams to her.

4

Laura, weary from last night's nightmare, was up and dressed by 4:30. She walked a very sleepy pajama-clad Erin to the rear seat of the Land Rover and put a pillow under her head and a light blanket over her.

Then Laura returned to the Whitfield's where she filled her travel mug with black coffee and took two bagels. *I'll stop at a drive-through when Erin awakens; we'll be near the City around noon and home in Danbury by early evening.*

Laura headed north to NY 17 East. This would take her through the Finger Lake Region and then to the City itself where she was going to stop by the townhouse Nick had kept for them. It had come in handy for family visits to the City, and Nick had used it on the occasions when he had needed to stay over, but he always did his best to sleep at home in Danbury.

During summers, when school was out, Laura and Erin had sometimes ridden in with Nick on Friday mornings, and they would spent the weekend in New York enjoying special things.

Once on 17, Laura allowed her mind to shift to the events of the previous day.

. . .

Will these nightmares ever cease?

. . .

Thank goodness Erin actually ate a meal, a whole meal. Maybe she is starting to come to grips with reality.

. . .

Why was I so negative with Ted Weaver? Lord knows I guessed it was he the minute I noticed the black Labrador in the Suburban. . . . Sam always talked so fondly about Ted. And Sam never tired of telling Erin and Nick hunting tales that involved Rowdy and Ted.

. . .

Ted was a big help after Sam got sick, too. He even shortened his hunting trips so Sam could make them.

He made a real effort to include Sam in everything right up to the very end. . . . He saw to it that Sam got to all of the nearby games and that some members of the team visited with him after the games he had to miss. . . . I guess I owe him.

. . .

Once when I insisted that Sam come to the City where he could take his treatments at Sloan Kettering and where I could look after him, Sam told me that between Sally Ann and Ted he was given the best care possible. He said he was comfortable with them and with his doctor in Wellsboro.

Probably more comfortable with them than he was with me.

Laura frowned remembering that Sam had once told her Ted was the son he had never had.

But you did have a son! . . . Damn you, Sam. How could you forget so easily?

She shook her head. *Shut down the memories. . . . Erin's getting some real rest. . . . I don't think she has slept well a single night since Nick.*

Laura felt the tears begin to sting her eyes. *Shut it off, Laura. One hundred, ninety-nine, ninety-eight, ninety-seven. . . .* When she reached number one, she reached for her special water bottle and took a deep drink.

After some deep breathing, her control returned.

"Where are we, Mommy?"

Laura looked in the rearview mirror and saw Erin sitting up and wiping the sleep from her eyes.

"Hey, sleepyhead. Ready for a rest room break and maybe some breakfast?"

"Yes. But where are we on the road?"

"Binghamton is coming up; I'll find a McDonald's. Okay?"

"I love McDonald's. Oh, and I have to pee, but it isn't real bad yet."

"I brought us a bagel from the Whitfield's. Want yours?" . . . "Oh, look there's a food exit."

The sign directed her to turn right at the intersection. They could see the golden arches when she made the turn.

After Erin went to the rest room, they went to the counter. "I'd like an egg McMuffin with an orange juice, please."

"I just need a black coffee." Laura smiled to herself. *Thank goodness for cigarettes and coffee.*

. . .

"This is good, mommy; you want some?" Erin took another bite of her breakfast and chewed thoughtfully then downed some juice. She began swinging her right leg sideways. "Wasn't Max a great dog, mommy? I never knew a dog could be that smart."

Then, remembering her loyalty was owed to Rowdy, she quickly added, "'Course, I never saw Rowdy work, in the field, I mean. And Grandpa Sam always said that he was the best he had ever hunted behind. . . . But Max was sure a good dog."

Laura inhaled deeply, held it for a second, and exhaled. She caught the look of disapproval in Erin's eyes and decided to try to sidetrack the old quarrel about smoking before it got started.

Mimicking Ted, Laura leaned forward and lowered her voice. "Guess what."

"What?"

"I got some shots of your working him."

Erin immediately laid the McMuffin, halfway to her mouth, down on the table of the booth. "Did you? Oh, did you, mommy? That is so cool."

Laura nodded enthusiastically. *Whew! One avoided! I really have to stop arguing with a seven-year-old. If I can just pay attention to Erin, I can maneuver around most of our spats.* "I think maybe I got a couple of really good ones."

"Oh, mommy, will you process the film as soon as we get home?"

Laura's art major had included several courses in photography and the processing and printing of film, and Nick had had a darkroom built for Laura before they had moved into their home in Danbury.

She found work in the darkroom relaxing and thrilling at the same time. It was relaxing because she was alone in an environment which she understood well and had complete control over. It was thrilling because seeing an image gradually appear on a white sheet of paper was, for her, like a cloud moving to reveal the moon.

She smiled as Erin began to gobble her food in an effort to waste no time at this stop. "Remember to chew, kiddo. We're making good time."

5

Ted's alarm sounded at 5 a.m.

He and Max went for a short run before taking a quick shower and dressing. He put a rod case, a small duffle, and two coolers in the Suburban where he had left his vest, nets, waders, etc. He and Max were pulling into the parking lot at the PennWells Hotel at 5:45.

When Chester Justice had phoned about a guided fishing trip through the grand canyon of Pennsylvania, he had mentioned a friend who had given Ted high praise.

The Justices were staying at the PennWells.

Betty Justice loved old hotels and had heard from golfing friends about the beautiful old dining room.

The men would meet in the lobby at six a.m.. Ted would take Chet to the Diner down the block for breakfast. Then they would hit the stream where Ted would stay at Chet's side, help him read the water, select the proper fly, tie his flies on, etc.

Ted would also give advice on technique and proper landings. He would net the fish, take pictures, and release the fish until eleven when they would reel in and return to the hotel, lunch with Betty, and then float the gorge with Chet fishing from the boat while Betty took pictures.

Ted was one of the few fly-fishermen who choose to become guides primarily to save the sport:

"More licenses mean more money in the wildlife division, so more fish are released each spring."

"If a guide teaches a little stream ecology, there'll be less pollution of habitat, and more fish will winter over.   And, hey, when there's a genuine need for a national aquatic environmental voice, the voice will be louder."

When going to the stream alone, Ted rarely wore a watch of any sort, but, when guiding, he wore a watch with a vibrating alarm primarily as a marriage-saving device for his clients.

Once at the PennWells, Ted entered the side door from

the parking lot and took the two coolers to the kitchen.

The man sitting in the lobby looked to be in his mid fifties. He was on time and appeared to be reasonably fit, dressed in tan pants and a tan long-sleeved shirt.

Looks like he's fished some before.

The man checked his watch then looked up expectantly through wire-rimmed trifocals as Ted and Max walked into the lobby.

"Chet?"

Chet Justice nodded as he rose.

"Ted Weaver." Ted covered the distance between them, hand extended, a smile on his face.

The men shook hands and took a moment to size each other up a bit.

They found each other to be tolerable and headed toward the side entrance which led to the parking lot.

"Your gear in your vehicle?" Ted asked as he opened the door for Chet.

"Yea, mine is the gray Durango." Chet tilted his head toward the sport utility.

"Mine's the black Suburban. I'll get her opened and help you load; then we'll grab some breakfast while Max holds down the fort. I need to grab a cooler from the kitchen too."

In under five minutes the two men were heading a block away to the Wellsboro Diner.

Ted led Chet to a booth.

The waitress automatically brought water with a smile. "Hi, Ted. What can I get for you gents this morning?"

"Mary Jane, I'd like you to meet Chet Justice. We're gonna try to empty the streams today."

After Chet and Mary Jane exchanged hellos, Ted ordered his usual: oatmeal, dry whole wheat toast, sausage patty, tomato juice, and black coffee.

Chet decided to try the oatmeal with grapefruit juice and coffee.

"Have you fished this area before, Chet?"

"No, I get out around the Finger Lakes a few times a year, but I don't have enough time to venture far from home. I keep reading about the Pine Creek Gorge, and I told Betty this summer we were going to give it a try. Betty has some golf friends who come here once a year on a golf outing sponsored by the hotel. So she was ready to come anytime. "

Ted took a pull of his coffee. "You golf?"

"No. Had to go to trifocals a couple of years ago. Too much reading I guess." Chet shook his head. "Once you get these damn things, you can't see anything unless you're looking straight at it."

He paused and sampled his coffee. "Never was any good anyway, but Betty likes it. My hours can be a little long when we're closing a big project, so it's a nice hobby for her. . . . You don't need glasses yet, Ted?"

"Only the polarized to help me see fish in the water."

Chet rubbed his thumb across his chin. "Enjoy it while you can, brother."

Mary Jane arrived with their breakfast and topped off their coffee.

Both men ate quickly, each wanting to get to the water.

They walked back to the parking lot and climbed into the Suburban.

Ted gave Max one bite of the sausage patty. Then the three of them got down to business and headed out toward the gorge; each was quiet with his own thoughts.

"Look around, now, Chet. You turn on this dirt road to drive to the bottom of the gorge. It gets a little rough in spots: narrow and steep, but I've seen more than a few Explorers and Durangos down there if you want to come back alone. Just remember to take it slow and let the transmission do its work. I think I'll close the windows and turn on the air."

Chet got his bearings.

The Suburban began its descent. It rocked to one side as a wheel dropped into a water hole in the tracks

What the hell? Chet's hand went up to the dash. He sheepishly pulled it back a little.

"Go ahead, brace yourself; remember I've got the wheel to keep me stable."

Fred didn't say anything about this. This isn't a road;

hell , it's more like a path that has car tracks in it: no gravel, just clay and exposed rocks. "What happens if you meet someone?"

Ted grinned, "One of you learns to back real well."

Chet returned the grin and added a grunt as a leaf-filled limb scraped along the outside of his window. He swallowed. *This will be one to talk about!*

The last bit of the road was especially steep; then the flat area opened up. Ted pulled into the parking lot beside a Jeep. "Let's give it a try."

Afterwards, Chet had to admit that they had enjoyed a near-perfect morning. Ted had lent him a wading stick and had taken him into the creek itself. There had been no sign of the other fisherman.

Chet's first few casts had been off the mark, but Ted quickly had him drifting the dry-fly over the rise.

The two men talked easily about fish and good streams.

By 9:30, Chet had caught three nice browns and a rainbow.

"What say we take a break, Chet. I have drinks in the cooler. Let's chew on some nuts and drink something cool while the next hatch gets a start."

"Sounds good." Chet used his walking stick to make his way to the bank. Once away from the slippery rocks, he inspected it more closely. "I'm going to get me one of these things, never used one before. They work."

"I always carry one. No sense taking a bath unless you're dirty."

They took time for refreshments.

Chet made a trip to the toilet while Ted attached a new fly.

A couple of trout were lost; one was landed and released Just after Chet caught a nice rainbow, Ted's watch began to vibrate.

Wet waders stored in the rear, both Ted and Chet chose a cold bottle of water for the ride in. Max was given time to relieve himself and half of Ted's bottle of water.

Chet settled into the front seat for the climb up the

mountain. "You took me to some good ones, Ted."

"You brought the meat to the skillet, partner." Ted noted Chet's nod of satisfaction. "I need to stop by a little restaurant to leave Max for the afternoon."

"I wondered how he and Betty would get along in a boat. She's not much for dogs."

Betty was sitting in the lobby of the PennWells reading a novel. She looked up and smiled as the men approached. "Well, how'd it go?"

"Great morning. Absolutely perfect. Three nice browns and two rainbows." He turned toward Ted. "I hated to put that last rainbow back."

He winked in Ted's direction. "Play your cards right, and I might take you down there before we leave."

Then his hand went to his head. "Where are my manners? Betty, I want you to meet the legendary Ted Weaver. Everything Fred said about him is true, in spades."

The conversation over lunch went well. Ted learned that Betty had never been on a float trip. "You want to be sure to put on sunscreen; the reflection from the water can give you a good burn. And a hat with a scarf or something to tie it on with is a good idea if you have one."

"I brought an extra fly hat with a face net and a neck skirt for her."

"Looks like Chet has you well-covered, Betty."

Ted collected the afternoon cooler and headed for the upper boat launch where he knew Jerry would be waiting for him with a pickup and a trailer carrying Ted's relatively flat-bottomed drift boat.

. . .

"See that rise, Chet?"

"Yea. I caught it out of the corner of my eye."

"Let me ease us a little closer. He'll be laying in the shadow of the bank waiting for something tasty to pass by. Cast a little upstream of him and let the fly just drift through the center of the rise. . . . That's it. . . . Mend your line some. Mend just a little more. . . . Ha. You've got a good one. Let him play a little; let Betty see his action." Ted turned to give a quick glance toward Betty. "Can you see him, Betty?"

Betty had her camera out. She ripped the hat from her head and threw it into the open bag. "I can't see to shoot through that net."

She looked toward Ted. "Will he jump again? I want to get one of him in the air."

She glanced at Chet. "Make him jump again for me, honey."

Chet certainly didn't try. *Can't let this one get away.* But the fish obliged with a good leap.

"Careful he doesn't throw the fly, Chet. This old boy knows what's going on. . . , Easy now, don't try to power him; he's too big."

Ted turned slightly to smile at Betty. "This may be one for the wall, Betty."

His attention immediately went back to his client. "Just play him out 'til he tires a little. . . . Good. Good. That's the way to do 'er."

Betty and Ted watched the action for a while. "Now I'm going to move the boat a little to bring you in closer. Watch your balance and keep some tension on him."

Ted smiled as Chet brought the trout in near the boat. "Well, okay; that's the way to handle one."

After removing the fly, Ted kept his attention on Chet who was lowering the trout into the water. "That's it; just let him rest in your hand a little. He'll know when he's ready. . . . There he goes. . . . Thank you big guy; hope to run into you again next year."

After many casts, several hits, and two more nice catches, the sun was beginning preparations to set. Chet looked at Ted. "I sure hate to call an end to an absolutely great day, but this old man is beginning to feel it in his back and shoulders. Let's wrap her up, Ted."

"You're the boss."

Ted put his strong frame to work: legs braced, arms coordinating to move the boat steadily in the direction of the lower boat launch where Jerry, one of his baseball players, would be sitting with the Suburban and trailer.

Ted glanced up when he heard Betty's voice filled with excitement. "Look, Chet. Look up, honey. Is that an eagle, Ted?"

He steadied the boat. "Sure is. There's a nest down here." He heard the auto wind again.

. . .

"Eyes on the water, Chet; you never know when one will decide to tease you."

"I'm finished, Ted, but I sure thank you."

In a short while, the boat bottom touched gravel, and Ted stepped out to bring it to shore.

Jerry was in the water too, helping to steady the boat. After their clients were on shore, the boat was pulled onto the trailer.

Chet and Betty chose the rear seat, so Jerry climbed in front with Ted. All four took an orange juice, and, until Ted pulled in at the upper launch for Jerry's dad's pickup, an easy conversation prevailed that comes from having shared a good experience.

Ted pulled a white envelope from his shirt pocket and handed it to Jerry. "Thank you, Jerry."

Jerry smiled as he climbed into the old half ton red Chevy. "See you, Coach."

Soon Chet and Betty were climbing out of the rear seat and stretching in the parking lot of the hotel.

The men made short work of stowing Chet's gear in the Durango.

Chet extended his hand. "Ted, I can't tell you how much this has meant to both of us. What a great day! Come on in, and we'll buy you a drink."

"I'd love to, Chet. I could talk with you and Betty all day, but I need to catch up with Max and finish some things up at home. I sure thank you. It's been a real pleasure for me."

Chet handed Ted 2 hundreds and a fifty. "Thank you, Ted; we both sure enjoyed it. We'll talk about this all winter." He handed Ted another fifty.

"Well, thank you, Chet. It's been my pleasure. . . . You might want to hit the gorge again before you leave."

6

Ted headed for Sally Ann's and Max.

He averaged a couple of guide trips a week during the summer. Most were good. Fly-fishing is one of those activities capable of renewing a person's spirit, rejuvenating the better self.

To Ted, it seemed almost like formula:

Take a person who is tied up in knots with stress. Put him in a different place, an outdoor environment peopled with folks who value others. Walk a little. Keep the chatter to a minimum. Catch a fish or two. ... You can almost see the blood pressure drop. Add a friendly lunch, an afternoon of partnering on the stream, and a man or a woman can go home revived.

Guiding, coaching; they're really the same thing. Know the game yourself well enough to read the situation. If they have the basics, work to get 'em to relax.

Of course, it won't work for everyone. Some folks just hurt so much they can't quiet their minds to concentrate on a physical activity.

. . . .

Sally Ann had a light take-out supper for him when he stopped to get Max.

He told her about having met Sam's daughter and granddaughter the previous day.

Then he headed home for a shower and supper. After cleaning out the SUV, Ted turned on the TV and made his favorite Saturday evening snack: popcorn with a beer.

The phone rang just as the eleven o'clock news was starting.

"Ted Weaver here."

"Ted, this is Neil Bradley. Sorry to catch you so late, but I have a letter at the office for you. I've tried to reach you off and on all day; you must have been guiding."

"I had a couple of good trips, Neil. When am I going to get you away from the office and out on the rocks with me?"

"It's amazingly rocky here at the office some days," Neil

chuckled. "But I would like to get out soon. I haven't had time all spring. How's the water?"

"Great today. We got into some nice hatches. My client landed some good twenty-inch trout." Ted paused to take a drink of the cold Coors. "You say you have a letter for me?"

"Yes, Sam Barnsworth wrote it before he died and asked me to see that you got it after school was out and before we read the will. He left one for Sally Ann and his daughter too; you were each to get them at the same time."

"I sure do miss Sam, Neil."

"We all do, Ted." Neil paused. "Anyway, I've asked his daughter Laura to come to the office at two this Wednesday. It's time we got started on this. Sam had also asked that you be there for the reading if you can."

"Two on Wednesday? Sure, Neil, I can be there if you think it's necessary."

"Well, Sam requested it."

Neil paused again. "I thought you might want to read this letter before we meet. Sam wrote it at home and brought it in sealed and addressed to you. I would have got it to you earlier, but Sam had made it clear that he didn't want you to bother with it until you were finished at school."

"Sounds like Sam." Ted took a couple of pieces of his popcorn. "How about I drop by the office Monday morning?"

"Good. I'll be in court first thing." Neil thought a bit. "Probably be over by noon, but Janice will have it if you come in early."

"I'll get it from Janice, then Neil, and I'll see you on Wednesday at two. By-the-way, I met Sam's daughter this weekend. It's a shame she has to drive back down here so soon."

"That's strange."

"How so?"

"I just got off the phone with her. She never mentioned that she had been down. We could have held the meeting up for a couple of weeks."

"Well, maybe she'd just as soon get it over with."

"Must be."

"Hell of a thing isn't it? First her husband and then Sam.

Must be hard. She has a great little girl left, though."

"Oh, yes. I remember Sam's talking about that little girl. She was the apple of his eye. What was her name again?"

"Erin. Erin McCort."

"That's it. Well, thanks for being flexible, Ted. Sorry for the short notice."

"Don't think of it."

"See you Wednesday then."

"I'll be there."

Ted hung up the phone and brought the bowl back to his lap. *What's that about? It wasn't like Sam to be secretive; Sam was as straightforward as they come. What could he have had left to say?*

Max had come to sit by his side during the phone call. Ted ran his fingers over Max's head and let them trail off one of the ears. "You want some popcorn too, boy?"

Ted turned off the news. *I'll get the scores in the morning's paper.*

He stood up and stretched. "Come on, Max, time for bed."

7

Ted took the envelope from Janice and walked down the street. Normally he would have gone to Sally Ann's, but he wanted the relative privacy that the Diner would give him.

He chose the booth at the rear and sat facing the wall. After his coffee arrived, he opened the letter.

"Dear Ted,

"If you're reading this, I hope I have joined Rowdy in a place where the birds are plentiful."

Ted looked toward the ceiling as the tears stung his eyes. *I do too, Sam; I sure do too.*

"First, I want to thank you for having been one of my very best friends. You brought a lot of pleasure to my later years, almost as a son. In a lot of ways, you reminded me of the man I like to think I once was.

"You and Sally Ann certainly worked magic to make my last days not just bearable, but as enjoyable and pleasant as possible. Not many are comfortable watching over a friend through his last days. You have enough compassion to know this time comes for each of us and that the smile of a friend can sure make the time pass easier.

"May God always bless you, Ted Weaver.

"Now, of course, I have some favors to ask. I don't want you to take on anything which you really don't want, but, if you can, without harming yourself, I would appreciate it if you would do the following for me:

"First, attend the reading of the will. There are some directives in there that I want followed to the T.   I don't want my wishes to be second guessed.

"To that end, I am asking you now to administer my estate.

"Please feel free to share any of your thoughts with Sally Ann. She is receiving a letter also as is Laura.

"Now for the other favors:

"Ted, I want you to try to help my Laura and her little girl, Erin. It won't be easy with Laura; it may well be totally impossible, and I want you to have enough sense to recognize that situation and get out with no regrets if that is necessary.

"Laura came late to Emily and me. I was forty, and Emily was thirty-eight; we had given up hope. Like you, my students had become my kids. Then suddenly there was this little towhead trying to walk and calling me daddy. What joy the baby Laura brought us!

"You can imagine the shock and joy when five years later another little towhead came along, this one a male. Yes, Ted, I had a son, Samuel Lucas Barnsworth. Trouble was I didn't have him long enough. More about that later.

"Laura is a very troubled woman, Ted. She has been for many years, and she has responded to very few attempts at help. Nick could bring her closer to normalcy than anyone else, but even he could not completely crack the shell with which she surrounds herself.

"She wasn't always like this, Ted. Until the spring before her senior prom, she was a lot like Erin, her daughter. Laura took delight in life. She loved to dance. She was a good student. She belonged to the local riding club. We took her skiing. She was the photographer for her yearbook and had been a cheerleader in junior high.

"Laura was a beautiful girl. She had her mother's natural blond hair, and those beautiful blue eyes once sparkled like diamonds dancing with the pleasure of life itself.

"Of course, she had a big date planned for the prom. She and Tom Watkins had been sweethearts for a couple of years. Tom was a good basketball player, handsome as they come. He was a charmer.

"Our school always crowned a prom king and queen, and there was, honestly, little doubt that Tom and Laura would receive the crowns that year. I was teased about it daily in the teacher's lounge.

"Well, of course, that meant a special dress and shoes and the beauty parlor. Tanning beds were just getting started, and Laura had a gorgeous tan as the prom approached. That was probably the last tan she has ever had.

"Her mother and I were so proud. She had been accepted to the University of Virginia. She was going to study to be an art teacher: art because she loved it and a teacher because I was one.

"She wanted to get away from Philadelphia and strike out on her own, and we couldn't say no to her. She was spoiled; it's hard not to spoil the kind of girl she was.

"She, her mother and little brother, Sammy, had to go to the city to find the perfect dress. Nothing in our suburb was elegant enough. Of course the girls would have rather had Sammy stay home, but he put up such a fuss that Emily decided it was easier to let him have a day off school and to take him than to listen to him. You get that way when you're an older parent.

"They took our new Ford convertible, and Laura drove off just as I was loading my briefcase into the station wagon.

"The top was down, even at that time in the morning. Laura and her mother sat in front; Emily's hair was neatly tucked under a scarf. Sammy sat in the middle of the back seat waving at everyone he knew who had to go to school that day. What a scamp he was!

"I knew they would be home fairly early because Laura and Tom had a pre-prom dinner date for that evening. I supposed she was going to tell him all about the gown.

"I got the call just before school was out for the day. They had seen a storm coming in and had stopped and put the top up. Laura was still driving.

"Emily, that was my wife's name, was in front beside Laura, and Sammy was still in the back, over behind Emily now to make room to guard the dress.

"The five years between them had, amazingly, made them very close. He just plain worshipped her. I guess we all did.

"They were almost home when the lightning and wind really got started. They stopped behind another car for a red light on the corner where Mrs. Jackson's big house sat.

"The streets in our suburb were lined with mature trees. A limb broke loose from the big birch tree.

"Sammy and Emily lost their lives, crushed by the limb as it tore through the convertible's top.

"I pray it was over in an instant.

"Laura didn't have a scratch on her. But, Ted, I've always wondered if it didn't kill a part of Laura's soul.

"Since that moment, she has never been even close to her former self.

"She was, of course, hysterical. She was too drugged to attend the funerals.

"I don't think she has ever quit blaming herself even though, with the red light and cars before and behind them, there was absolutely nothing she could have done that would have prevented the terrible accident.

"I have never seen that special spark in her eyes after the accident, not even on her wedding day. Oh, she was happy to marry Nicholas McCort, and Nick was a good man: good husband, great father, hell of a provider.

"You see, Nick had grown up poor: broken family, ugly stuff. He had been fortunate to get a full ride to Michigan where he had studied hard and graduated with honors in business.

"He had been an intern at Merrill Lynch the summer before his senior year and was a senior broker and junior partner working in the Towers on September 11.

"Nick probably never knew what hit him. I hope not. He was a good man: good to Laura, adored Erin, worshiped his God. He liked to fish and enjoyed a drop or two of Glenlivit, nothing excessive.

"The streams had been his sanctuary growing up in Michigan. Having grown up poor and learned to fish with nothing but the bare necessities, he grew to want every new gadget, every gimmick there was.

"He was hard-driving and tough on the outside and probably thought the stuff would make up for form lost due to lack of time in the water.

"Nick came here to fish the spring hatches and enjoyed the fall runs too. I never asked you to guide him. He was in too big a hurry. But he was a good man, Irish to the core, but without that maudlin personality that is viewed by some to be the curse of the Irish.

"Nick carried a twinkle in his eye, and it was genuine.

He was a man who loved life, and wanted a chance to grab all of it.

"I didn't mean to ramble on so.

"Anyway, the long and the short of it is that Laura has flatly refused to allow anyone to get truly close to her from the day of the car accident to the present.

"I begged her to take counseling, but she would have none of that once she heard delving into memories from the past played a major role in therapy.

"She pledged a sorority in college but flatly refused to live in the sorority house; didn't want the closeness.

"After graduation with honors, she stayed an extra year to get her masters in art education and took a teaching position in New York City.

"You see, it is relatively easy to be anonymous in the City if one so desires.

"Laura met Nick the first year she was there, and they married the next summer. It was a beautiful wedding. Erin was born in the fall three years later.

"There were no other children. Although Nick was earning a very substantial salary and major bonuses, Laura flatly refused to be a stay-at-home mother.

"They hired a nanny, and each of them spent time with Erin at night and on weekends. Modern sure isn't always better, Ted. Poor little Erin.

"For a man, Nick spent an unusual amount of time with the baby Erin. He loved to sing her to sleep in his arms while rocking in a big antique rocker. He had a good voice; I think most Irish do.

"As quickly as possible, Laura had worked her way out of the classroom into the position of assistant director of art for her school district. Her goal was not one of advancement, but one of distancing herself from her students. She took the same type of position when they moved to Danbury.

"I trust you get the picture; hence, my warning.

"Always remember, son, the first person you have to save is yourself.

"Take care, my friend.

"Your old shooting buddy, Sam."

Ted sat quietly for a while unabashedly letting the memories of times spent with Sam wash over him as the tears washed over his cheeks.

Finally, he swallowed a couple of times and stood. He left two dollars on the table and walked out the rear door of the Diner.

Katie shook her head as she collected the money and wiped the table.

Wonder what's up with Ted. He never hides in the back, and I swear that man has never left by the back door before.

8

The flat mailer had arrived while Ted had been in town collecting Sam's letter.

Ted's name and address were printed in neat, understated black calligraphy. _Do Not Bend_ was stamped in red front and back on the mailer. Inside was a brief note thanking him and Max for having made Erin's first trip to Wellsboro, since Sam's funeral, less painful.

The glassine envelope held a 12 inch square photo of Max entering the water on the first retrieve.

Laura had caught a profile of Max in perfect form, eyes locked on the distant dummy, just as his front feet had broken the water. The setting sun had turned the water droplets into a mist of diamonds surrounding the big black Labrador.

Has to be a custom print job. He studied the sepia print. _The lady has talent._

Ted held the photo at arm's length and admired it. In fishing parlance, this was _one for the wall_. The matte finish on the ivory stock was perfect for the deep sepia-toned print. _Who would have thought? . . . This gal could be a pro if she wanted._

"Come here, Max. See the great picture the little girl's mother took of you. We'll have to put this one up in the den."

Ted studied the wall of his 16 by 24 foot den, his favorite room in the house, the one where he and Max spent most of their time. Dead center in the home, the room, originally a living room, had no outside windows.

Ted had immediately converted its fireplace with a Vermont Castings wood stove with glass panels in the doors. _Too much of the heat escapes through an open chimney, but I sure like to look at the fire._

He had placed interior windows and glass-paneled French doors to every room surrounding the former living room. _I like to see out._

He and the shop teacher had rewired the room and added

natural light fixtures in the ceiling.

"Hope no one thinks you've gone to raising pot," the friend had quipped.

Then Ted had paneled the walls in new poplar tongue-and-groove siding, and had finished it and the new matching beams in a stain the color of honey when morning sun shines through it.

It had taken most of the winter to put a real hand-finish on the wood, but, with ceilings painted ivory and faux-ivory stone floor tiles, it was a beauty.

Ted had furnished the room with two deep green recliners, a couch, and a rocker. Three deep blue pots of pink geraniums, his mother's favorite, mixed with ivy were added along with a live lemon tree.

He had asked Madge who ran the local antique shop to keep her eyes out for a big old desk. "Nothing wimpy, now, Madge. I need drawers on both sides and a big top surface. I like to leave some things out while I'm thinking on them, and I'll still have to be able to see the computer and phone," he had laughed.

It had taken her almost a year, but the wait had been worth it. Madge had hit on an auction where the equipment of a small local newspaper which had been eaten up by a chain was being dispersed. The editor's walnut desk, chair, and two file cabinets had sold as a set for $325 because they were "too dark, too big, and showed too much age."

Madge phoned the night she got home, before she had even cleaned them.

Ted came right over and had been so happy that he had insisted on cleaning them himself.

"Well, if you clean them, I'll let you have them for my price plus fifty for Harry's hauling them home and bringing them to your place."

"Hey, our deal was that you would find and buy them, and I would pay your usual markup."

"No, Ted, you're a friend," Harry had called from the adjoining room. "I'm not sure Jesse ever would have graduated if you hadn't got hold of him."

"I'll drink your coffee, Harry, and eat Madge's pie

anytime you offer, but I won't steal from you. You make a livin' doin' this."

Ted had written the check for $700 plus tax and had thought he had a real bargain.

After cleaning and more hand-rubbing, the rich walnut made a perfect contrast against the soft honey of the walls and really set off the green recliners and couch.

"Dead center over the desk; that's where you'll be, Max."

. . .

Ted was back in town at the frame shop by 11:30.

He was in luck; Cassie kept an excellent stock of suppplies. His former student promised results before closing.

. . .

Max's photo hung over the desk by six.

Stepping back to admire it, Ted noted, again, that all of Erin's gifts hadn't come from her daddy. Sam's daughter had more than a little talent herself.

9

The package was on Laura's desk when she arrived home Saturday evening, but she had promised Erin the picture, so she had ignored it until Sunday afternoon. *Nothing can be that important anyway, not anymore.*

Inside was a note from Neil Bradley and an envelope addressed to her in her father's handwriting.

Since Maria was out shopping, Laura made herself a cup of tea and sat at the kitchen table to carefully open the envelope.

Funny, I haven't sat at my kitchen table in years.

Her elbow came up on the table and braced the hand that went under her chin as she stared off into space. *The four of us used to spend a lot of time around the table at home. We almost lived in that kitchen 'til after supper. That's what we called it, supper. When did I begin calling it dinner?*

Laura shook her head and took the letter out to read.

"My dearest Laura,

"I pray that you and Erin are all healed by now. Don't mourn my death, dear. I lived a good, full life. My passing was as comfortable as possible.

"Laura, I wish I had been able, in life, to make you know that you were the best thing that ever came to me. After years of wanting children and finally giving up hope, I fell hopelessly in love the first time I laid eyes on you.

"There you were in the circle of your mother's arm; one look told me that my life had been worthwhile. If I never did another thing, I had done my part in bringing life to you.

"And, Laura, nothing since that moment has changed that feeling, not even a smidgen, not for an instant.

"I thought maybe Nick would be able to help you. I know he tried. The Easter you were down here pregnant with Erin, after a little Scotch, I asked him if you had ever told him about the accident.

"He shook his head in wonderment as I shared our story.

"Laura, my dear, I believe, on that horrible day, you decided that you would never allow yourself to care so much for anyone, ever again, that another's pain, even his death, could hurt you the way the results of that storm hurt you."

Laura's tears started.

So he had known all along. . . . He had understood. She wiped her eyes. Please forgive me, daddy. I never believed that anyone could understand, least of all you. . . . I stole them from you!

"I think you made that decision, not to hurt others, but to save yourself. I suspect you convinced yourself that you were not strong enough to ever hurt that much again.

"I know Nick got close a few times, but you did not trust either life or yourself enough to let him inside that wall. Not even little Erin has made it completely inside.

"Oh, I know you love her in your way. I believe you would die for her with absolutely no hesitation, but I sometimes wonder if you will _live_ for her.

"There are many degrees of love, Laura, many different kinds. You have the fierce love that all good mothers have for their children. There is another love, the I-don't-give-a-damn-how much-pain-it-brings-me, I-will-always-give-you-my-total-heart kind. It's the best there is. I know.

"I never told anyone else your story. I always figured it was yours to tell, but I felt I owed it to Nick. There was no sense in his feeling that your pain was his burden, somehow his failure."

Laura heaved a sigh of relief. *At least he betrayed me only to Nick.*

"Laura, dear, another person is reading the next part of this letter, the part that begins 'Dear Ted.' Please read what I have written him."

Laura read all of Sam's letter to Ted. Then she threw the pages on the table. *How dare he? . . . How could he do this to me? . . . What right did he have?*

She snorted. *Well, I can never face Ted Weaver again; that's for sure, no matter how much I think he helped Erin.*

Laura gathered the pages, angrily preparing to shred them, but then felt she owed it to her father to finish reading what he had written. *After all, he used his strength when he was losing his fight with cancer to write this, and it is the last time I will hear Sam's thoughts.*

She continued to read.

"Laura, dear, don't be angry. Someone has to know to be able to explain should that ever become necessary.

"Ted Weaver is a good man; I can assure you that he will never repeat your story unless it is absolutely necessary. You can trust him. I do, completely.

"But I owe him in almost the same way I owed Nick. Laura, I have asked him to be the administrator of my will, and Ted is a busy man. I know he will do as I have asked, but I also know that unless you change, it will be very difficult for him to deal with you. You see, Ted is a man who values memories as much as you try to wall them out.

"I can hear you telling him to take what he wants and burn the rest, that you want nothing: 'That part of my life is over.'

"He wouldn't have been able to understand and would have done his best to reason with you if I had not told him. That scene would have hurt both of you.

"I want him to know your anger is not directed at him.

"You would never have allowed yourself to care enough to sort through my things because, in sorting, you might discover something which you want to forget.

"I will love you and Erin to my last moment, dear, and take memories of you both with me if that is possible. I ask one thing:

"Try to tear down the wall. Forgive yourself, my darling, of a guilt that was never yours.

"Daddy."

. . .

Daddy, that is what I used to call him all of the time. I started calling him Sam after the wreck.

. . .

Laura dropped her head to her now-folded arms and began sobbing. *Oh, daddy, did the pain I have caused you bring on your cancer? . . . Would you be here now if only I hadn't wrecked?*

. . .

Laura cried softly for some time, then took a deep breath. *This is doing no one any good.*

She stood and collected the pages of the letter returning them to the envelope.

She placed the mailer in the trash but carried the letter to her room and put it in her safe.

Then she went to her bathroom and took a deep drink from the water bottle which she now kept on her sink.

Erin must not see me like this.

10

The reading of Sam's will provided some surprises.

Neither Ted nor Laura had known that Sam had become very wealthy through his only stock purchase: 1000 shares of Microsoft when it first went public.

Ted and Sally Ann were each to have one fifth of Sam's stock account, ending any money worries for them.

The remaining three fifths of the account was to be shared by a variety of charities since "Nick left Laura and Erin with more wealth than they can ever spend."

Neither Ted nor Laura had expected Sam would require that his home be kept open and ready for visitors for a period of 24 months following the reading of the will. At the end of the twenty-four month period, Laura was to decide whether to keep or to sell Sam's home. If sold, the proceeds were to go to Laura.

Other provisions were of a more normal nature.

Erin was to be given her grandmother's jewelry.

Ted was to retain Sam's gun collection which he had taken for safekeeping when Sam's end was near, and Ted was to take the entire contents of Sam's library.

Sally Ann was to take Sam's Bronco.

As they left Neil Bradley's office, Ted paused in the doorway. "Laura why don't we go over to the hotel and treat Erin to a lemonade or an iced tea? We can talk a bit and maybe decide on a time to go to the house. I'd like to be with you and Erin when you go there for the first time if I won't be intruding on your privacy."

"No, you won't be intruding. It will be nice to have someone there." She looked at Ted, "I don't do well in lonely spaces. ... An iced tea sounds good."

"Want to leave the cars here and stretch our legs a little?"

"Yes, a walk might feel good. Erin has been sitting still like a good girl for a long time, haven't you, honey?"

Erin smiled up at her mother. "It will be okay, mommy. We'll do just what grandpa Sam wanted. He knew best about a lot of things."

They walked the block and a half to the PennWells, pausing as they passed the Wynken, Blynken and Nod statue on the Green across from the town library.

"Say, Erin, have you seen the statue up close?"

"Yes, grandpa Sam took me there a couple of times." She smiled. "He read me the poem too."

She looked up at Laura. "He said that he and grandma Emily used to read the poem to you at night when you were a little girl, mommy."

Laura agreed. "They did and to Sammy too." *How long has it been since I have even said Sammy's name? . . . Poor little Sammy.* A shiver went over her body.

Erin took her mommy's hand. "I know about Sammy. Grandpa Sam told me he had had a little boy."

Erin looked at her mommy as she felt Laura's body stiffen. "Grandpa Sam said Sammy died when he was just a little guy."

Laura made no reply.

Ted breathed deeply. *Lot of tension right here at the moment.*

He opened the door to the PennWells and held it for Laura and Erin to enter. He paused at the desk clerk's office window. "Is it too early to get a cold soft drink, Terry?"

"Not at all, Ted. Three?"

"Yes."

"Right this way." Terry seated them himself and motioned for a waitress. "Been doin' any fishin'?"

"You need to get out there. I took a couple through the gorge last weekend. It was a good day. I'm hoping to get some in tomorrow too."

His glance at Laura reminded her of his phone call the night before.

Ted and Laura chose iced tea, and Erin asked for an orange juice.

Laura opened the conversation. "We should go over

to the house after we drink this. You probably ought to get started moving the books." She looked meaningfully at Erin. "And if you two plan to fish together tomorrow, we'd better get something done today."

Erin's eyes lit up. She looked at Ted, then at her mother. "May I, mommy? Are you going to let me fish with Ted and Max?"

Erin's sudden enthusiasm brought a smile to Laura's face. "Well, I don't know what Max's plans are, but we brought your gear, and Ted promised to bring you back to me safe and sound."

"You could come too, you know."

"I don't fish, Ted."

"Well, lots of people who don't fish enjoy just being out in nature. To tell the truth, that's one reason I like fishing so much. It's quiet and peaceful with birds and butterflies and lots of wild flowers this time of year."

"I hadn't thought of that. . . . I might take you up. It's been a long time since we've been outside much. And I would feel better about Erin if I could see her." Laura looked at Ted. "Are you sure I won't get in the way?"

Ted stood and got Laura's chair. "We'd love to have your company wouldn't we Erin?"

The red pigtails bounced off Erin's back. "Yes, mommy, I really would."

"Let's walk to the cars. We'll meet again at Sam's."

Sam's house sat well back on a double lot that fronted Route 6 at the edge of Wellsboro. He had built the house when he learned that Laura was pregnant. *Can't have them crowded in here with me when they come visit, and I want plenty of visits with my grandbabies.* He had drawn the plans for the 3600 square foot home himself and then had polished them with Bud Johnson, the contractor. Sam had wanted a nice front porch which ran the front of the 16 by 22 living room.

The living room, the library, and the eat-in kitchen made up the central core of the house. The library had a fireplace, and there was an 8 by 12 sun room facing south off the kitchen. "My Emily always loved a sun room for plants. This is for you, Emily." An 8 by 10 laundry completed the rear wall.

The central core was flanked both east and west with 20 by 44 foot wings. The interior of each wing had a six foot inner hall with skylights. The outer wall surrounded two 14 by 15 bedrooms, each with a three foot closet running the length of the side wall. An 8 by 14 bathroom separated the two bedrooms of each wing.

A bedroom, bath, and a den for Sam had claimed the east wing. The west wing was for guests.

The inner hall on the west also gave access to the second story which was a finished 44 by 22 foot space crossed by four exposed beams which divided the ceiling into eleven-foot sections, " play room for the grand kids or more rooms if Nick and Laura are really productive."

Naturally-weathered gray shingles covered the outside of both home and garage. Everything was trimmed in white.

It was a pretty place with the double lots providing ample room for a spacious fenced front yard, "a safe place for the kids to play while we watch 'em."

The front yard was flanked by a driveway on the east and an open side yard to the west. Both were edged with garden.

Sam had liked his tomatoes fresh and had always planted a variety of vegetables and flowers each spring.

The gardens were empty and mowed this year.

Ted pulled the Suburban in behind Laura's Land Rover. He allowed Laura and Erin to go to the front porch first. *Just take your time; you can do this.*

Laura unlocked the front door to her father's home and walked in. Erin and Ted followed. Ted set about flipping switches and opening windows. He soon had lights on and ceiling fans going.

Laura headed straight for the kitchen. *I hate to even open the refrigerator door. I should have cleaned this when we came for the funeral. I wish Maria were here. Oh, well.* Laura swung the door open. A sparkling refrigerator interior greeted her. "Ted, did you clean this?"

"No, Sally Ann beat me to it. She cleaned it the day after Sam's funeral. She emptied the freezer too. She didn't know about Sam's 24-month plan."

Laura walked back to the living room and ran her hand over a tabletop. "No dust."

"Sally Ann again. I told her we were meeting at Neil's today. She wanted the place to look the way Sam always kept it."

Laura looked at Ted. "Sally Ann? She's the person dad left his Bronco to, isn't she?"

"She's the one."

Laura's brow furrowed. "He left her some grave spaces and part of his stock account too. Were she and Sam? . . ."

Ted laughed. "No, no. Nothing like that. I don't think your dad. . . .   Well, I know he and Sally Ann and I were just good friends. She came here from the West Coast and opened a sandwich shop a few years ago. Your dad and I immediately became regulars when we discovered that she welcomed hunters, fishermen, and sensible dogs."

Ted looked at Laura. "Not many places will let a dog in even when it's cold outside, and we never liked to leave a wet dog in a cold car. She knew Rowdy and half a dozen others. Kept a dog there herself."

Ted grinned and shook his head. "No, not your dad and anyone as far as I ever knew." He paused, then added, "And I think I would have known."

He walked to the doorway. "Laura, if you would like to keep the Bronco to drive when you're down here, I know Sally Ann would never claim it. She has a perfectly good vehicle, and she has never appeared to be hurting for money."

Laura shook her head. "That won't be necessary. I use the Rover, and we have a Jeep at home. Maria, Erin's nanny and our live-in, uses the Jeep for errands." She motioned toward the library. "Dad wanted you to take the books."

"If you don't mind, I'd like to leave them here until the house is closed, Laura. I'll need to build more book shelves, and I want you and Erin to go through the books and keep what you would like."

Laura looked at Ted through vacant eyes. "We have a library in our home and in the townhouse, Ted. I can't imagine dad would have anything either of us would want."

She walked into the library. Except for the door and

the hall to the kitchen, the walls were completely covered with shelves. Books, videos, pictures, and souvenirs covered the walls. "It's up to you. Leave things here until we close the house or gradually take things as you make room. What you don't want, give to the Salvation Army or whomever."

"Thank you, Laura." Ted swept the room with his eyes. *How can she do this? These were Sam's treasures. Maybe with time. ...* "If there's nothing you need, I'll be going on home. What time would you like Erin to start fishing tomorrow?"

"I'm not sure. What would be a reasonable time?"

"A lot of my guides start at six. If later is better for you, we'll start whenever you like."

Laura lowered her voice and nodded toward Erin walking into Sam's den. "I'd like to have her sleep as long as possible."

"Well, why don't you and Erin drive on out to my place when you get ready tomorrow. I'll be there all morning, and we'll take it from there. There's a map to my place on the back of my card." He brought out his wallet and pulled another card from it. "Here's a spare."

"That sounds good. We'll see you sometime in the morning."

"After some fishing, we might want to come back here and go through the files. We need to get them cleaned out. This is a safe town, but you never know when a house is empty. No stranger needs to know Sam's business."

"Okay." She turned away and then turned back. "You're sure she will be safe?"

Ted put his hand over his heart. "I swear Erin will always be safe with me."

11

Ted's cottage sat three miles out of town. His 17 acres on Little Pine Creek bordered state ground on its north side. The land sat high enough to prevent flooding and to provide a dry basement.

He had restored the cottage himself. His first effort had gone into converting the former living room into a den. The living room was moved to the former dining room.

His second undertaking had been the conversion of the smallest bedroom into a 10 by 16 locker-style bathroom with a 5 by 7 shower which he and Max always shared after Max had been in the water.

Max and he also shared the master bedroom. Max's bed, one foot off the floor, was set in a bay that had once held a window seat.

Ted had hired a former student who was now making his living as a stained glass artist to create three stained-glass panels in which lots of frosted glass had been used between the pinks, yellows, cobalt blues and emerald greens. *I want to know when it's daylight.* The flower garden design glowed when the sun was in the east.

Ted's bed was situated so he could check the weather by looking straight ahead and then enjoy the sunrise by glancing to his right.

To the left of his room and directly behind the den was another converted bedroom. This 16 by 10 room was now a walk-in closet. One area of the shelving was devoted entirely to fishing gear: special clothing, nets, boots, waders, etc. Some was bagged; some sat in clear plastic containers so logically arranged that Ted could have packed the Suburban blindfolded. Beside these shelves were floor-to-ceiling vertical supports for his fishing rods.

Another area was similarly devoted to hunting gear; two locked gun cases had been bolted to the wall. All gear was kept cleaned, repaired, and at-the-ready.

Max's gear rested on horizontal shelves

Sam had once groused that Ted's closet was better organized than most libraries.

Outside, a small two-acre, spring-fed pond took pride of place. Ted had put some fish in it over the years. When he caught a really pretty brookie on Lyman Run at the end of the day, he sometimes brought it home rather than turn it loose. He had put a few browns in the pond too, not many of either, just enough to see some once in a while.

Ted had never fished there nor had he allowed fishing there; this was just for looking at.

He had created a place of peace for some of the species who had given so much to so many over the years, sort of his gift back. He fed the fish often enough to make them come near the surface when he walked out on the dam or the small dock where he kept a blue L L Bean Predator Canoe by Old Town in summer.

The pond was surrounded by a bed of flat stones seated in pea gravel. He kept the next twelve feet mowed close to the ground. Then four feet of semi-naturalized plants created a barrier between the close mow and the fields beyond; nothing fancy, it was just a mixture of seasonal perennials and any small shrub which produced a berry for Ted or the birds.

Ted could see this area out his kitchen window and, of course, from his deck. He always kept his large lawn mowed close: *mountain rattlers. Never seen one out here.* The remainder of his land was brush-hogged every fall.

Laura had barely parked the Rover beside his garage when Ted and Max started down the walk to meet them. "Good morning, ladies. Come in and let me show you around."

He winked at Erin. "Then we'll go down and see if anyone in the pond is hungry enough to take a fly."

Laura noticed the floor to ceiling bookshelves covering one entire wall of the living room. More bookshelves had been fitted into the den and even the bedroom.

Bookshelves holding an assortment of cookbooks and gardening books along with team photos and antique crocks and pitchers had been built in the kitchen.

"You certainly must have shared my dad's love of books, Ted; I'm glad the library is yours."

Ted nodded in agreement. "We spent a lot of time talking about the books we had read and movies and plays we had seen."

He paused by the door. "We went into Phily once or twice a year to see a weekend of plays, and, in the summer, there's a nice little theater in the Finger Lakes."

"Ever come to the City for the some real theater?"

"No, but we had talked about it."

He led them out to the deck. "I thought you might be more comfortable if Erin and I try our luck here, Laura. You're welcome to use anything in the house, or you could sit here on the deck and watch us. You might want to go down to the picnic table or move around the pond if you want to get some shots."

He raised an eyebrow and smiled in her direction. "Of course, you could fish with us; I have one or two extra rods."

Laura shook her head and almost smiled. "So I noticed. That is some closet you have in there. We have walk-ins too, but yours is wider than ours, and I have to admit I have never before seen a window, a ceiling fan, or a dehumidifier in a closet."

"Well, it was a bedroom before I bought the place. And we have to watch the humidity up here in the mountains, especially since I come in a little damp from time to time."

Ted turned to Erin. "Did you bring your gear, Erin?"

Erin's pigtails bobbed. "It's all in the car."

"Well, come on; we're burning daylight, kid." They headed for the Rover with Max between them.

Once Erin was outfitted, Laura walked with them to the pond. "You know this is really lovely, and there are so many birds. You must feed them."

"Guilty. The wildlife circle gives them cover from the hawks, and the water is right there. I've put some houses in trees and on old posts. A lot of them build their nests in the pines." He took Erin's hand. "Let's walk around her once, Erin, and see if we can spot a fish."

Erin started concentrating on the surface of the water. "Oh, look, Ted; lookie, mommy. Right there." She pointed, "See?"

"Look out, Mr. Fish; she has good eyes."

A smile settled on his face. "What do you usually do first, when you start to fish, Erin?"

"My Daddy taught me to strip off some line and get my fly in the water and then false cast to bring the fly up and try to get some line out. Then I cast."

Ted looked off toward the long sand pit he had used primarily as a place to have semi-private practice with his pitchers and catchers for the last few years. *That would be a perfect place.*

"You know, Erin, I always need to loosen up a little when I haven't been casting for a while. Let's walk over to the sand pit."

Ted laid his rod down. He proceeded to twist his body, roll his arms in big circles and roll his shoulders. As he did some squats, he noticed out of the corner of his eye Erin was doing the same. *Gotcha!*

Then he picked up his rod, laid out some line, put it in the air, and aimed for the limb on the holly tree.

"Well, would you look at that. Must be a little rusty. Why don't you go ahead and do some dry casts, Erin, while I get myself untangled." *Buy her some time to cast without my watching. Let her relax in private.*

Laura didn't know much about fishing, but she had seen Ted purposely put the fly in the holly tree. *It's easy to see why dad liked him so much. He's a gentleman; just like Sam.*

She sighed. *Oh, daddy, I wish things had been different. If only I hadn't made us late by insisting on trying on that black sheath, and that wasn't even the dress we bought!*

Laura's head raised, and she heaved an audible sigh. *Mother and Sammy would still be alive. How old would Sammy be now? . . . I wonder what he would have done with his life?*

Tears filled Laura's eyes. She blinked them back, but they returned. She proped her elbow on the picnic table and rested her chin on the back of her fist as she tried concentrating on Erin to bury the memories. *Everything lost. All over a simple dress.*

"Say, you sure know what to do with that thing, Erin.

I'm finally unhooked. Let me give you a fresh fly."

Ted walked toward the laughing little girl who had managed to put her fly in the sand every time she had cast. " I'd better just watch and net for you today; my control's a little off."

Taking his feigned distress as real, Erin encouraged, "Maybe you didn't warm up enough, Ted. I know you can do it; mommy and I saw you at the creek the last time we were here."

She allowed her lower lip to cover part of her upper one. *Is it okay to give him a tip?*

She squared her little shoulders and put a smile on her face. "I think about casting a lot, Ted. I never want to forget how, and my Daddy can't help me any more, so I lay in bed at night and think about how to do it. I go over and over it in my mind." She met his eyes. "It helps me."

"Well, thanks. That's a good idea. You know what that's called, Erin?"

Her expression became a little defensive, and she looked at her feet. *Did I make him mad?* "No."

"It's called imaging. Great athletes do it all the time: pitchers, batters, high jumpers, basketball players. Did you figure this out all by yourself?"

I'm glad he didn't say it was bad to give him a tip. Jamie always says secrets are bad; that they make me sick. A smile appeared on Erin's face. "Yep. All by myself."

"Well, we're not gonna catch any fish up here in the sand. Come on."

Ted walked her to the side of the pond which would allow Laura a good shot if she was so inclined.

Erin put the fly out reasonably well and brought it in correctly.

Ted saw a young brown come up a few feet away. He touched Erin's shoulder. "See him? Just off to your left," he whispered.

Erin nodded, angled her body toward the fish, managed to get her line in the air, and put the fly down close to where the brown had been. The fly had landed with a tiny splash.

She'll have to make the landing a little more delicate. Ted rubbed his chin as Erin gathered her line. *How do I get her*

to ease off just a little without making her tense? . . . She still
has to put enough energy in the line to get it out far enough.

Another brown came up about fifteen feet out. *That just might be the answer.* "Did you see that one, Erin?"

She nodded. "He's out pretty far."

"Go ahead and give it a try."

By extending her normal cast, Erin had caused the line to eat up most of the energy, and the fly landed gently as a feather.

The brown trout was fooled. He took it.

"Keep your tip up, Erin. Play him out some; he has a real tender mouth."

Erin was all business now, watching the line move from side to side in the water, letting the trout take a little more line, keeping the rod tip up.

"Okay, bring him in a little when you want. He'll still want to go sideways with you. Let him. Don't tug. Play him like a Stradivarius."

He heard Laura chuckle behind him. Out of the corner of his eye he saw her crouch for the shot if Erin got him to the net. *Love is always stronger than fear.*

He didn't want to break Erin's concentration, so Ted said nothing. *Looks like he may have swallowed the fly; don't bite the leader, Mr. Brown; Erin needs this so much.*

Ted crouched beside Erin and pulled his net from his back. He slipped the net gently below the surface of the water. "Quit reeling now, but keep your hand on the reel. Keep your tip up and back slowly around behind me."

Ted waited until she had the nice trout centered over the mouth of the net. "Got him! Look at that color, perfect dark leopard mottling with just a touch of red-orange for contrast. What a beauty!"

He reached for Erin's rod in order to shift the net into her hands. "Here, feel his weight, kiddo. This is no baby; I can tell you that. Take both hands."

Erin just beamed. "Look, mommy, look. I caught him. I really did."

She looked at Ted then at the ground for quite a while. She raised tear-misted eyes to his face. "I never did catch one all by myself before. My daddy sometimes gave me his rod, when he had one in close, but I never did catch one all by myself before."

She looked at Ted through happy tears. "Thanks, Ted. Thanks a whole bunch." She handed the net back to him.

Ted had heard the camera's lens recording each movement. He looked at Laura as he bent to wet his hands. "We'll need a special picture of Izaac Walton Jr. here holding her first fish."

Ted carefully looked at the brown's mouth. One reason Erin had been able to land one this size was that he had, indeed, swallowed the fly. *Being hand-fed had made him careless. Sorry, big fellow.* Ted cut the line near the trout's mouth. *Well, you went for a good cause.*

"Wet your hands, Erin."

Erin walked to the pond's edge and bent carefully to wet her little hands.

Ted clamped a small vice on the brown's lower lip. *This one won't make it back to the water, but she needs this.* "Wipe your right hand on your shirt sleeve. That's the way. Now here, take this vice and hold his head like this and put your wet hand back here under his tummy."

As he stepped back, he looked at Laura who was ready. He heard the lens.

Ted stepped in and took the trout from Erin. He looked at her then to Laura. "Now the three of us have to make a decision. I decided I wanted that picture to hang next to Max more than I wanted to put this one back. Do we clean him and have him for lunch, or do I clean him later and have him for supper?"

Erin didn't hesitate. Her voice was a little high from excitement, and her words came out in a rush. "My daddy had a black skillet, and we cleaned them, and he cooked them, and they tasted so good."

Ted lifted his eyes to Laura. "Can you clean potatoes?"
"I think so."

"Well, Erin has got us lunch. We shouldn't waste him."
Ted took time out to make a quick phone call.
The kitchen was big enough for three work stations.

Erin went to the bathroom. When she came back, she proudly announced, "I washed my hands real good. I'm ready."

Ted tied a kitchen towel around Erin's waist. "You have to work for your lunch here, kid." He moved a stool to the small sink, gathered fresh vegetables from the crisper, and pulled down a Tupperware bowl. He handed her a knife. "Know how to make a salad?"

"Yep."

"Laura, you take this double sink. If you'll peel and dice these potatoes while I go outside and clean this critter, I'll cook everything when I get back in."

Laura and Erin set themselves to two very unfamiliar tasks. *It's been a long time since I have cooked. Darn, taking too much potato with the skin. Mom always scolded me about that.*

Ted came back in and grabbed a bite of salad. "Um, good fresh vegetables; I love them. Laura, will you set the table while I get this stuff on the stove?"

He looked at the cabinet to the right of the sink. "Dishes are up there. Set four places."

Laura had just finished with the table when the front screen door squeeked. "Hello. Anybody home?"

"Get on in here, Sally Ann. You know better than to hesitate. We are in desperate need of dessert."

Ted glanced at Laura and lowered his voice. "I phoned Sally Ann to come join us. Give you ladies a chance to get to know each other."

A smiling white-haired lady placed a lemon meringue pie on the table.

Ted made quick introductions and left the girls to get to acquainted while he cooked.

The lunch was great. Erin ate like a little pig. She washed it all down with two glasses of milk, matching Ted glass for glass.

Sally Ann's pie made a perfect ending to a rural feast.

"Thank you, Erin, for this special treat." Sally Ann patted Erin's hand. "It isn't often I get good fresh fish like that. Thank you so much for sharing."

She turned to Laura. "Oh, Laura, I can see so much of your father in you: the color of your eyes, the way you carry yourself; your no-nonsense approach to things. It was sure good to meet you."

"And I want to thank you for all the friendship you shared with Sam, Sally Ann, and for the care you took of the house and everything."

"Oh, think nothing of it, dear. That's just what friends do." She smiled at Laura again. "I hope we'll be friends, too, Laura. Next time, you make Ted bring you to my diner; I'll feed us all there. Just now I need to hurry back and get ready for the early evening rush."

Sally Ann took time to stop and pet Max on the way out. "You be a good boy, Maxie."

Max gave her a kiss on her hand as his tail thumped the floor.

Ted gathered the plates. "Want to work on the files this afternoon, Laura?"

"This has been better than you'll ever know, Ted, but I want to go back to the Wakefield's this afternoon and get some rest before the drive home tomorrow. I'm eager to get a look at the pictures. I know we agreed to go back to dad's this afternoon, but . . ."

Ted nodded in agreement. He could see that both Erin and Laura were pretty drained. "I think that's a good idea. Sometime in the next couple of weeks give me a call, and we can meet over there."

He bent and gave Erin a hug. "I still owe you a trip to the creek."

"Why don't we decide now, mommy. Ted has a calendar in his den. He can write it on there, and we'll know when to come. . . . I might leave my things here if that's all right." She looked at Ted for permission. *That way I'll have to come back.*

"Good idea. No sense in dragging gear home and back up here when you'll be back soon. Max will guard it for you."

Max's tail thumped the floor at the sound of his name.

Ted turned to look at Laura. "Do you want to set a date now or would you rather call?"

"Summer is fairly open with school out. We just have to arrange with Erin's counselor." Laura looked at the big calendar on the wall of the den. *Erin probably needs a couple of sessions with Jamie after Sam's will.*

She mentally counted off two weeks. "I suppose you're busy the week of the fourth."

"July fourth? No, I have no commitments."

"Why don't we drive down the first of July?" She turned to Erin. "And we'll go home the fifth. Erin can see how they celebrate Independence Day in a small town; maybe she'll learn to appreciate the big city celebrations more."

Laura prodded Erin out the door, then stopped and turned toward Ted. "I really appreciate all you did today."

"I enjoyed every minute." He paused. "Want me to air out Sam's house and have the beds made up for next time?"

"That's a good idea; we would probably have a difficult time getting reservations at this late date. That way we'll be there, and I can sort through dad's files a little each day. I have a key. I'll phone when we get in."

"Sounds good. Oh, and, Erin, that brown was close to twenty inches, in case you want to tell someone."

The Land Rover pulled out of the drive.

. . .

"I didn't know you could cook, mommy."

"And I didn't know you could make a salad." Laura paused. "Or catch our lunch." She smiled at Erin who was beaming again.

"My very first one all by myself. Will you print my pictures right away, mommy?"

"I'll be too tired to see when we get home, but I promise I'll print them the first thing the next day."

"Okay. . . . I think I might try to draw him. Jamie says it would be good for me to draw and color. I know just what he looked like. . . . And, mommy, he was so heavy. I wasn't even sure I could hold him when Ted gave him to me."

"Well, you did just fine, kiddo. I'm proud of you."

My Daddy would have touched me even if we were driving.

12

Sally Ann Truesdale had come into town a few years ago from the West Coast after having traveled a lot with her husband who had been an officer in the Army.

She said she had never really had a permanent home after marriage; now she wanted to put down some roots.

She had purchased a small house with a tidy yard downtown and a second, larger, house with a big yard on a corner at the edge of town where small businesses and homes mingled. The second house was repainted a soft yellow with pine green shutters. A red front screen door trimmed tastefully in pine green was added.

The interior walls which, originally, had formed three large rooms across the front were carefully eliminated. Chair railing was added, and the entire area was painted a rich cream.

The top third of the two side walls of the shop were covered with pictures when the shop opened. On one wall were pictures of Sally Ann's family and places she had lived. There was a nice family portrait of Sally Ann, her husband, and their only son. There was a single of her husband in uniform along with another candid shot taken when he had been fishing while standing in the surf. There were three pictures of her son: a baby on a rug, a teen with a group of friends, and a teen in a baseball uniform, holding a catcher's mask.

The opposite wall held framed posters of scenes in the United States and Europe.

The interior walls across the rear had also been removed. A large stainless steel kitchen with a counter that served as a divider from the front area centered the rear space. A pantry bordered one side of the kitchen, a similar room (a tiny den where she could relax in private with her dog) bordered the other side, and a bathroom on each outside wall finished off the remaining space.

Both the side yard and the front yard were then paved, and stones were set near the building to define a parking lot and on the corner itself to protect the traffic.

A sign was added to the corner of the parking lot: "Sally Ann's Sandwich Shop" was the header; "Open weekdays 7 a.m. to 7 p.m.; Closed Sundays and holidays;" "No Smoking or Cussing;" "Teens, Fishermen, Hunters, and Mannered Dogs always Welcome."

Sally Ann was in her mid-sixties, short, no-longer thin, but still an easy smiler with a twinkle in her eye. Her little sandwich shop instantly became a haven for the town's teens. She had rules, but they were sensible.

If she asked you to leave, you left, and you didn't come back until school opened the next fall. "Everyone starts fresh in September."

Sally Ann enjoyed teenagers, but she believed in tough love. She wanted them to grow to be good men and women who knew to be honest and fair with others, a philosophy which did not allow for what she called "trashin" regularly along the way.

After she opened, she put a computer in the shop. "E-mail's the best invention of the twentieth century," she would often say. She firmly believed that the 'kids,' who only needed to ask to share her computer, had introduced her to it's opportunities and had kept her updated.

Although she enjoyed all sports, it was no secret that she loved baseball best of all. When the game was home, Sally Ann was there. Professionally, if the Cubs were playing, the game was on the shop's TV.

From the day she had met him, she had liked Ted. Over the years, she had grown to respect him a lot and, now, treated him with the love she would have given her own son.

Sam had been another favorite, and she had somehow talked him into putting Rowdy with her own good bitch.

Sam had sworn he would never do it. He had never bred Rowdy, and he "wasn't about to start on some used-up show dog who did nothing but lay behind the counter and attend high school sporting events."

Sally Ann had countered that Emma carried the best English lines in America, had a pedigree full of close-up English champions, and that, in England, a Labrador Retriever had to do more than walk around a ring to earn a championship. . . .

"And neither dog is getting any younger."

Sam had said the only championships that he counted were the field champions and added that, although Rowdy was by and out of the same, he (Sam) wasn't convinced that some field champions were much more than trained monkeys. "Hunting is what proves a dog, and Rowdy is the best I have ever taken to the field! ... And I've hunted behind a few dogs."

On and on it had gone, frequently after baseball games when Sally Ann was all worked up about some call which the umpire had "obviously made with his eyes glued shut," and Sam was looking at a long summer which afforded no decent bird hunting.

He could have gone to the pheasant farm, but Sam held that he would just as soon shoot chickens as some poor, pen-raised, hand-released pheasant that had "never had a chance to live a normal life."

Amazingly, somehow, four years ago, the arguing had stopped; and Emma and Rowdy, both well-past their primes at eleven and twelve respectively, had been mated.

Sam was to get pick-of-the-litter male.

Sally Ann was to take pick-of-the-litter female.

They were to split the money from the sale of the remaining pups with Sam controlling the sales.

Emma produced one pup, a black male.

It was as though both old dogs had relinquished their personal best to their sole prodigy, for each had died before the start of the next baseball season.

Rowdy and Emma would lay with that pup in Sally Ann's den, taking turns washing him with their tongues.

Rowdy would spend hours on his belly with his stout forepaws in front, the pup snuggled between them.

Emma did her duty on her side offering him the best that her body could produce.

Before the pup was weaned, it was mutually agreed that neither Sam nor Sally Ann could take the pup. Max would go to the one person they each loved.

They both knew Ted would bring him on the right way, and that Max would always be a part of their lives too.

So Max saw his first basketball game with Emma and Sally Ann.

He filled his nose with bird from a wing that Rowdy and Sam had brought him.

He took his first swim with Rowdy and Emma at the boat launch as Sam, Sally Ann, and Ted had shared the potential they each frequently noted in the fuzzy, slightly awkward pup who that day, to a less biased observer, would have resembled a clumsy little bear cub much more than the poised wonder he had become.

13

Laura followed her previous procedure for getting an early start from the Whitfield Bed and Breakfast. She glanced in the back seat to check on the sleeping Erin, and then turned east on NY 17. Not needing to go into the City this trip, they should be home in Danbury by late afternoon.

Once she had the Land Rover settled into the pace of the early morning traffic, she reached for a sip of coffee. *It was a good weekend. Ted Weaver went out of his way to let Erin fish in a spot where I would feel comfortable and have something to do other than just sit and watch them.*

The driver of a red sports car sped by and then, seeing the sign that warned of single-lane traffic ahead, cut abruptly in front of them.

Jerk! Laura tapped the brake softly. *Wonder if he has a sleeping child on the rear seat.*

Laura hit the power to the c d player and immediately turned the volume down low. She took a deep breath. *Well, maybe they don't know what can happen in an instant in an automobile. . . . I do, and I pay for that knowledge every day of my life.*

She used the rearview to glance at Erin again. *No harm done. . . .Erin certainly ate well yesterday. I wish I could get her to gain a little weight. . . . It was nice of Ted to fix lunch for us. I'm sure the man has lots of other things to be doing. That place of his was neat as a pin.*

Laura smiled at the thought of one of her dad's favorite sayings. *Those two must have got along like Nip and Tuck.*

From time to time, Erin moved a little on the seat to adjust her pressure points, but, for the most part, she slept soundly.

Probably really wore her out yesterday.

Laura changed lanes to pass an older couple in a pickup truck. *Looks like they're having fun: he's talking and gesturing with his right hand, and she's laughing. . . . Nick and I will never have the chance to be like that.*

Erin began to stir as they approached Binghamton.

Must be when her bladder wakes up. Laura smiled into the rearview mirror. "Hi, there, sleepyhead. What you doing back there?"

"Hi, mommy." Erin rubbed sleep out of her eyes and sat up. "Where are we?"

"Close to Binghamton. Shall we pull in for some breakfast and a pit stop?"

Erin arched her back as she leaned forward and placed her palms on the inside of her knees, stretching and rolling her neck and shoulders. "Yes, please. That would be nice, mommy. And I'll get up front then."

Laura remembered the exit and put on her blinker. "McDonald's again, okay?"

Erin scratched her forehead. "Sure, I liked it last time. Did you, mommy?"

Laura grinned again into the rearview. "They must have built it for us. It's a perfect place for us to stop and stretch our legs and grab a bite to eat." She brought the SUV to a stop.

Erin headed straight for the rest room. Laura followed. *Got to watch that coffee on long trips.*

After washing their hands, they came to the counter. "I'd like an orange juice and an Egg McMuffin, please."

"I want a black coffee and a McMuffin. Oh, and two bottles of water for the road."

They went to a table by the windows and unwrapped their breakfast sandwiches.

Laura took a bite. "Are they always this tough?"

"They're not tough, mommy; just chewy. My Daddy always got his on a biscuit."

"Do I still ask for McMuffins if I want a biscuit?"

"I don't remember. My Daddy just knew what to say, and they gave it to him." Erin took some juice.

Yes, Nick always knew what to say. Laura looked at the ceiling. *He had a way with people. But it wasn't just bullshit. He really liked people, cared about his trust accounts, and not just because it was his job either. He and Sam were a lot alike in some ways.*

Erin brought Laura out of her reverie. "Mommy, do I have a will?"

Laura's brows tightened as she stared at Erin in mild shock. "Why on earth would you ask that?"

Undaunted, Erin replied, "'Cause I want to know."

"Of, course not, Erin. Don't be silly."

"Why don't I have one?"

"Because you are just a little girl; you don't need a will." *I'd better get my own updated, though.* "Little girl's don't have wills."

"Why not?"

Laura rolled her eyes. *Oh, Lord, why does she get like this?* She looked at Erin and cleared her throat. "Because wills are for adults so, when they die, their possessions can be placed with those they choose to have them."

She paused for a second then continued. "Like grandpa's will told us what he wanted done with the things that he owned."

"I have things."

Laura could feel the tension, almost anger, building. "I know you have things, Erin, but wills are for people who might die."

"I could die."

"It is not probable. That means that it is not likely to happen soon."

"My Daddy died." Erin chewed on the last of her McMuffin. She swallowed. "Did you think he was likely to die soon?"

So that's where this is coming from. "No, of course, not."

"But he had a will. I know he did because I remember the day you went to the lawyer's office after my Daddy died just like we went after grandpa died at Easter."

Erin took a drink of juice. "So my Daddy had a will."

She looked squarely at Laura. "Didn't he? . . . Didn't my Daddy have a will?"

"Yes, of course, Nick had a will. Now will you please get off this subject before I become ill?" Laura stood, gathered the trays, dumped them with a definite thump, and walked to the

Land Rover. "Are you going to sit up front?"

"Nope. I'll stay in the back." *That will fix her!*

"Here's your water. Don't spill it!"

"I won't!"

Laura worked her way back onto 17 east. She looked in the mirror. Erin was staring out the window. *Why in the world didn't I handle that better? Why can't I just answer her damn questions and become involved with her without becoming emotional?*

Laura lifted her chin and rolled her head and shoulders. She could feel the tightness getting worse. *Does she have any idea what this obsessive talking about death does to me? Why won't she just drop it? I've told her often enough.*

The flashing lights behind her caught her attention. *What now?*

"Look, mommy, the cops."

Laura pulled to the berm. "Police, Erin. Not cops. I will not have you using slang."

The patrol car stopped behind her.

She lowered her window.

The officer left the warning flashers on and walked to the side of Laura's car. "Morning, Ma'am."

Laura didn't bother to smile. *Why go through a farce?* "Hello, officer."

He noted the little girl in the rear seat. She had her seat belt fastened. A pillow was beside her. He smiled at her. "How are you, miss?"

Erin smiled at him. "I'm fine, sir; how are you?"

"Just fine thanks." He moved his attention back to Laura. "I need to see your license."

Laura started to hand her wallet to him.

"Please remove it from your wallet."

Laura did as she was asked.

"I'll just be a second. Please stay in the car." The patrolman walked back to his car. ... He returned to Laura who was rubbing the back of her neck.

"Are you ill, Mrs. McCort?"

"No. I got up early this morning to try to get my daughter

home to Danbury at a decent hour."

"Do you know how fast you were going?"

"No. But I couldn't have been speeding. We had just pulled out of McDonald's."

"Which McDonald's would that be, Mrs. McCort?"

Laura pointed over her shoulder with her thumb. "The one right back there, at Binghamton."

He took a close look at her eyes. *Pupils look okay. No previous violations.* "Mrs. McCort, the McDonald's at Binghamton is seven miles back. I've been behind you for two miles. You were driving 78 miles per hour when I stopped you."

Laura looked at him and released a sigh. "Seventy-eight?"

"Yes. Is that your daughter in the rear seat?"

"Yes."

"Well, if I had a little girl like that in my rear seat, I sure wouldn't want to be speeding. Something tragic could happen." He shook his head. "People die everyday."

"I know that officer, and I am sorry I was speeding." She shook her head. "My mind was elsewhere."

He nodded. "I believe it was. But 78 with a child in the vehicle is way past my patience level. Do you have a history of speeding?"

"No; I am normally a very careful driver."

"Something have you upset today?"

"You might say so. I just spent two days in Wellsboro opening my deceased father's home for the first time after his funeral."

The officer fingered the rim of the hat under his arm. "I am truly sorry, Mrs. McCort. But you know you weren't thinking about that little girl when you were speeding, and you weren't thinking about her just now either. You said I, not we, just spent two days in Wellsboro. I assume she was with you?"

"Yes, Erin was with me."

"Well, maybe you'd better take a drink of your water there and calm down a bit. Under the circumstances, I'm afraid I'll have to cite you."

Afraid my ass. Laura looked straight ahead and involuntarily gritted her teeth. *Everyone knows you have to make a quota.* Laura sighed. *I wonder, does he specialize in stopping women?*

He handed her the ticket.

She reached for her purse. "I want to post bond."

"You may do that at the next exit, Mrs. McCort. You'll see directions to downtown as you pull off. The courthouse is on Main Street in the center of town."

"You mean you can't take my money?"

"That's right, ma'am. Please have a safe day." He paused. "You're free to go now."

Laura pulled out into traffic while he was walking to his car. *Have a safe day, my ass. We haven't lost enough time as it is. Now we have to find the courthouse and then waste more time paying our bond.* She exhaled noisily, but drove very carefully.

Laura parked in front of the finely detailed old building. "Come on, Erin."

Once inside, Laura entered the first office door to her right.

"May I help you?"

"Yes. I'm sorry to bother you, but I'm from out of town; I need to post bond for speeding."

"Oh, gracious, I'm sorry. Their office is on the second floor." The older woman pointed to the right of her door. "Take the elevator, then the first door to your right."   Laura never bothered to answer.

Erin turned and smiled at the nice lady. "Thank you." Then she followed Laura to the elevator. "My Daddy told me to always say thank you after someone helps you. He said it was even okay to do with waiters, no matter what Emily said." A thought just occurred to her. "Was Emily grandma?"

Laura took a deep breath. *I guess it's not her fault.* "My mother's name was Emily, Erin, but the Emily Nick was referring to was Emily Post, an expert on proper etiquette. It is not considered necessary to thank waiters in a restaurant; their job is to be as invisible as possible in order to provide a private experience for their customers."

"Invisible? Like Harry Potter when he has the cape on?"

Laura expelled a breath in exasperation. *I can't take any more of this!* "Oh, Erin, will you please just shut up for a while?"

Laura jerked the door open and made eye contact with the first clerk she saw. "I need to post bond for a speeding citation."

The young woman could hear the anger in Laura's voice and sense it in her body language. She tried to dispel some of it with a pleasant smile. "I'm glad you found our office. Some folks have trouble with us being on the second floor and all."

Laura's eyes shot bullets at the clerk. *Look, sweety, I am in no mood for chitchat with the likes of you.*

She simply handed the clerk the ticket.

The young woman looked at the ticket. "Oh, 78. That's in our serious range." She looked at Laura. "I'm afraid I have to take $156 for that."

Afraid? Laura gave a small snort. *Afraid? What is it with these nitwits? Do they ever break down and speak English?* Laura handed her 2 hundred-dollar bills.

The clerk hastily wrote a receipt and placed $ 44 in front of Laura. She smiled once more. "The receipt indicates your court date. You need to be back here in municipal court at 9 a.m. next Wednesday."

Laura collected the receipt and the money. *Fat chance, honey!* Without a word, she turned and walked toward the door.

Erin smiled up at the young woman. "Thank you; we'll see you on Wednesday."

Laura grabbed Erin's hand with enough force to make her wince. "Come on, Erin."

"Mommy, that hurt." Erin rubbed her hand as she climbed into the front seat.

When they finally got buckled into their vehicle, Laura rested her crossed arms on the steering wheel and dropped her face into them. For the first time in many months, she allowed herself a good cry, but not for long.

She reached in front of Erin and opened the glove compartment. She took a water bottle out and took a deep drink. Then she replaced that water bottle and opened the bottle from McDonald's.

She pulled herself together. *I will not allow myself*

to feel this. She banged her right fist on the dash. *I cannot wallow in the mess that my life has become!*

She squared her shoulders and turned the ignition key, ignoring a frightened Erin who was slightly huddled in her corner with her head tilted toward Laura, a curious expression on her face.

Once the Rover was moving, Erin put her hand on her mother's thigh. "It's okay, mommy. I won't tell."

Laura turned on the c d player and raised the volume until conversation was impossible.

She drove with care the rest of the way home.

Erin sat quietly and looked out the window.

14

The first thing Erin did when they got home was to go to her bedroom. She took the green crayon to her wall calendar and put a diagonal through each day until July 1. *I'll make one into an x each morning, and then I'll be sure to know how long until I can go fishing in the creek.*

She unlocked her closet, took her bath, and got ready for bed. She wasn't hungry, so she got herself a bowl of cereal and some juice and made this her cold dinner.

After she had eaten, she went to her mother's room. "Good night, mommy." She hesitated, but wanted some assurance that Laura's anger had gone. "I love you," she said to Laura's back.

Laura stopped brushing her hair and turned. "Come here, Erin." She held out her arms to the little girl. When Erin got to her, Laura gave her a big hug. "Are you sure you don't want some dinner? I could call for delivery."

Erin wrinkled her nose at her mother's faint smell, "No, thanks, mommy. I ate a lot yesterday, and I had lunch and then cereal after we got home. I'm not hungry." She kissed her mother on the cheek and went back to her room.

Erin went to her closet, took one of Nick's sweaters out of the plastic bag that she kept each in, and carried it to her bed where she put it under her pillow.

She went back and locked her closet, then returned the key to its hiding place in her slipper.

After she knelt and said her prayer, she climbed into bed and moved her pillow enough that she could breathe in Nick's lingering odor. *Oh, Daddy, I had the best time yesterday; I know I told you about it last night, but I want to tell you all about it again.*

Her lips never moved, but she replayed the entire story in her mind. *It was my very first one all by myself, Daddy. I wish you could have been there. ... I love you, Daddy. Good night.*

The first thing Laura had done when they got home had been to phone Jamie for a next-day appointment for Erin. "I really think she should come in first thing tomorrow, Jamie, if you can manage some room in your schedule; she had to sit through the reading of my father's will."

"How did she react to that, Laura? . . . Any noticeable flashbacks?"

"No, not that I noticed." Laura paused. "Oh, and she caught her first fish since Nick's death. Nick used to take her fishing with him."

"How did that go? Did she cry or express any emotion at all?"

"Of course she didn't cry; she was happy." *This woman is a counselor?*

"I'm glad she was happy, Laura, but we need to get some of that pent-up emotion out of her. She is so tight. It's almost as if she has a lock on her emotions."

"Erin has always been a strong person, Jamie; she will, thankfully, never be a crybaby."

Jamie shook her head as she opened her appointment schedule. *What will it take to get through to this woman? I have begged her to take some counseling herself. . . . Poor little Erin; she's the one who will pay for all of this. . . . Well, Erin needs this more than Mr. Wilson does. I can re-schedule him for an appointment at the end of the day.* "I can see Erin at nine, Laura. It will be an hour-long session."

Laura had poured some Stoli into a glass which held ice chips. She took a drink. "I'll see that she's there, Jamie." Laura took a drink. "Oh, and Jamie, can you do something about her questions?"

"Questions?" Jamie's antenna went up.

Laura made a face at herself in the mirror. "Yes, she has been asking the most preposterous questions lately."

"What kind of questions, Laura."

"Oh, you know, just silly questions about things."

"Can you give me an example? It might help me break through."

"No, not really."

"It might be very important, Laura."

Laura took another drink. *Aren't you supposed to be the expert?* "Just talk with her about asking too many questions, Jamie."

Jamie clenched her right hand into a fist. She released a deep breath. "I'll be looking for Erin at nine, Laura."

"She'll be there." She paused. "Thanks, Jamie."

Laura set her alarm for seven. She finished her drink and got into bed. After a few minutes, she sat up and fluffed her pillow. She stretched after she had lay back down. *Why didn't I just tell, Jamie some of the questions?*

She rolled over on her back and stared at the ceiling. *Why should I have to tell her our business; isn't she supposed to be counseling Erin about her reaction to the Towers?*

Laura exhaled with a snort. *Counseling! It's more like nosing around in someone's private life.*

She turned back on her side and lay quietly for some time. *I am so tired!*

Laura moved again in bed in an attempt to find comfort. *Where is sleep?*

. She lay quietly a bit longer. *Well, I know how to fix this.*

Laura sat on the edge of her bed and poured more vodka into her glass. She downed it straight in one gulp and lay back down. *Now if I just lay perfectly still. . . .*

Sleep finally came, but it lasted only long enough for the dream to surface again. "Oh, Nick, Nick, I didn't mean it. You. . ."

Laura was suddenly wide awake. She was shaking as she sat up on the edge of the bed and reached for her decanter. *No! No I will not. I will not take another drink tonight.*

Laura switched on the light beside her bed. She stood and walked to her bathroom. She ran a tub of warm water scented with lavender.

She removed her bed clothing and sank into the deep soaking tub. Laura rolled her shoulders and stretched her neck from side to side as she inhaled the scent. After half an hour, the lavender and the warm water, combined with the effects of the earlier Stoli, had done their job; Laura toweled and returned to bed.

The alarm went off at seven. Laura lay still for a couple of minutes. *I feel like shit!*

She got to her feet, padded to the bathroom and took a couple of aspirin. Laura returned to her bed and lay down again.

Her hand suddenly went to her forehead. *Oh, God, I forgot all about Erin's appointment. I have to get her awake and fed. Why in the hell did Maria have to go home right now?*

Laura sat up and pulled on a robe.

When she walked into the family room, she was greeted with a smile.

Erin was up and dressed. She was sitting at the round cherry table with a glass of orange juice in front of her along with a half-empty bowl of cereal. Off to the side was an empty glass that had contained milk and a plate on which toast crumbs, a remnant of scrambled egg, and the juice from a sliced tomato were in evidence.

Erin had the news channel on. "Good morning, mommy."

"Hi, honey. Mommy has a headache this morning." Seeing the plates, Laura hit the buzzer for Maria. *She must have made it back from her vacation in time to be here and fix all of this.*

Maria's rich voice sounded. "Good morning."

"Hi, Maria, will you bring some dry toast and coffee to the family room?"

"Right away, Miss Laura."

Laura turned to Erin. "How do you feel today, Erin?"

"I feel fine, now, mommy. I was real hungry when I woke up." Erin looked at her mother. *Poor mommy; she feels bad a lot.* Erin gave Laura the volume control and a few minutes of quiet.

"Maria made me my breakfast. She had a real nice vacation. She got to visit with her sister and see her new baby." Erin looked to see if Laura was showing any interest and then went on. "He's really cute. He has big brown eyes. She has a picture that she will show you if you ask."

Laura rubbed her forehead. *I almost care about some brat in Spain.* "Maybe later."

She smiled at Maria as the smooth-skinned Spanish girl

wheeled the tea cart into the family room.

"Good morning, Laura." Maria paused to give time for a reply.

She received another smile from Laura.

Maria began to pour the strong black coffee into Laura's cup. "I really missed you and Erin while I was gone. I hated to leave you two, but I need to get back to the sun and the beach once in a while.

She smiled at Erin. "It restoreth my soul."

Maria loaded Erin's empties on the tray, left the coffee carafe on the table, and began to leave the room. *Miss Laura likes peace and quiet in the mornings.* Nevertheless, she turned. *Maybe I can brighten her day a little.*

"I brought some special gifts back with me. Should I bring them in now while you two are having your breakfast?"

"Erin has an appointment with Jamie at nine this morning, Maria. We'd better wait until lunch. Have you had time to market at all?"

"Oh, yes, I made sure I got in early enough to pick up the basics. Lunch will be no problem, and I will shop and fill the larders this afternoon."

Maria beamed at Erin. "You ate a very good breakfast, little one. That makes me happy."

Erin took on a proud look.

Maria stopped at the doorway, *transportation?,* and looked back at Laura. "Should I phone for Mr. Sam to come around 8:30?"

"Thank you, yes, Maria." Laura thought a moment. "Remind him to collect Erin and bring her home. Her session ends at ten."

"Yes, ma'am."

Erin smiled as she thought of Sam. The big black cab driver and Maria always had time to visit with her, and they were always in a good mood. *They never seem to have headaches.*

She watched as Laura lit a cigarette and began drinking her coffee. "Eat some toast, too, Mommy. It's real good today; I think maybe it was special bread."

"Has 'real' become your only adjective, Erin? Honestly,

you sound like a little street child." Laura did, however, begin to eat some dry toast. *I don't need stomach cramps on top of this headache.*

She looked at Erin. *Why am I such a bitch with her? She can't help it. . . . I'll do better. . . . Just as soon as I get over this headache, I'll spend some extra time with her.*

Laura smiled warmly at Erin. "Did you sleep well, honey?"

"Yes, I did, mommy. How about you?"

"Once I finally got to sleep."

"Weren't you tired yet?"

Laura continued to smile at Erin. "I was tired enough, but I just couldn't seem to drift off. I finally got up and took a nice, warm bath. Then I went to bed and fell asleep. How about you? Did you get to sleep okay?"

Erin nodded. "The last thing I remember is laying in bed and thinking about my Daddy."

The smile left Laura's face. She tilted her chin and looked critically at Erin. "I've told you not to do that. You need to let go of Nick, Erin. If you think about him all the time, especially when you go to bed, you won't be able to sleep either."

"But I did. I did go right to sleep, mommy!"

Laura stood. *I will not allow my daughter to determine my emotions today. I'm going to be a better mother, spend some real time with her each day.*

She started toward the master suite. "I need a morning shower, Erin. If I'm not out when Sam gets here, don't bother to say good-bye; we'll visit when you get back."

"Are you still going to print my picture where I was holding my fish, mommy?"

She looked at her mother. "Remember? When we were in the car coming home, and I asked you if you would print it last night, that's when you promised that you would print it first thing this morning."

Laura drew a deep breath. *Did I? . . . I must have; Erin doesn't lie.* "I may be in the darkroom when you get back, but I will print the picture and give it to you before lunch. Okay?"

Erin went to Laura and gave her a hug at the waist.

"Thanks, mommy. I can hardly wait to see it. Wasn't he beautiful?"

Laura smiled, "Yes, it was, sweetie. Now mommy needs a shower." She stood and walked toward the master suite.

15

Sam stood outside his cab holding the rear door for her. "Hello, Miss Erin."

Erin smiled at one of her best friends. "Hi, Sam. How have you been?"

Sam shut Erin's door and went to the driver's seat. *Ain't that just like her? None of this I, I, I stuff. That is sure enough one sweet little lady.* He hit the ignition and pulled out of the circular drive.

He looked in the mirror. "I been havin' a fine time, 'cept for missing my favorite little girl." He gave her a big smile. "But I sure am interested in hearing all about your trip."

"Oh, Sam, I had the best time." Erin paused. "Well, at first it was kind of sad. . . . Mommy and I had to go to the lawyer's office where he read my grandpa Sam's will."

She stopped as the thought hit her. "Gee, Sam, grandpa's name was Sam too; Samuel Dawson Barnsworth was his whole name. Is yours really Samuel too?"

"Sure is." Sam's head turned slightly sideways to check for oncoming traffic. "Samuel Johnson." He looked in the mirror. "You know who he was?"

"Your daddy?"

"No, my dad's name was Francis after the saint. . . . Samuel Johnson was a famous English writer."

Sam thought a bit. "He wrote in the 1800's, I think. Wrote some important stuff, too. They still read him in college."

"Anyway my mama used to work cleanin' the library here in Danbury, and she named me after him." Sam laughed easily. "Always said she hoped some of his smarts would come through in me."

He shook his head. "Some gal, my mama. Remind me to tell you about her some day."

He pulled into the parking lot of the complex where Jamie had her office. "Ole Sam will be right here when you come out that door at ten, Erin."

"See ya, Sam. Thanks for bringing me." *I have to remember to tell him about my fish on the way back.*

Erin walked through the double doors and toward the elevator. *Imagine that: Sam was named for a famous writer! Wonder if I was named for someone special.*

Jamie Winters, Ph.D. was standing at her open door when Erin got off the elevator. *Erin looks different. Happier? Healthier? There's more color in that face.*

"Hi, Erin." Jamie extended her hand which Erin took as they walked into her comfortable office. "How about some freshly squeezed orange juice? I'm going to have some myself."

"Thank you, I will, Dr. Winters."

Jamie poured from a carafe and then brought two glass mugs to the table where she and Erin always sat: Erin on one side, Jamie across from her. *Her posture is much better.* "Did you have breakfast this morning? I have some fruit."

"I'm stuffed; I had a big breakfast this morning."

"You did?" *This is a first. She hasn't been eating much at all.* "What did you have that was good?"

Erin smiled. "Maria came home last night. She was there when I woke up this morning. We were happy to see each other. She fixed me a scrambled egg and a piece of toast with a glass of milk. Then I ate a bowl of cereal and had an orange juice. I like orange juice."

Erin ran her finger along the handle of the clear mug. She looked up at Jamie. "I really like these mugs, Dr. Winters." She lifted hers and took a sip. "They're easy to hold."

Jamie smiled. "That's why I like them too, Erin. Sometimes a regular glass just slips right through my hand if I'm not real careful."

Erin looked at Jamie's swollen knuckles. "Do your hands hurt, Dr. Winters?"

"Sometimes. But mostly my arthritis just makes me awkward; it can make it difficult to grip things tightly, that sort of thing." Jamie took a sip of her juice. "I hear you took a fishing trip this past week."

Erin nodded enthusiastically. "I sure did. I caught my

first fish." She stopped to correct herself. "Well, not really my first fish; I had caught fish before with my Daddy, but this was my very first fish to catch all by myself."

She beamed. "It was great. And, the best part is that I get to go back over the Fourth of July and catch some more."

"Oh, Erin, I bet that will be a lot of fun."

Erin, again, nodded enthusiastically.

"Tell me all about your fish."

"Well, he was big." Erin stretched her arms apart. "And he was sooo beautiful." She closed her eyes to get the picture in her mind. "He was brown with spots, and he was shinny, and he was sooo heavy. I had to use both hands to lift him when Ted handed him to me. Mommy took a picture, and I'll bring it next time, so you can see him."

"Oh, I'd really like that, Erin." *She's actually beginning to bubble. She's finally beginning to loosen up, maybe beginning to normalize.*

Jamie unconsciously took a deep breath. *That's a relief. I've been so worried about her.*

Jamie reached into the drawer on her side of the table. *I want to keep her in this frame as long as possible.* She withdrew a piece of sketch paper, a pencil, and a box of crayons. "I'd really like to see him; I don't know much about fish. Could you draw him for me, Erin? Just until next week when I can see your picture."

As Jamie watched, Erin brought the paper and pencil to her side of the table. She let her upper teeth come out over her lower lip and squinted.

Always so thoughtful and eager to please.

For a seven-year-old, Erin produced a remarkably good likeness of a trout, stopping occasionally to erase and re-draw.

She likes to get things right, but thank goodness she doesn't obsess.

Erin reached for the crayons and colored her trout in bold colors trying to make him as beautiful as he had been in real life.

I'm glad to see she's not tentative about color. Strong color is a good sign at this stage. "Oh, Erin, I can really see why you like to fish." Jamie held the picture at arm's length. "He *is* beautiful. Are they all as pretty as this?"

"Just the really good ones."

Jamie continued to admire the picture, then shifted her gaze to Erin. "Is that the only reason you like to fish, because they are so pretty when you catch them?"

"No, my Daddy loved to fish. He taught me how."

"Did he really? I never knew that about Nick." Jamie paused a minute to observe Erin's reaction. "So he taught you to fish."

"Yep. He bought me a whole set of gear for a little girl. And he showed me how to use it and how to clean it, . . . just everything." Erin released a happy sigh. "He took me fishing with him, too."

She stopped and looked directly at Jamie. "And sometimes when he had a little fish on, he handed his rod to me and let me land it, but this time I did it all by myself."

"How'd you feel right then when you caught him?"

"Real happy and. . ." Erin's voice dropped and the smile left her face. "and sorta sad too."

"Why were you sad, Erin?"

Erin looked at the top of the table. She twisted her little hands. Finally she took a deep breath and made eye contact. "'Cause my Daddy wasn't there."

She stopped. A tear trickled down one cheek. She turned her tear-filled eyes up to look at Jamie. "Cause my Daddy will never be there anymore. . . . My Daddy is gone forever."

Breakthrough!

Jamie allowed Erin some quiet time. This was the first time she had talked this openly about her feelings, the first time she had cried.

Jamie walked around the table and put her arms around Erin. "I know it hurts, Erin. I know." Jamie gently rocked Erin in her arms for a bit. Only after she felt Erin settle, did she go on. "When my husband died three years ago, I thought I might have to quit my practice. It hurt so much."

Erin snuggled closer to Jamie's chest and allowed her counselor to pull her really close this time, to hold her tight.

Jamie felt no resistance. She could feel Erin's heartbeat

as well as the nodding of her head. *Finally! Thank you, Lord. Thank you! This is such a special little girl.*

After a bit, Erin collected herself. She pulled back slightly and looked at Jamie. "Do you still think about him?"

"Almost every day."

"It didn't make you crazy? The thinking, I mean."

What's this? "No, Erin; just sad at times."

Erin saw the glossiness in Jamie's eyes. "It still hurts when you remember?"

Jamie smiled at her. "Sometimes."

"But you could make it stop. You could. . . . You could just put your memories in the back of your mind and not bring them out. Couldn't you?"

"Yes, I could do that." Jamie looked directly at Erin. "But I don't want to, Erin. I loved James a long time; he was a big part of my life. I don't want to lock him away. I like to think about him from time to time."

She could see Erin identifying. Jamie walked leisurely around the table and sat again across from Erin. She leaned forward a bit. "Not all of the time, you know."

She smiled at Erin. "I didn't think about him all of the time when he was alive, so I'm not tempted to think about him all of the time now, but almost every day I think about him a little." She grinned. "And it hasn't made me crazy."

Erin seized the moment. "I do that too." Erin leaned forward. Her voice dropped almost to a whisper. "Know when I think about my Daddy the most?"

Jamie let her voice model Erin's volume. "When?"

"At night when I'm in bed. First I say my prayers. Then I get in bed and tell my Daddy all about my day. He always used to tuck me in at night, and we'd talk about our day."

Her expression became one of mild defiance. "So I tell him all the stuff I think is important." She looked at Jamie. There was a hint of a question in her eyes.

Jamie Winters nodded encouragement and smiled at Erin. "And after you tell your daddy about your day, what do you do, Erin?"

"I roll over and go to sleep."

"Just like that?"

"Just like that." Erin broke eye contact and looked at her hands for a while before deciding to go on.

She raised her eyes and looked at Jamie. "See I know that Daddy is up in heaven, and I know he's watching me down here, so he sees what happens. I know because my Daddy taught me about God and heaven. But I have to tell him stuff he can't see, like how I feel and stuff. That's what we mostly talked about after he tucked me in. How we felt about things." Erin looked out the side window for a while.

Jamie sat quietly. *Please don't let me lose her now.*

Erin shifted her gaze back and looked at a place somewhere in the vicinity of Jamie's right shoulder. "Mommy has trouble sleeping, but I don't."

Erin moved her eyes closer to Jamie, but still refused to make contact. "Mommy had a headache this morning. Oh, and I almost forgot to tell you." She swung her eyes to Jamie's. "We got arrested."

Has she begun lying? Could she be hiding in a fantasy of some sort? . . . No, Laura told me she had caught the fish. Jamie laughed. "Arrested? With a policeman and everything?"

Erin nodded but said nothing more.

"Well, that must have been exciting. How in the world did that happen?"

"Mommy was speeding, and the policeman made her stop, and he gave her a ticket. We had to go to a courthouse and find the right room and pay the nice lady behind the counter so we could come home."

"Well, when you two have an adventure you really have one don't you?"

"Yep, even my Daddy never had to pay a nice lady so we could go home."

"Oh, Erin, dear, look at the time. Sam will be waiting."

"Is it time already?"

"I'm afraid so. It has really flown by this morning hasn't it?"

Erin nodded.

Jamie thought a minute. "Erin, would you like to see me

again on Monday and then have your regular Friday appointment also? It would be okay since we missed last week. Or you may just want to wait until your regular Friday morning appointment."

She smiled at Erin. "What do you think?"

"Better call mommy; she likes to decide everything, but I would like to see you on Monday morning 'cause I'll have a real picture of my fish by then . . . and on Friday too. I liked today. I liked it a lot, Dr. Winters."

"I did too, Erin. And I do want to see a photo of your fish. Do you want take this fish picture home today? I have a folder for it."

"Yes, thank you, Dr. Winters. That would be nice. I had thought that I might draw him, but I didn't yet. I'll put it on my bulletin board, and then I'll bring them both with me on Monday so we can see both of them. . . . Oh, and this way, I can show him to Sam when we go home; he'll want to see the picture too."

"That will be wonderful. And on Monday you can tell me about how you actually go about catching a fish like this. I'd like you to give me some fishing tips in case I ever have a chance to go."

She handed Erin the folder. "I'll phone Laura, and she or Maria will tell you what we'll do about next week when you get home. Okay?"

"Okay. See you." Erin started for the door, then stopped and came back to Jamie.

She gave Jamie a quick hug at the waist then turned and hurried through the door.

16

"It's coming back to you, Button."

A smile broke across the face so porcelain-like that, even with s p 20 and a proper hat, it was beginning to show a definite blush from the sun.

"What say we reel in and take a rest at Sally Ann's? She has a new soft ice cream machine and is practicing up making ice cream sodas."

Erin began reeling in at once, running her line through her fingers to clean it a little.

When finished, she attached her fly to the hook ring on the rod heel and turned to meet Ted, carefully placing her feet to avoid the moss-covered rocks that showed in some places in the shallow riffle just above the hole.

As they slowly made their way hand-in-hand toward the bank, she squinted up at him, "I like it when you call me Button, but we'd better not do it around mommy."

"Why not?"

"'Cause she doesn't like nicknames."

"How do you feel about them?"

"Oh, I like them; they make me feel special, but we'd better do it when it's just us."

"Um. . . ." Ted pushed his cap back on his head a little and adjusted it. "Well, that presents a dilemma."

He glanced at her. "Do you know dilemma?"

Erin began thinking about the word's meaning as they made their way up the bank.

When she reached the road, Erin leaned her rod against the Suburban and turned to face Ted. "When you don't know what to choose, that's a dilemma."

Ted nodded.

"But, Ted, I don't know why it's a dilemma to just call me Button when we're alone and call me Erin when mommy's there."

Ted pulled a top stem of grass from its joint and put it

in his mouth. "Well, I'm not sure it's right to behave one way when someone else is around and another way when it's just the two of us. See, I always think that if I don't want someone to know what we're doing, maybe we shouldn't be doing it."

He smiled at her. "That smells like sneaking to me, and I don't like to sneak." Ted continued, "I guess to me that would be sort of a lie, so I think we need to decide what we'll do."

Erin didn't reply immediately. They were loaded and heading for Sally Ann's before she spoke. "We could try it once and see what she does. I could tell her how it makes me feel and you could say some stuff."

Ted considered this and then nodded. "But can we agree that however we leave it, that's the way it will be; no sneaking around, no behind-the-back stuff?"

"Yep, no lies." She was quiet again; then she turned to look at Ted. "Lying is against one of the commandments."

"It sure is."

She squirmed sideways in her seat to look at Max who had taken to sitting in the middle of the second seat when Erin was with them.

"Will Sally Ann let us bring Max in?"

"Well, she'd better; she's his grandma."

Erin giggled, "Oh, Ted, a person can't be grandma to a dog."

"She can if she owned his mother."

Erin caught her breath and turned toward him. "Did she really? Does she still have her? . . . Does Max know his mother? Does she know Maxie? . . . Can I see her?"

"I'll explain it all after we get there while we have our sodas. What flavor do you like best?"

Erin studied her toes. "I'm not sure what ice cream soda is. Is it another name for a shake?"

"Well, it's a little more like a cross between an ice cream Sunday and a soft drink, I guess." He grinned at Erin. "You put some ice cream in the bottom of a big glass, and you fill the glass with pop or juice, and you serve it with a special long-handled spoon and a straw."

He gave her a wink. "I think you'll like it; I sure do."

17

A cheer went up as they opened the door to Sally Ann's.

Sammy Sosa had just knocked one out of Wrigley. The Cubs were ahead two to nothing. Harry would have been ecstatic.

"What's the score?" Ted asked as he and Erin walked to a table.

"It's two to nothing in the fifth; wind's been giving everyone fits."

"Hey, Coach. Did you catch Sammy's homer?"

Ted shook his head. "Gentlemen, I'd like you to meet Miss Erin McCort." A crooked grin shot in the general direction of the young men. "Erin, this is part of the sorry crew that makes me appreciate pretty young ladies like yourself."

"Ah, don't you believe it, Erin; he loves us. Why coach loves us so much that he hangs out with us after school."

"Yea, and he gives us free tips about stuff like, 'if you can't quit tippin' that shoulder in, I'm gonna' come out there and put it where it belongs for you'."

Sally Ann gave them a 'careful, boys, you don't know this little girl' glance as she came to the table. "Pay them no mind, Erin. They're just trying to impress a pretty new girl."

"High school boys!" Sally Ann shook her head, sighed, and grinned. "Now what can I get you three?"

Ted looked at Erin. "Want to try one of those sodas?"

"Yes, please." She moved her smile from Ted's face to Sally Ann's. "I'd like a berry one if they come in berry."

"We have red raspberry."

"I'd like a red raspberry please, Miss Sally."

Sally Ann nodded, "Good choice. . . . Ted?"

"I'll go along with Erin."

"Small dish of vanilla ice cream for Max?"

Max's frantic tail wagging told her that he not only understood but also fully approved.

Ted nodded his head.

Sally Ann moved toward the counter.

Erin leaned forward. "Miss Sally lets Max eat out a dish?" she whispered.

Ted nodded, "It was his mother's."

A deeply tanned young man approached the table. "I don't want to interrupt, but Jerry was looking for you a while ago, Coach Weaver."

Ted gave the young man his full attention as Erin began to pet Max. "What's up with Jerry, Tom?"

"He got a call last night from the coach at Marietta. He'd like to see him hit. Their main bat will be a senior next season; I guess he got hurt on vacation. Marietta's coach wants someone hot in the wings."

Ted rubbed his hand over his chin and looked at Tom. "That could be a fit. Marietta's tough academically; but Jerry can cut that." Ted thought a minute. "Just might work."

Sally Ann appeared with two glasses of ice water and two raspberry sodas. "Enjoy."

"At ease, Max."

Max followed Sally Ann behind the counter where fresh water and a dab of soft vanilla ice cream had been placed in his mother's bowls.

Ted looked at Tom. "Any idea where Jerry is at the moment?"

By then the three additional young men, having sensed that they would not be intruding on a client, had moved to a table beside Ted and Erin.

"Said he was heading home; I think he was gonna' look up how far it would be to drive."

"I could call," Sally Ann offered.

"I'd appreciate that. Tell him Erin and I are taking a break from the sun for an hour or so."

Ted rose, "Gentlemen, I'd like you to formally meet my friend."

Four young men rose and removed their baseball caps.

"Erin, may I present Tom Mackey, a fine outfielder; Judd Thompson, a math wizard and top catcher; Matt Swensen, our team's starting pitcher, and Leigh Morgan, our closer."

"Gentlemen, Miss Erin McCort, Sam Barnsworth's

granddaughter, a young lady who knows how to use a fly rod."

Judd, the team flirt, took Erin's hand and looked into her eyes. "You sure must be something special, Erin; he never takes ole Judd fishing with him."

Erin giggled.

Leigh angled his chair toward Erin. "My dad and I hunt; I've hunted with your grandpa. He sure could shoot. We'll miss him."

"The whole team misses him; he came to most of our games, even some away ones, especially if he thought it would be tough going. Mr. Weaver had taken us on a trip to Cooperstown, so we all missed the funeral. But we buried the ball from the last home run of the season by his headstone," Judd explained.

The screen door swung open and six-foot-two, two-hundred-five-pounds of eighteen-year-old walked in.

Erin sucked in her breath. To her, he resembled the pictures of a Greek god: tanned from hours in the sun and sporting wavy, sun-bleached hair, he even had the bright blue eyes.

Ted rose as Jerry Thornton hurried toward their table.

Jerry smiled apologetically, "I sure didn't mean to interrupt a guide, Mr. Weaver, but I didn't think you'd be busy today."

"Pull up a chair, partner. . . . Jerry, I'd like you to meet Erin McCort, Sam Barnsworth's granddaughter."

"Erin, this is our legendary slugger, Jerry Thornton."

Jerry blushed, handsome and talented as he was, he was equally shy and unpretentious. Ted had actually had to fix him up with a date to the prom.

A fine a math student, Jerry was analytical about everything: classical literary passages, factors which affect both the pitcher's idiosyncrasies and his own, and hard-core scientific data. In short, Jerry, the product of two latter-day hippies, was one of those magical people who could be successful in many fields.

Ted often thought of him as a sunshine boy.

"Sit down and tell me about Marietta."

"Well, there's not a lot to tell, Coach. I guess some scout caught our semi-final game and gave Coach Neeley at Marietta

College in Ohio my name. Coach Neeley called the school to get my number and then called me. He told me he was interested in talking with me about my future plans. I told Coach Neeley you had tapes of the state tournament that we could send, but he said he wanted to see me bat in person."

Jerry paused; a questioning expression came on his face. "Coach Neeley told me he had once known a Ted Weaver, and that the man he had known could sure enough coach some. He wondered if you were that man."

Ted didn't reply, so Jerry continued. "I looked at the map, and I think I could drive it in a day. He said he would put me up in a dorm for three nights and keep me fed while I was there. He said I should find my own way out and back. He wants to see me hit four times in two days."

Ted began thinking as he scratched his right wrist. He gave Sally Ann a signal to bring Jerry's standard drink, a tall apple juice over ice. "What's he offering?"

"A full ride if he takes me."

"When does he want to see you?"

"This week or next."

"Did he say why all of this is happening now? It's late."

"Maybe something the doctor has told him. He did tell me that his main bat had been in an accident."

"Did he ask why you were still available?"

"No, he just asked if I had signed with anyone yet."

Ted thought for a minute, then went to the counter and talked quietly with Sally Ann.

Sally Ann's "Why you know I will, anytime" carried to the six at the tables.

Ted walked to the rest room.

He returned to the table and looked over his kids. Four would be seniors next year, and one just might decide to leave home and be a freshman again. They had been tight as glue for the last three years: no secrets, best friends, much more than teammates.

"Tell you what, gentlemen. If Jerry's willing to let us tag along, Sally Ann said she would keep Max. I'm guiding Saturday and Sunday, but we could pull out of here early Monday morning and eat supper in Marietta."

Ted had no idea what kind of personal reception he would get from Neeley: the last time they had seen each other Ted had ended up with a split lip, and Neeley had been flat on his ass. Neeley, however, was never one to let prejudice keep him from talent, and Jerry packed a full barrel of that.

Everyone agreed it was the way to do it.

Jerry will show his stuff a lot easier if he has some people watching who know what he has, and I sure don't want him trying to get there on his own with his parents' old Buick or the pickup.

Ted was sure the athletic boosters would pay for the food. Allowing their four best juniors to watch a college tryout would be a worthy experience. He would provide the transportation. And surely Neeley would get Marietta to spring for their dorm rooms.

Sally Ann appeared at the table, "Erin, honey, I hate to ask you, but I've got a pile of people coming in this evening. Would you care to help me dish salads?"

What a wonderful woman! I need some time with the boys just now.

Erin looked at Ted, received the if-you-want-to shrug, and agreed at once. She liked Sally Ann a lot, and it was great to be treated like someone who could actually do something to help; Maria sometimes did that too.

"How out of shape are you all? Remember, it's been ten days."

All five admitted that they had been meeting at the field at 6:30 and going through their regular forty-five minute morning workout.

Judd was the first to suggest it. "You know we could beef up to our regular batting practice."

"Yea, Leigh grinned; we wouldn't want old Jerry to let his eye get rusty."

"Good idea," Ted said, "but only one set." He gave them a firm look, "And I don't want to hear otherwise."

Judd stood and saluted, "Yes, sir, Mr. Weaver, sir."

Everyone laughed, Ted most of all. He turned his attention to Jerry. "Remember those aluminum bats we put in storage?"

Jerry nodded.

"Go in the locker room and find one that has a feel to it. Hit a little with it each day. All colleges use aluminum, you know. NCAA rules."

"I hadn't thought of that."

"Want me to call Neeley to set the dates and get us bunks, Jerry, or would you prefer to work out the details?"

"If you don't mind, coach; I'd like to keep things the way they've been: I'll work on the little picture; you work on the big one."

"Okay. We'll load at the field at six Monday morning."

Ted stood, "Max. Erin."

Erin came laughing out of the kitchen; Sally Ann had worked her magic.

"We're burning daylight, kid. There's fish just snoozing out there thinking we've quit for the day. Let's go give 'em a little wake up call before we go home to the files. Come on Max."

Ted handed Sally a five and a ten and waved off her protests.

When the three of them were back in the Suburban, Ted looked at Erin. "I'm sorry, Erin, that I got a little tied up with the boys."

"I had a good time, Ted. Sally Ann needed me, and I like to help."

"What did you do for Sally Ann?"

"We dished salads and put them in the cooler. Then we made some special peanut butter cookies for your trip, and I marked them for her."

Sally Ann's peanut butter cookies with raisins and chocolate chips. How many local kids has she helped raise with those treats?

"She said I was a good helper." Erin thought a bit. "I might just help her again next time I'm down. She said she could use me anytime."

Erin smiled, proud of her accomplishments. "Oh, and she said to tell you the Cubs pulled it off; Sammy put one over the ivy in the 9th."

18

Erin sat on a rock at the stream edge picking at the nail of the third finger on her left hand.

"What are you thinking about, Erin?"

"Mommy."

For a minute, nothing more was said.

Erin finally looked at Ted. "It's just the two of us now. Me and mommy. She's all I got."

Ted reached out and tugged on a braid. "Try to say mommy and I, Button." He gave her a wink. "Make them think you know your English."

Erin twisted her slightly sunburned neck toward Ted in order to observe his profile. She feigned a British accent while batting her eyes and extending her right hand with the little finger dramatically dropped. "I must say, dear chap; it is just mommy and I now."

Pity the boys when she starts dating. They won't know what's hit 'em.

They both burst out laughing as Ted took her right hand with his left and grabbed the waist of her bibs in his right. He first lifted then stood her knee-deep in water while doing his best to sound colonial, "How about a Boston Tea Party for you Brits?"

Erin, laughing hard now, turned and raised her arms for Ted to lift her out.

They gathered their gear and settled into the Suburban for the ride to Sam's, Laura, and some dry clothes.

Erin looked up at Ted. "Is your mommy alive, Ted?"

"No, Button, she died about ten years ago."

"What killed her?"

"She had cancer."

"Like grandpa Sam?"

"Um hum." Ted rolled his index finger under his thumb. "Different place; same deal."

They drove a mile or two in a comfortable silence,

each off in his own memories.

"Was she a good mommy?"

"Yes, Erin, she was. She worked hard and kept dad and me fed and clean." . . . Ted smiled and shook his head. "Wouldn't hear of one of us wearing a shirt that hadn't been properly starched and ironed. . . . She attended all of my school functions." Ted shook his head in disbelief. "Never missed a single game that I played in high school."

He glanced sideways at Erin. "Her apple pie won blue ribbons at the fair three years in a row. Then she quit entering it; didn't want to be unfair to the younger cooks. . . . And the best homemade ice cream you ever slid down your throat was made on her back porch." He nodded his head at the memories. "She was some lady."

"Homemade ice cream?"

"Um hum!" Ted was in full reverie now. "We had a cow, a Guernsey, when I was in high school."

"You lived on a farm?"

"More like a little patch of land. Beckley is a lot like around here." He smiled at his dad's old joke: "A lot of our land sat on edge."

He glanced at Erin to make sure she understood and was rewarded with the change from a wrinkled brow to a smile and dancing eyes.

"I grew up in the mountains of West Virginia."

"Now you live in the mountains of Pennsylvania."

"Yep."

"Please try to say, yes. It would be nice if people thought you knew your English being as you are a teacher and all." She poked him in the ribs.

"Snot."

"Do you still miss your mommy?"

"Um hum. It's strange: some days I don't even think about her, and then I'll be watching an old movie and hear a song." . . . He shook his head, "I'll catch a glimpse of an indigo bunting; they were her special favorite, or I'll smell apple pie fresh from the oven." He eased into a favorite memory for a minute. "Cinnamon; she always used cinnamon, or I'll overhear a certain kind of laugh."

Ted's voice coarsened, "Suddenly, she's right there with me, telling me to keep myself neat and walk like I'm going someplace; reminding me that nobody is born knowing it all: 'everyone has to learn'."

Ted wiped his eyes, "Right then there is a big old hole in me for a while."

Erin looked at him, saw the moisture in his eyes, and nodded. "I sometimes smell my Daddy's aftershave on someone else." She studied her hands. "And, I never told anyone, but I took. . ."

She stopped abruptly. "How do you get homemade ice cream?"

Ted respected her privacy and ignored the change of topic. "Well, we had this Guernsey cow when I was in high school. Guernsey is a breed of cows noted for their rich, creamy milk. They're buckskin colored with some white markings."

"Mom milked her every morning and every night. She'd bring the milk in the house, strain it from the bucket into a big crockery bowl, and put the crock in the refrigerator. Next morning you could take a spoon and pull the cream right off that milk, and there would still be cream to stir into the milk for breakfast."

"One of us kids took a pint of milk down to Pappy Smith each morning. He used what he needed and gave the rest to his dog, Ginger."

Ted smiled, "Named her after Ginger Rodgers, a famous movie star back in those days. He sent three dozen eggs our way every Saturday morning and shared any extra fish that he caught."

Ted looked at Erin. "He got me started fishing."

"Was Pappy Smith a relative?"

"No. He was a nice old man who lived alone with his dog. Kept his little piece of earth neat. Always raised a garden. He was a good person who never hurt anyone and helped when he could. Dad saw to it that Pappy had coal for the winter." Ted looked off to the side of the road and cleared his eyes.

Erin didn't want to interrupt Ted, but she did want to learn about homemade ice cream. "So did Pappy help with the ice cream?"

Ted grinned, "Only to eat it. Well, that and the eggs; eggs go in the custard for the ice cream."

"Custard?"

"Yea. You cook milk and beaten eggs and sugar and a pinch of salt together over low heat until it thickens. After it cools a bit, you add vanilla and cream and more milk. You have to be careful not to use too much cream or it turns to butter when you start cranking."

Erin's forehead was wrinkled again. "Cranking?"

"You blend all of this and pour it in the pre-cooled metal cylinder of the ice cream freezer. Pour in the mixture, put on the top, drop the cylinder in the freezer, and fill the freezer with chipped ice and a little salt. The salt melts the ice and holds the water at the perfect temperature to cool and thicken the custard. You don't want to freeze it; just hold it right above freezing."

"Then you take turns crankin', excuse me, cranking, the handle. Of course, you eat chips of ice and throw some bigger chips at your best friends when your Mom isn't around."

"After a while it gets hard to turn. You clean back the ice and open the cylinder real carefully so you don't get any salt or water in it. Then you pull out the paddle and pack the freezer down with ice and wait until your mom says it's ready to open. If you're really lucky, she has made a chocolate cake."

"What was your dad doing?"

"Oh, he'd help crank some and pitch horseshoes or hit some ground balls for infield practice. He might whittle some little kid a whistle, that sort of thing. He was a coal miner and worked hard six days a week, so some days he would just rest, but most times he would try to make sure all of us had fun while we were helping and waiting for our special treat."

Erin suddenly got serious, "So he was a coal miner like those guys who got stuck in all of that water in a mine close to where the bad guys crashed a plane the day they killed my Daddy."

"That's right. Miners are a special breed, Erin. Every day they put their lives on the line so the rest of us can enjoy heat and electricity. They sure are special people, hard workers."

He pulled the Suburban into Sam's drive.

As she and he and Max walked toward the door, Erin slipped her hand into Ted's and grinned up at him.

"Are your feet still wet?"

"Yep." Bigger grin.

Hand in hand, they faced Laura.

"Ted Weaver, what have you let Erin do?"

"He dumped me in the creek, mommy."

"He what?" Laura's eyes snapped. "I told you I will not have her endangered!"

Erin grinned up at Ted. "We went to the gorge. I really like it down there. We saw an American eagle!"

"Really? An eagle?"

"Oh, yes! He flies sooo high."

Erin's eyes got big. "The gorge is really steep. "I hold on to the seat going down, and Ted tells me to lean forward to help the car when we come up."

Laura rolled her eyes in Ted's direction and got down to business. "Go change into dry clothes, Erin."

Erin put her lips together and looked at Laura. "In a minute, mommy; I have to ask Ted something."

Laura walked into the house as they settled in the porch swing.

"Does it make you sad, Ted; to remember that they aren't here anymore? Your mommy and daddy, I mean."

Ted thought a bit. "No, not really. . . not very often. They're here; they're a part of me, always with me, as long as I am able to remember."

He looked thoughtfully at her. "You'll never be alone, Erin. You have your dad and your mother and grandpa Sam and Sally Ann and me and Rowdy and Max right there and there." He pointed to her head and her heart.

"Did your dad die first too?"

Ted looked down. "Yes, he had a disease that coal miners sometimes get called black lung."

He raised his eyes to took at Erin.   "Do you know what job your lungs do for your body?"

She nodded, "So you can breathe."

"That's right. They collect and process the oxygen for your blood. Your body has to have oxygen. Well, with black lung, your lungs lose their flexibility, so you can't get enough air in them. The lungs get so they can't process the oxygen that they do get very well, and eventually you die. It's one ugly disease, Erin. It sure is mean to men who have worked so hard."

"Is it quick or long?"

"It takes a while. It's hard to watch a man who has always been strong as an ox gradually get so he can't even walk and spits up his own blood. Dad died the year I graduated from college."

They were both silent for a while, each recalling the loss of a father.

Erin saw Ted wipe a tear from his cheek. "You cry?"

"Sure."

"Mommy says it does no good to cry."

"Well, people are different. Maybe it doesn't help her, but it sure doesn't hurt me. . . . I wouldn't like me very much if thinking about having lost someone I loved didn't make me hurt. And when I hurt, I need to get it out. Everyone has to find his own way. What works for you?"

Erin loved it that Ted had never once talked to her like she was a kid. He always told how he did it and asked about how she handled things. Never said things like "That's sick." or "You must not let yourself." or "You have to." He also never wrote things that you said down on a tablet or made you tell things over and over. She never hesitated to tell him the truth.

"I don't really think anything works very well. When I say my prayers at night I sometimes ask God to watch over my Daddy and to tell him that I love him, and then I cry, but only in my bed where mommy can't hear. Mommy says I have to be strong."

Ted didn't allow himself ponder the ineptitude of Laura McCort in this area. He could only imagine the demons she must be carrying. Beginning, apparently, with her own mother's death, she had tried to isolate herself from Sam and all of the memories which being around him had caused to surface in her mind. From that time, she must have been in a constant battle to control her life through isolation.

Poor little Erin. The seven-year-old was trying to find her way pretty much on her own.

"I never knew your daddy. What was he like?"

Erin looked off toward the Land Rover for a while, not worried, just dazing back into memory. A warmth came over her, and she turned back toward Ted. "In a way my Daddy wasn't a thing like mommy. He worked hard like her, though. But when he took me places, we always had fun. I always learned stuff with him, but it was different." She paused to let a memory come.

"Once, when we were walking in the park there must have been about a million butterflies on the butterfly bushes. There were so many different colors all flying around, and they let us get so close to them!"

Her eyes danced with the memory. "Well, my Daddy found this perfect little place between two of the bushes, and he laid right down on the ground between them."

She focused on Ted; "Mommy would never do that."

She giggled and shook her head. "Anyway, my Daddy said for me to come sit on his tummy. And I did. And we watched the butterflies for the longest time. They were sooo beautiful, the way they can just sit in the air and then dart in and out."

She gave herself some more quiet time to remember. "Oh, and some hummingbirds were there too. Do you know how long their beaks are? And when they fly, . . . My Daddy said that they sounded like dive bombers: zoom, zoom."

"We stayed there for the longest time. People would stop and point to us sometimes, but my Daddy didn't care. He said we had been careful not to hurt any plants, and we weren't scaring the butterflies or the birds, so it was okay. It must have been okay 'cause no one made us move. We had a great time."

Erin was quiet for a bit again.

Ted noticed that the smile had never left her face.

"On the way home we stopped for an ice cream; we each had one dip of strawberry. My Daddy said it was close to what the hummers were eating, only cold."

She smiled and heaved a little sigh. "And then he took me to a bookstore where we bought a coloring book for me that had pictures of butterflies to color, and he got me a story book about a hummer who almost stayed too long in the fall. But he finally figured it out just barely in time and hurried real hard and caught up with his friends on their way south, and they were so happy to see him."

Erin pulled her upper front teeth over her lower lip and wrinkled her brow a bit. Her left index finger came up to rub the side of her nose.

When she had the idea just right, she made eye contact. "See that is how my Daddy was different from mommy. Mommy takes me places and buys me anything I ask for and lots of stuff I don't even want. But mommy would never do anything silly; she would never, just for fun, stop for ice cream and dab some of hers on my nose and say that is how the hummers got it, and then giggle with me and let me put some on her nose so she's a hummer too. Mommy is good, but she isn't like my Daddy."

What would Sam have done? His letter had made it clear that Sam wished he had done differently when Laura's mother had died, that he had not allowed Laura to withdraw.

Lord knows I have no right. ... The hell I don't! I have a damm mandate!

"Did I make you mad, Ted?"

"No, Button, I was thinking of something else."

He paused. "If a doctor is on a train, and the train wrecks, do you know the first person the doctor must save?"

"The moms?"

"No. Himself. If he doesn't save himself, he can't help anyone else who needs him. The first person we each have to protect and save is ourselves. It's normal to grieve. It's normal to cry when you're sad so others will know who you really are, what you really value, how you really feel."

"Cry when you're sad, Erin. Talk about your feelings, especially the feelings that you think maybe you should keep to yourself, the ones you're a little ashamed of having. They're the very ones you have to get out in the open so someone can talk 'em over with you. See, if you do that, then you'll be strong and can help the next person. That's what God wants."

Ted thought for a moment and then went on. "Don't let

anyone tell you that being strong means that you bottle all of your pain up and keep it inside. Being strong means that you take your pain out and look at it and try to understand it so you can help yourself and be able to help others."

"Like grandpa Sam?"

Ted looked at Erin and nodded. "Exactly. Sam knew that he had cancer, and he told me what he wished he had time left to do."

"Did he cry?"

"Yes, he did, not hard, but he cried." Ted paused to consider what he wanted to say next. *Would it hurt her?*

He drew a deep breath and decided to tell Erin the truth. "He said that what he would miss the most was seeing you grow up. He knew you were special."

Erin leaned forward. "What did he want me to be?"

"He wanted you to be just exactly what *you wanted to be.* He was sure you would figure it out."

Ted paused. "He wanted you to live in a way that would make you happy and satisfied with life."

Erin started picking at her finger again. "I hope I can."

"Trust yourself, Erin; you have good instincts. Ask when you need help. You'll get there."

19

Ted picked up the phone and dialed the work number of the athletic boosters' president.

. . .

Bud Johnson had been an all-around athlete during his high school years. During the late sixties, he had played the big three: football, basketball, and baseball; he had made all state in football where he had been a legendary pass receiver.

Bud had not gone to college for three reasons: although intelligent, academics had never meant a lot to him; his family didn't have much extra money; and he sure-as-hell didn't want to be a draft dodger. So he had taken a job as a carpenter's assistant with a local fix-it man who was getting on in years.

Otto Brimner had been a good man who took a lot of pride in his work. "Do it right the first time; saves time in the long run; good for business too." He had taken time to spit, then winked at Bud.

Originally, Otto had looked at Bud merely as someone whose back was in a lot better shape than his own, but he had been pleasantly surprised to find that Bud also took pride in everything he did and was eager to learn to do new things with his famous hands.

Otto had no family. At his death in the late seventies, Bud had, surprisingly, found himself the inheritor of Otto's small estate and his business.

Bud had dug in and made the most of it; he now employed six men full-time and used another dozen during the heavy season.

. . .

"Johnson Construction."

"Hey, Bud, how you doin'?"

"About half crazy with a concrete job, but otherwise good, Ted. What's up?"

"Jerry Thornton has an offer from Marietta College, Bud. He's been flatly against leaving home for a big school, but I think he might go to a small one like Marietta. It's a good college. I'm thinking about driving him down there. Might take the four juniors along too; it'll be good for them to watch a tryout, and their being along will make it easier on Jerry too."

Bud chuckled, "You know they call themselves the four horsemen now?"

Ted laughed, "What next?"

"You're the one who works with kids, buddy. I stick with wood; most times I can control it."   Bud thought for a minute. "Hey, it's a little late for offers isn't it? Bad coach or something?"

"No, he's a good coach. I know him personally. He's good. ... Not my favorite person on this earth, but that's a personal thing. Anyway, he lost his bat to a little white water adventure that went wrong: took a spill in rapids; the shoulder will heal, but he'll never have his former power. Might stay on the team if everything heals just right. Damn shame; the kid's a senior. They have a some decent younger players, but he's been pretty much carrying the team. Jerry's still available, so Coach Neeley talked with him."

"I'd sure like to see that kid get out of here long enough to get away from his parents. Don't get me wrong, but you know how it is. I mean, they're good people and all, but Jerry can make something of himself if he just broadens his horizons a little."

Bud drew on a cigarette. "I like his dad a lot, but as long as they're warm and not hungry," ... Bud shook his head. "Well, maybe he has the right idea. They seem happy enough, and both kids are great. That little one, Matt; has some shoulders on him already; might make a linebacker."

"Could be."

"So you're gonna drive five kids down to Marietta. How far is that anyway?"

"We can make it in a day if we get an early start."

Bud's brows tightened. "Planning on just down and back?"

"No, I figure a day down, three days there, a day back. The coach won't know we're there the first day. I want to get Jerry settled in real comfortable; work the butterflies out. It's not easy when you've always stayed pretty close to home."

"Good thinkin'; glad to hear that. Where you planning to stay?"

"Two nights in motels, three in the campus dorms."

"Why don't you stop by the Tavern around seven tonight. I'll have a check from the boosters for a thousand and one from Johnson Construction for another thousand."

"We don't need even half that much, Bud."

"Ted, sometimes I wish you would just shut up. Those kids played their hearts out, and you know it. Cash the checks and see to it that they enjoy the trip. Don't try to cheap-ass this thing. Hell, the kids earned a lot more than that; you won't believe what the boosters made off the sale of championship stuff: T-shirts, team pictures, our share of the state gates. We're rich, buddy."

"In that case, will do."

"See you at the Tavern, then."

. . .

Ted was sitting in a booth when Bud came through the door. Both men were a little early. Bud waved at the bartender, "Couple of cool Sam's over here pronto, and a plate of appetizers when it gets ready." He slid into the booth. "So, how's the fishin' this season?"

Ted shook his friend's hand. "Still good, buddy; that bottom water has stayed cool. How about my taking you out and showing you tomorrow morning? My way of saying thanks for the support."

Bud shook his head as the frosted mugs were put in front of them. "Not tomorrow; I wasn't kidding when I told you that concrete job is driving me nuts."

He made a face. "First it's rain, and we have to wait for the ground to dry out some, then it's the damn sun puttin' a crust on it."

He paused and grinned at Ted. "Turnin' into a crybaby, ain't I?"

He noticed the disappointment in Ted's face. "But, I'll tell you what. When you get the trip planned, call and give me the date you'll get back. I'd like a float though the gorge. Just the two of us, and you can fill me in on the trip. How's that?"

"Plan on it."

The appetizers arrived.

Bud handed Ted the checks and tapped the table top with his index finger. "Now I mean it; show the boys a good time. The boosters have a fat reserve, and it's there for our kids."

He dipped a fried shrimp into the sauce. "One of the things I love about a small town: they support their kids. How in the hell do you suppose people live in the cities where no one knows anyone?"

He took another shrimp. "Ought to be a law against towns bigger than twenty thousand. People need to know each other." Another shrimp. "You in a hurry?"

"Not tonight, Bud."

"Good, then lets eat this and have dinner here. You can give me the details of the trip, and I can whine a little more about the weather." He gave Ted a rueful smile. "Sammy's really slammin' this year. How long you think he'll last?"

Ted thought a while. "You talking about his career or his run this season?"

"His career."

"Some last longer than others. He seems fit, and I think he loves what he does. My dollar goes on his being around a while."

The bartender took their orders for steaks. Ted's medium. Bud's rare. Both men took rice, a salad, and fresh green beans for their sides.

In his early fifties, Bud was still fit. Six-one, 225; morning workouts at the hotel's fitness center after he had hit forty had paid off. Brown eyes sat in a broad face that was tanned by the sun, not machines. His salt and pepper hair was cut short but stylishly. "Hey, I heard Sam Barnsworth's daughter was in town. How's she doin'?"

"Laura, that's her name, is wound pretty tight just now. Erin, her daughter, is havin' a tough time too."

"Must have been real close to Sam. Funny though, I don't remember ever seeing them around here."

Ted's hand went to his chin as he considered how much he ought to say. "Well, Laura was an only child most of her life; brother died young." Ted cut into his steak. "And they hadn't got over Nick's death before Sam left us."

"Nick?"

"Laura's husband." Ted chewed and swallowed. "He was a broker, had an office in the Towers."

"Oh, shit." Bud ate in silence for a while. "Quite a looker according to Walt Whitfield."

Bud appraised his friend's expression. "Hear you gave the little girl some fishing lessons."

"Yea, Nick had started Erin fly-fishing. She thought she couldn't fish any more until she grew up some." Ted took a draw on his beer. "I invited them out to the pond." Ted smiled at the memory. "Erin caught a nice brown; it made her feel real good." He raised an eyebrow. "She's pretty good for a little girl."

"The sacred pond. I don't believe it. You never let anyone fish there. Don't even fish there yourself, do you?"

"No. No need to." Ted looked up as the tavern door closed after another diner. "That little girl needed to get some confidence."

They finished their dinners. Ted shook Bud's hand again. "Thanks a million, Bud. I'm gonna hold you to that drift trip."

"You won't have to hold a gun to my head. It's been too long. Take care, pal. Don't let 'em drive you completely crazy."

. . .

Bud shook his head and called over his shoulder as he walked toward his truck. "Any man who will volunteer to ride herd on five wild-assed state champions is already teetering on the edge."

20

At 5:45 a.m., Ted nosed the Suburban into the parking lot at the high school. Just as he had suspected, the boys were waiting.

They loaded their gear in the rear. He and Jerry got in front; Matt and Leigh took the middle; Tom and Judd got in the third seat. Ted had put a pillow between the front arm rests and two pillows in each of the rear seats.

"Everyone buckled? Got the aluminum bat? Gloves and spikes? Sunglasses?"

"Yea, coach. We've done the drill a time or two before. Let's get this show on the road. Go, Jerry!"

Judd must be wound.

"When you need to stretch, let me know. And make use of those pillows 'til we hit Ohio. The rest of the way south may be kinda new to you. We'll stay in a hotel when we get in town tonight. We'll look around some on our own tomorrow morning and loosen up a little. Then we'll let the coach know we're there and settle into our rooms for three nights."

Ted looked in the rearview. "We'll leave early Friday. Pittsburgh has a home game, and Bud Johnson surprised me late last night with six complimentary tickets behind home plate in the middle of the big spenders."

After a few miles, Jerry glanced in the back seats. "They're all snoozing, Coach. Did Mr. Johnson buy those tickets for us?"

"No, you know Bud. He has a way with words." Ted braked as a car pulled onto the narrow road. "He called the ticket office and told them the kids who had won the state would be in town on Friday. They offered the seats and lunch or supper in the club-level restaurant; our choice. The passes will be waiting for us at the front gate."

"Wow! That's really nice of the Pirates."

"Sure is. Lots of real nice things get done by the pro

teams, Jerry. They do plenty of payback. No one ever hears about most of it. The media only reports salaries, scandals, and the score of the last game."

"You ever think about goin pro?"

"Not seriously. I wasn't that good, and I wanted to get married and help my family some. You make more money coaching than you make on one of the farm teams."

Jerry stared off into the distance. "You think I can make it?"

"Jerry, if you can't, the world's even crazier than I think. You have a ton of talent: good eye, judgment, power, and a brain." Ted smiled at his former standout. "You do just like you did in high school. Just because you're away from home doesn't mean you have to go crazy. Keep to your principles. . . . You don't need to become anyone else; stay you."

"Would you leave home if you were me?"

"I did, Jerry. I came out of the mountains of West Virginia on a scholarship to Marietta."

"That's where you played?"

"Four years."

"Baseball scholarship?"

"No, academic. I walked on. The coach took a liking to me, and I played all four seasons."

"He left three years after I graduated, went to assist in Florida." . . .

"I had taught those three years in my hometown near Beckley. My wife had been from Williamstown, West Virginia, right across the Ohio from Marietta. Her mom called and told us that both the high school and the college had lost their baseball coaches. I applied and ended up with the high school. I stayed there until I came up here."

"What if I don't like it, or I don't fit in? I've had the same friends all of my life."

Ted reached across and rested his hand on Jerry's shoulder. "Wellsboro will always be here, Jerry. You can always come home. And you can also always decide to stay home if you don't like the lay of the land at Marietta. You aren't committed to anything. . . . If I were you, I'd just look at this as a little vacation where I'd get to hit a few balls in front of some new people."

Ted paused, then continued. "If things felt good, I'd consider it. If not, I'd enjoy the Pirates' game and write a real nice thank you letter to Coach Neeley."

. . .

Arriving in Marietta, Ted drove through the campus, pointing out historic buildings and other landmarks. He drove slowly to give the boys a feel for the atmosphere of the old, private college.

Back downtown he pulled into the parking lot at the LaFayette Hotel located on the northeast side of the confluence of the Muskingum and Ohio Rivers. Upon entering the formal lobby, Ted bypassed the registration desk for a while and took them to the salvaged wheel that had once been used to pilot an old boat.

"Geez, I never knew they were this big." Matt took the holds in his hands. "Look at this thing."

"There's a nice river museum in town. We'll take a look tomorrow if you want."

After unpacking, the boys elected to eat in the hotel's tavern where they could watch the river traffic.

Ted was relieved when, Jerry, who had been a little quiet on the way down, looked at the tavern's fine wood paneling and announced, "You know, except for the view of the river, it looks a whole lot like the PennWells in here."

Tom Mackey had been admiring the interior too. "It sure does," he said as he plowed into his baby-back ribs. Tom looked toward Ted. "Are all old hotels like this?"

"A lot of the nice ones share certain things: fine wood, a good chef, an unusually courteous staff. . . "

Judd interrupted their coach, "Small rooms, funky smells, hard water stains in the bathtubs."

"And wiseoffs sleeping in the halls in their underwear, Juddie." Tom finished.

Tom and Judd were best buddies, but Tom never let Judd forget the way Mrs. Thompson had called for her son when he was little: *"Juddie. . .Juddie, honey; it's time to come in now."*

After dinner, Ted took Jerry and 'the horsemen' for a ride across the older of the two bridges over the Ohio. "You're in God's country now, boys, West Virginia." As he named the state, he hit the tape player, and John Denver's voice filled the interior with one of Ted's favorite songs.

. . .

Tuesday morning the six were up by 5:30. They ate a light breakfast and headed for the fairgrounds at the edge of town. They started with their regular pre-game warm-up and then went into a practice session with Jerry using the aluminum bat which he had come to like.

Matt Swensen, who loved Jerry like a brother, understood Sally Ann's tough love theory; he and Leigh Morgan had sworn to each other to cut Jerry absolutely no slack from the time they had learned of Neeley's call.

They gave him everything they had, and that had been enough to bring the state trophy home.

Jerry hung tough and showed why the press had loved his performance in the finals.

When Jerry had had enough and went to infield, Ted followed the lead of his best pitcher and the team's closer. He put the ball through all the tricky maneuvers he had in him, that is, when he could get a piece of it.

The kids showed him no mercy either.

Damn. The slider had dipped at the last minute. Ted took a minute to reset his feet and scratch his neck. *Kinda tough on the old man.*

They took lunch at the LaFayette and went to their rooms for some quiet time.

Then it was back out to the fairgrounds to repeat the morning workout. Ted's body was feeling all of its various parts by the time they unloaded at the LaFayette. "Pool anyone?"

"Yea. Now you're talkin'."

. . .

Another half hour of quiet time in their rooms, and they were back to their old selves.

"Time to go meet Coach Neeley, gentlemen."

Neeley was in his office when the six were announced

by his secretary.

He looked up and smiled at his former best friend as he stood and walked around his desk, "Ted Weaver! Damn it is you in the flesh! How the hell are you anyway?"

"Still able to dance." Ted shook Bill's hand and then clasped him on the shoulder. "It's good to see you Bill."

Bill Neeley looked into Ted's eyes. "God, the times I've wished I could talk with you and pick your brain like I did in the old days!"

Bill turned to the kids. "Did you men know that your coach and I used to have strategy sessions every Tuesday and Thursday night?"

Five heads shook sideways.

"Well, we did. We both started coaching in Marietta the same year. . . . Ted was the college's first choice for head baseball coach. Fortunately, he was also the first choice of the high school. Ted chose to coach high school, and that let me take the college."

He smiled at Ted; then turned his attention to the boys. "Let me guess now." He focused on Jerry. "You're the bat, right?"

Jerry nodded. "I hit my share. Everyone on the team can handle a bat."

Ted stepped forward again. "Bill, let me introduce the team's four starting juniors. Bill Neeley, Tom Mackey. Tom will be our big bat this year; he plays a mean outfield too. He and Jerry saved us a lot of times."

"This guy is Judd Thompson, Bill; he's a catcher who can give you the statistics and preferences of every batter we met last year."

Ted put a hand on Matt's shoulder. "Matt Swensen was our team's lead pitcher. He managed four no-hitters last year, one in the semi's."

"And this, Bill, is Leigh Morgan, our team's closer. He held them for us in some tough times, and he took a freshman under his wing last year and has personally trained his alternate."

Neeley shook the hand of each young man as he repeated the name and position of each. Then he took a step back and surveyed the group. "No wonder you took the state." He shook his head. "It's a hell of a thing for a small town to be able to pull that off."

He eyed Ted again, then smiled at the boys. "You must have had a good coach."

Five heads nodded in agreement.

"Well, let's get out of this office and let me show you around campus. Then we'll get you settled in a dorm."

Once outside, Neeley turned to Jerry. "What do you think you'll major in, Jerry?"

"I've thought some about chemical engineering."

"Good choice. Lots of opportunities there. Our department is ranked nationally."

He walked them though the student center and the library and down past the old buildings explaining the significance of each.

He saw Ted walk to the steps of Erwin Hall and rest his right hand on the hollow surface that more than a century's worth of footsteps had created in the steps. "Still a damn sentimentalist."

Ted grinned, "Guilty. I think that's one of the reasons I moved to Wellsboro. It's an old historic town too." He glanced up at Neeley. "Ever been there?"

"No, Malinda and I stay pretty close to home."

Both Judd and Leigh noted a slight coloring of Ted's complexion.

"She's always wanted to travel, but you know how it is. Never enough time to do it all."

Bill Neeley turned to Jerry. "Now, this is our chemistry building, Jerry; nice facility, practically new; top professors, respected nationally. You'll get a good education."

Neeley looked at Ted. "And maybe a chance at the pros." He hesitated only a moment. "Ted got an offer when he graduated. We've had a few off and on since."

Judd Thompson looked at Ted. "You never told us that, Coach. . . . Geez, an offer to go pro!"

"Still too humble?" Neeley shook his head. "I don't know what's wrong with you, Ted. Hell, if I had your story,

I'd write a damn book about myself."

Bill hasn't changed much either. Ted grinned and shook his head. *Oh, well, this is about Jerry; not us.*

The boys were beginning to wonder what to think.

Judd read the situation. *Coach isn't acting quite like himself. ... Motor mouth acts like he's Coach's best friend, and Coach seems friendly enough, but me thinks there might be something rotten in Marietta.*

Neeley looked at the sky. "Well, it's starting to get dark. I'd better get you folks settled in for the night."

"Actually, Bill, our boosters got the boys rooms at the LaFayette." Ted paused. "Sort of a reward for their championship."

"Well, good support from the home crowd. That's important. ... Tell you what. I'll phone the hotel and tell them to put your meals on the athletic department's tab. And I don't want you skimping any. Don't look at the prices. Order what sounds good."

Bill looked at Ted. "Let's meet at the field at ten in the morning. I rounded up some kids from Marietta High's team to come in and play a little. A pitcher from Belpre is coming up too." He looked at the horsemen. "You men bring any gear?"

"Never leave home without it," Judd joked and made the gesture of getting a credit card out of a wallet.

"Good. Come dressed; bring something to change into after we shower for a break at lunch. We'll use all of you too." He looked them over again. *Ted never was one for overrating his players.* "Maybe I'll get an idea or two for next year's recruiting."

Once they were in the Suburban, it was Matt who spoke first. "You didn't tell us we were staying at the hotel, Coach."

"Bud and I talked late last night. He felt strongly that we should stay put, let you get used to a bed, be in air conditioning, that sort of thing. It's a lot more humid down here than it is in the mountains. After I thought about it, I agreed."

"And you sure never told us that you had had an offer to go pro," Judd added. "I agree with Mr. Neeley; you ought to write a book."

Ted drew a deep breath. "Bill Neeley is a good coach;

at times he approaches greatness, but he sometimes lets his enthusiasm get the best of him. We hadn't seen each other for several years, and we had once been close. He was just trying to make me feel welcome. You know how it is."

"Well, but you did get an offer didn't you?" Judd wouldn't let up.

"It's not that big a thing, Judd." . . . *I need to defuse this one fast; we're here to talk about Jerry's future not my past.*

"The pros make hundreds of offers a year. People who accept go to a farm team and start trying to work their way up. They don't make much in the way of salary at that level; just about enough to live on. . . . I had other things on my mind. And I never thought I'd make it to the big time; just wasn't heavy enough. . . . Let's forget about history and concentrate on Jerry's career choices. I made mine a long while ago, and I'm happy with them."

"Sorry, Coach."

"Now, Judd. No offense was taken. . . . Think we can get out to the fairgrounds by 6?"

"Easy."

"Good. There should be enough light by then. Let's plan on that. We'll prep out there for an hour, come back here to shower and eat breakfast. Then we'll take some quiet time and load up around 9:45; the field is real close."

The edge had worn off Jerry. Everyone was tired enough to get a solid night's sleep.

. . .

The next day, they worked their plan, and pulled in at the college baseball field with a few minutes to spare. The five unloaded, stretched out, did a quick warmup and walked over to the dugout where Neeley; Jim Riley, the Marietta High School coach; and the local kids were waiting.

Neeley introduced everyone, remembering the names and positions of each of Ted's five. Then he created Riley's team from Ted's kids and some of the locals; he would coach a team that had been created from the best of the local talent. He announced that they would play a short game of five innings in the morning and another of five in the afternoon.

They went at it. Ted's kids executed fine form; Jerry was dead on, but they couldn't carry the local reserves. Riley hadn't used the 'horsemen' in their regular positions.

Neeley's team won seven to three.

. . .

At lunch Ted's kids mingled with everyone, commented on the good plays, and gave encouragement to those who had tried to make something happen.

Ted stayed out of it, eating with Bill and Jim Riley. He noticed his kids huddling with the locals before they left the dugout for the afternoon session.

Ted's kids walked on the field in their regular positions. The reserves filled in.

Neeley sent his team on the field.

. . .

The five innings went fast. Final score Riley, nine; Neeley, two.

Ted was ecstatic when they were driving to the hotel. You could see it in his face, hear it in his voice. He didn't dwell on it, but he was glad his kids had showed their stuff.

Five pit bulls. They'll stand as long as anyone will. Dear Lord, I thank you for the life I have.

"Gentlemen, you showed them how it can be done. I was so proud I had to keep myself from coming on the field at the end. Let's hit the fitness center. We'll eat and take in a movie afterwards."

. . .

The six went through Wednesday's routine on Thursday morning.

They pulled in at the field a few minutes earlier. With the exception of the Belpre pitcher and Neeley, everyone was new: Parkersburg coach, Frank Ogre; some of his team; and a few kids from Athens were present.

Ted headed for the bleachers again.

Neeley assigned the teams and announced that they would play a regular game; some unexpected commitments had come up.

Of course, the odds were stacked in Neeley's favor.

He still wants an edge.

Well, I guess we all do. A win tastes good, almost as good as seeing a green kid grow into a strong young man who respects others as well as himself.

Helping to make a good man, keeping 'em healthy; that's where it really is.

The game started at 10:30. It was over a little after one: Ogre, eight; Neeley, five.

All of Ted's kids had been used along with some of Ogre's reserves since Neeley had taken Ogre's best pitcher, and the Athens' pitcher, and the Belpre pitcher.

Ogre came over while the kids were cleaning up. "I want to shake your hand, Weaver. What a great group of kids! With my first team and those five of yours, I could have won the damn world."

Ted rose and shook hands with the winning coach. "I watched your decisions." He nodded at the man. "I'd put my money on you any day, Frank. Where'd you go to school?"

"Ohio U. I played there, and they kept me for one year as an assistant."

Ted raised his eyebrows, impressed.

Frank was cool. "Na, isn't a big deal. They take care of their athletes up there. If a kid works hard on any of their teams, they usually offer him a year as an assistant. Gives him a year of free graduate school and some time to look at it from the other side of the bench. Marshall offered me an assistant's job after my year with OU, but Parkersburg High had a nice package too."

He looked aside for a minute or two. "I like high school."

"Good for you. . . . And real good for your kids. They're lucky to have you."

"Well, there come my bunch." Ogre shook Ted's hand again. "Congratulations on the great year. If it can't be us, I love it when an underdog can take the big one."

He started to walk off toward his kids, then turned. "If Jerry comes here; I'd like to contact him, sort of let him know he has someone local to talk with from time to time. That is, if you think that's okay."

"Thanks, Frank. That would be great. You know how it is; they get to be like your own after a while. I always wonder a little when we send a kid off. I'd really appreciate it; I know Jerry's folks would too. They're tight."

They were shaking hands one more time, the mutual respect obvious, as Neeley approached. "I thought you two would hit it off."

"Hey, Ted, I'm sorry about this, but I need to hit the road. You have a swell bunch of kids. That Morgan kid really impressed me as a closer. He and Jerry make a perfect outfield team too. I have Jerry's verbal acceptance. I'll take care of the paperwork when I get back."

The men shook hands and walked toward their respective cars.

. . .

"You guys showed them how we play ball in Pennsylvania again today. I'm proud of you. You made a good impression, Jerry."

"I really liked Coach Ogre. He shook our hands before we went to the shower and told us to get in touch if we ever think he could be of help."

"Yea, imagine that from a guy named Ogre." Leigh shook his head in disbelief. "How do you suppose that's affected him?"

"Oh, please don't go all psychological on us, Leigh. Your name's just your name, Leezy Weezy," joked Judd.

"What's first? Lunch or the fitness center? . . . It's up to you, Jerry."

"I'm not tight, Coach." He glanced at his teammates. "To tell you the truth, after the first set of five innings yesterday morning, I never used a full load. I did during that first set. I really wanted to win that; I didn't want to embarrass you or anything."

"But then I remembered what Coach had told me about thinkin' of this as a little vacation where I got to hit some balls from some new pitchers. I was sittin' there thinkin', and all of a sudden it came to me that when I 'm concentrating real hard on slamming the thing over the fence, I don't see the ball quite as well. At least I don't think I do. So I just started concentratin' on seein' the thing, and it worked out."

Ted smiled. "I've always believed control trumps

power. You know, the body is sort of like a machine. It only has so much power. The more power it throws toward one task, the less it has for another. That's why we practice until most reactions come pretty much automatically from muscle memory."

They went to the fitness center to stretch out first. After lunch and some time in the steam room, they hit the pool.

. . .

As they were heading to their rooms, Ted cleared his throat. "I have a couple of stops to make this evening. How about you guys doing the dinner thing yourselves? I'll meet you back in the room later."

"Sure, Coach."

"Jerry, are we still bunking together tonight."

"Yes, sir."

21

Ted drove to the florist shop a couple of blocks up the street where he bought a single red rose in a water vial.

His next stop was at Mound Cemetery.

He walked straight to the tombstone he hadn't seen in a long time: *John Theodore Weaver, 'Teddy.'*

"Hi, son." Ted stood and looked at the stone for some time.

A thousand thoughts swept through his mind. He held the image of his infant son kicking his little feet and waving his hands as he smiled up from his crib wanting to be held. "You were loved, Teddy, and your memory is still cherished."

Ted knelt and said a prayer. He laid the red rose across the grave, kissed the stone, turned, and began to walk away.

"I thought you might be here."

Ted turned, slightly startled, at a voice from the past. She stood in the twilight two rows back from their son's grave.

"Lindy." Ted walked toward her and gave her a hug. "It's good to see you, Lindy. I wasn't sure what you might want, so . . . "

"Well, I'm glad you left it up to me. I wasn't sure what I wanted either. . . . Or what you would want for that matter. Bill had told me you were bringing some kids down. Why didn't you ever let anyone know where you were, Ted?"

"I just couldn't do it, Lindy. I knew that you were happy with Bill, and I wanted you to be happy."

He looked at the ground and then back up at her. "I, I wasn't sure I could stay out of the way if I hung around. . . . I wanted to give you space because I knew it was the right thing to do. . . . I couldn't help it, Lindy, I still loved you, so I left town."

He paused, then went on. "I still love you, Lindy, but in a different way, the right way."

He smiled a crooked grin at her. "You're safe."

Warmth showed in her eyes too. "And I love you,

Ted Weaver. I'm married to Bill, and I love him, but I still love you, like you said, 'in a different way,' and I want you to be happy too."

She turned, and they walked toward the Suburban together, not touching, but comfortable with being close. "So, have you married and had that big family you always talked about?"

"No." His voice was hoarse.

Malinda Neeley turned and looked into his eyes.

He noted that her's were glistening as he felt the sting in his own.

"Well, Ted, that's a shame. You were a wonderful dad." She pulled a Kleenex from her jeans pocket and saw the look of concern come over his face. "I'm okay. It's just that, after all these years, I owe you the truth, Ted. ... Bill and I had an affair because I had no self worth after Teddy died, what they now call postpartum depression mingled with a lot of grief."

She looked at her hands. "Bill had been a friend of both of ours, and I could tell him things I refused to tell you."

Ted was totally puzzled. "Why couldn't you talk to me, Lindy?"

She looked at the ground. "Because I loved you too much."

"Loved me too much?"

What the hell is this? ... Loved me so much you divorced me? ... Keep it buttoned, Ted. No need to cause more pain.

She dropped her head; a little sigh escaped. "Ted, Doctor Hawkins told me right after Teddy's birth to cherish him; there would be no more children. The lining of my uterus was too soft to allow another egg to implant. We were lucky to have had Teddy."

She studied her hands. "You know how Doctor Hawkins was; he was old-fashioned and kind. He told me to break it to you when I thought the time was right."

"He said we could always adopt as many more as we wanted. I never got around to telling you before. ... before Teddy, and ... and I couldn't force myself to tell you later. We were both hurting too much for that."

Ted took her gently in his arms. "Lindy, Lindy, Lindy."
He rocked with her slowly for a while until he felt her head
resting against his neck. Then he released her and stepped
slightly back. "Oh, God, Lindy; I am so sorry."

"Well, so am I, but since I can't change the past, I just
want to try to explain it." She blinked back tears and went on.
"So, after Teddy's death, I had to talk to someone. I talked to
Bill. He promised to keep my secret. He and I got closer."

She paused again and then gave Ted a bit of a smile as she
blinked more tears, "And the rest, as they say, is history, just old
history."

She took a couple of steps toward the white Corvette
which was parked a bit back from the Suburban. Then she turned
once more. "Bill had always said that he didn't want kids, didn't
even like little kids. Remember?"

Ted remembered.

"Well, that was why I could talk to him." She bit her top
lip. "When I was pregnant, he used to joke that he would quit
visiting us when the baby was born. He said he'd come back when
it was a teenager; those he could, at least, tolerate."

She faced Ted as she leaned against the side of the car.
"So, you see, dear one, I could no longer give you what you had
always wanted: a big family."

Her voice hoarsened with emotions. "And I loved you far
too much to make your pain worse."

She cleared her throat and continued. "I could give Bill
what he wanted: a wife with a guarantee that there would be no
little rug rats." She blew her nose.

When she had regained her composure, she looked Ted
full in the face and forced a smile. "I am so sorry, Ted. Sorry for
all of us."

She quickly walked around the Corvette and opened the
door. "Good-bye, Ted Weaver."

She started the motor which muffled his response.

Ted made it over to a bench. He slumped down on it. He
wasn't sure how long he sat there and couldn't really remember
much about his thoughts.

He finally realized it was getting dark and went to his SUV.

He drove to the hotel, glad that he had Jerry with him tonight.

Jerry doesn't pry. He might have some questions about his future. . . . I hope so, something to take my mind off this until I get home. I can't ruin this trip for the kids; they gave it their all. . . . Suck it up, buddy.

. . .

Ted walked into his room.

"Well, see there; I told you the police would turn him loose. The guys were afraid we'd have to sell our championship bags to get bail money, Coach."

Ted smiled. "I managed to talk them out of it, Judd. I told them the only way I could stay was if I brought the five of you in there with me since I was sworn to look after you 'til I got you home."

Ted and Jerry said their good nights and tried to settle in. Each was restless, and each could hear the other moving in his bed.

Finally Jerry broke the silence. "Coach," he whispered in case Ted had drifted off. "What if I get down here and I don't like it?"

"Come home, Jerry. Wellsboro will always be there."

"But won't I have a sort of contract? I gave my word today."

"I always try to honor my word, Jerry," Ted paused.

"Me, too," Jerry interrupted.

"If. . . . and it's a mighty big if . . . if the other party to the agreement is honoring his."

They were quiet for a while.

"I always try to think about what the possible contingencies might be and what my major concerns are, . . . what my positions would probably be before I give my word or sign a contract."

Ted paused, searching through the fog of his own emotions for the right words. "Then I make sure I talk those things over with the other person. If he gives me his word on those things, I sign the contract feeling that I need to honor it so long as he does as he promised. . . . You and Coach Neeley have time to talk things over yet."

Ted paused again. "But, Jerry, if the other party breaks his word, then that breaks the contract to my way of thinking."

Ted was quiet for a full minute. "It's the beginning that is important. You know no one can see into the future, so I have no right to expect the other person to do what I 'thought' he would do or behave as I 'assumed' he would behave if something we hadn't clarified comes up. But I have every right to expect him to honor his stated intentions."

There was another silence. "Used to be I didn't think like that. I used to feel I had to honor my word no matter what happened; I felt the onus of honor was on me. But the onus is shared in a contract. Both people have to behave honorably."

Ted was quiet for a while, the events of the cemetery washing over him once more. . . . "It took me a while to grow into that. Am I making any sense, Jerry?"

"I can see where you're goin', Coach. It makes sense. Before I sign, I voice my concerns and listen to Coach Neeley's answers. If I can, I agree to the terms." Jerry thought a while. "But you're sayin' that really we both agree to the terms, and that the contract is void if either of us fails to keep his word?"

"That's how I see things, Jerry."

"It's fair. That's really the way things should be."

Ted thought a little more. *Might as well share today's lesson , too.*

"And, Jerry, when you're talking with people, always try to make abundantly clear what it is that you're really saying."

"What I mean is if your love your mom, tell her that you love her; tell her how much she means to you. Don't tell tell her that she's great because she makes the best pumpkin pie in town."

Jerry wasn't exactly sure what Ted meant, but he was getting sleepy, and the idea seemed really important to his coach. "Okay."

With things settled in each of their minds, they drifted off.

22

True to his word, Ted had phoned Bud Johnson and invited him to an early breakfast on Sunday morning. Both men knew the weather was making the water a little warm, but they would get out early and enjoy the quiet.

The porch light was on and the coffee ready when Bud's pickup pulled in at five. Bud didn't bother to knock.

Ted laid the thick slices of peppered bacon in the big cast iron skillet. "Come on back here, Bud. Get a cup of coffee and make yourself comfortable. I just want to brown off this bacon a little and wait for the biscuits to come out of the oven. By the way, Jerry's in."

"Good. Damn good. I'd like to see him make what he can of himself."

Ted put a pitcher of tomato juice on the table and dished up the hash browns. He added the browned bacon slices to the platter that held a thick slice of ham and an egg over-easy for each of them. The biscuits completed the offerings.

Bud reached for the honey at the center of the table. "Hey, you ever think about opening a bed and breakfast?" He laughed as he put honey on his warm buttered biscuit. "You put on a nice spread for a boy from the hills."

"Dig in, partner; we'll get lunch at the Diner."

The men ate with relish.

"I never cook. I live at the Diner, Sally Ann's, and the Hotel." Bud finished his meat.

Ted stood. "You know where the bathroom is. I want to clear the table a little, then we'll load up."

By 5:45 they were headed for a spot above the gorge.

. . .

Ted loaded Max in the boat before he backed the trailer to the launch. He stopped and disconnected the straps on the boat and threw the bowline to Bud. Ted eased the SUV back a few more feet, and the boat floated free of its trailer. Jerry would pick them up later.

In the water, Ted held the side of the boat until Bud settled in. Then he pulled the side of the drift boat near the shore and stepped in himself. He used the oars to take them to the current, positioned the boat to float, and rested the oars.

Both men were quiet, appreciating the birds offering up their morning songs and the sounds of the water gently slapping the boat from time to time.

Soon the sky was showing enough pink to put a light glaze on the surface of the creek, enough for them to note the fish rise from time to time.

"Which side?" Ted asked his guest.

"I do better to the left," Bud acknowledged.

"Good, I just saw a nice rise off to the right."

They didn't chatter, just allowed their minds to drift much as the boat did.

Occasionally, Ted would use an oar to reposition them in the current.

Once in a while, when the thoughts got a little deep, each man directed his mind elsewhere.

They caught and released a few, changed flies, at times suggested a favorite fly to the other.

This was the best part of any day for each of them, the quiet peacefulness of dawn.

Both liked people, but each needed privacy. Each had been married once with the marriage ending in divorce. Both lived alone, dated sometimes, worked hard, and loved athletics.

Talk between them was frequent and to the point. Neither man was one to mince words.

Ted reached into the cooler. "Thermos of coffee. Juice, water, apple?"

"Coffee would be good."

From the right angle, they would have made a perfect subject for a photo: two men and a dog in a drift boat formed a silhouette of various shades of gray against the lightening pink of the sky. A light fog was still rising from the water. The steam from the coffee cups was clearly defined from the less dense fog.

Bud took a long drink. "Ever wish you could just freeze time? Stay right where you are for a year or two?"

Ted raised an eyebrow. "Or maybe go back for a year or two." ... He took a deep breath. "This is close to perfect isn't it?"

"What's the name of that movie? ... 'As Good as it Gets.'"

Ted chuckled. "I was thinkin' of 'Grumpy Old Men.' ... But, if this is as good as it gets," he paused to mend his line, "well, it won't disappoint me much."

23

Laura and Erin left Danbury around ten on Sunday morning.

Erin had been up since six pestering, eager to get a chance to fish again.

She was glad she had left her gear with Ted: that had saved her a lot of lugging; normally, Laura wouldn't help her carry anything that involved fishing. Of course, Maria would have, but Erin didn't bother Maria with anything she could do herself. *Maria takes real good care of us. Thank you, Daddy, for getting us Maria.*

The trip was fairly easy. They knew their favorite spots along the road by now.

Erin was always happy when they reached the Binghamton exit. She knew the trip wasn't going to be much longer then, and all of the heavy traffic was well behind them. *Mommy can relax.*

She had wanted to phone Ted the minute they got to Sam's old place, but Laura had insisted they would unpack and go to the grocery for breakfast things first. *Might as well stop at the hotel for dinner too.* "You may phone when we get back to the house, Erin. Ted knows you're planning to fish with him tomorrow."

They were seated in the front corner of the PennWells dining room which was busy with the usual Sunday dinner crowd.

They waited until Annie had taken their order before going to the big salad bar. Erin chose one spoon each of beets, cottage cheese, and green bean salad along with a wedge of tomato.

She eats more like Nick every day; . . . when she decides to eat. Laura made a light mixed salad for herself and put two slices of the hotel's special bread on a plate for them.

They had ordered the home-cooked turkey dinner.

Erin ate all of her salad and most of her dinner. "Look, mommy, there's even cranberries. I love cranberries."

Laura rose to excuse herself for a trip to the Rover to pick up her water bottle.

"Mommy, there's water in your glass."

"I am able to see, Erin. I want my water bottle, okay? Besides I need a cigarette; I'll be right back."

. . .

After they had settled themselves back in the house, Erin used Laura's cell phone to call Ted.

"Weaver here."

"Hi, Ted. It's Erin."

"Well, hi, yourself, Erin Mc Cort. Are you in yet?"

"Yep." She looked around the living room as though to assure herself. "Right here in grandpa Sam's house."

Laura's hand shot across to Erin's arm. "Erin, I want you to quit saying 'yep.' You sound like some hillbilly."

Ted ignored the overheard remark. "What time do you want to start tomorrow, Erin?"

"Real early!"

"Well, okay; you're my kind of gal." He paused. *How early would Laura tolerate?* "Ask your mother whether 7:30 would be too early for me to come by."

Laura cleared it. *I might just as well get it over with.*

"I'll be there. I'll bring your gear with me. . . . How about Max? Yes or no?"

"Oh, please bring Maxie, Ted." A smile spread across her face. *I like it that he asks me about things.*

"Max will sure be happy to see you, Erin, and he loves helpin' us fish." Ted took time to gently scratch behind the Lab's ears. "I'll see you at 7:30 then. Ask Laura to give me her cell number in case something comes up."

Laura gave Ted the number. "You're welcome to come by early for cereal with us if you'd like, Ted."

"Thanks, Laura, but Max and I eat pretty early." He didn't miss the sigh of relief. "Say, you know the county fair is ready to open tomorrow. Did you bring a camera with you?"

"Yes, I always have one or two with me anymore."

"Well, Sally Ann and I make an afternoon visit on opening day. You and Erin might want to join us. You could get some new material, and I'm sure Erin would enjoy seeing the animals."

Has Laura ever been to a fair? Does she even know what one is?

"The local kids have their 4-H animal projects judged at the fair. And there's a variety of adult art projects: quilts, fancy needlework, baked goods, and carved pieces. We always have a Ferris wheel, merry-go-round, bumper cars, stuff like that, and fair food: candy apples, funnel cakes, and cotton candy."

"I think she'd like that, Ted." Laura paused, then decided. "Let's plan on it. It will be easier to get her off the water that way too. I don't want her to stay out too long."

"You're welcome to come fishing with us."

"No, I need to stay here and start going through Sam's file cabinets."

"Okay. I'll see you in the morning."

Laura shut the phone off, then turned to Erin. "Ted just invited us to the county fair with him and Sally Ann tomorrow afternoon when you two come in from fishing, Erin. There'll be animals and rides and treats."

Laura smiled as Erin's expression showed enthusiasm. "Sounds like fun, huh?"

"I bet it will be lots of fun, mommy. I've never been to a fair, but my Daddy told me about 'em.."

. . .

Ted and Erin were standing in six inches of water in Pine Creek. Erin had enjoyed the ride to the gorge.

"Did the coach like Jerry?"

Ted adjusted his footing. He'd just seen a nice rise off to his left. *Too far for Erin. Might as well try him.* "He offered him a full ride."

"So Jerry got on the team? He'll be their star."

"He might. . . . Got one on, Erin. Don't move, honey. Remember the rocks are slippery. Stand still until I get him landed."

Ted moved a few feet away from Erin; he could see her out of the corner of his eye. The trout made a hard run downstream. Ted eased him back up a little at a time and then let him take another run. Ted played him gently and gradually brought him in close.

The rainbow was beginning to tire. Ted, still gently playing the fish, eased back toward Erin. *Not too big for her.* ... *I think he's tired enough.* "Stay put, Erin, but reel in."

Erin, trying to help, had been thinking about moving out of what appeared to be Ted's way as he had begun to inch toward her. Instead she stood quietly and began bringing her line in.

Ted stopped beside and slightly to the rear of her. "Plant your feet. Now let's trade rods. You bring him on in, and I'll net him. Sometimes one like this takes more than one person."

They managed to trade rods without Erin's falling or Ted's losing the rainbow. "Nice and easy now, honey. He's a little tired, but he's a fighter."

"Watch him; he might try for another run. If he does, just let him go; keep a little pressure on him. ... Keep your tip up. That's the way. Now try to bring him in a little, just a little at a time. ... Hold some pressure on the line; we don't want him to throw the fly. ... He's a cagey one. He might try to run at you. If he does, keep your tip up and remember pressure on the line."

Ted took hold of the back of Erin's vest and felt her start to look at him. "Watch the fish, honey. I'm just going to give you some balance if he takes off."

"Oh, lookie, Ted. I can see him in the water. He's right out there." Her voice was pitched high with excitement. "See him? Right out there." She nodded toward the spot where her line entered the water.

"Yep, he's right where he should be: on the end of your leader. Bring him in easy. ... Easy now." Ted was reaching toward his back for his net. He slipped it into the water. "Okay, bring him over the mouth of the net, Erin. Don't move your feet. Use your rod. ... Easy now. Don't power him; you'll tear the fly lose. ... Easy, easy."

A smile broke over his face. "There; we got him. ... Take a good look at him; he's a real beauty, Erin. Just look at that color. ... Remember your feet now. You're too big for me to dip up out of the creek."

"Now let's see if we can trade rods again. ... That's the

way. Good girl. Put your rod in your left hand and use your right to release your walking stick like we practiced."

Erin did exactly as she was asked.

"Good. Do you want to try to get to the bank by yourself or do you want some help?"

"I can do it, Ted. I know I can." Her face slightly colored by the morning sun and the excitement, she had confidence in her voice. "I'll take baby steps like you showed me."

"Okay. Use your stick for balance and turn slowly. The turn is the hardest part of this maneuver just like it is for Max when he's swimming in the water. ... Easy. ... Oops. ... Good girl. Damn! You have good balance, Erin."

She smiled up at him.

He watched as she made her way. *Courage enough to try and sense enough to listen; she's one in a million.*

Ted had stood quietly in the water until Erin was standing at the bank. *Don't want to distract her with my movements.* He didn't want her to fall, but she had to keep developing her sense of confidence. *False confidence is worse than none at all.*

He walked to the bank, pausing twice to wet the trout which was still in the net. She had already laid her rod in the grass and had turned toward him to bend and wet her little hands. The smile on her face said it all.

The trout was of legal size, so Ted kept him in the net. He had decided to let Erin extract the fly by herself.

Before they had gotten in the water that morning, he had taught her to use two sets of pliers, one to grip the fish's mouth and one to grip the fly. Her fingers were still too tender to take a chance with. He had brought a chunk of strip steak along for her to practice with while he at first steadied the meat and then wiggled it to aggravate her as a fish would. She handled her pliers well.

"Careful with the fly now. Don't let it swing loose; take it up to the patch on your vest. That's a girl. Now seat it. Good. Okay, release your pliers and cut the leader. Good girl! Great job, Erin. I know full grown men who can't do that as slick as you just did."

She beamed; her shoulders squared.

"Now, let's take a look at this critter."

They admired the fish, and Ted slipped it into the ice in the cooler.

He pulled two bottles of orange juice and some oatmeal cookies from the second cooler. *The excitement really drained her. . . . She'll recoup.* "Let's go sit with Max for a while."

They sat at the picnic table.

Erin took a swig of juice and a big bite of cookie. She rinsed the cookie down with some more juice. "Ted, why did you say Jerry *might* be their star? . . . If the coach likes him?"

"The best hitter isn't necessarily the best person for the team, Erin."

"Well, that's dumb."

Ted scratched his chin. "You ever been on a team of some kind, Erin?"

She shook her head. "No."

Suddenly Max's muscles tightened with alertness. Most of his body remained inert. Three things moved: his muzzle went up, his ears opened and formed a straight line across the crown of his head, and his dark eyes went the sky above the gorge.

"Listen, Erin. I think Max just heard some geese. Sit real still like he is, but look up the gorge and listen real hard."

Max glanced at Ted, then back at the sky.

Ted nodded when he heard the first faint sounds. "Hear 'em?" Ted's whisper was coarse. "There, did you catch that?"

Erin was excited. "Yes, yes, I did; I really did." She had kept her volume low as she mimicked Ted's actions.

Suddenly the geese came out of the curve that the gorge made above the parking area. Now they could hear them plain enough, and see them too. "At, ease, Max."

Max got quietly to his feet for a better look, but he remained at Ted's side.

"It's okay, boy; they're way up there. Go take a look. At ease, Max," Ted said a second time.

Max went into the tall grass and walked near the creek.

"Oh, Ted, aren't they wonderful? They are sooo pretty. There's a lot of 'em, too." Erin watched until they were nearly out of sight. "Just look at them go." . . . She sighed. "It must be nice to be a goose and be free to fly anywhere you want."

Max watched until they were out of sight. Then he came back to the picnic table where he sat and looked so wistfully at the cookies that Ted broke down and gave him half of one. "Good boy, Max; here's half a cookie, but you can't have much sugar."

"I wish I had brought my sketch book. I'd like to draw them. Or maybe mommy would have taken a picture."

"Just remember them real hard, Erin. Right now think about what they looked like 'til you get their image in your mind."

Erin squinted her eyes almost shut and wrinkled her brow in total effort. . . . A smile came across her face as she shut her eyes completely. She breathed deeply and finally opened her eyes to look at Ted. "There, I think I can draw them when I get back to grandpa Sam's; my sketch book is there. I'll draw our fish too. . . . Just like you said: we both had to work to get him."

"That's right. It took both of us to bring him in. And it took all three of us to see the geese."

"Did you notice that Max stayed real still when he heard them before us even though every part of him was excited and wanted to see the birds? . . . Remember how he went into the tall grass when I released him? . . . Know why he went to the grass instead of walking down the path?"

"No."

"So he wouldn't been seen so easily. Geese have real good eyes. They watch the ground to find food and to find safe places to land. Remember how you watched the trout, so you could bring him in and how you gave careful attention to the rocks as you were going to shore?"

"He's so smart; he's a great dog, isn't he?"

"He sure is. He has a lot of qualities that make him a star. He's loyal: he never runs off doin' his own thing. He's honest: he doesn't sneak and do bad things, and, if he tells you something is coming, you'd best look for it. If I ask him to try, he tries with every ounce of his being."

Ted stopped to give Max a good rubbing. Then he looked directly at Erin. "Most important of all, he's a team player. He didn't just sneak out there so he could see the geese;

he wanted us all to get a chance. That's what a team player is: Someone who wants everyone to have his best shot, someone who wants to share, doesn't want all the attention, all the glory."

"So Jerry has to be a team player?"

"Exactly. See every coach dreams of having a great performer because that can make the difference. But experienced coaches know that a great performer can destroy a team if he forgets that he is only one of many who need to work together."

"T E A M, *to each a minute* of fame. That's a saying I have my kids chant before practice and before games. It's just something I made up, but I think attitude makes or breaks a team of any kind. Confidence in performance makes the player, but attitude makes the team."

"See, Erin, Jerry has to fit in with and support the team that is already established." Ted thought a minute. "It won't be easy. Jerry is a great kid with a lot of talent, and he's as unselfish as he needs to be, but he only knows how our team did things."

"The kid he's there to replace didn't graduate; he got hurt real bad. Hopefully, he'll be back trying to play a little too, and that team has relied on him in the past."

"Jerry and the recovering batter have to feel at ease with each other. Neither can be selfish; they and Coach Neeley have to think of what's best for the team on a given day."

He looked at her and shook his head. "It's not easy. Their established hero is going through some tough times."

"Like mommy is."

He reached across the table and took her hand. "Yes, you and your mommy and daddy were a team. And now you've lost a key member of that team, and " . . .

She jerked her hand away from his.

"We didn't lose him!"

Erin stood up and stamped her foot. "They killed him! The dirty bastards."

Tears streamed down her face. "My Daddy is dead, and he can't come back home. He's dead!"

She looked defiantly at Ted. "You don't know anything! We weren't a team; we were a family. You don't know anything about a family." Erin threw her nearly empty bottle at Ted. Her eyes snapped.   "You don't even have a family."

Suddenly Erin threw herself down and began pounding her fists on the ground. "I hate everyone who is alive! . . . My Daddy is dead. . . . My Daddy is dead."

Still needing to give more punishment, she turned and glared at Max. "And I hate him too. He's just a stupid dog who does what you tell him. He's not a family."

Max's ears dropped, not at the words, but at the sound of her voice, at the strange smell of anger coming from Erin. He made a little half whine, and let his tail move a little, but his eyes were sad.

She lay there and beat on the ground until Ted thought she had cried herself out, but then she stood and started kicking the picnic table. She swore and sobbed and pounded the table top and hated everyone and everything she could think to name.

Finally she walked off to the tall grass and stood quietly looking off downstream remembering the flight of the geese.

Ted stood up. "Let's take our rods and check out that upper hole.   They sometimes rise there about this time of the day." *Anger is better than hopelessness.*

She turned and stood looking at him as he gathered his rod and took the empty bottles to the bear-proofed trash container. Erin stamped her foot. "Didn't you even hear me?"

"I heard."

"Well?"

Ted sighed deeply and came to her where he knelt to her eye level. "Well, what, honey?"

She looked totally exasperated, "You don't even know how to fight."   She paused. "Yell at me for being mean."

. . .

She dropped her head and kicked the ground.   At the same time she began to sob softly. "Aren't you going to say something?"

Ted looked into her reddened eyes as he felt the sting of tears in his own.

He swallowed. "I don't know what to say, Erin."

"Say I'm mean and selfish and that *you* hate *me*."

"That would be a lie, Erin."

"Say I'm a big girl, and I have to understand that we have no control over life, that bad things happen, that I have to learn to accept the fact that life is just a crapshoot."

She paused to get her breath. "Say it could have been worse; mommy and I could have been there too. . . . Say I'm not the only little girl who lost her Daddy that day, and they all manage. . . . Say I should draw a picture of the. . . the . . . plane hitting the Towers. . . . Say it was all just part of God's plan and that I should quit thinking about my Daddy."

She was beginning a deeper sob now.

Her voice had become hoarse.

Ted lifted her to his chest. He held her so tightly she could hear his heart beat, feel the wetness of his cheek as she nestled her head between his chin and shoulder.

He gently rocked her body as she once again sobbed herself to exhaustion. He walked as he rocked their bodies, walked until he reached a big flat rock sitting in the sun. He sat there holding her, never loosening his arms from her body.

They sat in the sun for a time. Finally she drew three choppy tries into one long breath. "Are you cryin' too?"

"Um hum."

"Why?"

"You hurt so much, and I don't really know how to help."

"Do you feel sorry for me?"

"Yes."

She drew back and looked at him. "You're not supposed to say that. You're supposed to tell me that every single person has awful things happen to him, that that is just the way life is."

"Why?"

"If you don't, I might. . ." She paused searching for the proper word, then substituted slang. "Crack up."

It came out before he thought, "Is this the kind of shit they've been feeding you?"

She nodded solemnly. "Yep."

Ted shook his head. *What's wrong with these people?* "Is this the first time you've said these things out loud to anybody?"

Erin sniffled and nodded her head. "Yep."

"And cried like this?"

"Yep. . . . They always make me stop before I start crying too hard and maybe can't quit."

She looked at him, then lowered her eyes. "I'm sorry, Ted."

"Sorry for what, Erin?"

"I was so mean that I made you say shit. And that's a bad word."

He smiled and pulled her to him and rocked again. It was a gentle rock this time. "Oh, Erin." *Help me here, Lord; help me to say it right.* "Shit is a bad word, and I'm sorry I said it, but you didn't make me say it."

"Yes I did, and I made you cry too."

"I'm not smart enough to explain this, Erin."

It was Ted's turn to draw a long breath. "But I cried with you. . . . Not because of you. And I said shit because, for a minute there I caught a glimpse of how it has been for you. Everyone loves you so much and just wants you to be better, but no one really knows how to help."

He breathed heavily again and shook his head buying time to search for the right image, the right words. He looked up at the sky for a while.

If I can just find the right way to explain, . . .

. . .

Ted cleared his throat. "I'm not a psychologist, Erin, but I think pain and anger are a little like splinters." He stopped to look at her. "You ever have a splinter in your finger?"

She nodded; she had had one.

"Would you tell me about it?"

"Well, I got it fishing with my Daddy. And my finger got all red and started to hurt."

He looked at her. "What happened then?"

"Well, when we got back to grandpa Sam's, grandpa said that it had to come out so I could heal up."

She looked up at Ted. "Grandpa Sam said it would hurt a little to take it out, but that it would hurt a whole bunch more if we let it stay there 'cause it would fester."

She made a face. "That means get worse with stuff

called pus. So he made me wash my hands real good. Then he got a needle out and held it to a burning match. He wiped my finger with some stuff and wiped the needle with it too."

She paused remembering the experience. "He said we had to be awful clean when we did surgery. Then he," . . . Her upper teeth came out over her lip as she worked to remember exactly what had happened. "he stuck the needle in my finger; . . . pretty far I think; I didn't look 'cause it hurt. And then he squeezed my finger. That really hurt." Her brow tightened at the memory.

"And?"

She giggled a little. "And the splinter came flying out and splattered stuff on grandpa Sam's glasses."

"Right on his glasses?"

"Yep." She shook her head. "He had to wipe it off, and he put the splinter in a little piece of wax paper and put it in a book."

Ted's eyes misted again. *Just like Sam; may the good Lord treat you well, pal.*

"Which finger?"

"This one." She extended her right index finger.

"Does your finger hurt now?"

"No; it all healed. See?" She examined her own finger.

Ted stayed quiet and watched her. *Sometimes, Ted, you just need to keep quiet and let it happen.*

He watched and hoped and silently asked God to help her make the connection for herself. *She is such a smart little thing. She might do it. She has surely been 'told' enough.*

Erin was quiet too. She stared at the water. Then she moved on his lap. She got down and knelt in front of Max. One tear came down her cheek. "Oh, Maxie, I am so sorry that I said mean things and hurt your feelings. I don't hate you."

She patted his shoulder. "I could never hate you, Maxie."

She patted his shoulder again. Another tear appeared. "I love you, Maxie."

She put her arms around his chest.

Max kissed her: first on the cheek, and then, seeing that he wasn't corrected, on the mouth. She made no attempt to stop him and, instead, gave him an even bigger hug as his tail made dust.

She stood and took Ted's hand.

They walked, by unspoken agreement, to the Suburban.

She's had enough for today.

It was always a slow drive up out of the gorge, and Ted continued to take his time on the highway.

They had just nosed into town when the silence between them was broken. "Ted?"

His gut told him to stop the vehicle.

He pulled over and looked at her.

"You think that's the way?" . . . She looked at her hands in her lap, "If I keep the bad stuff inside, it'll all fester up and get lots worse?"

Thank you, sweet Jesus.

Ted smiled. "Could be, Button."

Erin studied her hands for a while, then she raised her eyes to meet his. "I'm sorry that I said mean things to you and Max 'cause you're good, and I love you both."

"And we both love you."

She squirmed in her seat to touch Max who thumped his tail and kissed her hand. "I'm glad Max isn't mad at me." She looked questioningly up at Ted.

"Oh, Max wouldn't be mad at you any more than I would. We love you. We understand that people get upset and sometimes have to let off some steam to work through their problems."

Ted started the motor and pulled out into traffic. "Emotions are good things, Erin. They," . . . He searched for the right analogy again. "They're like little pressure valves." He glanced her way. "You know what a pressure valve is?"

"Yes, Maria uses a pressure cooker in the kitchen sometimes. She showed me the little spot on top that will let the air out before the pan blows up and makes the whole kitchen a mess. She said that little dot keeps us safe. It's made out of something special. . . . I can't remember what Maria said it was, but she told me not to worry: she wouldn't blow us to," . . . Erin searched her memory for the strange word which Maria had used. "smithereens!" Erin giggled, "That's what she said. You know smithereens?"

"I sure do." He drove slowly while he thought things through. *Point me in the right direction.*

. . .

"You know, Erin, emotions are a little like the pressure in the pressure cooker: good for what they are intended for, but things you don't want to let get out of hand. Sometimes you get so much love built up that you have to say 'I love you' and hold a person close or you'll just burst," he glanced at her, a twinkle in his eye, "and blow great globs of love all over the floor."

She giggled, "Great globs of love all over the floor. That's funny."

"Well, that's what I think. And it's the same way with the bad stuff. Sometimes it just builds up, and you have to open your mouth and let 'er out."

"Or you'd blow great globs of bad stuff all over the floor!"

. . .

Laura was waiting on the porch when they drove into Sam's drive.

"Hey, you two, I've been worried; you were gone a long time."

She shot Ted a glance.

"Erin, have you been crying?"

Again, Laura looked sharply at Ted who glanced at Erin, wondering what Erin would share with Laura.

Erin looked squarely at Laura. "I'm okay, mommy. I feel good."

She smiled up at Ted. "We've spent the morning catching fish and gettin' rid of globs."

"Globs?" Laura hadn't taken a single step toward Erin.

"Now I got to go pee, mommy."

Ted recognized a perfectly executed flanking maneuver when he saw one.

"She caught a nice rainbow. I put it on ice to hold its color in case you wanted to get a shot of it." *Surely I can flank as well as a seven-year-old.*

"Oh, yes, let me get the camera. I have it ready for

the fair this afternoon."

Laura paused on her way to the door. "Why don't you come in and wash up some? Sally Ann called and said we should come out there for lunch, and then she would go to the fairgrounds with us. I'll drive if you're tired."

She saw the hesitation. "Max can ride in the Rover the same as he can with you. Or had you made other plans?"

"Max and I would love to ride in a Land Rover. We've never been in one."

"You can drive it."

"No, thanks. It'll be good to relax."

24

"So, where is this fairground?" Laura asked once the four of them were in the Land Rover.

"Drive east on route 6; it will be off to your left, honey," Sally Ann explained. *Oh, I wish I hadn't called her honey.* "Laura, I'm sorry."

Laura glanced to her right. Erin, Max, and Ted had chosen to ride in the rear seats. "Sorry for what, Sally Ann?"

"Oh, I'm afraid I probably offended you when I called you 'honey.' I didn't mean anything by it, Laura. It's just a holdover from my youth. Back then 'honey' wasn't a bad word to call a lady. It was what we called people we liked. I'm sorry; just consider the age of the source."

Laura smiled. "Sally Ann, don't fret as Sam would say; 'honey' is a nice word." Laura maneuvered carefully as she passed three horseback riders heading single file along the berm of her lane. "Look, Erin, see the horses?"

Erin caught her breath. "Oh, mommy. They're beautiful. Look at the one with all of the spots on his back end."

"I think that's an appaloosa, Erin." Laura looked questioningly toward Sally Ann.

"That's right. That's Meg Randall riding. She owns a real estate office." Sally Ann smiled. "Meg sure does love her horses. The others belong to her too. She takes friends riding with her when she can. Horses always need exercise."

"I'd sure help her if she ever wants," Erin piped up.

"Erin McCort! Where are your manners? You wait to be asked, young lady; you do not try to push yourself in."

"But, mommy, I wasn't. I just said I would help. I didn't ask to ride." Erin looked at Ted for support.

Ted was busy studying his fingernails. *Stay out of it, buddy. Laura's her mother.*

"There! There it is on your left, Laura." Sally Ann

pointed, "See? We turn to the left just ahead a little. Up there where the flagman is."

Ted reached for his wallet. "My treat, ladies." He found the correct button and got his window down just as Laura pulled to a stop beside a man wearing a white carpenter's apron. "Four, please Jim." Ted handed him a twenty.

Jim handed Ted four ones and a string of white tickets. Then he directed Laura to the man with a red flag who was in charge of parking cars in neat rows on the big grass lot to the right of the display area.

Ted handed the tickets to Erin. "Try not to lose them, Erin. These are tickets to the rides." He looked at her eyes big and shiny with a new adventure; she was taking everything in. "Have you ridden on a Ferris wheel, Erin?"

Erin licked her upper lip. "I'm not sure what that is."

Ted pointed to the tallest thing in the midway. "There, that big thing. See; it's a double Ferris wheel this year. We'll walk over there when we get out so you can watch it for a while."

As soon as Laura locked the car, they started walking through the grass stubble toward the midway.

"Wow," Erin said when they were standing outside the rope that formed a perimeter around the Ferris wheel.

She rolled her eyes upward and lifted her chin. "Look, mommy; just look how tall it is." She watched as each wheel turned independently while the connecting bar and the two wheels formed a unit which also turned slowly in a big circle.

"Boy, those people way up on the top must be able to see clear back into town. . . . Ut, oh, it's rockin'!" Erin grabbed Ted's fingers and pulled back a little.

Ted laughed. "It's supposed to, Erin. See that's what makes it fun. You go way up and see all over the fairgrounds, and, when you're really lucky, your seat stops on the very tiptop while someone is getting off on the bottom. Then you get to rock, like on a porch swing."

He studied her profile a moment. "Want to try it?"

"Will you take me?"

"Sure. I will." He looked toward Laura to make certain she didn't object.

"Give mommy and Sally Ann two tickets, and they can get in the car behind us. We'll wave at them and show 'em how it's done."

"Max, stay."

Ted and Erin climbed in the next available car.

Sally Ann and Laura loaded right after them.

Erin's eyes got big as they started to move, and she took a firm grip on Ted's hand as she wedged herself into her corner.

Ted moved a little closer to her.

She actually held her breath and closed her eyes about halfway when they rounded the very top, then she heard Sally Ann go, "Whee" as she and Laura began their rolling decent.

Erin looked up at Ted and grinned. She released his hand and put her hands on the protective bar at the front of the car. They made another round. She kept her eyes open this time and pointed, "Look how little everything looks. We're up really high, huh, Ted?"

Nick must never have taken her to work with him. Maybe he was saving that for when she was older. . . . I never thought, but this could have been bad for her. Pay more attention, partner; remember, this is no ordinary little girl.

On their third and final circle, their chair actually stopped at the very top of the arc. They sat there swaying slightly with the momentum from the stop, feeling the warm wind on their faces.

Ted watched Erin for any sign of stress, but she had settled in completely. She was leaning slightly forward and peering down; then she moved a little sideways and looked over the side. She wasn't one to scare herself.

She turned back to look up at him. "This is fun; I like it."

"Look back and wave at mommy."

She did, and Laura and Sally Ann waved back at them.

After they got off the ride and collected Max, Sally Ann looked at Ted. "I've waited as long as I can, Ted. I have to go to the art hall and see about my cake."

Sally Ann wasn't given to displays of personal pride, but she made the best coconut cake anyone had ever tasted, and she had taken both the blue and purple ribbons with it every year she had lived in Wellsboro: blue for best cake with cream filling; purple for best cake regardless of type.

She led the march to the art hall.

They went straight to the display of baked goods. "And, once again, the winner and champion," Ted teased her as soon as he saw the ribbons.

Laura got a camera out. "Stand over there by the cake, Sally Ann."

Sally Ann took Erin's hand. "You come too, honey."

"Erin, move to the other side of the cake so I can frame the cake and the ribbons with you and Sally Ann." Laura focused, then asked them to move in just a little, and shot.

When they moved out of the way, she stepped forward and took a close-up of the cake by itself. It sat on a short-stemmed, round crystal cake plate. A single slice lay temptingly atop a matching crystal serving plate. The three layers of white cake were separated by a rich-looking cream filling. The vanilla frosting had been covered with what looked to be lightly toasted slivers of fresh coconut. The slightly browned edges of the slivers made a perfect foil to the otherwise delicate tones.

Laura fiddled with her camera a bit. She reached into her camera bag and took out two regular flashlights. She handed one to Ted and one to Erin. "Take those lights behind the table on either side of the cake. Now, Sally Ann, go in and stand there beside it again. Okay, guys, turn those lights on and point them at that beautiful cake stand. ... Good. ... Erin, lower yours just a little. Good. Hold it right there." Laura shot again.

She turned and smiled at them. "We got us a good one."

Erin smiled up at Ted, "And it took all of us."

Ted and Sally Ann exchanged looks, ironically both were thinking the same thing: *Laura's a completely different person when she's so involved that she forgets herself.*

Laura smiled at Sally Ann. "Thanks for indulging me, Sally Ann. I wanted to get a good picture of you, but I wanted a picture of that cake too. My mom used to make the best coconut cakes." She shook her head sideways. "Dad always loved them; Sammy too. I never cooked much, so I didn't take mom's cookbooks when ... well, when dad offered them to me."

She took a deep breath. "It's strange, I can almost taste her cake right now. Hers always had that rich cream filling between the layers too."

Laura quickly batted her eyes. "Right now I wish I had taken the books though I never would have used them, but they're lost. . . . Another lost opportunity." . . . She sighed, her shell cracked for a minute, then she squared her shoulders. "Oh, well. You can never go back, can you?"

Sally Ann was beaming as she walked to Laura and gave her a warm hug: "Sometimes you can, Laura."

"I suppose."

"Yes, Laura, you really can."

Sally Ann looked at Ted. "Ted, can you remember what I have always told you about that recipe?"

Ted thought a minute. His brow furrowed, "That it wasn't really yours?"

"That's right. Laura, honey, that *is* your mother's cake. Sam brought me a box of cookbooks and decorating books, shortly after I opened the sandwich shop and got to know him. When I looked through the cookbooks, I took several recipes from them. Most of the ones I took had handwritten adjustments in the margin of the page where the recipe was printed."

She smiled and touched Laura's arm. "Your mother's coconut cake has won the county fair every summer since I've lived here. That was one reason I wanted you and Erin to come with us today. I hoped you might remember. I'll bring the books to you tomorrow; they should be yours."

Tears were falling from Laura's eyes. "Oh, Sally Ann." Laura made the first move and put her arms around the older woman. She looked deeply into Sally Ann's bright blue eyes. "Please, you keep the books. I really don't cook. . . . It's nice to know that someone who loves to cook is using them. My only pain was thinking they were lost in some landfill with no one benefiting from them."

"Well, I'll tell you what then. The next time you come over here there will be a cake waiting for you." Sally Ann looked at Ted. "Just let me know. I'd gladly give you that one, but the filling goes bad if the cake isn't kept cool."

"I will look forward to that." Laura's eyes misted again. "It's been years." She put the flashlights and camera back in her bag. "Where in the world did you get that beautiful cake stand, Sally Ann?"

"My Charles got that for me, Laura. Charles and I used to go to Czechoslovakia to buy crystal when we were stationed in Germany. If you like crystal, I'd love to show you my 'treasures' anytime you're in the mood. You don't need a special invitation; just stop by."

"Nick always loved crystal. He bought us several nice pieces, and Erin has some crystal figurines that she puts on her window sills." Laura shouldered her bag. "Do we have to leave now or could we look at the rest of the things?" Sally Ann smiled, "Let's look."

Erin ran ahead when she saw the quilt display. She delighted in the colors and the patterns. Suddenly, she came running back. "Come look, Miss Sally; you won another blue ribbon."

Sally Ann clapped her hands with joy. "My grand-mother's log cabin took a blue. She would have been so proud." Sally Ann bent to speak to Erin. "That quilt was made from scraps of clothing, not from pieces of store-bought cloth like they are today."

She reached across the barrier and fingered the quilt. "My family's history is right there in the pieces of this quilt."

"I thought you made it, Miss Sally."

"No, honey, the quilt show has a special class for quilts which are owned by local people, but which someone else made. I have three quilts that my mother's mother made; and I put one in the fair this year."

"Family is real important to you isn't it Sally Ann?" Laura asked.

"Oh, my, yes! . . . Family! . . . Well, that's just like the bloodlines on the dogs; we're all products of what has come before."

They went through the cattle barn which intrigued Erin because it was round, "I never knew you could make a round barn, did you, mommy?" and through the horse barn, where they had to keep a close eye on Erin; she wanted to pet the horses so badly. She loved the goats, especially the miniature ones, and the rabbits. "Look these have floppy ears, oh, and there's one that looks just like a Siamese cat, its color, I mean."

The chicken barn had a smell that made Erin wrinkle her nose; the hog barn smelled worse and was "real noisy!"

Dusk was beginning as they wandered back toward the midway.

"Now, Erin, you may choose one treat, but I want you to eat a sensible meal when we leave here."

"Then I want to look at all of them first."

As they were walking the midway, Judd saw Ted and came hurrying over. "Hi, Coach Weaver, Sally Ann."

Judd backed up a step and made a little bow, "Well, well, Miss Erin McCort is in town today too, I see."

Erin beamed. *He knows me. He remembered from Sally Ann's. I remember him, too.* "Hi, Judd. You're the catcher for the team."

Ted turned to Laura. "Laura, I'd like you to meet Judd Thompson from our baseball team. Judd, Erin's mother, Laura McCort."

"Pleased to meet you Mrs. McCort. I sure like the little spitfire here." He turned again to Erin. "Hey, Erin, do you like stuffed animals?"

Erin's head bobbed. "Sure."

Judd smiled. "Well, come with me, my friend. Ole Judd will show you how they're won."

Laura stayed close enough to grab for Erin should it be necessary.

Ted, Sally Ann, and Max walked over to the cotton candy trailer. "You never cease to amaze me, Sally Ann. You were certainly generous with Laura about your cake and the books."

"I like her, Ted. She's all wound up, tense, tight as a bow string, but she does love that little girl, and, every once in a while, I get a glimpse of the woman she once was."

Ted raised his eyebrows.

"Sam left a letter for me, too, Ted. Probably not the same as yours, but he shared the important things with me too, and asked that I try to help. He had some suggestions."

As the vendor handed Ted and Sally Ann cones of rainbow- colored cotton candy, they heard a whoop.

They turned in time to see Judd hand Erin a big black dog. Erin came running to them, her pigtails flopping on her shoulders. "Look, Miss Sally. Look, Ted, at what Judd just won for me."

She turned to smile up at Judd. "Thank you, Judd; I didn't know you could pitch too." She looked back at her mother. "Judd knocked all the bottles down with the first throw on his second try."

She hugged the big stuffed toy to her and looked up at Ted. "I'm gonna call him Maxie."

Her eyes shifted back to Judd, her new hero. "Thank you, Judd, thank you a whole lot. I never had anyone win me anything before."

Judd, a natural flirt; appreciated the feminine side of life, and attention from any source was greatly enjoyed.

Judd took Erin's hand as he addressed her mother. "If it would be okay, I think I know a game where Erin just might be able to win another prize all by herself." He looked at Erin who was all ears. "You fish don't you?"

Erin nodded eagerly. "Ted took me this morning; we caught a big rainbow."

"Well," Judd hunkered down to Erin's level and lowered his voice, "there's this fishing game just up the way. You drop a circle of plastic over a bottle that is standing up. Then, if you can lay the bottle on its side without letting the circle slide off the top of the bottle you get to choose a prize. You get three tries for a dollar. . . . Now if you can stand it back up, you get to choose a bigger prize from the top row. But you only get one prize for each three turns." He leaned in closer. "I've got a couple of dollars." He looked up at Laura who was smiling.

They walked up the midway.

Erin was on a mission, completely ignoring the food stands and holding 'Maxie' tightly against her body with one arm while keeping the other hand free to hold Judd's hand.

The adults followed. Ted put his hand on Laura's arm as they neared the booth. "Let's give her some space. Judd will take care of her. He doesn't have siblings. That's a real shame because he loves kids. He's helped coach Little League for the last three summers. He won't let anything happen to her."

Laura's expression darkened, and her eyes snapped. "That's easy enough for you to say. You don't have a child."

Ted turned slightly away as his mind returned to Erin's emotional morning. *Why in the world don't people realize that when they fight in front of a child, they're teaching the child their own tactics? If you fight dirty; they'll fight dirty.*

He turned back and smiled at Laura. "Trust me on this one, Laura. Erin is one hundred percent safe when she's with Judd."

Sally Ann touched Laura's arm. "Ted's right, Laura. Judd would die first. And this isn't the City, dear; no child has been snatched since I've been here."

Judd handed the vendor a dollar. Judd smiled and shook his head; then pointed to Erin.

Erin handed 'Maxie' to Judd for safekeeping and took the short fishing rod in her hands. There was no reel, just a fixed length of line with a plastic ring the size of a half dollar at the end.

Erin's expression became totally serious. She managed to drop the ring over the neck of a bottle on her first try; this was no mean feat in itself. Each attempt to put the ring over the bottle neck counted as a turn; three turns for a dollar.

Erin stood still for a while; she watched the teen next to her as he tried to manipulate the bottle. He could get the ring over the neck, but he could not lay the bottle down. He walked away.

On Erin's first try, the ring slipped off just as she was an inch from getting the bottle down on its side. She quickly went for another bottle but failed to get the ring around its neck.

She scuffed her feet on the ground as though she were planting them in the stream. She settled herself and went for the third try.

All four adults held their breaths. The ring went over the bottle neck and, by taking her time, and moving the tip of the rod up and down as she moved her body back and forth, she got the bottle to lay down. She took a deep breath and went for it.

The ring slipped off the neck on her first try to stand it up.

The man inside the booth pointed to the choices.

Erin selected a small object.

The man handed her a key chain with a plastic catcher's mask on it.

Erin handed the key chain to Judd who tried, at first, to refuse it, and then bent to kiss her cheek as he accepted it.

Erin turned to leave, but Judd touched her shoulder.

He held up two fingers. They returned to the booth. He handed the vendor another dollar.

The vendor smiled, "The young red-haired lady has a gaming spirit, ladies and gentlemen," he called to the midway as he handed her a rod. "Gather round now."

She raised and lowered the rod and took it sideways a couple of times.

The vendor leaned forward as Erin asked him something; he smiled and handed her a different rod.

She managed to get the ring over the bottle all three tries. She got the bottle down on the first try. The ring slipped off about midway down on her second try, but it stayed with the bottle all the way down on her third.

Erin stood still for a while. She tested the tip of the rod a few times and made some wiggle movements with the ring. Her face went through some contortions. She set her feet again and slowly and patiently worked the ring as far back on the neck of the bottle as she could.

She stopped again to consider.

Judd couldn't help her; he had never been able to win with the rods.

Erin glanced back at Ted, who stood looking at her with a smile on his face.

She moved her feet slightly sideways and lined up straight with the slight diagonal on which the bottle lay.

She planted her feet again then moved the rod tip quickly upward and eased her upper body forward just a bit as the upward motion started. It worked!

Even the vendor clapped.

Laura caught a glimpse of Ted in her side vision.

He was discretely wiping a tear as he ran his hand

up around his mouth and under his nose. *How in the world did she figure that out?*

Erin studied the items on the top row. One was a ballerina stick toy. The ballerina was dressed in pink satin shoes and costume with a white net crinoline that made her skirt stand out. Fine string ran from the tip of each hand and the tip of each foot to the wooden handle that allowed you to use its four tiny bars to position the arms and legs. With practice it would be possible to make her dance.

The vendor reached into a plastic container under his display and pulled out a clear box that held a ballerina.

He handed it to Erin. "Enjoy your prize, dear, you earned it."

He switched to his midway voice. "Now who will try to do the job this little lady just did? ... Ladies and gentlemen, a mere child can take one off the top rack!"

Erin walked proudly back toward Max and the adults.

Judd followed closely with 'Maxie.' "How about that, sports fans?"

"Why did you ask to change poles, honey?" Laura asked.

Rods, mommy, rods. Erin did not correct her mother. Instead, she smiled sweetly at Laura. "I asked him for one with a green ring, mommy. My Daddy always told me that green was his favorite color, and that it brought us luck."

Laura pulled Erin to her in a big hug. "Well, it certainly brought you luck today, Erin. But I think, maybe, you made some luck of your own, too."

25

It was Labor Day 2002 when Erin dug her toes in. "I don't care what you say; I am not going to the memorial service."

Laura was firm, "We've talked about this before. You *are* going. I will not tolerate defiance from you."

She leveled her eyes at Erin. "Now enough, young lady! You *are going* to the memorial to show respect for your father. You need this for closure. You must get past Nick's death, and this will help."

"But, mommy, I. . . ."

"You *are going*, and that is it! We're both going." Laura took a sip from her water bottle. "We'll have to get up early because there will be a crowd, and security will be an issue."

She paused. "Maria is going with us. We're going to drive down to the City on the tenth and spend the night in the townhouse. That will give us a little more sleep. Emil's will deliver a good dinner for the three of us after the ceremonies. We'll drive back up here the next day."

Erin turned and went to her room. *Why can't I ever decide anything? . . . It's my life, too, and it was my Daddy!*

She jerked the center drawer of her desk open and took out a sketch pad and her markers. *Jamie said to draw when I feel frustrated.* She turned the sketch pad horizontally and picked up her black marker. She printed in square capital letters I R A Q. . . . She spit on the paper and grabbed up her red marker and tried to scratch out the letters. Then she tore the page out, wadded it up and threw it in the waste can.

After thinking about it, she took the paper out of the can and smoothed it enough to tear it into little pieces which she then took to her bathroom.

She urinated on the pieces of paper and flushed them. *Take that!*

It had felt good, so she repeated the process not bothering with the waste can this time.

She sat at her desk and looked at her Daddy's picture for

a long time. She drew a blue sky and left a white cloud in it. She put a red heart in the cloud. Then she used her black pen to write 'Daddy' in the heart. She removed the page from the pad and centered it on her bulletin board using the plastic-topped tacks which Nick had given her.

After admiring her picture, Erin left her room and walked to the kitchen.

"Hi, Erin. How's my sweet girl today?"

Erin sat at the butcher-block table in the center of the big room. "Sad, Maria."

Maria stopped adding spice to the fish broth which she was making and came to sit beside Erin. She put her arm around Erin's shoulders and pulled her close. Maria didn't say anything; she just held Erin and kissed her hair.

After a while, Maria stood and walked to the refrigerator. She looked back over her shoulder as she opened the door. "I am so glad you came to the kitchen. I need help with the cookies." She looked tenderly at the little girl. "I am busy with the fish broth for tomorrow's chowder. If I roll the cookie dough, will you cut the cookies for me?"

"Sure, Maria."

Maria put a disc in the CD player. Soon light-hearted Spanish music softly filled the kitchen. "I feel like a cup of hot chocolate to get me started." Her brown eyes twinkled at Erin. "Care to join me?"

"Oh, yes, please."

Maria made the hot chocolate and added a topping of small marshmallows. She sat beside Erin again and stirred until most of the marshmallow was dissolved. Then she looked at Erin and winked. She scooped the remainder of the marshmallows into her spoon and plopped them into her mouth.

Erin did the same.

"Heaven," Maria signed.

Erin smiled in agreement.

Maria softly hummed with her favorite songs, and she smiled when, during the first repeat, Erin hummed along with her as she cut the cookies. Soon the smell of lemon cookies was adding to the ambiance of the kitchen.

Well before the cookies were done, Erin's black mood had lifted. When she went to the living room to join her mother, Laura was watching a program about the Louvre. Laura talked along with the commentator and played a professionally produced tape of a tour of the Louvre for Erin after the program ended.

Maria came to announce dinner.

The three of them went to the dining room whose mahogany wainscoting and framing glowed in the warm light of the candles which centered the round mahogany table.

Nick had found the table, capable of seating twelve when leaves were added. The antique shop in the City also had the matching chairs, a tea table, a buffet, and two beautifully engraved corner cabinets.

He had had them shipped as a surprise birthday gift to Laura.

She had immediately fallen in love with the pieces.

Originally, the dining room had seemed too large to Laura, but the finish on the antiques matched the wainscoting perfectly, and there were just enough pieces to produce an elegant, yet cozy feel.

Laura had often marveled at how a man who had grown in poverty could have acquired such perfect taste.

His taste had been one of the first things attracting Laura to Nick.

"He's a class act," Sam had commented. "He likes the best; that's why he loves you so much."

He did love me, unconditionally; he always gave me the best of everything.

Laura looked at Erin, *including himself.*

Oh, Nick, I wish I had been a better wife. I'm sorry, Nick. So sorry.

Laura squared her shoulders and pulled herself together the instant she felt the sting in her eyes.

"Maria, the table looks beautiful, and dinner smells delicious, doesn't it Erin?"

Erin agreed. She inhaled deeply. "Maria takes good care of us, mommy."

"Yes, she does." Laura turned to Maria. "Thank you,

Maria, for putting up with us. We couldn't make it without you."

"I love you both, Laura."

Maria bent her head to ask the blessing.

As soon as Maria had finished the blessing and the food had been passed, Laura excused herself for a trip to the bathroom and her special 'water.'

I can't get through this without a little something. She poured a double shot of Stoli into a water glass, added water, drank it down, and returned to the table.

"There, now. Let's enjoy this wonderful meal. Lots of people are just eating burned hot dogs today. We're lucky to have this wonderful slow-roasted chicken and trimmings."

Laura smiled at Maria. "You really are a wonder. Happy holiday."

26

When Erin got home from school on Thursday, September fifth, Laura told her they would go to Wellsboro on Saturday morning if Erin would quit quarreling about the Memorial Service "which we are going to attend!"

Erin had immediately gone to her room and packed. She was ready before Maria had had even called them for dinner.

Laura watched as Erin approached her dinner with some interest. She decided then and there that they would leave at noon on Friday.

I won't tell her; it will distract her too much at school; her teacher has called about that. That isn't like Erin; she always pays attention. . . . I'll just let this be a pleasant little surprise.

Erin had, of course, been delighted when Laura brought her home for lunch the following day. She had helped carry everything to the Land Rover. She hadn't once criticized Laura's driving during the trip, a habit which she had taken up lately.

. . .

Ted collected Erin at 7:30 Saturday morning, and they had fished the first two holes.

Since Erin was getting a rough start, Ted decided it was time to try some fresh water. "Let's reel them in, Erin. I know a nice place just down the road a bit."

They had come to the Suburban. Erin looked up at Ted as they sat on the logs marking the parking lot to remove their waders.

"Ted, what's a bitch?"

"In dog circles it's what breeders call the mother dog." He grinned at her. "Why? You gonna buy a dog?"

"No; I just wondered." She made a face and wiggled her spine as she stood and extracted her left foot from the waders. "What is it in people?"

"Well, it's not a nice word to use with people, Erin." He thought for a moment. "When a person calls a woman a bitch, it means she is unpleasant, selfish, doesn't think about others; that sort of thing. It is not a word to use lightly. In fact we should not say that word at all."

"So, what's a son-of-a-bitch?"

"Another bad word: a scoundrel, a person without principles, a dishonorable person, sort of the male version of the word bitch." He looked at her. "Have you begun saying bad words, Erin?"

Her pigtails flew horizontally. "No, my Daddy would hate that. I just wondered what those words meant."

"Well, I'm glad to hear you're not into cussing and swearing. We shouldn't use those words, Erin, and we shouldn't hang out with folks who do use them on a regular basis."

Ted stood. "Let's get in the car and try the next hole. It's just down the road a little."

They rode along in silence. Ted's peripheral vision told him Erin was picking at the skin along her thumbnail.

"Mommy called my Daddy a son-of-a-bitch the day he died. ... That morning before he left for work. But he wasn't one. He had principles." She looked up at Ted. "That's rules to live by, right?"

"Right."

"Well, he had them. He had a lot of them."

They stopped to inspect the stream.

"Looks good to me, Erin. Want to try it here or go on a little further?"

"I vote for here."

"Good girl. Let's see if we can discover what they're feeding on. Why don't you take your collection net and see what's in the water."

Ted watched as Erin went to the stream, used her wading stick to get down the bank, and walked out a bit before she used her little net to collect a sample from the stream. She made her way back to Ted and handed him the net.

Ted studied the contents. "Lets try a blue-winged olive."

Erin had decided to pick up right where she had left off. *Ted's the only one who listens to me; well, and Jamie and Maria, but Jamie gets paid, so she doesn't really count. ... Mommy won't listen to anybody. . . . She is a bitch; just like my Daddy said, a selfish bitch.*

"Well, my Daddy had rules to live by."   She held up her index finger. "'Always tip the waitress even if she is having a bad day; people need to be encouraged.'"

Another finger came up. "'Don't say bad words, especially if you're little; God listens to little people harder than He does to big people.' 'Don't drink too much; a little is okay, but don't overdo anything.' 'Listen to people politely when they tell their thoughts; nobody has all of the answers.' 'Respect other people's opinions, and, if you disagree, do it nicely; don't try to hurt.' Stuff like that. So he had principles." She looked squarely at Ted and gave a firm nod of her head.

She took her rod as he held it toward her after he had attached the blue-winged olive.

In a couple more years, she can do this all by herself. . . . She just has to work her way through this stuff today.

"My Daddy called my mommy a selfish bitch that morning. They thought I couldn't hear, but I listen real well."

She looked at Ted who appeared to be busy tying a fly to his leader. "They were arguing about my mommy drinking too much. My Daddy said she was cutting herself off from me and that that wasn't right. He said she should not drink until after dinner; that way he'd be there to keep me company at night. My mommy said she would drink whenever she damn well felt like it."

Erin tipped her chin up. "That's when My Daddy called her a selfish bitch, and then she called him a controlling son-of-a-bitch."

Erin followed Ted to the stream; they entered quietly. Ted gave her room to find her own spot but stayed near enough to help her if she got in trouble. He watched as she selected her rock.

She has good judgment for someone her age. She'll make a good one. He smiled. *She's a good one right now. But she sure is worked up this morning, tryin' to talk it out.*

Erin cast her line into the air above her and then laid it in the stream. "Well, my Daddy went out the door, but he came back and tried to kiss mommy. He told her he was sorry, and that he didn't mean to try to control her, that he was just worried about her health. And then he said, 'I don't want to leave like this, Laura. Darling, I love you; I certainly don't think you're a bitch.'"

"She shoved on my Daddy's chest, but he still tried to be nice. He said, 'I'm sorry, darling. Give me a kiss; let's make-up before I leave.'"

Erin brought her line in and put it out again. "And my mommy just said, 'Leave me alone you son-of-a-bitch. I don't know why I ever married you.' Then my Daddy left."

Erin brought her line in again. "Ted, are you hungry?"

"I could eat a little something. How about you?"

"I'm hungry."

He began reeling. "Where do you want to go?"

"Is Sally Ann's too far?"

"Not at all; it will just give us time to decide what we want to have."

They headed for the Suburban.

Sally Ann saw them as they came through the door. She smiled at Ted and called out, "Hi, there, Erin McCort."

Erin smiled back, "Hi, Miss Sally."

Sally Ann brought water, black coffee and orange juice to the booth as soon as they were seated. "You were supposed to tell me when to expect Laura and Erin, Ted. I would have made Laura that coconut cake."

She looked at Erin. "See your mother's pictures over there on the wall, Erin? Just look at the the the one with your grandmother's cake and me! Your mother made that cake plate look like it was cut from diamonds."

Erin was still mad at her mother, and she wasn't about to let her garner much praise. "Ted and I helped; we held the lights for her. It was the lights that did it. She just pushed the shutter button."

Sally Ann gave Ted a look over Erin's shoulder then smiled warmly at the little girl, "What are you hungry for, Erin?"

"I'd like a pancake, Miss Sally. Just one with two bacons, please."

"Ted?"

"I'll stick with the kid, Sally Ann. She's got me this far."

Erin started picking the skin beside her thumbnail again. "Sometimes I get so mad when I think about that morning. She was mean to my Daddy."

Ted took a drink of his coffee. "What does Jamie think about all of this?"

"She doesn't know . . . . I never told her. Mommy says that it's bad to tell other people our secrets, that family stuff is to stay family stuff."

Ted looked at Erin. He took a deep breath. "I think she's a little bit confused about that, Erin. Of course family business isn't something you go around telling everyone you meet." He paused. "But, in this case, things are different. Jamie, that's your counselor's name isn't it?"

Erin nodded her head and leaned forward, all engrossed in the concept of the bitch being wrong. *She thinks she's right all of the time. Anyone who disagrees with her is STUPID.*

"Well, Jamie's license depends on her keeping your private business completely confidential with a few rare exceptions." He paused. *Erin's a Catholic.* "She's a little like a priest in that respect. Do you know that a priest wouldn't likely repeat a confession?"

"That's right; it would be a sin."

"Okay, well, Jamie isn't a priest, but she would lose her license if she told other people your business unless she did it to protect you or someone else from violence. That's about the only exception."

"So it's not wrong to tell Jamie?"

"I'm sure it isn't; she needs to know what bothers you. She can't help you much if you don't open up to her. . . . She can help fix minds, Erin, but she can't read them. She has to have some facts to go on; otherwise you're just wasting time and money."

Sally Ann brought the pancakes and bacon. "I brought good maple syrup from a local bush and some fresh sliced peaches to go with the pancakes. You two eat it all up for me now. Don't let them get cold. I don't want to think I've lost my touch." *Erin looks like she's losing weight again.* Sally Ann shook her head. *Dear Lord, Please help us to help her.*

Erin's tummy was ready for the food.

. . .

Laura had awakened with a headache and had only provided Erin with dry toast from some bread she had left in the freezer on their last visit. They had arrived too late last night to get groceries.

Laura had pulled into Sam's drive and gone right to bed after she had set the alarm. *Thank heavens I left a message for Ted on his answering machine.*

. . .

Erin emptied her plate and finished her juice and a glass of milk which Sally Ann had brought to the booth, 'by mistake.'

They went back to the streams until 11:30.

Laura's message had said she wanted Erin back by noon; she wanted to leave around 12 so they could spend Saturday night at home.

Ted would comply, of course, but he wished he had been able to have more time with Erin. She was in pretty bad shape.

For the first time she had seemed unable to concentrate on fishing, unable to lose herself in the act.

Laura came out and said hello, but she was showing signs of increased stress too.

She certainly wasn't the Laura who had enjoyed the fair and who had sent Ted and Sally Ann professional-quality photos. She had even sent a candid photo for Judd, a picture that showed the back of Erin and Judd at the booth where Erin had won the ballerina and the key chain.

Judd was proud of the little key chain. He used it for his car keys, and he had stuck the picture up on the bulletin board in his locker.

27

Laura, Maria, and Erin had arrived at the townhouse on Sept. 10, 2002, in time for lunch at one Laura's favorite bistros. They sat outside and enjoyed the busy street scene while they tasted flavors that can only be found in the City.

After lunch, they returned to the townhouse.

Laura planned to visit an art exhibit.

Maria had carefully packed provisions and intended to put them away and prepare the evening meal.

Erin, much to Laura's disappointment, elected to stay with Maria.

"Honestly, Erin, you should come with me. This art is here on loan from the Louvre. You need to develop a sense of who you are."

Erin had not argued with her mother. She simply repeated that she wanted to stay with Maria.

Laura changed clothes and left in a huff.

Erin went into the kitchen. "Hi, Maria."

Maria turned and came to Erin; she knelt and gave her a big hug. "Hi, little one." Maria rose and smiled. "Has your mommy left us?"

"Yes." Erin went to the table and sat on a stool. She used her feet on the leg braces to turn in slow circles for a while as she watched Maria placing things in the refrigerator. "Do you have to come with us tomorrow too, Maria?"

"Oh, I am coming, dear one." She turned to look at Erin. "But not because I have to. I want to go there to pray for the souls of all who were lost. I will say a special prayer for the soul of your daddy." She came to hug Erin. "Your daddy was a fine man, Erin."

"When you pray are you gonna ask God to be sure the bad guys go to hell where they belong?"

Maria sat on a stool across from Erin. "No, Erin, it is not my place to judge for God. It is not my place to ask God to hurt; it is my privilege to ask God to show mercy on us."

"Well, that's just not right!" Erin shook her head. "The bad guys should burn in hell! My Daddy burned!"

"I have faith that God will know what to do, Erin." Maria stood. "I think I would like to go to church this afternoon after Laura comes home. I want to ask for forgiveness and pray for guidance. Would you like to come with me?"

Erin considered. "Yes. My Daddy went to your church, and he always took me with him. Mommy didn't go very often, just when I was real little. She never goes now."

Erin decided it was important for Maria to know that she had stayed true to her teachings. "I still say my prayers each night, and then I tell my Daddy about my day before I go to sleep. I say my morning prayer every day too."

Erin looked at the floor, "But I haven't been to church for a long, long time, Maria. I would like to light a candle for my Daddy."

Driven by love for Erin and good intentions, Maria had created a predicament for herself: Laura did not attend church. Nick had. Did Maria have the right to encourage Erin? Maria considered this for some time.

She went to the phone and called Spain. "Mama. It is Maria. How are you today, mama?"

After they had caught up on each other's lives and had enjoyed a bit of a visit, Maria confessed her dilemma to her mother.

"Oh, Maria, how could you ask such a silly thing? You are a good Catholic. Mr. McCort was a good Catholic; he was rearing his daughter to be the same. She was baptized in our church! Your teachings tell you that it is your privilege and obligation to help little Erin keep her faith. Frankly, I am ashamed that you have not been taking her to church with you at every opportunity. You must not hesitate further."

They finished their visit, and Maria hung up.

Erin stared at her. "Well? May I go or not?"

"Of course, we'll go together, Erin. Let's get ready, and we'll go right now. I will leave Laura a note telling her where we will be."

I will do my best to give Erin a chance to prepare for

tomorrow. If Laura is angry, she will not hesitate to tell me that I was wrong. . . .   I will not sneak. No one should have to sneak to church. . . . But I will, this one time, leave before she returns just in case. Maria phoned for a taxi.

They went to a cathedral that was familiar to both of them. Maria, Nick, and Erin had attended it when they were in the City on weekends.

Erin waited while Maria went to confession. *I wonder what Maria would have to confess? She never does anything bad. . . . Does she have to make things up?*

Erin shook her head. *No that would be a lie, and that would be a sin. It's probably a big sin to lie to the priest.*

Maria came to Erin and took her hand. "It is time for us to talk to the blessed Virgin Mary, little one." They each prayed.

Maria took her hand again. "Now we go to the beautiful sacred altar." Again they prayed.

Maria had given Erin a five dollar bill before they had left for church.

They each took a candle and completed that ritual.

They rose to go. "I wish we could just stay here forever, Maria. It's so nice and quiet."

Maria knew Erin was feeling the peacefulness that Maria had asked God to grant her. "We can stay and have our thoughts as long as you like."

Erin looked up and smiled. "I would like to stay for just a little longer, Maria."

She bowed her head and sat quietly for some time. Finally her little hand lightly touched Maria's. "Now, I'm ready, Maria. I've talked to God, and I talked to my Daddy."

The sun had come out while they were in the cathedral, and Erin asked Maria if they could take their time and walk back.

They did, each enjoying the exercise and respecting the other's quiet mood. They walked hand-in-hand much of the time, but remained silent until they neared the townhouse.

Laura was still out, but Maria left the note where she had placed it. "Let's have a hot chocolate while we fix us some dinner." She put a compact disc featuring gentle Spanish guitar music on the player and made each of them a mug of chocolate.

"Tonight, we will have a shellfish paella, little one. I brought the spices. I will make a nice bread to go with it. Do you want to make the salad?"

Erin nodded enthusiastically. She had been helping Maria with the salads since the day she had caught the fish in Ted's pond.

Maria laid the vegetables out for her and got a stool where Erin could stand while she chopped and sliced.

She is so happy when she works. She will make a fine cook one day.

They were enjoying the soft music when they heard the door.

Laura came to the kitchen.

Oh, dear, I think she has been drinking . She should not do that when she is out. "Hi, Laura, how was the exhibit?"

"Oh, Maria, you should have been there. We can go back tomorrow if you'd like. It's just wonderful, truly wonderful."

Laura came to Erin and bent to kiss her on the cheek. "Did you have a pleasant afternoon, honey? You look better."

"Yes. mommy. Maria took me to church with her. We went to the church where my Daddy used to take me."

Erin smiled up at her mother and took a deep breath. "I just love it there, mommy."

"Well, that's good, Erin. . . . Yes, that's just fine." Laura steadied herself a little on the counter, then squared her shoulders "Nick was a very faithful Catholic. I am not, but, if you like it, you should go whenever you want."

She smiled at her daughter then waved her index finger in Erin's direction. "Just don't try preaching at your mommy. Your mommy has a tin ear when it comes to religion."

Laura walked to Maria. "It sure smells good in here, Maria. I think walking around at the exhibit gave me an appetite."

"There is a snack plate in the refrigerator, Laura. Sliced apples and pears with a nice smoked cheese. There's a bowl of mixed crackers to go with it. Would you like me to bring them to the sitting room with something to drink? We have fresh coffee."

"Do we have Kahula?"

"Yes."

"Then I'll take you up on the offer. A nice hot coffee with Kahula and the snacks would be fine; maybe dinner around seven? I might want a nap or a nice hot soak."

"We'll be ready."

Erin went to bed at 8:30. They would have to be up at 5 a.m. in order to dress properly and get to the site in plenty of time to go through the security screenings.

Erin flatly refused to eat breakfast.

"Oh, well, she ate a good dinner; don't fuss with her, Maria. With my headache, it's just not worth it."

Maria packed bottles of water and of orange juice along with packets of almonds, sliced apples, a wedge of cheese, and three chocolate bars.

Her backpack was heavy on her thin shoulders, but she would have what her family needed.

Going through the security check was a long and tiring procedure.

The service, at times touching elegance, missed the mark at other times.

Many people did seem to find a sense of peace during the ceremonies which, thankfully, went off without an interruption.

. . .

The three of them were exhausted by the time they returned to the townhouse.

They had each broken down more than once.

Erin had actually thrown herself on the ground at one point, sobbing, "My Daddy, my Daddy; the bastards killed my Daddy, and they didn't even know him or give him a chance."

Emil's delivered the exquisite dinner which Laura had pre-ordered.

The good smells could not tease Erin into eating.

Maria checked on her after cleaning the kitchen.

She saw that Erin's sketch book was out.

When she checked Erin's bathroom, she found what looked like a piece of torn sketch pad paper on the floor. It was wet with something that looked and smelled like urine.

It couldn't be.

28

Since her differences with Laura on Labor Day and her experiences at the first memorial service, Erin had become more and more disagreeable.

Her teachers were complaining that she no longer mingled willingly with her classmates, preferring to sit alone with her sketchbook rather go out to the playground.

She seemed to have a limited attention span.

She demanded more frequent rest room breaks than were normal and sometimes returned smelling of both urine and human feces!

At home, she was experiencing her 'bad dream' more often and had begun awakening screaming from new dreams as well: running in Central Park with a giant bird trying to land on her, sitting at her desk at school with both the ceiling falling and the floor of her classroom collapsing, and running while choking on air filled with a white dust.

She was eating very little, mostly what Maria was able to allow her to fix by herself. But, strangely, she had, kept some distance from Maria after the Memorial Service.

I can't get too close to her; she could always go home to stay.

Swearing was becoming a more frequent occurrence.

She had begun talking softly to herself. She refused to tell either Maria or Laura what she had said.

When home, she spent most of her time in her bedroom. Frequently the door was locked, although, so far, she had always opened it when one of them knocked.

Laura found herself talking with Jamie after nearly every session.

Jamie was insisting that they begin at least two sessions per week; she really wanted three until "we can get to the root of this; we're losing her, Laura. She is in deep depression, and she is, suddenly, a very angry little girl."

One night in mid October after too much Stoli, Laura

called Sally Ann.

She's the only woman I really know well enough to talk with. . . . What the hell? She's nothing to me; what do I care how she thinks of me!

In this state, Laura had little false pride. She poured the whole dreadful mess out to Sally Ann, hanging up after an hour and a half only to call back crying fifteen minutes later. This second call lasted for almost an hour.

Sally Ann had done her best to soothe Laura while protecting Erin. *Telling her everything will be fine is a lie; if something doesn't change over there, we may lose Erin.*

Sally Ann suggested that Laura bring Erin for one last fishing trip while the leaves were turning. "It's a beautiful time to come over here, Laura, and Ted has always had such a good effect on Erin."

"I don't want him to think I'm dumping her on him. She's not his problem."

"Oh, Laura, he isn't like that at all. He and Erin both just love the streams. Why don't you leave school early and drive over Friday? I'll tidy the house a bit for you and put some things in the fridge, and I'll call Ted and talk with him so you won't have to. Just come on over and get a good night's sleep. I can leave a note on the table about what time to expect Ted to pick Erin up."

Laura stopped crying. *We'll leave after lunch. . . . Thank heavens for Sally Ann. She's just the way my mother would have been if I hadn't killed her. . . and Sammy, poor little Sammy.*

She went to the bathroom and poured some 'water' into the waiting glass.

. . .

Sam's house was spotless and smelled of lemon Pledge when Laura opened the front door late Friday night. The note on the table told her two things: 1. Ted would be by to get Erin at nine the next morning. 2. She should open the refrigerator immediately.

What now? Doesn't the damn fool know I'm almost at wit's end?

Laura opened the door with a jerk. There sat her

mother's cake on Sally Ann's cake server.

There were also two plates covered with plastic wrap: a thick slice of meat loaf had been laid on a slice of bread. The meat loaf had a light gravy over it. A mixture of carrots and green beans dressed the side.

A note said to push the power button on Sam's microwave, set the power at 50 percent and heat each plate for three and a half minutes. "Please eat something before you go to bed."

Both she and Erin cleaned their plates.

Erin had asked for a glass of milk with her slice of cake, and Laura joined her with both.

I've had enough 'water' for one night.

I don't need Ted getting into my business. Men! They're always so good about knowing exactly how someone else should live.

After giving the other contents of the refrigerator only a precursory glance and setting their alarm for 8 a.m., they had gone straight to bed.

At eight the next morning, Laura went to the kitchen and started the coffee. *Thank goodness dad had a Bunn. Coffee hot and quick; that's what I need to handle this headache.*

She had failed to notice the small, heavy stainless steel skillet sitting on the stove the night before.

She walked over to examine it and found that it had a note lying on its Teflon lining.

"Now, Laura, call Erin and tell her that you need her help in the kitchen. She likes to help. While she's dressing, go the fridge and take out the bread, milk, butter, jam, and orange juice."

"Take the egg carton out and put it next to the stove."
"Tell Erin to start the toast and pour the juice and her milk. There are glasses and plates on the counter. Let her put the silverware on the table while she is waiting for the toast."

"Now turn the burner on medium, put a teaspoon of olive oil (it's on the counter to the right on the stove) in the pan. When the upper rim of the skillet feels hot enough that you fear you might have burned your finger, break five nice, big brown eggs. Put them in the skillet as you break them. Sprinkle salt and pepper on the eggs. Open the top drawer to the right of the stove. Immediately use the nylon turner in there to break up the eggs."

"Turn off the eggs and set them on another burner when they still have a shine and look a little runny. Give them one last stir. Put them on the plates where Erin will have the toast waiting."

Laura's head had a real ache, but it was not as bad as it had been recently. She followed Sally Ann's directions step by step.

Erin was delighted. "Oh, boy, mommy, real food. Last time I fished with Ted I got hungry too soon."

"Oh?"

"It was okay; I told him, and we worked it out." She gave Laura a big smile.

Oh I wish she could do that more often.

Erin continued, "But this is the best breakfast ever." She came around the table and gave Laura a hug and a slightly sticky kiss. "See, we can do it." She kissed Laura again. "I love you, mommy."

A single tear began its way down Laura's cheek. She quickly wiped it away before Erin could see it.

Grow up, Laura. Be strong.

. . .

Erin and Ted were standing on the bank of Tioga Reservoir.

The sun was to their left, causing Erin's fish to have to look into the sun when it rose to take her fly.

"They get a little spooky this time of year. We need to take every break we can," Ted had told her.

Erin brought the small rainbow in and managed to release it properly with no instruction from Ted.

She had been quiet all morning, but making a successful catch seemed to have opened her spirit a little. She turned to Ted. "I'm mad at Maria."

"You are? I thought you two were buddies."

"Well, I still like her, but I'm mad at her right now."

"Why?"

"She wouldn't pray to God to make the bastards who

killed my Daddy burn in hell where they belong. That's why."
Erin gave him a defiant glance.

"Did you ask her to do that?"

"Yes, the day before the Memorial when she took me with
her to my Daddy's church in the City. I told her that I wanted her
to tell God to send them to hell. She wouldn't do it."

"Did she say why?"

"Yep. She said that it wasn't her place to tell God what to
do." Erin, a defiant look on her face, turned to Ted. "What do
you think of that shit?"

"I think she's probably right, Erin."

Erin gave him a cold, hard stare. "You do?"

"Yes."

"Why?"

"I believe God is much wiser than we are, Erin. It is to be
His divine will, not ours. We ask for God's blessings, but I don't
think we need to tell God to hurt others."

Ted cast to a nice rise to his right.

"But they were bastards, the sons-of-bitches." Erin
turned to look at Ted, ignoring her fly. "Even President Bush
calls the terrorists evil doers."

"God can figure that out, Erin."

She laid down her rod, unattended, and put her hands on
her hips. "Well, I want every single one of the bastards dead and
in hell, every last one of them. I hope we bomb their country until
they all burn alive just like my Daddy did."

Ted continued to refuse to give her eye contact. "Even
the little kids?" . . . "The mommies?" . . . "The daddies?"
. . . "What did they do to hurt us?"

Erin refused to reply; she stomped over to retrieve her
rod. On her next cast, her fly hit the water with a splash. She
ignored Ted for quite a while. "There's nothing here." She
turned to him, angry, disgusted and wanting to get some action
from Ted.

"I just released one."

"Well, they're not taking my fly."

"How's your presentation? . . . You're in a perfect spot.
I'm getting hits. . . . We're using the same fly."

She settled down a little. Her fly landed properly, and she got a hit but did not react quickly enough.

She settled herself a little more. She got one on, but it fought its way loose.

Erin turned to look at Ted. "Did you ever tell a lie?"

"More than one Erin. . . .   I'm not proud of that. I try never to lie, especially about anything important."

"How do you know when it's important?"

"Well, now that's a good question." Ted repositioned his cap. "Probably the best thing is just to avoid telling any lies; that's what I try to do."

"Really truly?"

"Really truly."

"Is lying a sin?"

Ted nodded. "'Thou shalt not bear false witness.'"

Erin looked at her toes. In a very quiet voice, she ventured, "I think my Daddy told lies."

"What makes you say that?" *Keep this light.*

"Mommy. . . .   Once mommy called my Daddy a dirty, drunken liar. I heard her with my own ears."

"What did he say about that?"

"He said she was a cold bitch who didn't want anything to do with the real world."

Erin waited for a reaction. When there was none, she reminded him, "And you said bitch was a bad word to use."

"It is."

"Then why did my Daddy do it? He was a Christian. He went to church, and he taught me to say my prayers."

The Memorial must have stirred all this up. Don't overreact, partner.

"If I had to guess, I would say he was angry and that, at that particular moment, he wanted to hurt your mother a little, not hit her or anything like that, but hurt her feelings. . . .   That word would make any woman feel bad. . . .   He probably didn't mean a word of it; he was probably just upset about something else."

"Well, she threw a lamp at him, and he went out and slammed the door."

"It was probably good that he left; sounds like everyone

needed to cool off and think things through, figure out who and what were really important in life."

"But if my Daddy lied, can he go to heaven?"

Ted was quiet for a while. "Well, I'm not Catholic, Erin; I'm a Lutheran, but I believe if you admit that you have sinned, and you ask God to forgive you, you will be forgiven."

Erin looked at Ted. Surprise and shock were on her face. "Of anything, even killing people with planes?"

Ted paused to consider, then he turned and nodded at her. "If you truly repent, I think so."

"So if those sons-of-bitches who killed my Daddy," . . . She kicked a rock.

Ted interrupted. "That's what the Bible teaches, Erin. . . . A person has to truly repent, to be sorry for an act, not just be trying to weasel out of something. . . . And God would know a man's heart."

Ted looked at her. "Do you know the word repent?"

He could almost see her brain trying to make the connections. Erin liked words and had a strong vocabulary for a child who had just turned eight last month.

She shook her head, "No."

"Well, let's say you have a bad habit, you pull dogs ears, for instance. Let's say you finally realize that that is wrong because it hurts the dog. When you realize this, you are sorry that you ever behaved that way, and you decide that you will do your very best never to pull a dog's ear again. You tell God that you're sorry, and you ask Him to guide you to quit pulling ears and being mean. . . . And you really, truly work at avoiding pulling ears. . . . Then if you ask God to forgive you for having done that bad thing, I think He will."

"That's repent?"

"Um hum."

"So you say you're sorry, and you stop doing the bad thing, and you go to heaven?"

"That's what I've been taught."

Her lip quivered. . . . "What if you didn't have time. . . time to get all of your repentin' done? What if you didn't have time to say your prayers?"

Ted resisted the strong urge to go to her, to pull her to him, to comfort her.

She needs to get this out, needs to know that it's okay to hurt, okay to cry. "I think God understands those things, Erin. I trust in Him to know a person's heart."

Erin reeled in and was quiet for a long time. Finally she made a decent cast. "Were you ever married?"

"Yes, to a fine lady."

"Did you ever lie to your wife?"

"No."

"Not ever?"

"Not a single time."

"Did she die?"

"No, she divorced me."

"Why?"

Ted took a deep breath. "Well, she was trying her best to make me happy by setting me free. That and another man, a good friend of ours, helped her through a very difficult time, and she came to love him."

"Do you hate her?"

Ted smiled. *Maybe she'll be an attorney.*

"No, Erin; I don't hate her at all. I wish things had been different, but I sure don't hate her or him either."

"Were you ever a drunk?"

"No."

"Was grandpa Sam a drunk?"

"No."

"Was he a liar?"

Ted laughed out loud. "No way. I can't remember a single one that he ever told."

"Is he in heaven?"

"I'd bet on it. Careful now for a minute, Erin; I've got a nice one on."

Ted played the fish a little. *Don't want you to use too much energy, fella.* Then he landed and carefully released the feisty rainbow.

. . .

"Grandpa Sam had a funeral, and he has a grave." Erin

was silent for a bit, then took her eyes off the water to look at him. "Do you have to have a grave so God knows where to find you?"

"No, Erin; God is omniscient. That means He is all-knowing."

Erin wanted this new word. "Om. . .knee?. .cent?"

"Almost." Ted gave her the syllables again.

She got it this time. Erin whispered the word again with its meaning. "That's a nice word to know."

She reeled in and laid her rod on the bank beside her. She walked over beside Ted and took his free hand.

He looked down at her.

"So you think my Daddy made it?"

"I'm sure of it, Erin."

"And those bad men in the plane; they went to hell?"

Ted didn't believe in dodging issues with young people, but he didn't want to attempt theological philosophy with an eight-year-old. "I've never been as sure about hell as I have been about heaven, Erin. God will know what to do. He's omniscient."

"But you think my Daddy made it."

Ted looked at the blue sky mottled lightly with clouds. "I believe he is up there right now, loving you and your mommy with all of his heart. He's sorry that you have these worries, but he is so proud that you are brave enough to be thinking them through and talking about them and getting things straightened out in your head and in your heart."

Ted reeled in and laid his rod beside hers, giving Erin his full attention. "It takes a brave person to face his fears, Erin. . . . Some folks think that a brave person is someone who has no fear, isn't afraid of anything. But that's all wrong. . . . A brave person recognizes danger, has fear, and admits it. He seeks advice and tries to figure out how to best handle that fear. That's real courage, real bravery."

"When you're a little older, we'll read some Hemingway together. He says it a lot better than I do."

Too deep, partner; remember she's only eight.

"Did I ever tell you that Max was afraid when he met his first bird that had some fight in him?"

"No, not Maxie."

She looked at Max for confirmation, but it was Ted who nodded. "Grandpa Sam and I had put him after about a half dozen birds that had been totally dead when they hit the ground. He had handled them just like his practice dummies."

"Then one cold morning one of us brought down a mallard."

Ted smiled at the memory. "Max was just a pup, not a year old yet. We had Rowdy with us too, and we had always sent him after the live ones.

Well, we both misread this tough old mallard, and we sent Max after him.

He went running in there, and the mallard bit him, bit him hard, fighting for his life, you know."

"We heard Max yelp, but he stood his ground."

"Then the mallard hit Max with his wing; now that can hurt more than a little. Let me tell you both of those things, a bite and a wing hit, can get your attention right quick like."

"Well, Max backed up. He kept his eyes on the bird, but he gave ground."

"Oh, no. Poor little Max."

"Yes. It had hurt him, and he was scared. Then the mallard sort of beat the ground with one wing and hissed to show Max that there was more where that had come from."

Ted studied Erin's face.

She was right there with Max and the mallard.

"Did you and grandpa Sam help Max?"

"Well, I wasn't sure what would be best. I hate to shoot a bird on the ground, and Sam would never do that. We knew we could send Rowdy, but we were afraid that might hurt Max's pride, maybe ruin him."

Ted glanced at Erin and noted the worry furrows across her little brow. "Finally, Max figured it out."

Ted looked fondly at Erin. "You know how he is; he thinks things through."

She nodded. "He's the smartest dog in the whole wide world."

"Well, Max backed up about ten or twelve feet. I was afraid he was going to turn and run, but his eyes never left that bird for a minute. I'll never know why, just automatic probably, but I yelled, 'Max, fetch' a second time."

"He went in low to the ground, like a streak of black lightning. Went straight for the bird's neck. Made a mighty shake. All of this happened in a split second, mind you, and that was a lot of bird for a pup that age to shake, but he had enough grit to break that old mallard's neck. ... Max never loosened his hold until the bird quit flopping its good wing. Then he laid him down and studied him a minute or two in order to catch his breath and to make sure there would be no more biting and flopping that morning."

"When Max was sure and had got some wind in his lungs, he picked that bird up and brought him right to us. His tail was going a mile a minute, and his eyes were dancing as if to say, 'see; you can count on me too.'"

Ted shook his head and smiled with pride at Max who was sitting by his feet now, having heard his name mentioned several times.

Ted's hand went out to fondle the Lab's neck. "Oh, we gave him a bushel of praise. Even Rowdy kissed him."

Erin's eyes were dancing. "That's a good story."

"Well, it's not over yet. You see, the real problem was with Sally Ann."

Surprise swept Erin's face. *Maybe I'll learn to hunt.* "Was Miss Sally there too?"

"No, but, of course, we had to high-tail it over to the sandwich shop to tell her what a wondeful pup her Emma had produced."

Erin nodded eagerly.

"Well, Sally Ann yelled at your grandpa and me."

Ted nodded at Erin's raised eyebrows. "Said if we couldn't shoot any better than that we should turn in our licenses."

He shook his head at the memory. "She made over that pup like she was his mother. Then she cooked him a scrambled egg."

Ted winked at Erin. "She only offered us a cup of coffee and spilled most of that when she slammed em' down on the table."

Erin was smiling. "Miss Sally yelled at you and at grandpa Sam?"

"Oh, you should have heard her. She called us stupid and careless, said we didn't know the meaning of the word patience. . . . But she didn't mean those things."

Ted studied his hands and then put his arm around Erin's shoulder.

"She didn't mean a single one of those hurtful things. She meant that she loved Max and was scared that we might get him hurt. . . . She meant that she didn't want us to let him get in a fix like that again."

"But she didn't say that."

"No; it's a strange thing about adults, Erin. We forget how to say the real message. We're afraid someone will think we're too sentimental or soft, so we say some other stuff that we think will get our point across."

"Young people do a whole lot better at saying the real message. Hang on to that as long as you can, Erin. Speak openly about your feelings. It's the way to be."

"The bird was brave too."

"He sure was. See that's what happens, an animal's instinct tells him that, when he senses danger, he should act brave, try to look bigger than he is."

"Well, people are just animals too, but they don't have feathers to fluff up so they get loud and say mean things and slam doors and throw things because they're scared of something. They don't mean the things they say or do at such times."

"They aren't, at that moment, as smart or as honest as Max was. They don't know to back up a little and look things over; to cool down and figure out how to best handle the situation."

Erin had sat down beside Max and had one arm thrown over his shoulders. She was petting his chest with her free hand.

She was quiet for a long time, letting her fingers run through the hair on Max's chest while she looked off across the water. "So mommy didn't mean it when she called my Daddy a no-good-drunken liar or when she yelled that she hated him?"

"No more than Sally Ann meant it when she called

Sam and me fools and said she'd kill us if we ever got that pup hurt."

"Did my Daddy know this stuff about how adults say things that they don't really mean?"

"He did; all grownups know it down deep, Erin. We just forget to explain it to our kids."

She nodded her head and continued to pet Max.

Out of the corner of his eye he saw a tear trace a path down her cheek.

He heard the sigh of relief.

She didn't break down. There were a few more tears which Erin didn't try to hide; she just brushed them away.

Finally she bent and planted a kiss on the top of Max's head between his ears. "I love you, Maxie. You are the best dog in the whole world. I wish my Daddy could have known you."

29

December 2002

Three inches of snow had fallen overnight, making Wellsboro a perfect setting for the annual *Dickens of a Christmas Celebration.*

Erin awakened early at Sam's, and her first look out the window made her rush to wake Laura. "Oh, hurry; mommy, hurry and look out your window. It's just perfect. It snowed and everything."

She pulled back the curtains. "Look at the pines in grandpa's yard. They look like they've been dusted with powdered sugar. It looks just like a fairyland."

With some effort, Laura finally managed to get her eyes open. *You'd think it never snowed in Danbury.* "Okay, Erin. I'm awake."

Laura rubbed her eyes. She stretched in bed: first her legs, then her neck and shoulders. *If just I didn't wake up with a lousy headache every single damn morning.* She sat up in bed and continued to roll her head and neck as Erin stood, impatient with her mother's lack of enthusiasm.

"Come on, mommy. Stand up and look at the trees."

Will the pitch of her voice ever lower? Laura gritted her teeth and stood. "I'm coming, Erin. I'll fix us some toast and coffee."

She swallowed and licked her dry lips. *Coffee; that's what I need.* "We bought some fresh bread and coffee and orange juice last night didn't we? When we got to town?"

Erin's head bobbed up and down. "Yes, and you got eggs and milk and sausage, too. You said you would make me French toast 'to start our celebration off right.'"

Laura's furrowed brows tightened. *I must have been hitting my 'water bottle' pretty heavily on the way here.*

"Yes, Erin, honey, I remember. Tell you what. You go pour us a nice big glass of orange juice. I'll brush my teeth and be right out."

After Erin had hurried off to Sam's kitchen, Laura stood and walked to the bath while rubbing her neck. She reached into her makeup kit, extracted the aspirin bottle, and carefully laid four on the counter. She walked to the door and locked it. She removed a bottle of Stoli, cracked the seal, poured a double into one of the glasses, and added water. She made a face as she downed the aspirin with the mixture.

She opened a new bottle of water and poured half of it down the sink. She re-filled the bottle with the Stoli.

There, 'water' to get me through the day. She smiled with satisfaction at her reflection. *One sip at a time.* Beginning to feel her pain relief taking effect, Laura giggled a bit at her clever update of an old proverbial saying. *Whew, that hit.* She put her fingertips on her scalp and pressed and rubbed as she breathed deeply and rolled her head and neck.

Better put the goodies away. Laura carefully tightened the cap and replaced the Stoli bottle in her makeup case next to its two buddies. She left the water bottle out to take into town with her.

Laura snapped the case shut and unlocked the bathroom door. "Erin, honey, mommy has one of those darn morning headaches. I'm going to take a hot shower before we start breakfast. Okay?"

"Sure, mommy. I'll make a slice of plain toast and drink some juice while I wait."

Laura heard the television click on. *Maybe a cigarette will help.* After the cigarette, she brushed her teeth and stepped into the shower directing pulsating hot water to her back and neck. Some minutes later, she turned around and lowered the water's temperature. She shampooed her hair, mostly to get the scalp massage, rinsed it thoroughly, and took a body shower. After a few more minutes of hot water on her back and shoulders, she stepped out and toweled.

Laura slipped on clean undies and her robe. She padded toward the kitchen. "Mommy wants a cup of coffee before she starts the toast. Okay, Erin?"

"Sure, mommy; I can wait." She stood and came to

give Laura a hug. "You've never made me French toast before. Maria sometimes makes it for me on special days, but you never have." Erin smiled up at her mother. "I'll bet yours is better even than Maria's."

Oh, yea. Laura slowly moved her head from side to side. *I must have been pretty well trashed to have promised French toast. Oh, well, we didn't hit anything.* She quickly got the coffee started then walked to the refrigerator and opened the door.

There they sat: a carton of eggs, a half gallon of milk, and a box of sausage patties. Laura swallowed a couple of times. *Did I get cereal, or did we plan to do this again before we leave tomorrow?*

She poured a cup of coffee and carried it to the living room where Erin was watching an old movie. The headache was almost gone by the time Laura had finished her coffee. *No more excuses. Time to pay the piper.* She went to the kitchen and found one of her mother's cookbooks that Sam had kept and used.

She sighed. *French toast coming up.* "Erin, did we get syrup too?"

"Yes, of course, mommy." Erin came walking into the kitchen giggling. "Don't you remember? You said we were going to have a good homemade breakfast before we 'go out and freeze our asses off on Main Street.'"

Laura looked directly at Erin. "Asses? I said asses?"

Erin nodded. "That's exactly what you said, 'before we go out and freeze our asses off.'"

"Well, mommy was tired from all of the driving." She stopped beating the eggs long enough to look pointedly at Erin. "I don't want to hear that word coming out of your mouth again, young lady."

"My Daddy said ass sometimes. . . and shit, and. . ."

"Erin McCort, that's enough!" Laura slammed the whisk down on the counter where it made a yellow splatter. "I will not have you talking like a child of the street. Do you hear me?"

Erin bit her lip. "Yes, mommy." Erin started to walk back to the living room, but stopped and looked at Laura. "Mommy, if your head hurts too much, you don't have to make breakfast. We bought some cereal too. We can just eat that.

It'll be okay."

"No!" Laura's voice was harsh and slightly raspy. "I said we would have a homemade breakfast, and we're, by damn, going to have one if it kills me."

They sat at the square white kitchen table in the bright blue and tan kitchen. Each was quiet.

Laura, whose headache had returned the instant she became angry, sat playing with her food.

Erin, not wanting to upset her mother again, gamely choked down the dry French toast and a slightly burned sausage patty. She drank a big glass of milk and a small glass of orange juice.

When she had finished eating, Erin took her own dishes to the sink and returned to take Laura's. "You didn't eat your breakfast, mommy."

Laura ignored Erin's remark. "We need to get dressed if we're actually going to do this. Be sure to dress warmly."

"I will, mommy." Erin hesitated then decided to remind Laura even though it might make her angry again. "Dress in layers, mommy."

. . .

Laura parked the Rover in Sally Ann's driveway.

It was nice of her to offer the driveway at her home to us; it saves a lot of hassle, and then she's doing dinner for us tonight too. I bet you couldn't buy a reservation in town today.

"Here we are." She looked at Erin who seemed to have lost some of her enthusiasm. "Might as well join the fray."

Laura reached for her water bottle. She slipped it into her shoulder purse. "I put a water bottle in the back seat for you, Erin. Put it in your backpack."

Erin slipped the bottle into her pack. She pulled the backpack straps over her shoulders and adjusted them as soon as she was out of the vehicle. "I'll be okay, mommy. Ted told me they sell hot chocolate." She smiled up at Laura. "And I love hot chocolate; especially with marshmallows."

Erin quickened her step. "Oh, mommy, I think I can smell it."

"Smell what, Erin? Hot chocolate?"

"No, it smells like the fair. I'll bet there are lots of good things to eat. Hear the sounds?"

They began the two-block walk to Main Street.

"Who introduced you to the wonders of hot chocolate with marshmallows?"

"Maria." Erin smiled at Laura again. "She made it for me a lot last winter, especially when it was real cold out or if I felt bad."

"Well, go easy on that stuff, kiddo. I don't want you to start rolling."

Matt Thornton, Jerry's younger brother had been watching for the little red-haired girl and her mother.

Jerry had told him about Erin, and Matt had decided he wanted to meet her himself.

Judd had mentioned her too. *Maybe she'll tell me how to win the fishing-for-bottles game.*

With self-assurance and single-mindedness, Matt put himself on a course to meet them on the street. "Come on, Tig."

Unlike Jerry, Matt never hesitated when confronted with opportunity. He walked to within a few feet of them and, after rubbing his nose, he extended his hand. "Hi, there."

Erin smiled, "Hi."

Matt never planned his approach for subtle nuances. He preferred a direct one. "My name's Matt Thornton. I guess you probably heard about my brother, Jerry; seems everyone knows Jerry since we won the state championship."

Erin extended her hand. "I'm Erin McCort, and this is my mother, Laura."

Matt sniffed a little. *Darn this cold.* "Nice to meet you." He turned and fell into step with them. "You ever been to the festival before?"

"No, this is our first time, isn't it, mommy?"

Laura smiled at the young boy dressed in his version of the fashion of the late 1800's. *He looks more like a Huck Finn than a child from London, but he seems sweet.* "Yes, this is our first time. I have a feeling you have been here before, Mr. Thornton."

Matt swelled out his chest. *Mister!* "Oh yea; I've been

comin' here since I was little."

He glanced toward Erin. "I usually win some prizes. All us Thorntons are real athletic."

They walked a few feet in silence. Erin smiled at Matt again. "I know Jerry. He goes to college in Ohio."

"Yep. Marietta. He's gonna show them how to hit a baseball come spring."

"I know him because I fish with Ted Weaver."

"Oh, Ted's a good guy." Matt looked her over. "What grade you in anyway?" Matt didn't hold much with older women. *Never had any luck there.*

"I'm in third. What grade are you in, Matt?"

Matt squared his shoulders as he kept his own pace in sync with theirs. "I'm startin' fifth." He looked off to the side and drew a long breath for effect. "Starts gettin' harder then."

Matt studied the snow-covered street. "Say, you gonna be in the dog-sled race?"

Erin's eyes grew large. "What's the dog-sled race?"

Before Matt could answer, she had made a decision, but she also had more questions. "Do they give you a dog and a sled? I will if they do."

"Na, you have to have a dog and a sled. If you want to race, I'll let you borrow my sled after Tig and me run."

"Would I use your dog too?"

Matt, imitating a frequent gesture of his father's, spit rather importantly sideways. "Can't help you there. They only let a dog run one time. A person can only go once; a dog can only go once, but a sled can go as many times as it wants."

They walked along a bit further.

"Well, I'll be around if you find a dog. . . . It's fun. It's the first event after noon; always draws a big crowd. Me and Tig will be there in the park; that's where it's held."

He glanced over his shoulder as he did a ninety degree turn to walk off, another gesture borrowed from his father, "We won it the last two years. . . . Yep, two trophies sittin' there in the bedroom at home." Matt reached down to pat Tig on the head as they walked off onto a side street.

Erin screwed up her face in thought as she looked up at

her mother. "Mommy, do you think Ted would let me use Max? He could win; I know he could."

"I hardly think Ted views Max as a race dog."

Before Erin could state her case, two ladies dressed in period costumes approached them. The younger one spoke first. "My, my, I see neither of you has her wooden nickels."

Laura and Erin exchanged puzzled glances. Laura smiled. "I guess we're guilty."

"Well, we can fix that." The older one reached into the large shopping bag which she was carrying and extracted two drawstring felt pouches each of which held ten wooden nickels.

She returned Laura's smile. "Everyone gets a pouch compliments of the chamber of commerce. Each time someone says 'Merry Christmas' to you before you get a chance to greet him, you have to give that person a wooden nickel to put in his pouch."

She smiled at their slightly puzzled expressions. "It's our little attempt to make the whole day a bit more cheery and festive for everyone." She glanced at the younger woman. "Helps to get everyone in the Christmas spirit, and the person who ends up with the most wooden nickels by 4:30 this afternoon is crowned The Spirit of Christmas right there on the Green and gets a nice prize too."

Erin looked up at the nice lady and smiled. "Merry Christmas," she said.

"Oh, my, you catch on quickly, dear." She handed Erin a wooden nickel. "You're on your way now."

Erin stood politely waiting to return the nickel to the lady, but the lady smiled. "And to you too. Remember, only the first person to say 'Merry Christmas' gets a nickel. Don't let someone tell you otherwise."

. . .

"Step right up for a sample of the finest roasted chestnuts this side of the Globe. Roasted almonds too."

Erin recognized Ted's voice before she recognized him.

Ted was dressed as a street vendor of Dickens' era, and he had covered his dark brown hair with a salt and pepper wig and had applied false whiskers and mustache.

Erin started to giggle. "Is that you, Ted?"

"In the flesh, miss," he said in a practiced London accent. "Oh, and I see your mam is with you." He tipped his cap to Laura. "Good day to you both."

Then he shifted to his regular voice. "Max and I have been on the lookout for you two. I see you made it in all right." He glanced at the pouches, "And someone got you started on your nickels."

"Merry Christmas, Ted." Erin's eyes twinkled up at him.

He dutifully handed her a wooden nickel from the pouch which hung around Max's neck. "Merry Christmas to you, Erin; and to you too, Laura."

Erin was looking at Max who had begun letting his tail sweep the snow behind him the minute he had recognized her. "We met Jerry's brother, Matt, and he told me about the sled races. He said that I could use his sled and enter if I wanted to."

She paused. "But I told him I couldn't because I didn't have a dog." She had never taken her eyes off Max. *My Daddy always said that it was mostly rude to ask, but it was okay to let them know what you were hoping for.*

"Erin!" Laura, in exasperation, rolled her eyes at Ted as she reached out and put her hand on Erin's shoulder. "I'm sorry, Ted; sometimes I don't know what comes over my daughter. Believe it or not, she has been taught basic manners," Laura paused to look pointedly at Erin, "even if she can't seem to recall them."

Ted turned to give another couple a sample of chestnuts. When he turned back, there was a twinkle in his eyes. "Hey, I was just thinking: You know Max has never got to run in that race. He always has to sit and watch the other dogs run and have fun. Would you like to run him, Erin?"

She beamed. "I sure would."

"Well, I work this gig until noon. So Max and I will meet you two at the Green at twelve. You tell Matt that you want to borrow his sled. He'll have the runners all slicked up. We'll see if you and Max can give Matt and Tig a run for their money."

Ted smiled as he remembered a younger Matt who had named Tig for a favorite Pooh character. The blue tick pup had grown into his name.

No way Max can outrun him, but he'll give it his best. Erin will have fun, and she won't get hurt.

Ted looked at Laura. "Don't forget to eat during the day, but be sure to save room for Sally Ann's dinner. She goes all out for this: roast goose and all the trimmings. Oh, and try to go see her in Santa's house. She's Mrs. Santa until noon; then she goes home to put the final touches on her feast."

"We'll save room." Laura smiled ruefully, "I just ruined the French toast breakfast that I had promised Erin." She paused a moment and then looked directly at Ted. "Is this race thing safe?"

"Perfectly. The kids hold on to a short strap attached to the dog's harness, and the dog pulls the kid on the sled the length of the Green. The kid can always let loose of the dog. Only one kid runs at a time, and the score is kept with a stopwatch. They give a nice trophy to the fastest dog." He winked at Erin. "You got a good grip?"

Erin nodded vigorously.

"Well, Max can move on out when he wants to, and he'll give his all for you, Erin. Matt's dog, Tig will be the one to beat."

Erin bent and began petting Max. "We can do it. Can't we, Maxie?" The big black dog gave Erin a kiss and swept more snow with his tail.

Laura was honestly impressed as they walked along Wellsboro's Main Street. Apparently all of the nearly 4000 villagers participated in the Festival.

Most Wellsboroians were dressed in some sort of costume according to their idea of what proper Londoners wore in Charles Dickens' time.

The majority of the out-of-town visitors were easily identified since they were dressed in normal clothing although some had come in period dress. *Must have been here before.*

Erin had been right about the smells: the air was filled with the scent of the good things one associates with Christmas.

Main Street was decorated beautifully with pine boughs and holly tied with red velvet ribbons; the posts that supported the natural gas lamps were wrapped in garlands that trailed to the street.

The fine old Victorian homes looked as though they would be right at home sitting in merry old London.

Laura inhaled deeply, savoring the sight and the scents while carolers holding lighted candles stood in front of the town library and sang the old songs.

The previous night's snowfall had added just the right touch to create a winter wonderland.

I'm so glad I brought Erin. Dad always wanted us to come. We should have; Nick would have been in full glory here. I can just see him, in costume, singing along with the music in that Irish brogue of his. Laura squeezed Erin's hand as she felt the first sting of tears. "Let's find us a sandwich and some of that hot chocolate you were telling me about. Then we'll go see Sally Ann before she leaves her station."

Just then Erin saw the horses. Three teams of work horses each pulled a type of wagon on which visitors could take a free ride.

The team's harness was decorated to the hilt. Every horse had a set of bells across his massive chest and shoulders.

One teamster had even put leather straps with more bells on them above each of the horse's hooves.

The wagons, freshly painted for the holidays, were decorated with pine and holly. A row of seats facing the rear of the wagon went across the front just behind the driver. A row of seats across the rear faced the front.

"Oh, mommy, can we ride? We just have to. They might go home."

Laura waved to the driver of the red wagon.

He pulled up beside them.

Just like New York taxis.

"Good morning, ladies. Welcome aboard."

His assistant stepped down to swing steps from the wagon bed to the ground. He offered Laura and Erin a hand as they climbed aboard.

The driver wove the wagon in and out around the vendor's booths and strolling carolers, past two street jugglers, and four children in period dress who were pulling a wooden wagon carrying a crate of geese, a pine tree on its side, and some brightly wrapped packages.

Three children racing rolling hoops cut in front of the horses who had seen it all before.

"Listen to the bells, mommy; listen to the horses' bells. . . . Oh, I just love this. Look there's the Santa house."

Laura leaned forward. "May we exit here, please?"

"Whoa, Billie. Whoa up there, Nel." The team stopped obediently. Nel tossed her head a little and made her bells ring.

"May I touch her?" Erin looked up at the assistant as he handed her down.

"Sure thing, miss; I'll need to lift you up so you can reach her."

Erin raised her arms. "Oh, please." She removed her gloves and stuck them in her pockets.

Erin leaned forward from his arms. She ran her hand along Nel's neck. She touched the braided mane and fingered its bright ribbons which matched the wagon. One more run along the neck, a deep sigh, and Erin was standing on the ground. She looked up at the nice man. "Oh, thank you so much, sir. Merry Christmas."

The assistant smiled at the pretty little girl and handed her a wooden nickel.

Erin almost dropped it; she had completely forgotten the contest.

"And a merry Christmas to you, miss." The assistant tipped his hat, returned the steps to their riding place, and climbed up to his seat.

They hurried toward Mrs. Santa's House as a few big flakes of snow began to fall.

"Oh, boy, it might snow even more." Erin walked through the open door. "Hi, Mrs. Claus."

"Well, goodness me, if it isn't Erin McCort and her mother, all the way from Connecticut. Hello, dear ones."

"Hi, Mrs. Claus. You look really pretty today," Erin said as she smiled at one of her favorite people in Wellsboro. "We came by to wish you a merry Christmas."

"Why, thank you, dear, and a very merry Christmas to both of you." Sally Ann reached into her pouch and handed Erin a wooden nickel.

She raised her eyebrows and looked at Laura. "See you both for dinner?"

Laura smiled at this woman who was fast becoming a dear friend.

"We'll be there. We're parked there now."

"Well, when you're done here, just come on over. No sense going back to Sam's house unless you have to. I'd enjoy the company."

"Then we might stop at your place. It looks like we may get some more snow. Right now we have to grab a sandwich before the dog races."

"Oh, my, yes. You don't want to miss that. The races always draw a crowd."

"And Ted's gonna let me use Max; we get race too."

"Well, good luck, Erin." Sally Ann waved good-bye as the next group of children came in to present their wish list.

Wellsboro never had a Santa at the Festival. He and Mrs. Santa were too busy at the North Pole making final preparations for the big run on Christmas Eve.

The local kids understood that Santa contacted the village officials and designated two local ladies to stand in for his wife on this day.

The local ladies collected the wish lists and, of course, e-mailed them to the real Mrs. Claus at the North Pole.

30

Laura and Erin had each enjoyed a pulled chicken sandwich and a mug of hot chocolate. They had splurged on sugar plums made by a local church group and had shared an apple turnover.

Fortified now, they walked to the 'Green'and stopped at the famous fountain where the bronze statue of Wynken, Blynken, and Nod sat.

Erin removed her gloves and ran her hands over the beautiful piece of art.

Laura read her the poem which was printed on the plaque. *I can remember my mother's having read this poem to me some nights before I went to sleep. She was such a good mother. . . . I wish she had been here to help with Erin. Things could have been so different.*

For the first time since they had left the house that morning, Laura opened her water bottle. She took two long drinks and drew a long breath. *At least this is better than drugs, I can control this.*

When Matt Thornton saw them, he and Tig came over to make certain Erin was going to enter.

Ted walked up while Matt was there. "Hi, there, Matt. Heard anything from Jerry lately?"

"Hi, Coach. He's about to come home for Christmas. The team's been doin' two-a-days. Their finals are after break. Team'll leave for six weeks in Florida a week after finals."

Matt glanced in Max's direction as he took time to pat Tig on the shoulder. "I guess Erin's gonna run your dog."

"That's right, Matt. You and Tig show them how it's done up here."

"We aim to. I'll run fifth, Erin; I do every time.   Five is my lucky number. I'll bring the sled over to you soon as we finish."

"Okay. Thanks for letting me use it, Matt. Good luck."

Matt smiled and walked off, sled in tow, Tig at his heels. *She's just a kid, but she sure is cute, and nice too.*

Erin was all eyes as the high school's track coach and his assistant set up their timing devices: one at the starting line; one at the finish. The instruments were attatched to shortened tripods in order to catch the movement of the sled in their lasers. Times were announced almost immediately.

Erin watched the first five kids who raced.

Tig and Matt were the easy leaders.

True to his promise Matt appeared at her side with his sled shortly after he had crossed the finish line. "Me and Tig will be waiting for you at the finish, Erin. Good luck." He turned and walked off. *No sense tellin' our secrets.*

Ted lifted the sled and examined its runners. He ran his gloves over them to dust off the snow and bits of ice. He bent to Max and slipped a reflective nylon harness on the big dog. He used it on Max when they jogged in the early morning and at twilight and always kept one in the Suburban. He attached a rarely used matching lead to the harness ring which rested between Max's shoulder blades.

"Lay down on the sled for me, Erin; we need to measure something."

Erin did as she was told.

"Which hand do you want to use to hold his strap?"

"This one." She held out her right hand.

"Okay, now grip the sled guide a little to the left of center with the other hand. You'll have to pull real hard on it to keep the sled straight. Max will be pulling off to the right, and you have to counter that by trying to cock the runners to the left." He looked down at her. "Understand?"

"Yep."

Ted made adjustments to the lead to shorten it. *I want this just long enough to keep the runners away from Max while Erin holds on. Too much slack will kill us for sure; he'll jerk the strap out of Erin's hand.*

"Okay, let's go back here for a minute." They found an open spot. "Now lay down. That's it. Here , take Max's lead. Now cock the runners to the left."

Ted jogged in front of the team. "Max, come."

Max strained a little to get the sled started and then followed Ted at an obedient easy trot.

Just then the announcer called, "Miss Erin McCort and Max Weaver are up next; get at-the-ready, Erin."

. . .

Ted placed Matt's sled beside that of the next runner.

Erin mounted.

Ted held Max as the next team began their run. "You're on your own, honey. I'll be on the other end."

Ted took off for the finish line to encourage Max. *He won't know to pull if I don't call him.*

The starter asked Erin if she was ready.

She was.

He waited until he saw Ted in position. "Ready, set."

Erin's hands took death grips.

"Go."

"Max, come."

They started at the same easy trot they had used before.

Ted called again, "Max! Come!"

Max surged forward.

Erin winced and held tight as long as she could stand it, but the strap slipped from her hand six feet from the finish. Luckily she had enough momentum to slide across at a decent clip.

Max left Ted's side to go bouncing out to greet Erin. *One more time! One more time; I got it now.*

Ted collected them.

While Ted had taken Erin and Max to practice, Laura had walked to the side of the run to get ready for pictures. She had placed her own tripod and had adjusted her camera to take continual pictures once she released the shutter.

Erin returned Matt's sled and thanked him profusely for letting her borrow it.

Matt allowed that they had, "Done pretty well for a girl and a first-time dog." He carefully spit sideways.

Ted and Erin walked over to Laura. They would watch the rest of the festivities with her.

"I hope we got some good ones." Laura bent and hugged Erin. "You were great." She turned and bent to pet Max. "You did okay too, big boy. You two made a good team."

"I can't wait 'til next year. Now we know how it's done. I'll get me a sled, and I'll learn to hold tighter." Erin was bubbling with the excitement of adrenaline.

Ted got them each a mug of hot chocolate. He bought Max a pulled chicken sandwich. *Sorry you can't have chocolate, but you deserve to celebrate too.*

They waited for the trophies. Laura took a picture of Matt and Tig as they collected their third trophy for that mantle in his bedroom.

She took a picture of the group of kids who went forward to have their wooden quarters collected.

Erin was in the group, but she hadn't spent enough time working the event.

The little girl who won and was crowned 'The Spirit of Christmas' was only six years old.

Laura took her picture and started to put her camera away when the announcer reminded the crowd that it was time for the 'Secret Question.'

"How many of you children under twelve want to take part in this event?"

Seeing Erin's hand go up, Matt raised his. *Might as well get another trophy.*

Five other youngsters raised their hands.

"Now, children, form a half circle in front of me. You adults have to keep quiet during this event. I don't want any cheating. I'll ask the question. The first hand up gets to try first."

He patted the shoulder of the woman next to him. "Mary, my wife here, will keep track of the order of the hands after the first."

He pointed his finger at the group gathered in front of him, "Remember now, don't call out your answer; just raise your hand like in school. Then one by one you can come up in the order in which you raised your hand. You'll whisper the answer in my ear."

He looked at the crowd. "First one to get it right gets

the prize."

All of the locals were familiar with the rules, but visitors were encouraged to enter too. Each year the question was kept a secret. It had to relate to one of two things: the history of Wellsboro, or the Christmas season.

The man cleared his throat. "The question this year deals with the Christmas season. Who among you can name Santa's eight reindeer?"

Erin's hand shot up.

"You're first, young lady. Come up here beside me." He glanced at his wife, Mary to be sure she had noted the hands of the other children. She was already forming them into a line representing their proper order.

Erin stepped forward and whispered; she paused, and whispered a bit more.

He laughed. "Well I guess that's so. Here's our winner, folks. What's your name, Missy?"

He held Erin's hand in the air. "I'm going to give the microphone to Miss Erin McCort. Erin, I want you to repeat exactly what you just said to me. Say it just like you told me."

Erin took the microphone and, for some reason, stood on tippy-toe. "Santa's reindeer are: Dasher and Dancer, Prancer and Vixen, Comet and Cupid, and Donner and Blinson. ... and Rudolph when it's a really bad night."

The crowd applauded.

Erin accepted the carved, eight-inch, wooden replica of Santa's sleigh which the announcer handed her.

She held it up for others to see, then pulled it to her chest.

Her eyes sparkled as she turned toward the master of ceremonies. "Thank you, sir. This is beautiful. I'll keep it always."

31

The McCort Christmas dinner had always been catered. Maria was only to present a festive table; she was to have the holiday too.

From the beginning, Nick had insisted that she join them for all meals. "We four depend on and love and appreciate each other. We're family."

By noon on Christmas Day, Laura had made so many trips to the bathroom for her headache that she was lightly touching furniture for balance.

As soon as the caterers delivered dinner, Maria asked Erin to come to the kitchen and help with the presentation. *I must hurry to get something into Laura's stomach, and I want Erin to be too busy to notice her mother's condition.*

. . .

Laura made it to the table.

Maria asked the blessing.

Erin served.

Laura slumped forward into her plate.

Maria jumped up and, with Erin's help, got Laura to her bedroom and on the bed. She then asked Erin to go straighten the table. "We'll eat in a few minutes, Erin, when your mama is resting comfortably."

There it was when Maria went to Laura's bathroom for a damp towel for Laura's face: A Stoli bottle right out in the open. *No longer bothering to pour it into a water bottle, I see.* Maria quickly put the bottle away.

Once Laura was settled safely in bed where she could sleep it off, Maria went back to the dining room.

"Your mother will be fine, Erin. She just needs to rest, so we must leave her alone for a bit. Let's enjoy our wonderful dinner and then go to her room and check on her. I want to give her time to get to sleep."

While they ate their dinners, Maria shared memories

of her childhood Christmas celebrations.

After dinner, Maria went to her quarters and brought out one of her scrapbooks and showed Erin pictures of the people and places precious to her.

Only then did they tiptoe into Laura's room.

Erin giggled. "Mommy's snoring!"

32

Monday, Jan. 6, 2003, Laura parked across from the impressive old stone Queen Ann after having circled the block twice to make certain there was absolutely nothing to indicate the building's present use.

The only identifying marker was the house number on the stone pillars just inside the property's entrance.

Laura sat quietly and studied the building. *Nick would have loved it; such rich architecture.*

Her hand crept to her face. Her second finger and thumb traced her face from her nostrils, around the curve of her mouth, and down to her chin then met at her throat as she unconsciously massaged the flesh under her jaw several times while analyzing the possibilities.

I should just go home. This is not at all necessary.

Laura's breathing had quickened. A faint gloss of emerging moisture was on her face though, according to the Rover, the outside temperature was an invigorating thirty- five degrees, and the temperature inside was its normal seventy. As she rubbed her hands together, she noticed the dampness of her palms.

Laura rested her head lightly on the steering wheel. She seriously considered shifting into Drive and moving the few blocks to one of her favorite museums.

She took a deep breath as she raised her head and reached for her ever-present 'water' bottle.

It's now or never.

Laura removed the bottle cap and took three deep pulls from the bottle, a good four ounces.

She carefully replaced the bottle cap.

She pulled down the visor and checked her makeup.

No matter how carefully she applied the multiple layers, she couldn't completely hide the slightly yellow-grey cast of her once clear complexion.

Laura snapped the cover over the visor's mirror.

She put one breath mint in her mouth, immediately chewing and swallowing it. Then she put a second in her mouth to dissolve slowly.

It really is now or never; I will not put myself through this again.

She took another deep breath and shifted into Drive. She merged with traffic and circled the block a third time. This time she used her left turn signal as she approached the drive.

She entered the nicely landscaped parking lot. After checking her makeup one last time and reaching for her purse, Laura hurried toward the steps leading to the white-columned verandah.

Once moving, she hesitated only a second at the door. After one last deep breath, she entered a spacious two-story foyer and turned left through an open doorway.

The woman behind the desk gave Laura a warm smile and immediately rose to come forward and extend her hand.

Laura took the hand, "I'm Laura McCort. I have a 10:30 appointment."

"Of course, Mrs. McCort; we've been looking forward to meeting you." The pretty redhead smiled warmly again. "My name is Ginger Geiger. Please call me Ginger. How should I address you?"

Laura did her best to return the smile. "Please call me Laura." She hesitated a minute and then went on. "I'm so very nervous, Ginger."

"Oh, Laura, everyone is at first. Here, let me help you with your coat."

She placed the coat in an office closet and closed the door. "There, now, let's go into a sitting room where we can deal with the paperwork in private."

The sitting room had been a small parlor in its former life and was furnished beautifully with some pieces Nick would have loved. The walls were a warm yellow above cream wainscoting. A fire was burning in the fireplace.

Ginger walked to a door between a wooden rocker and the desk. "There's a private powder room here, Laura, and a small closet where you may leave anything you wish. This room and storage closet are yours until you leave after collecting your coat in my office."

Ginger turned and smiled gently at Laura. "The wing-backs are recliners. You might want to rest in one of them after you finish with these forms and possibly again after you visit with Doctor Bratten. There is absolutely no rush."

Noting Laura's surprised expression, Ginger explained. "Doctor Bratten allows plenty of time between patients so complete confidentiality is maintained. He formalizes his notes between clients so little time is actually lost."

Ginger walked to the desk and laid a folder on it. "Thank you for having sent your autobiography and personal history forms to us in a timely manner. Your medical file and dental file arrived earlier in the week, so Dr. Bratten has had time to familiarize himself with them. These are the last of the forms needed from you, and they usually take around ten minutes or so to fill out. Push this button when you've finished or if there's anything you'd like while waiting. Please don't hesitate to ring me; we want you to be as comfortable as possible."

She turned to smile at Laura again just before she walked through the doorway. "This will always be your waiting room, so make yourself familiar with it."

Laura quickly answered the questions on the first page and read the consent forms. They were identical to the samples which had be sent to her. She stood and paced a bit. *If I don't do this now, I'll never do it. . . . I owe this to Erin . . . and to Nick.*

She walked to the desk, signed the consent forms, and rang the bell for Ginger.

Ginger returned and checked the folder. "Thank you, Laura. I'll take you to Dr. Bratten's office now if you're ready. Dr. Bratten will bring you back to this room at the end of your appointment, and no one will come in here until you come out and say good-bye to me. Oh, and feel free to excuse yourself to this room or the powder room if you need to during the session."

Ginger took Laura's hands in hers and looked into her eyes. "Believe me, it gets much easier and more pleasant after the first time or two."

Doctor David L. Bratten rose as Laura was escorted

into his office. The tall, trim black man appeared to be in his early fifties. Both his close-cropped hair and his mustache had gone salt and pepper. He had incredibly warm, dark eyes and the smile that goes with them. Dr. Bratten was wearing dark brown slacks and a cream-colored silk turtleneck.

"Hello, Laura. I'm glad to meet you. I'm David Bratten. Please call me David."

He took her hand. "Let's make ourselves comfortable in the wing chairs while we get acquainted."

Ginger entered with a tea cart and left without a word.

Dr. Bratten poured two cups of tea which Laura had indicated would be her drink of choice. He put one cup and saucer on a tray which also held cream, sugar, and lemon. He sat the tray on the side table to Laura's right, then brought his own cup and saucer to the chair across from her.

"How are you feeling today, Laura?"

"Nervous. . . . Frightened really."

. . .

Dr. Bratten studied the frail, tattered remains of a woman who had probably been quite beautiful at one time. The skin was taunt and gray; the eyes were sunken, darting around the room like those of a cornered animal. Both feet rested on the floor as though ready to make a run for it; hands were rubbing together.

Man's inhumanity to himself amazes me.

He took a sip of his tea and smiled at Laura. "You're safe here, Laura. Everything which transpires between us is, of course, completely confidential." He grinned almost boyishly, "My licensure depends on that."

He took another sip of tea and continued. "And I can assure you of one more thing: This is my twenty-second year in the field, so no issue will be new to me."

He stopped and looked directly into Laura's eyes, "We will work together to straighten things out. Now, tell me, Laura, what has caused you to seek my services?"

Laura's eyes snapped. "Perhaps when you've had time to read my autobiography you'll know."

David Bratten smiled warmly at Laura as he took another sip of his mint tea. "I have read your autobiographical notations,

Laura. And I could find many issues, but I need to hear you tell me what it was that finally brought you here."

He turned slightly as he placed his cup in its saucer, thoughtfully giving Laura time to compose herself, then turned back to face her.

He raised one eyebrow and patiently waited for her to fill the silence.

Nearly three full minutes, were filled with silence except for the sound of gently moving water.

Laura's eyes had searched the lovely room tastefully paneled in light cherry and filled with soft light. The wall opposite their sitting area was filled with living plants surrounding an aquarium.. No art adorned the walls. There was a fireplace on one wall, and a softly flowing copper waterfall fixture adorned the mantle.

That's where it's coming from.

Laura looked from side to side. She took a deep breath, held it as her eyes reluctantly focused on the man with the rich voice and the gentle expression. She looked at her hands. "I've never done this before."

Dr. Bratten nodded, leaned slightly forward and smiled again, silently willing her to break through her wall of silence, but saying nothing.

They sat in silence for a while longer. Then Laura began to pick her right thumbnail with her index finger. She studied the cobalt vase holding a trail of ivy vine.

When she could no longer stand the silence between them, she raised her chin and looked again at Dr. Bratten. "I'm doing this for my daughter."

"Did Erin ask you to do this?"

Laura was surprised to hear Erin's name. *He must have read it.* She rolled her shoulders then shook her head. "No, Erin does not tell me what to do."

Dr. Bratten nodded and smiled again. He tilted his head to one side. "Forgive me, Laura, but just now I'm lost." He hesitated for a few seconds. . . . "I believe you said you were doing this for Erin?" He took another sip of tea and looked quizzically at Laura.

Frustration was building in Laura.

How can he be so obtuse? . . . Surely he can figure it out. I answered all of his damn personal questions in my required client preview.

She sighed. "Well, I have to be healthier to take care of Erin."

"Healthier?"

"You know, stronger."

"Are you feeling weak, Laura?"

Laura stood. "This doesn't seem to be working."

Dr. Bratten gave her a warm smile. "Oh, it's working just fine, Laura. You can trust me to make that judgment."

"Walk about the room if you wish, but please help me to understand how you feel that you are not strong enough. I need you to give me some examples."

He paused and then, when there was no answer, gave options in hopes of teasing a response from her. "Do you feel physically weak? . . . Are you having difficulty making decisions? . . . Are you uncomfortable with your emotions?"

"Well, I find myself losing patience with Erin at times."

"I raised three of my own; believe me, I know parenting is not easy even when both parents are present." He paused and wrinkled his brow. "Please give me a concrete example, Laura; just so I can get a feel for what is going on."

When Laura didn't respond, Bratten continued, calmly refusing to acknowledge Laura's reluctance to engage. "Perhaps you could tell me about a confrontation that has happened recently."

He leaned forward. "The holidays always brought some interesting times at our house." He chuckled. "They still do. Tell me about one of yours." He reached for his tea and leaned back in his chair.

"Well, really, we haven't had a major confrontation; not a quarrel or anything."

"Oh, . . . well, tell me about something Erin has done which has upset you. Just anything within the last month which made you wish the situation had worked out differently."

. . .

And so it went for a full sixty minutes: long periods of silence, encouragement from Dr. Bratten, and a few reluctant details from Laura.

"I'm afraid we've come to the end of our first session, Laura." David Bratten rose and took Laura's hand. He looked into her eyes. "We have made some progress today; tomorrow will be a bit easier, and by the end of Friday's session we should be well on our way." He walked her to her sitting room and pressed the buzzer on the desk.

He turned as the door opened.

A fashionably dressed, middle-aged woman carrying a small leather satchel walked in.

Bratten smiled at her, then turned back to Laura. "Nedra is a registered nurse. She needs to draw a current blood sample for me, Laura. Sometimes the entire problem is based in an unsuspected nutritional deficiency or a minor chemical imbalance. We don't want to waste your time and money, so I require a thorough check on each of my new patients."

He smiled at Nedra, then turned again to Laura. "Let me assure you there will be no pain; the neonatal ward at St. Luke's calls on Nedra's skills when they have a particularly tender case."

He walked toward his office, then turned again. "I want to thank you for today, Laura. As you know, we've agreed to see each other each day this week while your school enjoys a vacation; we'll evaluate appointment scheduling after that."

"Hello, Laura, I'm Nedra Wallace." She opened her bag and extracted a small jar of pre-treated cotton swabs. "Please sit here behind the desk, dear; that's the way. . . . Roll up your sleeve for me. I need to take your blood pressure first. Now rest your arm on this towel and just relax your arm for me. That's fine."

"You'll be happy to know the sun has come out while you were with us. I just love to see sunshine; I think it makes the temperature seem a good ten degrees warmer. There now; all done. Just let me put a Band-Aid over that."

Laura finally lifted her eyes to meet Nedra's. "It's over?"

"Yes. I didn't think you were looking when I inserted the needle."

"I thought you were still searching for a vein. My doctor's nurse always has such a time."

"Well, you were a perfect patient, Laura." Nedra gathered her bag and walked to the door. "You have a wonderful afternoon."

Ginger looked up as Laura approached her desk. "I'll expect you tomorrow and the rest of the week at 10:00. We'll put our heads together to schedule further sessions after your Friday appointment. You know your workweek better than anyone else."

Laura nodded somewhat numbly.

What have I got myself into? . . . Oh, well, I took mornings off all of this week and did all of this simple paperwork just to get to see the man. . . . I'll stick it out through Friday. Besides, he's probably right; it's just a simple imbalance thing; a few pills, and I will be fine.

Laura began thinking about Nick as she walked toward the Rover.

. . .

Her thoughts wandered to the beginning of their argument on that last morning. The scene began replaying itself in her memory: "You think I'm an alcoholic, that I don't have enough guts to quit on my own."

He had come to her and had taken her in his arms. "Oh, Laura; believe me, I have no doubts about your willpower."

He had looked into her eyes. "I doubt that you are an alcoholic. . . . Yet."

He had allowed the intentional 'yet' to sink in. "But I do think you're using alcohol to fight your demons. And we Irish know a bit about fighting demons with alcohol."

He had held her tight to his chest and then had gently moved her back a little. "I love you much, much more than life itself, darling; I want to be closer to you, and I want you to be closer to our Erin."

"I am close to Erin. I love her. I love you."

"I know you love us, Laura. . . . It's just that in deep love there is a closeness we long for, . . . one we feel, one that we don't have to be told about, one that we sense. . . or we sense the lack of."

"Oh, you damned Irish and your nonstop sensing!" She had rolled her eyes at him. "Little fairies under the rocks, eh? Or is it witchcraft and psychics today?"

"I don't know what it is, dear, but it is legendary, and I believe it's true . . . when it needs to be."

"See . . . needs to be! There you go again. More sensing." She had waved her arms at her side while making a weird face and a ghostly sound.

Nick had known she was flanking him. Laura was a marvel at it. She could change any topic that she didn't want to pursue into an argument about something else.

. . .

Laura shook her head as the tears began stinging her eyes. She was determined to forget the rest of their argument.

She fastened her seat belt.

She reached for her bottle and took a deep drink.

. . .

There now; that's better.

. . .

The past is past!

33

"Got a minute, Coach?"

Ted looked up from the senior essays he was grading to make sure who was speaking to him. *Something's wrong when I don't recognize Matt's voice.* "Sure, Matt, what's up?"

Matt walked into Ted's office and sat across from him. He wallowed with the bill of the cap in his hands for a while, then looked up.

He studied his coach through worried eyes. *He'll know what's right. But I hate to dump this on him when he's busy with semester tests .*

Matt chewed the corner of his lip for a while and then spit it out. "Judd's sick, Coach."

Matt's expression and his unusual lack of composure told Ted this wasn't just the flu.

Ted gathered his papers into a neat stack in front of him. He moved them to his 'current' basket and gave his complete attention to Matt. "What seems to be the trouble?"

"He's pissin' blood."

Ted leaned forward. "How long?"

"A couple of weeks." Tears started down the senior's cheeks. "It scares me, Coach."

Matt twisted his cap some more and finally rubbed his right hand under his nose. "Scares Judd too."

"Has he told his parents?"

"No, and that's just it; he says he won't."

"Well, why the hell not? Does he think this will just go away by itself?"

"He says he doesn't want to ruin his senior year for them."

Matt searched his coach's face for understanding. "You know how his mom is; she'd go psycho if anything was really wrong with him."

"Yea, Jennie can be a little emotional," Ted rubbed his neck and the skull behind his right ear. He sat and stared out the window for a while then turned back to Matt. "I'll have a talk with him right away."

"Thanks, Coach. Try not to tell him I ratted him out."

"Don't count on that. How am I supposed to know?"

"Well, just try; but if you have to, it's okay. He'll get over it. Someone has to talk some sense to him; I tried, but I can't get him to talk to anyone but me."

Matt studied the floor. "He only told me because he wants me to watch his calls a little when season starts, make sure he's thinking straight." Matt stood to leave.

Ted walked around the desk. He put his arm around Matt's shoulder. "Thank you, Matt. I'll talk with you as soon as I finish talking with Judd and we get some sort of plan in place. Okay?"

He shifted around to face Matt and offered his hand as he studied him. "You did the right thing, Matt, the only thing a man should do under these circumstances."

Matt nodded. "Thanks coach." He stood and went to twisting the bill of his cap again. "I'm sorry to dump this on you."

Ted shook his head. "Come here, you big lug."

Ted took Matt in a full embrace. "Listen, son; it takes a man to care more about a friend than about a friendship! You did the right thing; made the hard choice. You didn't dump on me. Because you came to me, we can see to it that Judd has the chance to make the best decision about this thing."

He gave Matt a final pat on the back and pulled back. "Secrets kill, Matt. They kill people, and they sure enough kill relationships. I know that first hand."

Ted walked to his desk and picked up the phone. "Bessie, see if we can get Judd Thompson in here for a conference. It's important. Oh, and Matt Swensen needs a late pass to class, Bessie."

A few minutes later there was a tap on Ted's door. "Coach?"

"Come on in, Judd; just grading some papers." Ted studied his catcher. "How's life been treating you?"

"Okay." . . . Judd took on a wary expression.

"Sit down, Judd." Ted stood and went to look out the window for a while, then he turned. "I'm no good at beating around the bush, Judd. Is it true that you have blood in your urine?"

Judd was quiet for a while. He had never lied to Coach Weaver. *How in the world does he know? . . . Damn Matt; that's how.* "A little; probably just a bruised kidney or something like that."

"How did you bruise your kidney, Judd?"

"Well, I'm not really sure that I did, but, you know, we're always punchin' each other and stuff like that."

Ted shook his head. "How long as this been going on, Judd?"

Again, Judd considered lying but decided he didn't want to start now. He scratched the side of his cheek. "Maybe a couple of weeks."

"Maybe meaning a month or maybe meaning fourteen days, Judd?"

Judd sighed. "I don't inspect my piss, Coach; I noticed it two weeks ago tomorrow. It stung when I urinated, so I looked. There was blood in it."

"How do your parents feel about this?"

"I haven't told them, sir." Judd's demeanor became a little more defiant. He cleared his throat. "And I'm not going to, either."

"Why not?"

"Why worry them with it? They've been waitin' twelve years for my senior year. . . . You know how mom is, and dad's almost as bad."

"Judd, . . . Judd, we both know this could be a simple infection. Or some part of your urinary track could have become bruised."

Ted walked to the front of his desk and sat. "But, Judd, this is also an early detection sign for cancer."

Judd's eyes filled with tears. His voice was coarse, "I know, Coach." He gritted his teeth and finally got control. "I don't want to hurt them."

Ted drew a long breath and felt the sting of tears in his own eyes. He looked at Judd. *In the prime of his life; ... a sweet and gentle kid. Surely not! ...* He drew a deep breath. *Well, I sure as hell can't let him take a chance on this.*

Ted walked back to his chair and paused for a second to compose himself.

He sat on the edge of the desk looking at a boy he had never had to try to love. "Judd I'm going to tell you something that I've told only one other person. I consider it private and deeply personal."

He looked at the office door for a minute or so, then plowed on. "You remember last summer when we went with Jerry to Marietta?"

"Yes, sir."

"Remember that on Thursday night I went off by myself for a while?"

"Yes, sir."

"I went to visit the grave of my son."

Suddenly compassion was all over Judd's face. "Oh, gosh, Coach; I didn't know. ... None of us did."

Ted nodded. "I know, Judd. I know, and that was the way I wanted it, but, Judd, I learned something that evening, something that I sure wish I had known earlier. ... I learned that it isn't a good idea to keep secrets from people who love you."

Ted rubbed his knee. "It just causes a bigger mess."

Ted stood and went to the window again. "When our son was born, my wife, the only woman I have ever loved, was told by our family doctor that she would have no more children."

"Now we probably would have been able, eventually, to face that together, but Doc was a fine older man with good intentions, and he knew how much I cared for my kids at school. He meant well enough when he told her to tell me when she thought the time was right."

Ted turned toward Judd. "Before the time became right, our little boy died in his sleep."

Ted studied his hands for a minute, then raised his head, drawing a deep breath. "There was no way Dr. Hawkins could have anticipated that. Teddy had been a healthy little boy, not a mark on him."

Neither of them spoke for quite a while.

Ted drew a deep breath and looked at his hands again. "They call it crib death. It wasn't Lindy's fault; wasn't my fault, wasn't anyone's fault, just. . . "

Ted rubbed his nose. . . "Anyway, I had always told Lindy that I wanted a big family," he smiled foolishly at the memory, 'my own baseball team.' I loved kids and wanted a family, but what I thought I was communicating was 'I love you, Lindy, and I want to love you for the rest of my life. We'll have dozens of kids together.'"

Ted swallowed. "Lindy only heard my words; there was no way for her to know my unspoken meaning, so she took my words literally."

"When our baby boy died, she thought she would be unable to do her part to fulfill my dream. My only dream was to love her until I died, but she thought about the children who would never be born, thought about my 'baseball team.'"

Ted was silent. "I don't want to bore you with a long story, but she divorced me and married a man who had always told us he never wanted kids, didn't even like little kids, Bill Neeley."

Ted shifted on the edge of the desk. "That afternoon, when we were down in Marietta, I took a rose to my son's grave. I talked to him a little while and said a prayer."

"When I stood up, Lindy spoke to me. At first I thought I had imagined it, but she was there. I hadn't seen her since her marriage to Bill."

He looked at Judd. "That's when I came up here to Wellsboro. I wanted to give them space, a chance to make a happy life if they could. . . . And, truth be told, I wanted to avoid seeing the woman I loved walking down the street on the arm of another man."

Ted shook his head and took another deep breath. "Wasn't sure I could stand it." Ted looked at the floor, then back to Judd.

"Well, she told me the whole story that evening last summer. But it was too late for us then. My mind raced with a million things I wanted to say to her. 'We could have adopted. . . . I loved you! . . . We could have figured out what to do.' I didn't say anything; I knew it would just hurt her more."

"You see, Judd. That's why I know we have to go tell your parents tonight. Then you and they can form a team and decide what to do."

"I'm thinkin' that it's just a bruise or an infection; I bet it is, but we can't take a chance. If it's something else, the earlier treatment is started, the better chance you have. And the bottom line is that if, by some chance, the treatment doesn't work, your parents will have had some time to prepare for the worst, and you folks will have had time to tell each other the important things, the things most of us never get around to saying out loud."

Ted stood and cleared his throat. "Now that's not going to happen. You're not going to die, but you owe it to the people who love you and whom you love to be straight with them, Judd. I know that. I learned it the hard way."

Judd came to Ted and put his arms around his coach. "God, Coach, that's awful. . . . That's why you've never married someone up here; you still love her."

Ted nodded and looked at Judd through eyes glassy with tears. "A part of me sure does. . . . Don't do that to your parents, Judd. Let me go home with you tonight. We'll tell them together."

"I don't want to hurt them, sir."

"Then don't, Judd. Don't presume to decide what they can and can not stand or how they feel. Don't think more about your comfort than theirs."

Ted moved to look out the window again, then turned back to look at Judd. "You know, we have millions of words, Judd, millions of 'em, but most of us don't communicate. We hide behind masks of ourselves trying to save everyone who loves us from knowing how vulnerable we each are, and that just forces others to put on a brave front too."

Ted looked hard at Judd. "Tonight, Judd."

Judd looked at the floor for several minutes, then raised his eyes to meet Ted's, "Okay, Coach. . . . Coach Weaver, I was the only one mom could have too."

34

Doctor Hector Lyman had immediately agreed to an emergency appointment for the morning of Sat., January 18. He had arrived at his office early, around six, with a thermos of coffee and had spent two hours with the new *Physician's Aid Diagnostic Program* for computers which he had purchased as his Christmas gift to himself and his patients.

At eight a.m., he had gone to the Diner for his regular large oatmeal with fruit and was back at the office when the Thompsons and Ted Weaver arrived.

During a thorough physical, Doctor Lyman could find no easy explanation for the blood which was in the urine sample.

After some time in his office, he came into the examination room where Ted and the Thompsons were waiting. Dr. Lyman concentrated on Judd. "Well, Judd, there's good news and bad news. The bad news is that there is a strong possibility we're looking at a problem with an internal organ."

"You mean cancer," Judd interpreted.

"Possibly, but the good news is that you are in otherwise tiptop shape, and we have caught this at a very early stage." He paused, "So whatever it is, son, you have every reason to hope for a full recovery."

He allowed time for the emotions to settle, then continued. "Recovery will not happen until we get an exact diagnosis from an expert who lays out a plan of action. Mr. Weaver indicated that he wanted as much settled today as was humanly possible."

The family numbly nodded.

"So, I have taken the liberty of contacting the man I would send my own son to if he had a similar problem."

Dr. Lyman let his eyes shift to Judd's parents. "Dr. Rubin Shonk lectures oncologists, that's physicians who specialize in the treatment of cancer. He lectures across the country at the finest teaching hospitals we have; he has even lectured abroad. He's considered one of the nation's three top experts in a very specialized field, cancer of the bladder and urinary tract."

"He happens to be at his home in Sayre, Pennsylvania, this weekend. And he's a big fan of baseball. He and a friend attended the high school baseball playoffs last year. He remembers the Wellsboro catcher who called the pitches that won the finals."

His eyes shifted to Judd. "Doctor Shonk rarely takes a private client any more; research and teaching take up most of his time," Dr. Lyman smiled, "But he keeps an office at the Guthrie Clinic at Sayre, and he will see you this afternoon if you can make it."

Ted rose, "What time, Doc?"

"Whenever you can get there between 1 and 4, Ted. I have his cell number. I'll contact him when you leave. But you might want to alert him when you're at the town limits."

Ted glanced at the Thompsons. "Well, I'm driving to Sayre. Anyone here want to go with me?"

Judd took a deep breath as he got up out of his chair. "Might as well get it over with, Coach. Like you always tell us: study the opposition and start matching strengths and weaknesses. This Dr. Shonk sounds like our best shot."

Judd looked at his parents who were doing their best to contain their emotions; he knew he had to play strong, stay proactive, just to keep them in the game. "What do you want to do, Mom? Dad?, go home and lick our wounds or go to Sayre with Coach Weaver and see what we can do about this?"

Jennie Thompson stood. "We are surely blessed to have you and Ted, Doctor Lyman."

She swallowed hard and turned toward her husband. "We have to go, Jim; we have to fight this thing. I'm not gonna lose my boy."

She hugged Judd tightly to her as the tears spilled forth.

. . .

Ted held the door of the Suburban for Jennie as she and Jim loaded in the back seats. Judd sat up front with his coach.

"Judd, there's a Pennsylvania map in the glove box there, get 'er out and help me remember the best route to Sayre."

He needs something to focus on. We'll take 6 over and then 220 up along the river. ... It's 10:30 now; probably get an early lunch in Mansfield. Won't be much eating, but it will help to settle us.

Ted punched up the voice of John Denver.

A smile immediately spread across Judd's face. He turned toward Jennie. "This is it, mom. Remember I told you about Coach and this song and West Virginia?" The memories of the summer trip stayed with him as he and Ted reminisced until they stopped for lunch.

. . .

Ted punched the numbers into the cell phone as they passed the corporation limit at Sayre. "Ted Weaver for Dr. Rubin Shonk. ... It was kind of you to see us, doctor. I wanted to alert you. There are four of us. We're about two blocks away. ... Well, that would be great. See you shortly."

A tall, well-built man in tan Dockers and a navy turtle-neck extended his hand as they entered the lobby. "Judd Thompson?"

"Yes, sir. We're looking for Dr. Shonk's office."

"I'm Shonk, Judd. I shook your hand last summer at the finals. You signed my program along with around a hundred more. ... I always try to make the finals."

His friendly eyes shifted to Ted and then back to Judd, "I always try to get my program signed. I was amazed that you guys stayed on the field until the last request had been filled. You men were one class act."

Dr. Shonk shook hands with the Thompsons and Ted, then shifted his attention back to Judd. "Come right this way, Judd. Let's take a look at what's goin' on with you."

He took them into a room which was obviously his sitting room and study. Two books were opened on the large desk area which took up one wall. Two computers, one on either side of the opened books were turned off, and a simple desk chair sat facing the rest of the room.

A television with both dvd and video sat on an audio-visual stand. A couch, a love seat, a rocker, and a recliner were arranged in a half circle.

A small room refrigerator had been fitted with a counter across its top. A microwave and a coffee pot sat there.

"Well, here she is, folks. The blue door leads to a rest room. The tv is on cable; there's juice and water in the fridge along with some fruit and crackers."

He nodded at the coffee pot. "That's fresh; it's caffinated. Make yourselves at home. . . . Judd, I'd like you and your coach to come back here with me for a while."

They went through a music-filled room, lined with bookshelves and entered a third room.

Dr. Shonk turned to Judd. "Judd, I'll need some info and then I'll want to examine you, probably do some simple procedures too. We should be completely finished in three or four hours. We'll go back and forth and talk with your folks from time to time to keep them in the loop."

He pushed his horn rims up slightly with his index finger. "Before we sit down, I want you to think about something important. It's only important because I need you to be completely honest and as comfortable as possible. Do you want Ted in here or not? He can help keep your parents company or he can stay with us. It's your call right now, and, in either case, at some time, I'm going to need to see each of you two alone."

"I'd like Coach to stay for a while, sir."

"Good. Let's sit down."

He leaned forward and rested an elbow on his knee and his chin on his fist. "Now, Judd, you call me Doc or I'm gonna start callin' you Mr. Thompson."

He grinned and extended his hand to Ted again. "And, Ted, I would be proud if you would call me Rubin."

He twisted in his chair and turned on overhead cameras. "I tape everything. I use absolutely nothing specific about your case without your written permission; the tapes help me when I need to review. Either one of you can interrupt me or each other at any time."

He looked at both of them. "That's especially important if I use a word you're not familiar with or if I say something that you don't understand or need to question."

He grinned crookedly, "Imagine how lost I'd be if you

two started throwin' baseball lingo at me."

He stood. "First, I want to pull some blood, Judd." When he had finished the procedure, he turned off the cameras and went to a second door. "I'll be right back. Just want to walk this down to the lab."

Both Judd and Ted relieved themselves while he was gone, and Ted got each of them a bottle of water from the fridge.

Shonk turned the cameras on as he entered the room. For the next fifteen minutes Dr. Shonk questioned Judd about the specifics of his discovering blood in his urine and his general feeling of health. Then he asked him to strip to his shorts and step on the treadmill. When Judd finished, Shonk shook his head, "You sure as hell keep 'em in shape, Ted."

Shonk stripped to his shorts. "I need you to move over here and mimic my moves, Judd. You do just what I do and hold it as long as I hold it if you can. But if it feels even a little uncomfortable, return to standing immediately. This is part of the exam; I need to know the minute something is even a little uncomfortable. The cameras will get everything."

As they went through a series of maneuvers, Ted was surprised at how agile and fit the doctor was.

"That was good. Now come over and get on this table for me, Judd. Same deal; at the first indication of pain, say something. It's important; don't suck anything up."

While Ted and Judd were with Shonk, a nurse had come to pull Jennie's blood and Jim's blood and had had each of them fill out a complete medical history on themselves, each of their parents, and one on Judd. *'Someone always remembers something that the other one forgot.'*

At Shonk's request, Dr. Lyman had faxed complete medical records on each of the three to Shonk's office prior to their having arrived.

When Judd finished his movements, Shonk grinned and hit a buzzer. "We'd better get our cloths back on now, Judd. Ted and I will go catch up with your parents for a while. I want one of my assistants to take complete body scans then he'll bring you back where we are."

Shonk smiled at Jennie and Jim, "Well, I can assure you

folks of one thing. Judd is not in any pain." He grinned some more and nodded, "Muscles, tendons, joints, bones, all in fine shape."

. . .

There was a knock at the door; Judd appeared accompanied by a pizza delivery man.

"Let's have a piece of this before it gets cold and have something to drink. We need to relax for a few minutes while some lab work gets done."

When they had finished eating, Doctor Shonk leaned forward. "Folks, I want to tell you a little something about me."

"My dad died with lung cancer. Dad was a woodworker, laid and finished hardwood floors by day and made and installed cabinets at night and on weekends. I had two brothers and two sisters. Mom kept us clean, and Dad kept us clothed and fed."

His elbow went to his knee again and his head rested on his fist. He stared in silence for a minute or two and then came back to them. "I was in medical school when he was diagnosed, so I decided to become an oncologist."

He made a half-hearted grin and shrugged his shoulders. "I wanted to save my dad. . . . He died before I finished school. . . . I'd been practicing for about two years when my oldest brother was diagnosed with bladder cancer. . . . By damn, I saved him."

He drew a long breath. "Then I went into a specialty within a specialty. God has blessed me with a good brain, and I study and research nearly every day of my life. I don't know what we have here, but I *will* know. . . . If it is cancer, it's early, and I know how to give it more than it can normally take."

He looked directly at Judd, "You've got a body that won't quit on you, Judd. We can beat this thing."

He nodded, almost to himself, "We'll get through this; all of us."

Just then a buzzer made a faint noise. He stood, "I need to go back there and look at a couple of reports. I'll be back in a few minutes. Stay comfortable."

Research money, when placed in the right hands, is a wonderful thing. Before they had arrived at the hospital, two of

Shonk's top research assistants had previewed and correlated all relevant data from Dr. Lyman's records.

The minute the patient histories had been taken that data had been added, and more correlations had been identified.

Blood samples had had full spectrums run on each of the three; Judd's body scans had been processed and studied. More correlations had been made. Probabilities were noted and charted.

All data had been cross-indexed with the results of the physical which had been viewed on a screen by the assistants as it was being done. The film was kept for future reference.

Shonk had his own excellent mind, but he also had a half dozen others to relie on. And, luckily three had been within driving distance when Dr. Lyman had phoned early in the day.

He was back with the family in just under twenty minutes. "Judd, everything looks just the way we want it to look. I need to take some biopsies; they're just little snips of tissue, nearly microscopic. That will require a mild sedative, but you'll be awake during the entire procedure. There will be no pain, and you will be in absolutely no danger. When we finish, you can go home today and come back Wednesday afternoon when we'll have the results of the cultures. I'm gonna give you folks a few minutes to think and to talk."

They were back in the Suburban by five. Everyone felt relieved and confident in Shonk.

"Did you notice how he always talked to me, let me make the decisions?" Judd asked.

"Yes, and the office staff seemed real friendly and efficient too with several things going on at once," Jennie said.

Ted agreed. "I am glad we came." He cleared his throat. "I plan to take Wednesday afternoon off and bring you folks back. We'll go down this road together as long as you can put up with me."

35

They pulled into the parking lot of the hospital in Sayre at 2:00 p.m.

Doctor Shonk was, again, waiting in the reception center. "Hi, there, Judd." They shook hands. "It's good to see you folks. Let's go back where it is a little quieter."

When they had settled into chairs, Doctor Shonk rolled his chair near them. "I'm not one for small talk. . . . Judd, some of the cultures from your bladder were positive. You do have cancer in the lining of your bladder, but, and this is the big one, thank the good Lord, it's early enough that it is only in the lining. That means it has not gone into the bladder wall, and it sure has not spread anywhere else."

He paused to let this sink in. "We can treat it very successfully, Judd. I'm not talking about slowing it down; I mean get rid of it. I'd recommend a six-week series of treatments initially. We'd key the treatment to the molecular analysis of your tumor, go right after its very core. I'll explain everything in more detail later."

Both Judd's parents and Ted Weaver nodded, smiled, and said words of thanks.

Judd beamed, "Boy, what a relief. I'd rather die than miss baseball season my senior year."

Everyone in the room noticed Shonk's cringe.

Judd went on in an attempt to explain his statement. "That was why I wasn't going to tell anyone." He looked at Ted, "Just Matt so he could make sure I didn't mess up on the calls."

Ted smiled, "Well, you owe him; he made certain you didn't mess up in a big way."

Shonk was studying them, allowing the four enough time to absorb the negation of a possible death sentence.

Then he stood. "Judd, there will be no baseball this season."

"What do you mean?"

"I mean I won't let you play during treatment; in fact, I would prefer that you to drop school this semester.   I want your body to have its every resource at hand."

Judd stood. "Then, to hell with the treatment."

"Judd!" Jennie's voice was sharp as was Jim's.

Judd glared at Shonk. "I mean it."

"So do I." Shonk shook his head. "You know, Judd, I had you figured all wrong. When I watched you lead that team last summer, I would have bet my practice that you had to be a thinker: a smart, logical young man who liked to know the facts about everyone, everything; a man who used those facts to lay a course of action." Shonk looked defeated.

"I'd rather die than miss my senior year."

"Well, that's possible, Judd."

The two glared at each other for a while, then Shonk sat down.

Judd sat also.

"Now, look, Judd. You have the right to make any decision you want. I respect that. But you ought to have all of the facts before you make a final decision. ˙That decision should rise above what's best for this year's team. It should be based, . . . based on what you want to be doing ten, thirty, seventy years from now."

Shonk intertwined his fingers and rubbed his palms together. He looked off toward the microwave, then brought his eyes back to Judd. "Based on seeing your first son play his baseball, on seeing your parents through their final days and making them as easy as possible, based on your long-term future."

Shonk stood and began to pace. "I estimate," he turned to look directly at Judd, "and I'm so damned good at this that it sometimes makes me sick to my stomach, I estimate you have two weeks, three at the outside, until the cancer moves to the wall of the bladder. Once it's there, I can probably cure it, but that cure normally has an effect on your sexuality. The severity of the effect varies, and there are things we can do to help alleviate the effects, but, normally, there are residual problems."

He sat and pulled his chair close to Judd. "If you let me treat you right now, I can cure you. I *can!* And you'll be as good as new in six months. I have a 98.7 percent cure rate at this stage. It doesn't get any better than that, and, Judd, you're young and in otherwise perfect health."

Jim glared at Judd and then turned to Shonk and cleared his throat. "Well, he's going to take the treatment, Doctor Shonk. He's not eighteen yet."

Shonk shook his head. "Sorry, Jim; I won't treat Judd without his consent; it is his life that's at stake here."

"Well, I'll finish my senior year and baseball season and then I'll take your treatment."

"Let me give you some facts before you put that in stone, Judd."

"First, I will not treat you later. . . . I only treat people who value *life* above all else."

Seeing the shocked expression on the four faces in front of him, Shonk shrugged his shoulders. "Sorry, but that's just the way it is. You see, I decided when I started this war that someone had to be in charge. Since I 'm the one in this room with the most battle experience, I run the war my way."

"Second, I can guarantee you, Judd, that, fit as you feel today, you won't have enough energy to finish this year's baseball season regardless of what treatment decisions you make. The treatment itself will take a certain amount of energy, but, should you elect to postpone or refuse treatment, the cancer will take more energy from your body each day; that's how it grows, Judd, by taking your energy. . . . Without treatment, by the middle of March you'll be dragging; by the end of May you'll be lucky to walk to the bathroom by yourself."

Shonk stood. "You see, the term bladder cancer is a broad diagnosis. Within that diagnosis are several distinct types. Your particular type is, thankfully, rare, but it wastes no time, Judd."

"I've taken the prerogative of having called your school superintendent. He says the board will grant you a leave of absence for treatment for the second semester of your senior year. . . . That will allow you to return next September to begin your senior year again. You'll have to carry a full load both semesters, but you will be eligible to play high school baseball next year that way."

"My way you'll have two options: One, you'll be eligible to play your senior baseball season next year, and probably get a dozen scholarship offers to play in college.   Two, you can choose to take the treatments and continue school without baseball and graduate with your class.   I'm confident that, as fit as you are, I can keep you going.   In that case, you'll be healthy enough to go to a great camp this summer, collect a scholarship, and hit college in the fall."

"With no treatment, you won't finish the season; there's a good chance you won't even be able to begin it.   If you survive, and, in all fairness, you should with good treatment after graduation, you'll have to deal with the effects of treatment, and you will have shot yourself in the foot during your senior year."

"If you're lucky and have full recovery during the later treatment, there will still be camps and, possibly, scholarship offers, but they'll be at least a year away because later treatment will not give you the energy for summer camps."

Shonk swiveled his chair and clasped his hands on top of his head.   "I'm sorry, Judd, but those *are* the facts.   I wish to hell they could be different."

Shonk looked at his hands.   He shook his head as he raised it to look Judd.   "It's a worthy adversary, Judd."

"Oh, and, to complicate your decision a little, there is one other fact that you need to remember: Even at this stage, a little over one percent of my patients do not recover.   I've never lost one who was even close to as fit as you are, but that's the percentage.   We don't play around.   We go in there with a complete arsenal."

He sat still in the silence that pervaded the room, realizing that each of them needed to have time to let this sink in.

Finally, he rose.   "Now, Judd, I have a video set up back in the examination room.   I want you to go back there alone and watch it.   You can stop it whenever you want to think about a particular point, but turn it back on and watch it through.   Please do that for both of us.   Then sit there and think things through."   He paused.   "It wouldn't hurt to ask God to guide your thoughts. Come back out here when you've made up your mind.   If you'll do that for me, make an informed decision, I will support that decision with you."

He looked at the others. "No one is going to argue with you in my office; this is your life."

Judd walked toward the far room.

Shonk swiveled his chair around, "The refrigerator is stocked, Judd; use it; you need some grub."

Shonk stood, closed the door, and began pouring everyone a glass of juice. "We'll watch the same video he's watching, so we're all on the same page. He'll settle down. I know him. I knew him last summer."

Along with the juice, Shonk produced a snack tray and removed its cover. "Let's eat something while we watch this."

It was an in-house video tailored to Judd's specific case, explaining the physiology of the catcher's position as well as the demand which the cancer would make on the circulatory system and the resulting gradual, but continuous, changes which would occur in sight, reasoning ability, memory, physical stamina, and emotional stamina. It indicated that metasis was rapid with this particular type; typically its next location would be the lungs.

Ted was amazed that a specialist would have taken that much time to individualize and prepare for a patient. *This man is first class; that much is for sure.*

Probably has a string of degrees in psychology, too.

The idea of giving Judd the facts and then letting him study them out in private, fit Judd's personality to a 't.' . . . Let him stomp out, and his pride would make him defend his position, but, given time to think, Judd was one smart kid, a kid who had always studied the opponent's stats until he had a plan.

The second part of the film emphasized the proposed treatment which was approved only as an experimental procedure. It would involve, among other things, pumping genetically engineered tuberculosis bacteria into the bladder itself. This was not without risk, but when it worked, it cleaned the shit out completely.

Hypnosis, psychological counseling, and mind games along with a defined diet and an intensive exercise program to combat any loss of strength, endurance, balance or range of motion would be included.

Obviously there would be no time or energy for athletics, but continuing school was reasonable if the client so desired.

As each point was made, Shonk explained, in layman's terms, what was involved and the expected positives and negatives.

The film lasted forty-seven minutes.

One hour and fifty minutes from the time he had walked out of the room, Judd walked back in. He walked toward Shonk and extended his hand. "I want to thank you, Dr. Shonk, for respecting my thoughts about treatment. I appreciate all of the effort you have put into this."

He turned toward his parents. "When I was back there, I got to thinkin' about a conversation that I had with Mr.Barnsworth one night when I was riding home with him after an away game."

Judd fiddled with his hands for a while, then continued. "I asked him how he was doin'. He said that it was probably a little late for him, but that he was taking the treatments. ... He said that when an oncologist sets up a treatment program, it's a little like an experiment in chemistry, and, although he had never taught chemistry, he had always been fascinated by it." ...

"Mr. Barnsworth said he had decided to make the cancer kill him; he wasn't going to lay down and die for it, and maybe they'd learn something that would help the next guy."

Judd turned toward Shonk. "I've decided to take the treatment, sir. ... But I *will* stay in school with my class. I've taken my ACT and P-SAT tests, and I don't have to worry about an athletic scholarship. I'll get academic offers."

He turned to look at Ted. "Coach, I am officially resigning from the team roster as of right now. The team won't have much of a chance if they're always watchin' and worryin' about me. I won't even come to the games; that would just be a distraction."

He focused on Shonk again. "I'll put all of my energy into givin' this thing the fight of it's life and keepin' up with my studies."

He looked at his parents. "I *will* walk across that stage and get my diploma under my own power."

He thought a minute, then stepped back to survey all

of them. "This may not be important, but I never once in my life dreamed of being a big league catcher. That's no life for a family man, and that's what I want to be, a family man and a high school coach."

He took a deep breath. "I'll walk on at college because I *am* good. ... Coach walked on. ... There'll be something I can do if I just keep and review records." He looked at the floor, then raised his head. "I like bein' part of a team."

"So that's the deal, Dr. Shonk. I'll take the treatments, but I'll stay in school."

Shonk drew a deep breath. "If you haven't decided on a college major, you might consider labor negotiations, Judd."

He walked to Judd and offered his hand. "I'll treat you, and we *will* beat this thing."

He hesitated. "There's really no reason to bring this up, but you'll hear about it, so I may as well address it right now."

He took a deep breath and his expression changed. "Some oncologists stay with a patient until the tide turns one way or another and then back off to go on to new clients. They feel getting close adds too much emotional stress in their professional lives."

He walked to the refrigerator and removed a bottle of water. He uncapped it and took a drink. "I have never left a patient. I stay with them. We are a team now, and this is *our* battle."

"When will we start?"

"I can start you either tomorrow or Monday, Judd. You'll need to be in our hospital for the first six days. Then you'll come and go as needed. I'll be here with you for the first set of treatments. I'll be back for each evaluation and follow-up, and you'll have my cell phone number. Call *every time any question,* no matter how small, comes to mind."

. . .

"Let's start tomorrow, sir. Might as well take what edge we can get."

36

After the first week's daily sessions, Laura had agreed to see Dr. Bratten on Tuesdays and Fridays after her office at school closed.

Bratten had spent time exploring issues, noting body language, facial expression, mannerisms, and vocal tone while establishing rapport. This last had not been easy with Laura, but he was ready to bite the bullet. Now, on Valentine's Day, work would begin.

"Good afternoon, Laura."

She smiled. "Hello, David."

"Is there anything you would like to start with?"

"No. Same old, same old. I am desperately afraid I'll lose Erin. She's all I've got. I've lost everyone else: my dad, my husband." She began a soft sobbing. "I killed my mother and my baby brother, David."

Bratten intervened, "You were in an accident in which your mother and Sammy died, Laura. . . . You know, there is more than one way to lose someone: someone can be taken from you or you can wall someone out."

"So you think I, I who love my daughter more than life itself, am walling her out?" She started to stand. "That is too ridiculous to even talk about again."

"Again?"

"Yes, Nick once accused me of that very thing when he was in a drunken rage."

Bratten nodded. "Well, there is another area I would like to visit a bit if that's okay."

She nodded, relaxed and took a sip of tea. *I guess I showed you! . . . You can only push me so far. Go ahead try me; I can handle you.*

"We've had the results of your first blood test for some time. You remember that I had Nedra draw again last Tuesday?"

Laura nodded her head.

"I wanted to double check the results. It appears we are dealing with a two-pronged demon here, Laura. And one of those prongs is definitely chemical."

She smiled and leaned slightly forward. *I knew it was some simple chemical thing. Just a few pills are all I need to regain control.*

"Getting that under control, while it might not be easy, will enable us to make much shorter work of the other issues. And we can work on both simultaneously."

She smiled again. *Now we're getting somewhere!*

"I believe you have sensed all along that there was a chemical problem."

"From the first time you mentioned it; I knew it had to be some sort of an imbalance thing." Laura squared her shoulders. "I take great pride in the ability to control myself. I can't stand those who wallow in self-pity. Functional people have to learn to get on with it."

He nodded again and reached across to pat her arm. *Still in complete denial. . . . But not so cagey today. I just got a good look at you, Laura.* "Let's move to the desk where we can discuss the results of your blood work while we each look at a copy."

Dr. Bratten took Laura, item by item, through her complete blood profile. Then he carefully studied her. "You'll notice, Laura, that I have placed red indicators at five lines on your profile. Your calcium level is a little lower than I would like. Your cholesterol level is not where I would like it: your HDL is much too low, and your LDL is high. Your blood is carrying way too much alcohol; might be a digestive problem there. Your blood sugar is a little high. And, last, your liver function isn't what I normally see in a person your age."

He smiled at Laura. "Don't be alarmed. All of this is good news. We know where to begin a pathway to health. I have some tests scheduled for you at the hospital. You mentioned frequent severe headaches, so I have scheduled some tests for indicators in that area. I want you to have a brain scan and some additional tests to be certain we're seeing no abnormal growths and that circulation is normal."

"Brain scans?"

"Yes, Laura. We want to identify the enemy within, not guess at it. At this point, no indicator is such that it can't be brought back to the norm fairly easily, but I don't want to tinker with your health; I want to restore it."

He made eye contact. "In order to do that I need to know the root cause of the problems, not just the effects of the cause. You will need to have blood drawn once more, and that will need to be a fasting blood test, Laura. Nedra will give you the guidelines for preparation for all of the testing. For your convenience, I've scheduled everything to take place next Monday. I know you're busy, and I don't want you to have to string this out and miss several hours of work on different days."

Laura nodded in agreement. "One trip to the hospital is one too many in my mind, but I'll do it if you really think this is necessary."

Dr. Bratten smiled and released a deep breath. "Good. I know you are doing all of this for Erin, and I can certainly understand why, Laura. She is obviously precious to you, and she certainly doesn't need to be worrying about the possibility of losing you, too. She needs to know that you are in control of your health."

Laura nodded in agreement. "Yes, she's showing a lack of control herself; she doesn't need to see me losing it."

"Exactly. It is so much easier to work with someone who understands the need to work through these things."

"I decided a long time ago, Dr. Bratten, that I would be in control of my life, my emotions." She thought back to Nick's last morning. She winced involuntarily as the memories flooded her, then squared her shoulders and pulled back to the present. "Some have not always understood. I'm glad that you do."

"You know, Laura, I believe issues of control in one way or another actually determine the person we become."

"Yes, I do too."

"Good. Now let me clear up one little possibility here, Laura." He ran his slim fingers down the side of his cheek as he looked at the printout. "Do you normally have a drink with dinner?"

Laura smiled and nodded. "Yes. A dinner drink is just a normal part of life with an Irish husband. I have grown to enjoy an evening cocktail, sometimes even two."

Dr. Bratten smiled. "Most of us do." His face became thoughtful, and he raised an eyebrow. "Ever drink at other times?"

Laura's brow wrinkled, her complexion colored a little, then she smiled to herself. *He's sophisticated; he understands.* "Well, on rare occasions, I might have a glass of wine at lunch if we're celebrating something or a buttered rum in the middle of the day on a ski trip."

Bratten returned the smile. "That's exactly how my wife and I handle it." His fingers ran his facial lines again. "Something is making your blood carry too much alcohol. Why at this level you actually exceed the legal driving limits by a good bit. Any idea where that's coming from? . . . Has another doctor ever mentioned this to you?"

Laura's body stiffened slightly. "No."

Bratten smiled again and reached across the table to pat Laura's arm. "Well, don't let it worry you, Laura. We'll root out the cause and get it under control. Erin needs you."

He stood and smiled again. "Oh, Laura, now that I've presumed to 'know' Erin, would you consider bringing me a current picture of her? I'd really like to see a photo of your little girl, and I'd like you to consider giving me permission to speak with Erin's trauma counselor too. Of course, that's your decision. You're in control of your family."

Laura returned the smile. "I'll bring a photo to the next session. I'm an amateur photographer, so Lord knows I have a ton of them. As for your talking with Jamie, I see no problem there."

"What a wonderful talent photography is. I seem always to be cutting people's heads off in my pictures."

"I can tell you how to fix that."

"That would be great. My entire family would be grateful." Bratten smiled to himself as he walked Laura to sitting room where Nedra was waiting with the forms and instructions for the tests.

"Nedra, please tell Ginger I want to continue seeing

Laura on Tuesdays and Fridays."

He glanced questioningly at Laura. "That is if you can still manage to fit that into your schedule, Laura. I'm eager to get you back in tiptop shape for spring."

"I can handle it, Dr. Bratten; I want to get rid of these insidious headaches as soon as possible."

"We can do it, Laura. I know we can. Good medicine and a strong-willed patient can fix most things once we identify the root of the problem."

37

Late March 2003

Ted was in his office enjoying the warmth of the sun hitting his shoulders as he graded mid-term tests. *Good job, Nancy. You cited plenty of support for your conclusions.* He totaled the points and smiled as he found 94 and put an A- on the test. *Teach them to use facts as the basis of thought, not to regurgitate.*

He rubbed his neck and took a sip of lukewarm coffee while reaching for the ringing phone. "Weaver."

"Bill Neeley here, Ted."

A smile automatically spread across Ted's face. "Well, hi, there, Bill Neeley. How are things to the southwest?"

"You never should have left Marietta, Ted: shirtsleeve weather along the Ohio today. I suppose you're still shoveling snow up there in the mountains."

Ted chuckled. "Just about; that last storm hit us a pretty good lick, but the sun is warming my shoulders as we speak. How's Jerry?"

"Jerry Thornton is one hundred percent slugger, Ted. God, what a kid!" Neeley paused to shake his head. "His grades are solid. He's the first person at practice, starts warming-up before I even get to the gym."

Neeley smiled at his good luck in having found the kid who could fill a big hole. "I honestly think he can see the ball better than anyone I've ever coached. . . . You could always do that too, really see the ball; did you give him a secret of some sort?"

Ted laughed out loud. "I think maybe God did, Bill. I always thought he could see it right up to the bat, actually see the contact sometimes." Ted took a moment to remember some of Jerry's long ones. "And, on more than one occasion, it almost seemed that he could coax it a hair or two."

"Yea, I know what you're talking about. If he doesn't get hurt, he may be a major player in the big time in a few years."

"Well, if he makes it; he'll get us good seats. He was raised right."

Neeley scratched his cheek as he considered. "You know he probably would. He is one loyal kid. Right now he's pretty worried about that ace catcher of yours."

"Is it causing him trouble?"

"No, when he picks up a bat, everything else disappears from his mind; the only thing he thinks about is the ball."

"Good."

Neeley's voice, full of braggadocio, changed to one of concern, "Jerry told me Judd's havin' it pretty hard right now. How's he doin'?"

"If something like that ever comes your way, Bill, remember a doctor by the name of Rubin Shonk. He's one of the world's experts in his field." ... "Judd's just finishing a second round of treatment, and full recovery seems within reach."

Ted continued, "You know they caught it at the very beginning. His first series of treatments lasted six weeks. This short series is just to stimulate the immune system and enlist it to help kill any lingering cancer cells that might be unobservable at this time."

"His treatment seemed to carry a lot of risk."

"Well, Shonk is on the cutting edge."

"But with someone like that heading his treatment team, why is he just holding his own?"

"Well, it's early, Bill, and the treatments themselves take a lot out of a person."

"Hell of a thing to have happen." Neeley fingered a baseball from his *In* basket. "Hell of a thing. Makes me glad I never wanted kids of my own."

There was a moment of awkward silence.

"Oh, shit, Ted. I'm sorry. Really, I was just runnin' my mouth; I never meant. . . "

Ted interrupted. "Hey, Bill; we know each other better than to have to apologize for a slip of the tongue. No offense was taken."

He paused to gather his own thoughts. "You know, watchin' Judd this spring has reminded me of some important things that I had sort of let slip by the wayside. I need to find my way back to my better self." He paused again and took a sip of the coffee. "We were once the best of friends, Bill. I miss that."

"You're preachin' to the choir, Ted."

"I wish things had been different for Lindy and me." Ted rubbed the back of his neck again. "But the truth is Teddy's death and secrets and misunderstandings ripped us apart. You didn't." He was silent for a bit. "If I couldn't be there for her I'm glad another good man was."

Neeley's voice was coarse with emotion. "Ted . . . Ted Weaver, you are one hell of a man. . . . You always were."

Both men were silent for a bit, each remembering the special warmth of a friendship shattered by pain.

Neeley, his voice still coarse, broke the silence. "You remember my brother Pete?"

Ted smiled, "Sure, all of those freckles; Lindy used to say he had *Labbie* eyes: big, brown, dancin' with joy. What's he doin' now?"

"He's dead, Ted." Neeley continued. "Pete's been dead for six years now." He paused as the back of his hand crossed his lips. "Prostate cancer."

There was another pause during which each man recalled favorite memories of Pete Neeley.

"You know, Ted. I remember the first time he came to visit me at Marietta. I asked you to help me entertain him over Labor Day one year. You asked me what he liked to do and immediately set up a fishing trip down where you had grown up."

Neeley smiled as memories of the trip took center stage. "We stopped in and met your parents; and, before we left to come home, we stopped to say good-bye. Your mom had made a chocolate cake, and your dad had a canister of homemade ice cream packed in ice. . . Pete never forgot that, talked about it often: how you had taken us to your secret spots, how your parents had made us welcome. It was a fine memory; still is."

"Yea. I remember Pete insisting that he had never eaten ice cream as smooth as that, and he took two pieces of cake. Mom was just delighted. . . He was a good man."

After a pause, Ted chuckled. "I also remember that he joked he had never seen a little ole stream that he couldn't walk in." Ted laughed out loud. "And the splash he made when he fell flat on his ass. Remember? We stayed by that one hole with him fishing in his underwear while his pants hung on a bush to dry?"

Bill laughed, "Yea, and you never knew how sunburned his legs got; we went straight to Masen's Drug Store when you dropped us off. I rubbed calamine lotion half of the night."

"I'm sure sorry that we lost Pete, Bill."

There was a long sigh at the other end of the phone. "Me too. In fact that's one of the reasons I called. I want to offer Judd a scholarship."

There's a connection there somewhere. "You sure about that? We don't have any firm results yet."

"Yes. Full ride. One of the nice things about Marietta is that we get some pretty good players who come because their dads played here, kids who don't need a scholarship, so we have money for our big talent. If Judd is in remission or close to it by September, I want him here. Parkersburg Medical Center is really big now; he'll be close to some top oncologists, and Jerry will be here to watch him. It's close enough to his home, and I need a catcher who can read the opposition." . . . Neeley was silent for a minute. "You tell him; it will give him something to look forward to."

This is the Bill Neeley I remember. . . . "Maybe it would mean more comin' directly from you, Bill."

"Maybe, but I'm not sure I can talk to him about this without breaking down, Ted. Truth is my dad died of prostate cancer too. Dad's, we caught too late. Pete's, we caught early enough, but he had just been through a divorce, and he was too busy chasin' to take the time for treatment. . . . Damn fool! . . . If that kid has enough guts to face the facts and take the treatment, he has my respect. A kid like that deserves a chance, and the fact that he has the makings of a great catcher is just the icing on the cake."

Neeley came up for air. "So how do we do this

without my embarrassing myself?"

"Can you still write?"

"Damn you."

"Well, now, I think a letter would be just the thing, something he could carry around with him, look at when he needs it. You want his address?"

Bill Neeley carefully took down Judd's address. "Ted, it's probably none of my business, but are you okay?"

Ted was quiet for a little too long. "Physically? I think so, no indications otherwise. ... Emotionally might be another story. ... I learned some things last summer. I have some healin' to do after we get Judd squared away, Bill."

Always was the straightest, most honest man I ever knew. "Have you got a plan?"

"Yea, it firmed up today with our talkin' like we used to, not tiptoeing around each other."

Ted ran his hand through his hair. "I've been considering taking a sabbatical next year. I need to get away to where I have the time to clear my head out."

"You mean leave town or just leave the school?"

"Leave town. Otherwise, it wouldn't work. I'd still be doin' most of the same things I'm doin' now; just not teachin'."

"Any idea where you'd go; what you'd do?"

"I've always wanted to fish the western waters, Bill. For years I've promised myself I would before I got too old. I have a contact out in West Yellowstone who offered to let me guide out of his shop after I get my bearings. Pennsylvania allows its teachers a sabbatical with half pay every seven years. So I won't starve. It's just me and the dog."

A smile crossed Neeley's face. "You've always loved to be out somewhere, always needed a little time to yourself." He thought a bit. "Plan to leave right after school is out?"

"No, I'll hang around here until Judd gets settled; probably leave a little after Labor Day."

"Hey, Ted, guess who just walked in. I'm gonna let him talk to you for a while. I'll call you again after I practice up on my writing skills."

Neeley hesitated. "This has meant more to me than

you'll ever know. Guilt eats at a person, even an asshole."

Ted heard muted voices in the background.

Neeley's voice became clear again. "Hey, here's Jerry; see if you can get him to understand that the big wooden stick is supposed to *connect* with the little round ball."

38

On the last Friday in March, Laura seated herself across from Dr. Bratten.

"Laura, I am truly proud of you. Every blood test this month has come back showing a total abstinence from alcohol. I know it's tough, but you are one very strong woman when you set your mind to something!" He smiled, "Congratulations on a perfect record."

"Your plan helps." She shook her head. "I won't say it isn't a bitch, but it *is* possible. Maria cooks only foods that are on the diet for me. She packs me a lunch and snacks. I go to the fitness center every day immediately after school."

She shrugged. "At first, I hated that, but now I sometimes find myself looking forward to it, especially the massage therapy." She glanced at the floor. "I had never had a massage."

She raised her eyes to meet his. "But I absolutely hate going to those damn AA meetings; those people disgust me!"

"How are things going with your new sponsor?"

"Well, at least, I can stand Jim." Laura shook her head. "That Sherry really annoyed me. Every time I talked with her, I wanted to drink."

Dr. Bratten smiled and nodded his head. "Some people just seem to have that effect. I'm sure she tried, and she'll probably be able to help someone, but I am proud of you for stepping up and expressing your dissatisfaction out loud so something could be done immediately."

"You know it's strange, but I'm beginning to like Sherry now that I don't have to answer to her."

"It works that way sometimes. By the way, Jamie tells me Erin is making some progress too."

Laura nodded. "She is. We still have screaming fits with each other, but we always come to some resolution." Laura smiled ruefully, "She wins her share, let me tell you."

"Good. We don't want her to be weak. And we don't

want her to be unable to compromise. It appears things are moving in the right direction on all fronts."

"Maria cooks the same for all of us. Do you think diet may have been part of Erin's problem?"

"Do you believe that, Laura?"

Laura was quiet for a while, then shook her head. "No. I think I was the source of Erin's problems, a lot of them at least."

Tears filled her eyes. "I was only trying to help her. I didn't mean to hurt her or to hold back her progress. I really believed that if I let myself begin to cry, I might never be able to stop, and then where would she be?"

"Jamie tells me she has put Erin on an exercise plan very similar to yours."

"Yes, Erin goes to a different fitness center, one that specializes in youth. She works like a little trooper and takes dance, too. In fact, she's starting the balance beam. She gets a massage twice a week too."

"How about the blood tests, should we drop them to once a week?"

Laura studied her shoes for a long time. Then she raised her head and cleared her throat. "I really think we'd better leave things as they are. I still reach for that 'water' bottle. I wake up in the middle of the night craving a good jolt, especially if I've been dreaming."

She studied her hands. "I suppose it's childish, but sometimes the only thing that keeps me from giving in is the knowledge that I have to go to the damn blood sucker every single day."

She smiled at him. "Like I said, it's a bitch. But it works."

Bratten studied Laura. *Even her skin tone has turned the corner.* "That was a remarkably honest self assessment, Laura Barnsworth McCort."

He observed her for a long time noting the satisfied expression that came across her face. "Let's move into another area, Laura. Last session you were telling me about your freshman year in high school; that was the year you began taking riding lessons wasn't it?"

Laura took a sip of her tea. A full smile broke across her features. "Yes."

"How did that come about? Was one of your parents an equestrian?"

"No, but I had always loved horses. I went to every movie ever released that had a horse in it."

She was silent only for a second. "I read *Black Beauty* when I was a little girl, and I just fell in love with horses then. That's strange because it has some really sad parts in it, but I think I read and re-read that book until it actually fell apart. About that time, dad said, if I would get all A's on my final report card, there might be some money to let me join the local riding club; that meant riding lessons if I would take over the grooming of one horse each day of the summer."

She's becoming re-acquainted with the strong, trusting little girl she once was. I'm sure she likes that little girl; just look at those eyes shine! "So tell me, did you groom the same horse each day?"

"Oh, yes. Mine was Nancy. She was a little buckskin mare that knew way more than I did. And she absolutely loved to be brushed and to be talked to." Laura's smile broadened. "She got so she'd nicker every time I came to the stall area."

"Was she your mount too."

"Oh, yes. She actually taught me to ride. She took such good care of me."

So, she once trusted. "I've never ridden in my life. What is it like to control something that powerful?"

Laura shook her head, "You don't really control a horse. . . . I mean, it's not like a car. . . . The horse and rider . . . they trust each other; it's more like a mutual agreement."

Bratten feigned surprise. "And that works?"

Laura's eyes glowed. "At times, beautifully."

Yes!

39

Good Friday, 2003

The three of them made a fine silhouette against the sunrise from the opposite side of Pine Creek. Ted downstream, Erin upstream, and Max in the middle. The stream was wide here at a nice pool, too wide for Erin to cast to the other side, but the current was such that, if she aimed for the head of the pool and attended to mending her line, the current would bring her fly right to the fish as they sought breakfast.

They had been at it from the minute it was legal. Erin had had three nice hits and had brought two of them to the net.

Ted shook his head in wonder. *Who knows? She just might be the next Joan Wulff. She's gonna be tough; that much is certain.*

The next hit proved what Ted had been thinking: the sun's glare was beginning to bother Erin's eyes a little too much; she missed her chance at that one. *Time to take a little break.*

"Hey, Erin, what say we try our McMuffin and orange juice while the sun gets on up there where it belongs?"

Erin smiled in his direction and began gathering her line. "Is there one for Maxie?"

"You know it. Everyone eats."

"I am hungry." She looked at Ted. "Would it be okay if I go over there in the weeds first?"

"That's why they're here, Erin. . . . Okay if I take a glance before you go in?"

"Sure."

After he had checked the ground for snakes, he took Erin's rod and walked to a downed pine that lay at a comfortable height for their sitting.

He and Max checked the area around it, then he leaned their rods in the fork of a nearby sumac and opened his backpack.

Erin joined him on the pine and immediately started on the juice and sandwich which he handed her.

After she and Max had finished theirs, she scooted down to the ground and sat with her back against the pine. Max moved to her side. Her left arm went over his broad shoulders, and her hand patted his side.

Ted moved down to the ground on Max's other side.

Erin stared off into space; her breathing suggested that she was struggling with something. When she was ready to talk, she turned her worried eyes toward Ted. "Is Judd going to be okay?"

"We don't know yet, Button. He finished his treatments last month. We're all praying." Ted sighed and swallowed hard. "He goes for an evaluation again next Wednesday. We'll have a better idea then."

"Will you tell me if they say he's going to die?"

"Do you want me to?"

"Yes."

"It'll hurt."

"I know, but at least I'll know; it won't be like with my Daddy. . . . I really like Judd; I want him to get better, but I know . . . I know it may not happen; no matter how hard he tries."

"Okay, I'll phone you as soon as his doctor gives us a prognosis."

Erin twisted toward Ted and frowned. "Prog?" She wrinkled her nose. "What's that?"

"A prognosis is a doctor's best opinion about what will happen."

"So he'll tell whether Judd will get better or not?"

It was Ted's turn to stare and think.

Erin waited quietly.

Max feeling the tension sat alert and scanned the area around them, then rooted at Erin's arm which had slipped from his shoulder.

"Well, Erin, the doctor will tell us what he thinks will happen with the disease. But he may not know for sure. Judd's young; he was always healthy, and he's always been a fighter. If we lose Judd, the cancer will have to kill him. He won't quit fighting to live."

"It killed my grandpa Sam." Erin bit her lip, and a tear

spilled onto her cheek.

"I know, Button. I know." Ted reached across Max to rest his forearm on Erin's shoulders. "But he gave it all the fight he could."

Erin didn't look up. "You cryin' too?"

"Yep."

"Aren't you ashamed to cry? You're a big man."

"Big men hurt for those they love too, Erin. I love Judd. . . . I ache inside when I think about the possibility of losing him just like I ache when I think of the loss of your grandpa."

After a while Erin straightened herself, "You know that nice man, David Bloom."

"The reporter?"

"Yes, the one who went to war so we could know what was happening. . . . He died too. . . . And he has little kids. Now they'll have to grow up without their Daddy too; all they'll have is pictures."

"And memories, Erin; don't forget the memories."

They sat in silence for a while. "Is that all it is Ted? Does everyone just die?"

Ted was quiet.

They each drifted into their own memories.

Finally Ted broke the silence. "Sooner or later we all die, Button. But the thing is . . . the thing is to try to make sure you use your life force to make things a little better for the next guy."

After some thought, he continued, "Like your dad taught you to fish and to take care of things and to care about the people around you. And your grandpa Sam . . . well, we wouldn't even have had Max without Sam and Rowdy."

Erin nodded and pulled a handkerchief from her pocket. After she put it back, she turned to him. "Could we go to Miss Sally's for a while. I want to get happy, and that's a good happy kind of place."

Ted smiled and tousled her hat a little. "That's a good idea, I could use some happy time at Miss Sally's too."

"We can still fish some more today though." Erin looked to Ted for reassurance that they would come back to the streams.

"Sure, we have all day, Button, all day."

They gathered their gear and walked slowly toward the SUV.

Max was joyless because they were sad.

Ted was clearly worried about both Judd and Erin.

At times Erin appeared to be carrying the world on her shoulders, but she seemed to have gained some weight.

As they headed for Sally Ann's, Erin turned to look at Ted. "Do you know about mommy?"

Without waiting for an answer, she continued. "She's going to a psychiatrist because she is an alcoholic. He took a blood test to prove it. She passed out at our table on Christmas."

Erin shook her head and turned up her nose to make a face. "What a mess; her face went right into her plate. Maria had to take her to her room and clean her up and put her to bed. Then we ate."

Erin scratched her head. "I think she's being sober right now. She sure is grumpy, and she has to go to triple A meetings each and every day. But I think she's sober. Maria and I watch for the bottles. . . . We watch every day, but we don't tell mommy. Jamie says we have to let mommy be responsible for herself."

In spite of himself, Ted grinned at Erin. "They're AA meetings, Erin, alcoholics anonymous; triple A is for people with car trouble."

"Well, she goes there anyway, and she hates it, and she hates the other people there. She calls them self-pitying, drunken losers. . . . And she goes to see her doctor twice a week, and she hates that. She says he can't see the forest for the trees, . . . but I think she's sober."

She twisted in her seat again to look at Ted. "To tell the truth, mommy was nicer when she was drinking, not nearly so grumpy all the time, just when her head hurt real bad. Now she hates everything and almost everyone."

"I imagine she feels pretty bad most of the time, Erin; it's not easy to get off something once you're addicted."

Erin squinted her eyes at him. "Have you ever been a drunk?"

"No, Erin, I haven't. I guess I'm too much of a control

freak. I don't like it when I can't think straight and the world around me is a little fuzzy."

"Humph. You don't know what a control freak is until you live with mommy. Even my Daddy said she was a control freak."

They rode along a while in silence. Erin broke it. "So you think being a control freak kept you from being a drunk?"

"It helped."

"Then why didn't it stop mommy?"

Ted thought a while.

Erin waited patiently .

"Maybe when a person who likes control gets in a position where there's too much in his life that he can't control, it just gets so he can't stand the tension. So he does something to try to ease the tension, to make the world a little fuzzy for a while."

Ted lowered the sun visor. "Then maybe that gets to be too much of a habit, and the person gets so he's only comfortable with a fuzzy world."

He thought for a while. "Laura doesn't talk much about her feelings, she doesn't seem to enjoy exercise. Either of those things would have helped her cope with the real world, but she didn't do them, so she started doing things that were bad for her. She drank."

He turned to smile at Erin. "But the good news is her doctor seems to have her talking and socializing; he'll probably get her exercising, too."

Erin nodded. "He already has. She has to go to a gym every day where someone makes her sweat and then gives her a massage. That person reports to her doctor. And she has to eat what he tells Maria to cook for her."

Erin turned to look at him. "Jamie put me in a fitness center too. And I get a massage twice a week."

"I thought your were putting your line out a lot further. How do you like the fitness center?"

"Oh, boy, I really like it there, Ted! I stretch out, and then I do weights. Then I dance with other kids, and, now, I'm starting private lessons on the balance beam."

Erin became silent, considering, then she went on. "And I don't have to go have my blood pulled every day like mommy does. ... I heard her tellin' Maria that when we go back home, she has to start taking yogurt classes."

Ted's face broadened to a smile. *So smart for her age and yet unsophisticated.* "Yoga, Erin; not yogurt. She'll learn how to stretch and hold positions which help you relax, not how to make cheese."

They both laughed as they pulled into Sally Ann's. *Did she just set me up for a laugh on her? ...*

They each had a blueberry pancake with a glass of milk and split an order of bacon while Sally Ann visited with Erin.

Ted glanced out the front window and noticed clouds had started rolling in between the mountain tops. "Better get a move on, kid; fish will be looking for food before the water gets muddy."

. . .

They were walking through the sunbeams toward the creek when Ted decided. *She's ready, and I need to do this before I leave.* "Hey, Erin, want to make a bet about who makes the first catch?"

She smiled up at him and wrinkled her nose. "A bet with you?"

He nodded and smiled at her, his eyes dancing with mischief.

"Okay. What do we bet?"

"Well, it has to be something pretty important, something that means a lot to us, but that we're willing to lose." He thought a while. "I could bet a float trip through the gorge."

Erin's eyes danced. "Oh, Ted, really? You'll take me on a float trip? ... Really, truly?"

"Only if you win."

Erin got serious. "Okay. I'll bet ... I could bet one of my Daddy's sweaters. He had some real nice wool ones." She looked carefully at Ted, sizing him as best she could. "I think it would fit okay."

She looked at the toes of her waders for a while, then decided. "I'll bet a sweater."

"You're on, kid. Pick your own spot. I know where I'm goin'." Ted hurried onto a path which would take him to the shallow water just below the good hole. He could watch Erin from there, and she would be bound to find one in the hole. *She'll have to work, but she'll get one.*

Twenty minutes later Erin expertly eased her trout near enough the edge of sand and short grass at the creek's bank that she could lay her rod down to take line in hand and, ever so gently, while keeping the weight of her fish in the water, bring it to her.

"Ted! Ted, come see him; he's a beautiful brown."

40

On Memorial Day, the three friends met early at Ted's for a big breakfast before a trip to Pine Creek.

. . .

The sun was just beginning to cast a glare on the water when Ted noted a red fox making his way home from a morning run.

Jerry nodded. "Time to cash 'er in. Water'll be warm soon."

As he started reeling, Bud glanced toward Ted, reluctance in his eyes, "Damn! This morning was way too short. What say we go back to my place for a sandwich and a beer or two?"

Instead of picking up the oars, Ted folded his hands and let his elbows make a triangle on his knees. "Got time for a little heart-to-heart?"

Bud and Jerry stowed their rods and gave him their attention.

Ted was notorious for keeping things light. He had never talked much about himself except, possibly, to Sam.

Taking their silence for agreement, Ted plowed on; he needed to explain this to someone, someone who knew him well enough to either okay the decision or talk him out of it, someone who cared enough to know what was best: a man, someone who wouldn't get all emotional.

"You guys remember Tim Roberts from '95?"

Bud was the first to respond. "Yea, hell of a catcher. He went to college in Ohio somewhere didn't he?"

"Um hum. Graduated from Miami of Ohio in '99."

Jerry smiled. "I remember him. I was just a kid, but he took the time to help me learn to see the ball." The smile deepened with the memory, "He must have pitched me a million balls that summer after he graduated from high school. He gave me lots of tips; finally talked Willie Ames into pitching to me after I got so I could handle some speed."

Bud drew a long breath. "I haven't thought about Willie in a long time. Now he had an arm. Wasn't he supposed to go to State?"

Ted's hand swatted at a moth. "Yea, but he and Janie decided to get married, and he joined the Marines."

Bud looked down and spit into the creek. "What a damn waste! He died at boot camp. Cardiac arrest they said. . . . Why didn't he just go to State?"

Both Jerry and Bud looked at Ted who left the question hanging in the air.

"Well, dammit, I'm sure you know if anyone does. Why didn't he just go to State instead of rushing off to the swamps in the middle of summer?"

Ted arched his back and straightened on his seat. His hand made a couple of passes across his chin. "He did what he thought was best." *A kid discovers his girl is pregnant; he takes a job. Janie stayed somewhere in the South after the accident. Miscarried, finally remarried; never told. I'll be damned if I ever do.*

Ted shifted his shoulders. "In a strange way, that story leads into what I want to talk about. I've been thinking about making some changes in my own life."

"What kind of changes, Coach?" Jerry asked.

"I'm thinking seriously about taking a sabbatical."

The silence was as thick as early morning fog.

Ted continued. "Tim got his masters this year. He taught for a couple of years in Ohio and worked on it part-time; then he took a year off and finished up this spring. He's hunting a position for a year or two, then he'll go on for his doctorate." Ted smiled, "Wants to teach and coach at the college level."

"It's a damn good thing the Internet is free. I don't know how in the hell you have time to teach and coach and keep up with all of these kids and their dreams." Bud spit again. "When do you find any time to just think? That's what I want to know."

Jerry fished an orange juice out of the cooler. "Anyone else?" He closed the cooler and took a swallow. "One thing for sure, Tim will make a good teacher."

Ted grinned as he pulled the cooler toward himself.

"He was assistant coach at the high school in Ohio. They liked him enough that they kept him even during his year off. Would have advanced him, but the head coach wasn't going anywhere."

He swallowed some juice. "So I'm thinking he'd make a great replacement for me during my sabbatical. He'd get a year or two as a head coach. He'd be great in my classes. His major is the same as mine."

Changing now to a more convincing mode, he continued, "If I decide to come back, he's planning on leaving in a year anyway, so the transition should be smooth for both of us. Our coaching methods are similar; the team won't suffer any. . . . He's had experience. . . . He grew up here, so he knows how things are done."

Ted looked at Bud. "I'd like to tell him he could count on you, Bud."

"What the hell? A minute ago you were only thinking about this sabbatical. Now you're recruiting for him."

He pulled the cooler over to himself. "Sounds to me like this is way beyond the thinking-about-it stage."

He looked up from the cooler into Ted's eyes as he drew out a water. "Sure, I'd help him anyway I could, but just how set on this are you?"

"It's pretty much a done deal." He held up his hand. "I haven't told Sally Ann yet." He took a breath, "Or anyone else except Jim Pierson." He paused. "And, of course, Tim."

Bud chugged the water. "What the hell brought this on? This is about as out-of-the-blue as Willie was." He caught himself and gave a crooked smile. "You joinin' the Marines, too?"

"No. . . . I plan on hunting pheasants in the Dakotas this fall, then elk in Wyoming, and fishing the streams north of the Yellowstone in the spring. I have some part-time jobs lined up: Cabellas in Dakota and a guide shop in West Yellowstone, and I'll get half-pay during my sabbatical. Tim will stay at my place and take care of it."

He raised his juice bottle in Bud's direction and winked, "And I'll get some of that time to think you were so concerned about."

Bud shook his head and rubbed his thighs. "Well, I'll

be damned. . . . The rest of this discussion is gonna require more than orange juice and water. Let's get this thing behind the truck. I have fresh lunch meat and beer at the house."

. . .

The men rode in silence. Each was savoring his favorite part of the morning drift, storing it in that special memory place one goes to in times of need.

. . .

After potato salad and a couple of baked ham sandwiches, the easy banter began.

Bud looked at Jerry. "You're a bat; do you believe that shit about Sosa?"

Jerry shook his head. "No, sir. That bat just broke." He downed some water. "That or someone set him up. He doesn't need cork to knock one over the fence." He looked to Ted.

"I'm with you, Jerry. Besides Sosa has too much to lose. He's practically the king of Chicago. And he has plenty of power. Control might be a little off sometimes, but he sure doesn't need cork."

They were silent, each remembering Sosa hits that had made an imprint on their minds, paying a silent homage to a guy who had come a long way and was noted for giving a lot back.

Bud leaned forward and looked at Ted. "Think Rose will ever make it into the Hall?"

"I doubt it."

"Should he, Coach?" Jerry asked.

"Morals are hard to call, Jerry. There's lots of opinions. . . . Rose sure enough has a record on the field that entitles him. . . . Maybe the best thing would be to put him in the hall with a footnote about why it took so long: what the debate was, how long the discussion raged. Lot of kids might learn something from that."

Bud nodded in agreement. "That seems about right." He looked at his hands. "Speaking of kids. What's the latest on Judd. I haven't seen anyone recently."

Ted opened another water. "Man I'm dry." He patted his waist. "Out of shape. . . . They went on vacation after graduation. Down to Myrtle Beach. He's probably back by now."

"Let's hope so, I'd sure hate to fight that traffic all the way home tonight." Bud paused. "So how is he?"

"Doctor says he's looking good. Liver functions are normal. He's gaining weight and strength. The beach probably helped his appetite and exercise." Ted paused and looked at Bud and then at Jerry. "My money's on Judd."

Jerry stood and stretched then sat again. "Coach Neeley offered him a full ride to come play at Marietta. I hope he decides to come."

Jerry glanced at Ted. "Neeley's no Weaver, but he's a decent coach. It'd be good for Judd to get away a little; his parents need that too."

Bud nodded. "So what made you come up with this wild-ass decision about a sabbatical, Ted. I always figured we'd have to drag you off the field."

"Think you could do it, Bud?" Ted raised his fists in boxer formation.

"Really, Coach. What's up?" Jerry asked.

Ted took another long pull, sat his bottle between his feet, and scratched his right arm. "When we went to Marietta last summer, I realized I'd been keeping busy on purpose, in order to ignore some of my past."

He glanced at Bud, "I have my ghosts too."

. . .

"I need to get away, to spend some lonesome time: hunting, fishing, walking Max down some new trails in places where I don't have friends for ready diversions."

He turned back. "I'll be okay; I pretty much know who I am inside. I'll take my laptop, keep in touch, that sort of thing, but, mainly, I just need to sweat this thing through."

He picked up the bottle and took it to the trash barrel. "For the record, I plan to come back next summer. I'm not so sure about teaching or coaching."

A crooked grin settled on his handsome face, and his eyes began to twinkle. "I might just send you a resume in the spring, interview for a construction job."

Bud walked over and extended his right hand as his left found Ted's shoulder. "Anytime, buddy; full or part-time with guiding privileges. Anytime at all."

. . .

That evening the phone rang at 9:30.

"Weaver."

"Bud Johnson, Ted. How's about I swing by and we go watch the fireworks?"

"You're on."

41

Sally Ann was in high form as she sat across the table from Ted. "You promised her what?"

She glared at him. "What's wrong with you? I swear sometimes I think men are just plain mindless! ... It's dangerous; you know it is. You'll show her how much fun it is, and then you're going off to leave her."

She shook her head. "Not that I don't think you deserve your sabbatical, but, Ted, honestly, this just reminds me of you and Sam dragging little Max out hunting."

She stood, placing her hands on her rounded hips, and pushed her chain under the table with her foot as she turned away. "Honestly!" She snorted, then turned back deciding to sit down again and straighten him out once and for all.

He's one of the best men I've known, but sometimes. . .

Her eyes snapped. "Well, say something. Surely there must have been some feeble sort of reasoning behind this, some fiddle faddle, that made you dream this up."

"Sally Ann, I swear, I love you. If we were the marrying kind, I'd have been on bended knee long before this."

He gave her his most charming smile. "But you shouldn't try to direct plays when you don't understand the game."

Sally Ann sat straight, folded her arms across her chest, and gave him her full attention. *Don't try to charm your way out of this one, Teddy. This old gal has seen it all before.*

Ted leaned forward, putting his forearms on the table. "Sam and I did not hurt Max. We made him!"

He gave her a few seconds to consider this, then continued. "And I am doing this for the same reason."

"You see, for a retriever to be of any account, he has to have two somewhat conflicting qualities: he has to take direction, but he also has to develop judgment, so he'll know when to disobey in order to save himself. Well, Erin has to have the opportunity to develop judgment about new experiences too."

Ted shook his head. *How in the hell? . . .*

He thought for a moment. "Picture this: Max and I are in a blind, and I shoot a duck. I send Max after it. He's been trained to take the most direct route. He hits the water. The decoys have drifted around a little, and his forepaw touches a line."

Ted stopped and looked at Sally Ann who was leaning forward now, worried about Max, even in a fabricated example. "So he has to know to disobey, to give up the straight route, to backpedal like hell, and get away from the lines."

He paused and looked at her. If he doesn't do that, he can quickly and easily become so entangled that he panics. That will drown him!"

Ted, seeing the tension, smiled. "So he does backpedal, turn in the water and look to me for hand directions. I direct him around the decoys, and he completes his job."

He stared at her and leaned forward a bit more. "Because that *is* his job, Sally Ann. His second purpose in life is to do what is asked of him. His first is to stay alive, to be available."

"Most good retrievers have an inborn fear of being entangled; it's a genetic thing. But, if they aren't started carefully, they become so eager to please, that they'll quit thinking and become nearly automatic obeyers."

He continued, his voice indicating just how deeply the man felt about this issue. "It's the same with kids, Sally Ann. I don't want my students to parrot what I say to them. On tests, I want them to show me that they use the facts to form their own opinions."

"I don't want my team to follow my directions to the letter. God gave each of us a mind. If they see something that I don't, I want them to act on it. They know the game, and the stakes, as well as I do."

"I want Max to know when to ignore me in order to avoid danger, and I, sure as hell, want Erin to know that a drift can be, and usually is, somewhat dangerous."

He paused. "The danger can be easily handled, but it cannot be ignored. No one can go through life just thinking everything will work out. A successful life requires objectivity."

Ted caught himself and settled down some. . . . *Need a*

pulpit there, Teddy?

"I'm sorry. . . . You know Jerry's little brother, Matt has a crush on Erin. And Matt is just at the age where he *knows* he's totally invulnerable. If he thought for a minute that taking her on a drift would impress her, he'd figure a way to get a boat."

"Erin is not foolish when she understands the facts. I want her to know what to be wary of."

He sighed and looked at his hands. His eyes glistened. He drew a breath, "And the only way I know to teach her is by showing her, Sally Ann. Erin trusts what she has seen with her own eyes. She trusts my opinion, but her love of fishing will make her want to trust Matt's assurances."

He looked into Sally Ann's blue eyes. "I am not doing this lightly; God knows I'll be careful, but it's my duty to teach her about the dangers as well as the joys of fishing."

Sally Ann relaxed her arms and leaned forward. "Well, when you put it that way; I guess it might make some sense."

She raised one eyebrow in a questioning manner and looked at him. "What are you going to do about Laura?"

"Well, I didn't lie to her. I told her Erin had won a float trip from me, and that we were planning it for early June. She agreed since they'll be coming down in June after school's out."

He looked at Sally Ann. "Now I didn't tell the whole truth. I didn't tell her that a drift can be dangerous. I'll make sure she understands after Erin has a chance to learn, first hand, what precautions must be taken to keep it safe."

He reached for Sally Ann's hand. "Erin's a smart little girl, and she understands and remembers; she's in no hurry to get hurt and cause Laura more trauma."

Sally Ann extracted her hand and rose from her chair. "I could use another cup of coffee. How about you?"

"Sounds good."

She returned with a tray holding two coffees and two servings of her famous blueberry crumb cake.

Sally Ann waited until she had settled herself across from Ted. "Well, I guess I understand now."

She took a bite of her dessert and a sip of coffee. "Ted, I'm sorry. You were right; I do wade in unfamiliar waters from time to time, always have."

Seeing his raised eyebrow at her phraseology, she smiled and nodded. "You're right: straight from Sam," She glanced at her cake, "when he explained to me about Max and the mallard."

She shook her head and reached across the table to pat Ted's hand. "He was quite a man, and so are you, fella, so don't be gettin' on one knee unless you mean business."

Ted took a big bite of the crumb cake, leaned back, and smiled. "Since Jerry drove Judd and his parents down to Marietta to take a look, will you do it?"

"Yes. I'll come pick you two up down at the lower launch." She shook her head. "Can't get in the way of education."

She grinned at him; then frowned. "Now that we're clearing the air a little this morning, I just want to say I'm more than a little surprised about the sabbatical."

"I'll miss you, Sally Ann. But I'll be as close as the latest e-mail." He shifted in his seat. "And remember planes fly both ways; I can get here in a hurry."

"I'll miss you too, Ted; but that's not what I mean." She struggled to get it just right, not be too invasive. *A big part of Ted is completely private.*

"I guess I 'd let an old woman's imagination run a little wild." She ran her index finger around the rim of her cup and stared into it. "I thought I'd seen a closeness developing between you and Laura." . . . She looked up. "Maybe I even imagined love, marriage, a family of your own. You deserve one you know. . . . You need one; everyone does."

Her eyes searched his face. "And you can't deny that you love that little girl like she's your own."

Ted took a breath and looked into her eyes. "This is just between us?"

"If that's the way you want it, yes."

"That might have been, but I discovered last summer that I'm not completely over Lindy, and I'm sure not over Teddy."

"I may never marry again, but, if I do, . . . I want to be sure that my wife is the only woman I think about. . . . I've tried to help because of Sam and because they both need help, but

I've always kept some distance too."

Sally Ann gave Ted an encouraging nod, hoping that he might continue.

It worked. "Love is a funny thing. I'm not sure exactly what it is, but I'm certain it's not dependence, convenience, or plan B."

He looked around the room. "This is awkward because . . . because I've never really thought it through to put it into words." He sighed. "It's really just a gut feeling."

There was a long silence which Sally Ann refused to break.

"But I sure don't want either Laura or Erin to mistake something else for love. They deserve better than someone's taking advantage of a situation."

Sally Ann patted his hand again, then looked into her coffee for a while. "I think Sam wanted them with you, even allowed himself to hope the three of you would end up together. Lord knows he thought the world of you."

She paused to let this sink in, then went on, "I've thought that ever since the will with all of its convoluted stipulations: "Wait two years to sell the house; work there together." She raised an eyebrow, "Know what I mean? That wasn't like Sam. . . . Decide, then get on with it; that was Sam's way."

He smiled. "Yea." He fidgeted. "And I do honor Sam."

Ted looked up, glanced toward the door. "But no one can choose for someone else. At least no one should."

He rubbed his chin and bought some time with long breaths. "The best choosin' is done from a position of strength, not need. It's why I try to get my kids good enough that they can choose their way in life, get 'em to a place where they *know* they can make it."

Sally Ann got up and took their cups to the coffee pot. She sat a fresh cup of coffee in front of him.

His eyes, fighting tears, smiled love at her. "Lord, I am going to miss you. . . . But I want Laura and Erin to learn that they can live perfectly well without my presence. They need to get a look at Wellsboro through their own eyes, know that lots of people here will support them."

Ted's hand reached across to take hers. "And I need to figure out what role my past is going to play in my life: Have I said good-bye to my past? Do I even want to?"

He tried the coffee. "I'll be back next year, and we'll see how things go then."

"You're taking a big chance, Ted. She's a beauty, and her problems make her vulnerable. . . .Some men have a way of smelling money and can turn on plenty of charm."

He raised his eyes. "Sam's blood runs in those veins. Laura's no fool. . . . I trust things will go along the way the Man Upstairs wants."

He patted her hand. "Meanwhile if *you* need me, phone. Oh, and keep Christmas open." He pulled an envelope from his breast pocket and shoved it toward her. "It's my turn to cook Christmas."

Sally Ann opened the envelope. Inside were round-trip tickets to Jackson, Wyoming.

"I expect you in on the 20th and out on the 5th. No sense fighting the last minute rush. Max and I will be at the airport."

"Ted?"

His eyes took on a sheen again as he gazed at her. "Sally Ann?" . . . He swallowed, "I'd sure appreciate it."

"Well, then, I'll just be there."

She fussed with the envelope. "I never knew you could get tickets this early."

She smiled. "I'll consider this as payment for my carting you and Erin back home from the drift.

Ted smiled and rose from his chair.

42

Ted swung the Suburban into Sam's drive.

Erin was waiting at the door and was out it before he had come to a complete stop.

She ran to the SUV and pulled the door open. "Oh, Ted, I'm so glad to see you; it's been two whole months since we fished!" She hesitated. "Are you all tired from baseball and everything? Would you rather just rest today?"

"No, Erin, I've been looking forward to this. It will give me a chance to rest my brain a little. We've been playing hard, and that's kept all of us busy."

"But you won the league, even without Judd." Erin's expression became concerned as she studied Ted's face. "How is Judd? Is he still in remission?"

Ted smiled. "He's holding steady right now, Erin. Dr. Shonk is very pleased with his condition. It looks like he'll be able to go to college this fall."

She heaved a sigh. "I am so glad. He sure looked sick in April when I saw him."

"Well, he appreciated your visit. He told me it was the most fun he had had in a long time. He said you never once asked him how he felt or how he was doing; you just visited."

Ted looked at her. "That was a smart thing to do, Erin. He needed a break from the pressure to get well."

"I just know I get tired of people asking me how I'm doing. I figured he would too. Sometimes you just want . . . just want; . . . oh, I don't know how to tell it; . . . you just want to *be,* not to have people trying to figure out how you feel and makin' you think about it."

She looked at him as she was petting Max whose door she had also opened. "You know what I mean?"

"I do, Erin; it's called 'living in the present.' It means not forgetting the past, but not dwelling on it all of the time: paying a lot of attention to right now: a little to the past, a little to the future, but most to right now. It's a healthy way to live. They taught Judd that in his counseling sessions."

She closed Max's door and climbed into the front seat beside Ted. "So, are we really going to float today?"

"See that boat back there?"

"Yep." The smile went all across her face.

"The gorge is in perfect condition, and I'm going to show you one of my favorite ways to fish it."

"How will we get back?"

"Sally Ann has promised to come to the boat launch below town when I call her. She'll bring us the truck and trailer."

He grinned in her direction. "We'll spend half of the day on the water and half of it on the road, but it'll be worth it."

Ted scratched his ear. "Did you put on two coats of sunscreen like I told you?"

"Yep." She reached into her pants pocket. "I brought some extra too, and some lip balm, just in case."

"Well, I have our cooler and our vests. Max is going to ride with us, so I brought a sandwich for him too."

Ted pulled into the launch area for the float. He backed the boat up to the edge of the ramp. "Get out and put your vest on. Take Max and go pee if you need to."

Erin and Max went to the weeds near the ramp.

. . .

The boat tipped a little as Ted stepped in.

Erin giggled.

Max thumped his tail.

Ted untied the stern line and moved to the bow where he pulled the anchor. He came to the middle seat and took the oars grinning over his shoulder at Erin. "Mademoiselle, zee trip has begun."

"Yea."

. . .

Around 10, Ted maneuvered the boat toward a spot where a big willow tree hung over the creek. He brought them right up under the soft branches until the bow dug into the sandy bank. He dropped the anchor, put Max at ease, and helped Erin off the boat.

"Let's take us a little break, drink some juice, and stretch our legs a little."

He led them to a nice big rock where they could sit in the shade of the tree and handed Erin an orange juice and an oatmeal power bar.

Max received a Milk Bone.

Ted opened a juice for himself. "Well, what do you think about floating?"

Erin rolled her eyes, "Oh, Ted, it's the best." She was quiet for a while as she fingered her vest. "Wonder if my Daddy ever did this?"

"I'd bet on it, Erin. Nearly all fly fishermen try it either in a boat or with a personal flotation device."

"Is it your favorite way?"

"No."

"Really?"

"My favorite has always been walkin' the banks."

He looked at her. "I enjoy a float, especially if I need it to get to a place that's rough to get to on foot, but, given the choice, I'll walk if I can."

He looked off and smiled to himself. "I'll probably float more when I get older." Ted grinned at Erin, "Too stiff to walk."

"Boy, you really got to be careful when you float, huh?"

"You bet! Erin, I want you to promise me right now that you won't try any floats without me, not 'til you're a big girl in high school."

"Okay. I promise."

"Now I mean it, Erin; this is an important promise."

"Okay. I promise, and I do not break promises. My Daddy said that was wrong. I won't float without you until I am a big girl in high school."

"Well, that's really important because I'm going on a long vacation at the end of the summer."

"Where?"

"Out West. I want to go see Yellowstone and fish the western water."

"But you'll be back when school starts?"

"No." His thumb went up to rub the corner of his mouth. "I plan to stay the winter out there. Maybe take some classes at Montana State in Bozeman."

He smiled at her. "I want to fish the spring hatches and come back next summer."

He checked her for tears and was relieved to find none. "I've been pushin' myself really hard for a few years; Max and I need some time off to think things through and decide what we want to do with the rest of our lives."

"So, you're taking Maxie with you?"

"Oh, yea." He patted Max's shoulder. "Can't leave my partner at home."

"But you are coming back? For sure?"

He reached over and gently pulled one pigtail. "Oh, yea!" "I'm not selling the house or anything like that. The guy who's going to take both of my positions next year was one of my students. He plans to stay here only one year to save some money and rest up for graduate school, so he's taking a lease on my house. I'll be back next year for July 4th in Wellsboro."

Erin chewed thoughtfully on her oat bar. She was quiet for some time. . . .

She glanced sideways at Ted. "Will you take your cell phone with you?"

"You bet. And I plan to call you each and every Sunday evening. You figure out a good time, and I'll call. I want to know what you're doing with your life, Erin."

"So you'll call and talk with me every Sunday?"

"Yep."

Erin was silent. . . . She turned and smiled at him. "Well, I'm gonna miss you when mommy and I come down here, but if we talk every Sunday, that's more than we do now, so, in a way, we'll be better friends."

Ted shook his head in admiration. "That's the way I figure it, Erin. Oh, and there's a special favor I want to ask you."

"A favor from me to you?"

Ted's face became serious. "Yes, there's something at the house I want you to keep for me, something that I don't want to just leave there, and I can't risk losing it in travel."

Erin smiled. "Okay; I'm a good keeper."

"It's a box my dad made for me out of a tree that grew in our backyard when I was a kid. Our tree got blown down in a big storm. My dad had a lot of the trunk cut up into boards. He made my mom a nice, big, storage trunk and a pretty little jewelry chest. He made me a little treasure chest to keep my special stuff in."

Ted looked at Erin. "I'd like you to keep my treasure chest for me. It has some of Max's baby teeth in it, and my wedding band, some pictures, things like that. Nothing expensive; just things that are priceless."

He looked at her. "I think you know the value of the things I keep in there."

"Yes. . . . I keep stuff in my closet, my Daddy's stuff that mommy was going to throw away." . . .

Erin finished her juice and turned to Ted. "But I carried my Daddy's things into my room. I kept my Daddy's important stuff, and I put it in my closet, . . . and I locked it, and I hid the key!"

"Good for you. I knew we had a lot in common the first time I laid eyes on you."

She beamed up at him.

"Oh, and, Erin, I haven't told any other females but Sally Ann yet, so please don't tell my story for me. Wait until I have a chance to tell people in my own time."

She smacked her lips together and drew her index finger across them. "My lips are sealed."

She smiled at him again. "I'm proud you told me. I can keep secrets! And no one but you will ever look in your box."

She shook her head sideways. "Not while I have it. I'll put it right in there with my Daddy's things until you come back."

Ted stood and stretched; Erin copied his movements. They walked to the boat where Max loaded first, then Erin, followed by Ted, who cast them off.

43

Monday, August 18, 2003, Wellsboro, PA.

The heat had found its way to the mountains.

Ted's phone was ringing as he came through the door after cleaning out his office at school. "Weaver here."

Sally Ann's voice was an octave too high. "Ted. Oh, Ted. Oh, thank the good Lord I've caught you."

"Sally Ann, are you okay?"

"I am, but our Erin's not."

"Erin?"

"Yes, if you didn't live in a stream, you might find time to watch the news."

"News?" Ted paused as he leaned against the door frame. "Slow down, Sally Ann; I can't follow you. Take a breath and tell me about Erin."

"She's been kidnapped."

"Kidnapped? When? How do you know?"

"It's one of those new amber alerts; there hasn't been enough time, but Laura's trying to get one put out on Erin. She has been able to get it on the news. . . . Laura came home from school: she had been in to work on her room, and Erin was gone. Laura immediately requested an amber alert, but a period of time has to pass before that can be issued. Who knows what all could happen in the meantime?"

"I'll call Laura. I'll fill you in as soon as I talk with her. Thanks, Sally Ann." Ted hung up the phone and located Laura's number.

44

Laura was standing looking at the door of the still-furnished liquor cabinet.

Dear God, I have to stay strong for Erin; I beg you to help me stay sober.

She grabbed the phone on the second ring. Her voice was shrill, "McCorts."

"Laura."

"Oh, thank God. ... Ted ... Ted." ... The only sound was that of Laura's sobbing as her control vanished at the sound of his voice.

Ted gave her time to collect herself. "Laura, Sally Ann just phoned me about Erin. What can you tell me?"

Laura began sobbing again into the phone. There was a long pause as Laura fought to regain some control. Finally she said, "She's gone. ... Gone. ... Everyone's gone."

"Laura, I'm leaving right away. I'll be there sometime after midnight."

"I'll be up whatever time it is. Bring Max with you."

"We're on our way."

Ted hesitated but then went on with what had to be said. "Laura, I need you sober when I get there. Call your doctor if you haven't already. He'd want to be there. That's what you pay him for."

"Maria has, Ted. He's on his way here. I'm still okay, but it's not easy."

"I know." He sorted through his brain. "Laura, try to find something to do until he gets there. Anything. Hell, run the vacuum. Do something physical. It sounds simple, but it'll help; I promise. I'll be there as soon as I can."

45

Ted quickly gathered some things from his closet: a couple of changes of clothes, a shave kit, Max's food. "Come on, Max."

They were in the Suburban, and Ted was dialing Sally Ann on his cell phone within ten minutes.

"Sally Ann's."

"I don't know much, Sally Ann. Laura is convinced Erin has been kidnapped. I'm loaded to head for Danbury right now. I'll call as soon as I know anything. Meanwhile, if any news breaks, call me on the cell."

"Of course I will. And I'll run down and get Max."

"No, Laura told me to bring him. It was a good idea. When we get her back, Max will help settle her."

"Of course. Ted," Sally Ann paused remembering a horrible accident. "Ted, be careful."

"I will."

"Ted, did you have appointments or anything?"

"Damn."

"I'll go to your place. Do you still keep your appointment book on your desk with your address book?"

"I sure do."

"I'll take care of everything here; you take care of yourself, now."

"You're a Godsend, Sally Ann. Bye for now."

Ted put the cell phone on the seat beside him and started the Suburban. He glanced to the rear. "Sit tight Max; we're gonna push 'er a little where we can."

46

Seconds before his foot touched the accelerator, it hit him. *Had she checked?* He grabbed the cell, and punched Laura's number.

"McCort's."

"Laura, it's Ted again. We're in the truck ready to leave." He paused. "Laura, I wonder if you would do something for me."

"Anything."

"Go into Erin's room. Go right now while I'm talkin' to you."

"Why?"

"Please, Laura; I want you to look for something for me."

"What am I to look for?"

"I'm not sure. I want you to look around in there. Look carefully. See if anything is out of place or missing."

"No one broke in here and took her. This home has all kinds of security, and Maria has been right here except for a few minutes when she went for some fresh fruit. Erin must have stepped out on the lawn."

"Laura, please, just go into Erin's room and look."

"What is the point of this? No one broke in here, and, even if someone had, there's no note. We looked."

"Look in her closet."

"She keeps it locked." Laura tried the closet door anyway. "It's locked."

"Anything gone from her room?"

"Nothing I can see."

"Where could she get money? Did you check your purse?"

"She wouldn't steal from me!"

"Think, Laura, if Erin had to have money where could she get some?"

"Maria. But Maria didn't give her money; she would have told me."

"There must be some somewhere."

"Well, she has a bank that Nick gave her. He always gave her bonus money when she did something special."

"Is the bank still there? Is it broken?"

"No, Ted, her bank can't be broken; it's copper. Everything is just as it always is. ... If only they'd left a note, I'll pay them anything!"

47

Nick had always encouraged his only daughter to take preparation seriously.

"Preparation is the key to performance, honey. . . . Clean and take care of your gear, and it won't fail you when you need it. . . . Do your assignments carefully, Erin; then you'll be able to keep up with your teacher's thoughts. . . . Always try to think things through before you act."

. . .

At the beginning of summer vacation, Laura and Maria had agreed with both Jamie and Dr. Bratten that Erin might respond well to added independence and responsibility.

They had begun this year's summer vacation by leaving Erin on her own for a few hours at a time each day, even completely alone in the house while Maria ran short errands.

. . .

On Monday, August 18, 2003, Laura had begun two weeks of at-school preparation prior to the opening of school on Sept. 2.

Since Erin was now nearly nine and would be entering an accelerated fourth grade program at her school, she was to be on her own at home during the day; Maria would be there of course, but Maria was not to "baby-sit" Erin.

. . .

Following her Daddy's advice, Erin had thought a lot: Mommy liked big cities. She loved to go to the plays and the galleries and museums. She loved their spacious condominium in the City   She only *liked* their home in Connecticut.

There was little doubt in Erin's mind that she and mommy would move to the City when mommy thought she was old enough.

They had kept the large condominium after her Daddy's death and had continued to go to New York on many weekends and sometimes for an entire week during the summer vacations.

In fact they had just returned from a week in the City on Saturday.

Thursday and Friday had been a nightmare for Erin. The big blackout had started at 4 on Thursday.

Mommy had said it wouldn't last long and it was best for them to stick it out.

Their building had had backup generators to run the elevators and to keep lights on, but the air conditioners could run continuously only from midnight to 6 a.m. Friday morning it was back to running the elevators and lights, but there was not much air conditioning.

Still mommy had said they were much better off than most people around them; they should learn to control themselves and be thankful it hadn't been another terrorist attack.

Finally on Saturday morning, they had packed it in and driven home to Connecticut.

. . .

Erin had thought all of the way home while her mother listened to Mozart.

Her things were ready in her closet.

She remembered the night on which she had moved her Daddy's gear in with her things.

She had gradually sorted through everything, putting special things on one side of her closet and the rest in the rear of the big walk-in.

She was ready! She had been ready since September of last year when everyone was wondering whether the bad guys would try something on the anniversary of the attack.

She had hated attending the Memorial Ceremonies that mommy had forced on her last year.

She's gonna try to make me go again this year.

Erin reviewed last year's arguments: *"We need to finalize this once and for all, Erin. That is what these ceremonies will do. It will finally be over, and we can get on with our lives."*

Erin didn't need a simple ceremony to remember her Daddy; she had no intention of ever forgetting him.

. . .

Mommy had said ceremonies showed respect.

Erin's eyes tightened at the thought.

She didn't need to put a cut flower on a fence to show respect to her Daddy.

She showed respect by keeping Daddy's things safe from the trash and remembering their special times together.

She had collected all of her memories in her brain where they would stay as long as she lived.

Respect! Unconsciously, she squared her little shoulders against the Land Rover's seat. *Respect was remembering, not forgetting!*

Each night, after she had said her prayers, she told her Daddy about her day: the things she had done and the things she had seen that he would have enjoyed. She told him about the geese landing on the lake in the fog, the bird's nest that she had brought to her room after she had found it beside the holly tree, and the big black dog who had retrieved for her.

Then, she played one of her memories through her mind, seeing and hearing each detail. Then, and only then, she went to sleep.

. . .

So now, they had had breakfast, and mommy had gone to school to get projects ready for the art classes.

Now Erin began to work her plan.

First she went to her desk.

. . .

Her Daddy had always put money in a real bank account which he had opened for her when she had started school. He had taken her to the bank and had opened an account just in her name, and he would take her in and let her deposit her "bonus" money which he gave her after special accomplishments.

Mommy had thought it was crazy to trust a little girl with a bank deposit book, but Daddy had said that it was Erin's money and that she had sense enough to be responsible. *"How can she learn to be responsible if we don't trust her? We have to trust her, honey, so she will know to trust herself."*

. . .

She put the account book in her backpack.

Now she went to her copper piggy bank which Daddy

had bought her.

Does mommy even know it's a bank?

. . .

"That thing doesn't do much for her decor."

"Laura, honey, pigs are a good luck symbol to the Irish."

Daddy had fed *mad money* to Erin's piggy. *"Do you know why we call it mad money, Erin?"*

"No, Daddy."

"'Cause it's money no one else can get mad about. It is yours, in secret, to spend as you please, when you please."

He had winked at her. *"But now here's the thing that makes Mr. Pig really special. See his snout?"*

"Snout?"

"Um hum, that's what we call his nose. Now this is what makes this bank really great, Erin. First look in his ear."

"See how there are little knobs in his ears? Well, when you push on the knob in his left ear, it moves a little." Daddy had pushed on the little knob. *"See?"*

"Now hold him in your arm and twist really hard on his snout. Twist hard."

"Look at that. See, it twists off. That way you can get to your mad money when you want to."

Erin had looked at Daddy and had laughed with delight. She had tried to get her little hand in the pig's snout.

"No, no, sweetheart, not like that. Like this. Hold your pig with his tail up. Now shake him."

Erin had heard a faint metal-against-metal sound.

"Keep shaking."

The long brass tweezers had fallen out the pig's snout.

"These are tweezers. Hold them like this, and you can use them to pull money out of your piggy's tummy."

"See? That's why I always fold each bill before I feed him; so you can get them with the tweezers."

"Now put the tweezers back in Mr. Pig's belly so no one suspects and screw his snout back in place."

Erin had followed her Daddy's instructions.

"Look closely. His ear buttons look just like each other again."

Erin had checked the pig's ears, and, sure enough, they had been identical.

"Now you try it all by yourself." Erin had succeeded on the first try and had also been able to reinstate her bank. . . . *"That's my girl!"*

She had known that she never needed money from Mr. Pig. If Erin needed something, she just asked Daddy or mommy or Maria. But she had remembered how to get to it.

After the towers, Erin had pushed the button in the pig's ear for the second time in her life.

She had taken all of the money out of the pig's belly and had counted it. She had been starting second grade and had been able to add and subtract by September 11.

Erin hadn't had a good concept of amounts of money, but she had known that a little over a thousand dollars was a lot for a kid.

She had put the money back. She had reinstated her bank, and had kept her secret.

. . .

On the morning of Monday, August 18, 2003, Erin pushed the button in the pig's ear for the third time in her life.

I can't stand it here any longer!

She extracted the folded bills from the pig's belly, flattened them, laid 30 twenty-dollar bills on her bed, and placed the rest of the money in the bottom of her backpack. She reinstated her bank. Then, Erin refolded each of the twenties and placed them one-by-one in her jeans pockets.

I heard Maria leave for the grocery.

She called the cab company that Laura had always used to get Erin to her counseling sessions. She asked if Mr. Sam was on duty. He was. She asked that he come by to pick her up.

She pulled on her new navy backpack, and picked up her small suitcase and her little rod case.

She locked her closet and put the key on her backpack's key holder with her house key and a third key that she had taken from her Daddy's things.

She went downstairs to wait.

. . .

"Hey, kiddo, you usually go on Tuesday afternoons, don't you?"

Erin did something she could not remember having done in her life: she lied.

"Yes, Sam, but with school starting in a couple of weeks Mrs. Simpson thought we should have a special session."

Please don't be mad, Daddy; this is my only way. I'll lie today, but I won't be a liar after this, I promise; I'll repent.

Sam laughed as he put Erin's rod case and her small suitcase in the trunk. "Looks like you're movin' out."

Erin forced a giggle. "She wanted me to bring some stuff, stuff that she thinks will make me talk more. You know, stuff to help me remember more so I get better."

"Yea, well, I think you're mighty fine just as you are, kiddo. I bet you'll be glad when you don't need to go there anymore."

Erin released a sigh, "I sure will."

. . .

"Here we are. I'll get your things." Sam smiled at Erin in the cab's mirror. "Want me to carry 'em to her office for you?"

"No, thanks, Mr. Sam." Erin smiled back at him. "I can get it; I'm supposed to be responsible."

Erin paused and bit her lip a little. "But, Mr. Sam, thanks a lot. You sure have been good to me."

Sam tipped his Yankee's cap. "My pleasure, little lady. You have Doc call and ask for me when you get released." He gave her a wink.

"Mommy went in to school today, Sam, so she'll be picking me up for lunch. Remember to put this extra trip on our tab."

Sam nodded and smiled at the pretty little girl as she gathered her belongings and walked toward the office building. *Poor little thing. Why don't they leave her alone? She's not nuts. Hell, I'd be really crazy if I had gone through what she has.*

Sam gave a light tap on the horn and waved a salute as he pulled into traffic.

Erin turned, gave him a big smile, and, with purpose, walked resolutely toward the building. *Someone might be watching.*

. . .

The rest room was on the first floor.

Erin walked in, locked the door, and took off her back-pack. She took a piece of paper out of the left pocket of her pants and laid it on the counter. She pulled out her cell phone and called the number she had written on the paper.

"Sunshine Cabs."

"I need a cab at the front entrance of the Wharton building."

She listened for moment, "Yes, thank you."

Erin heaved a sigh of relief and pulled a navy cap from her backpack.

She lifted her braids to the top of her head and pulled the cap down over them. Then she tugged at the cap's edges until none of the mahogany-colored whisps showed. *People always say something about my hair; now they won't remember me.*

Erin smiled at her reflection in the mirror.

. . .

She was standing outside in the morning sunshine when the yellow cab pulled up. Erin opened the rear door and put her suitcase and the rod case in the rear seat as she had often seen her Daddy do. She climbed in. "I need to go to the bus station."

The cabbie studied her in the rearview mirror.

"You goin' to the bus station alone?"

Erin spoke rapidly, adding excitement to her voice. "Yes, my aunt Bess and Suzie are coming in from Marietta, Ohio, and I'm going to meet them at the bus. Then we're going to the train station to get a train to the City. Aunt Bess said she's going to show Suzie and me the Statue of Liberty before the terrorists blow it up too." Erin paused to check the driver's reaction.

He had nodded, "Awful thing to have to think about, but these days you just never know."

"We're going to spend two days there, and then we'll come back up here, and Aunt Bess and Suzie will spend the rest of the week with us before they have to go back to Ohio so Suzie can be ready to start school."

"Sounds like a plan." The man pulled the cab into

traffic. "Never saw the statue myself. Moved here from Akron. Been here for six years and never been to New York City."

He made eye contact via the rearview. "Be careful down there, Sis; I hear it can be a mess even on a good day."

"Oh, we will. Aunt Bess grew up in the City, so she is real careful."

"Here we are." He made eye contact again and added a smile. "You owe me six dollars thirty cents, young lady."

Erin passed him a twenty over the seat.

He turned and counted thirteen dollars seventy cents for her.

Erin handed him two of the ones. *My Daddy always tipped everyone.* "Thank you, sir."

"Well thank you, miss. Someone's been teachin' you some manners. You stay real careful now, you hear?"

"I will, sir. Have a good day." She hauled her cases out of the rear seat and started up the walk.

. . .

She carried her things inside the bus station, then paused just inside the door and studied the people behind the counter.

. . .

She walked confidently toward the ticket counter and put her bags down.

Erin stood facing the young blond woman who was talking to the older woman next to her. "And I told him there's just no way."

Erin cleared her throat. "Excuse me please. When is the next bus to Newburgh?"

The blond looked at her schedule. "One that will get you there leaves at 10:15."

Erin looked at her watch. "Okay, I want a ticket on that bus please."

The blond blew a bubble and let it pop, then she frowned and studied Erin. "You alone, kid?"

"Yep." Erin went through her Aunt Bess story again.

The blond bought it.

I don't even know a lady named Bess. I'd better be careful; this lying stuff sure is easy!

The blond handed Erin a ticket and change from her two twenties and turned back toward the older woman. "So I don't have any idea what he will really do."

Erin cleared her throat again. "Excuse me, but where will I get on the bus? I've never been in this station before. . . . If I get lost Aunt Bess will worry, and mom will have a conniption."

The girl frowned and sighed. *Kids! I have enough to do without being a tour guide!* She pointed to her left. "It'll stop right over there."

Erin picked up her cases and walked to the stop.

. . .

She handed the driver her ticket as she boarded the bus and made her way to a seat. *Not many people. Not at all like the subway my Daddy took me on.*

She settled herself and took an apple and a book out of her backpack. *Daddy always said people read so other people wouldn't talk to them. . . . My Daddy almost never read; he liked to hear their stories.*

The older man sitting in the seat in front of Erin turned and looked at her as the bus started to move. "Are you traveling alone, miss?"

"Only to Newburgh, sir. I'll meet Aunt Bess and Suzie there. They're coming in from Ohio. Aunt Bess said she wants to show Suzie and me the Statue of Liberty before someone blows it up."

"Oh, I see. . . . Well, it's certainly worth the trip. Have you seen it before?"

"No, sir."

"Have you been in the City before?"

"My parents took me there a few times."

"And Aunt Suzie; has she been there before?"

"Oh, yes; Aunt Suzie was born there."

"Well, you have a good time, and, when you get there, salute the Lady for me." He paused and studied Erin. "Do you know where she came from? The Lady, I mean."

"No, sir." *I can't act too smart or he'll remember me.*

"Well, the French people made the Lady as a gift for the United States and shipped her over here. They have a miniature of her in Paris, right in the middle of the Seine near the Louvre, that's a famous museum in Paris."

"You sure know a lot about Paris."

"Well, I ought to, young lady. I was born there. I came to our country as a young man in the fifties. I got a job at a news-paper and earned my citizenship here. Eventually I worked my way up until I was in charge of my department." He smiled with memory. "I retired a few years ago. I'm going to visit my daughter today."

He turned back toward the front of the bus. "Yes, sir, Lady Liberty has been mighty good to me and mine."

. . .

Erin got off at Newburg and went to the rest room. She went to a stall and relieved herself, then she opened her backpack and pulled out 4 fifty- dollar bills.

Oh, Daddy, help me. I don't want to worry mommy, but I can't stand it there any longer. . . . Mommy won't leave; she loves it. Help me get to Wellsboro. I have friends there. Ted and Miss Sally will help me. I've told you about them.

Erin paused and chewed her lip a bit.

Ted always tells me to listen to what mommy says, Daddy. But when I tell him about the blackout, he'll know what a mess the City really is. . . . And he likes the country too. He'll listen to me and help me. . . . I can help Sally Ann. You'd like her, Daddy. . . . I'm sorry about telling lies, but it's my only way.

. . .

Erin pulled herself out of her reverie. She walked into the lobby and studied the counter for a few minutes.

The agent she chose this time was a young man who was talking about last night's game.

"I like the Cubs," she told him.

"Ah, the Cubs never get anywhere, kid."

"You wait and see."

"You want something, kid, or you just want to argue about baseball?"

Erin nodded. "I want a ticket to Wellsboro, Pennsylvania. My grandma lives there, and I get to spend two whole weeks of vacation with her before school starts."

Erin rolled her eyes. "Grandma makes the best brownies in the whole wide world." *Mommy would kill me if she heard how I talk, but I have to sound like all the other kids.* "I'll bring you some back with me."

She fingered the four folded fifties that she had added to her pocket. *I hope this is enough with the twenties. I don't want to open my backpack here at the counter.*

"I can get you there, but you'll have to change buses."

"I know how to do that."

"I can get you a straight shot to Corning. You'll have to catch a different bus there to take you south."

"Okay."

He punched some information into his computer and waited while the ticket was printed.

He held it up. "I need a hundred twenty-nine dollars and fourteen cents for a round trip."

Good guess!

Erin handed him three fifties.

He gave her the change and the ticket. "Show this to the driver; he'll punch it and help you remember to get off at Corning. Then give this to the new driver when you head south."

"Okay, thanks a lot."

She started to leave the counter area when she thought of one last detail. "How long until the bus gets here?"

He checked his watch. "You'll have to kill about twenty minutes."

"Thank you." Erin checked her watch. *Better stay out of sight for fifteen minutes. Then I can go to the bus stop and wait.*

She walked back to the rest room.

. . .

Erin was waiting when the bus pulled in.

Mommy is working in her office, doing things for when school opens. . . . I'll go to school in Wellsboro. Ted will help me. . . . I can stay at grandpa Sam's and work for Sally Ann; she said she could use my help anytime. . . . I 'll fish with Ted and help him with Max until they leave for the West. . . . I might even go with them if Ted asks me.

. . .

Erin boarded the bus and found a seat by itself. She opened her backpack and removed a bottle of water, a napkin, and half of a peanut butter and jelly sandwich which she had made before she left the house. . . . *Better save the other half for later. Buses sure take longer than cars. We would be there by now if my Daddy were driving us.*"

Erin took some water and ate her sandwich. She wiped her hands and mouth on the napkin, refolded it, and put it back in her pack.

She took out her book and read a little from *Charlotte's Web.*

She watched Binghamton disappear behind her and looked out the window.

Betcha Mommy called home at lunch. Erin considered that possibility. *Maybe not if she was real busy.* Erin yawned and reached for her water bottle. *Lots of times Mommy gets to working and forgets about what time it is. I hope she forgot today.*

Maria probably hunted me for lunch. I should have thought better. Erin replaced her water bottle. *I didn't write her a note 'cause I didn't want to lie to her. I hope she's okay.*

She fingered the cover of her book.

I'll call home when I get used to things, and then they can come visit me.

The bus finally pulled into Corning.

Daddy always liked Corning. We came here to the glass museum, and another time we went through the art museum that was named for that western guy; that was a nice place. . . . Even mommy liked the little shops along that one street.

. . .

Erin went to the counter. "Excuse me, sir."

The clerk smiled at Erin.

Erin held up the ticket. At the same time her body did an involuntary shiver. *What's that smell? Smells like throw-up.*

Sure enough a man was wheeling a bucket and a mop toward the counter to Erin's right.

Erin angled away from the sight. *I don't want to throw-up too.*

Erin looked at the man behind the counter. "I'm supposed to get on a bus here that will take me to Wellsboro, Pennsylvania. I'm going to my grandma's for a vacation before school starts."

Erin looked at the older man. *Maybe he's a grandpa.* "When will that bus come, sir?"

"It's pulling in right now, miss. Hurry out there and get on. You don't want to miss your grandma."

. . .

Whew. Made it. Wonder how far it is from the bus station to Grandpa Sam's?

Erin got in her backpack and got out her Daddy's address book, not the big one, the little one he always carried with him on their outings.

She looked under the B's.

Sam's address was neatly printed in the first column. Erin said the address to herself. *Thank you, Daddy.*

She stared out the window a bit and then said the address again.

She checked the book. *I got it right!*

She slipped the address book back in her pack, and pulled out the other half of her peanut butter sandwich.

I'll get an ice cream when I get there. Then I'll take a cab to Grandpa Sam's. I'm not sure I can find his house walking; we always drove, but the cab can find it. . . .

I'll have to get me a bike. . . . Matt Thornton will help me.

Erin leaned back and relaxed.
Almost there!

48

They were moving. Ted was never one to drive reck-
lessly, but he knew every intersection, all of the deer crossings,
and every place a responsible person could make some time if he
needed to.

They had a few more in-town twists before they left
Wellsboro on Route 6 toward Mansfield. When they reached NY
17, they could open her up.

Max made a low bark.

Ted smiled to himself. *He knows we're speeding.*

Suddenly Max was standing on the seat over next to the
outside window and was barking hard, hair turned up a little.

"Max, sit down and shut up. I know what I'm doing.
What's wrong with you?"

Max, still barking, remained standing. . . . As they
approached the lane to Sam's house, he began bouncing his front
feet on the seat and then started digging at the window.

Ted swung into Sam's lane and hit the brakes hard,
intentionally throwing Max off balance, making him work to stay
on the seat.

When I get this thing stopped. . .

"What the. . ." Instead of jerking his door open to
correct Max, Ted eased up Sam's lane. "We don't really have
time for this shit, Max, but we'll have to make a quick check
before we call the police."

Ted pulled up beside Sam's front porch.

There was a faint light coming from inside.

Ted shook his head. *I wondered how long it would take.
But of all the nights to trash a dead man's home.*

Ted sighed as he got out of the SUV and opened Max's
door.

He tried the front door. *Locked.*

He listened. *Not a sound.*

He reached for his key and knocked. "This is Ted

Weaver. Open this damn door right now."

. . .

A sleepy little red-haired girl in pajamas opened the door.

"Hi, Maxie." Erin, in the midst of being covered with Labbie kisses, was on the floor with her arms around the strong black neck.

Ted knelt beside them. "Erin, honey, are you okay?"

She wiped at the sleep in her eyes, "Yes, just real tired. I've had a big day."

She smiled up at him. "My Daddy would have called it a whopper."

Ted pulled her to him and kissed her head. He began rocking her in his arms. "How did you get here? Did someone kidnap you?"

Erin wrinkled her nose, "Kidnap?"

"Your mommy thinks you were kidnapped, Erin." He was reaching for his cell as he said it.

"Sally Ann, it's okay. Erin's at Sam's. I don't have the details yet. I need to phone Laura."

"I've finished at your place and was just walking to the car. I'll be right there."

Ted started to punch in Laura's number.

A small hand reached up and placed itself on the phone. "No."

"No, what, Erin?" His voice took on a stern quality. "Your mother is out of her mind with panic, police in two states are hunting you. No, what?"

Erin drew a breath, pulled back from Ted's embrace, and corrected her posture. She looked Ted in the eyes as a single tear started down one cheek. "I won't go back. I've decided to take a sabbatical too. I love it *here*. . . . Here's where where I want to be while I think about things."

She looked at Ted, her eyes pleading for understanding.

She became firm. "I never will stay back there. If you make me go, I'll just run away again; only next time I'll go somewhere else." Her tone was both defiant and forceful.

"Well, what do you expect your mommy to do?"

"We should live here. You know that's what grandpa

Sam really wanted. I've thought about it a lot, and I'm sure; that's why he didn't want his house to be sold. He knew we didn't belong there; he thought pretty soon mommy would understand."

Erin looked at Ted again. "He wanted us here where we could live in peace like he did."

"Mommy had us in the City during the blackout. It was just awful, Ted."

Ted pulled her to him again and began rocking her in his arms. "Well, I need to tell your mother that you're safe."

The tone of his voice lightened but indicated no nonsense, "And I am going to do that now, Erin. And you are going to say something nice to your mother before we get in the car and go to her, so start figuring out what you're going to say."

Ted dialed Laura's number.

49

They headed for Danbury at a slightly slower pace.

Ted and Sally Ann were in the front; Erin and Max in the rear.

"Well, Maxie, Ted is probably never gonna like me again."

Ted glanced at Sally Ann and looked in the rearview. "What makes you think that, Erin?"

She was rubbing Max's chest.

The big Lab was laying down facing Erin. His paws were on her right leg. *Don't worry; she's not going anywhere.*

"'Cause I lied today, and you don't like liars."

"When did you lie, Erin?"

She yawned. "I lied all day long, Ted. I told some big ones to be able to get away."

"Want to tell me about that?"

"Well, first was to Sam, he's my favorite cab driver."

"I love Mr. Sam; he's always been so good to me. I would never lie to him, but I didn't want him to ever get in trouble, so I lied."

Tears ran softly down Erin's cheeks as she told every single thing to Ted and Sally Ann. No detail was omitted.

When she finished, they sat in silence for a while allowing time for each of them to think this thing through as they continued toward Danbury.

"Will I go to Hell now?"

Ted smiled. "I think we can save you, Erin. If I were you, I'd say a prayer tonight and ask God to forgive me and to guide me toward truthfulness."

He checked the mirror again, "Remember when we talked about what it means to repent?"

She nodded.

"Well, repentance might be in order."

Lord, keep me strong; I hate to make this rough for her.

I'm tempted to stop driving and hold her; she must feel pretty awful, and she has to be exhausted, but we sure as hell can't have her running away again.

They rode in silence for a while. Ted suspected Erin might be praying quietly. She took her religion seriously.

. . .

"Did you ever lie, Ted?"

"Yes, I have told lies, Erin. I'm not proud of that."

Erin could see his face by looking into the rearview mirror. "Did you pray for forgiveness?"

"Yes."

They rode again in silence.

. . .

"Well, then wherever I end up, there'll be someone I know. Grandpa Sam and my Daddy are in heaven 'cause they didn't lie."

She looked out the window into the blackness a long while.

Finally the silence was broken by Erin who spoke very quietly, "But if God can't forgive me then he can't forgive you, so it won't be so bad."

Sally Ann looked at Ted.

Tears filled Ted's eyes. "We'll make it, Erin. All of us. God knows we're not perfect. I think He just wants us to try really hard to follow the Commandments the best we can and for us to realize when we make mistakes."

"You sound like Maria."

. . .

Erin twisted in the seat and lay down, her body rested on Max's shoulders.

Her thumb did an unnatural thing; it went to her mouth.

She began making light, little girl snores.

50

They arrived in Danbury at three in the morning.

Dr. Bratten had insisted that Laura resist her strong temptation to immediately impress upon Erin the error of her ways. "Everyone will need rest; yourself included. So allow everyone to rest. Listen carefully to her explanation in the light of day."

"Make no harsh statements. Put no guilt on her. Listen, listen, listen. Put yourself in her place. Then talk with me before you take any action regarding her adventure. This family has experienced more than enough guilt and punishment for the time being."

Maria immediately showed everyone the layout and indicated where each would spend the night.

Erin would be back in her own room with Max.

Dr. Bratten was delighted that the dog was there. "Let him sleep with her tonight. It will give her someone to talk things over with."

He had made eye contact with Laura. "Unconditional love is a wonderful healer."

By mid-afternoon of the following day, everyone was awake.

Dr. Bratten, concerned about Laura's ability to follow his advice, had returned to Laura's home.

Erin had told her story.

Decisions had been made.

Ted, Sally Ann, and Max would remain in Danbury to sleep that night.

The following day Laura, Erin, and Maria would follow them back to Wellsboro to spend some quiet time at Sam's.

51

Once back in Wellsboro, Sally Ann cooked dinner for the five of them at her home. It was a simple dinner of roasted chicken with trimmings, the kind of home-cooked taste each of them needed to help settle the tension of Erin's little adventure.

As they finished, Sally Ann suggested they go to the living room; she wanted to visit a bit. She would bring fresh coffee and apple pie later.

When everyone was comfortable, Sally Ann cleared her throat. "Bear with me; I'm not very polished," she tried to smile, but there were tears in her eyes, "especially when I'm real nervous."

She cleared her throat again. "I don't want to hurt anyone's feelings."

She looked at her hands. "Lord knows I love each of you, but I'm not going to beat around the bush."

She paused to look around the group. "Fact is: Erin is the bravest among us."

She noted that Laura and Ted exchanged glances.

"She is, and the smartest too. She's smart enough to realize that the way we've been living is not healthy, and she's brave enough to try to do something about it."

Sally Ann gave Erin a big smile. "We're all in the same boat, honey. Each one of us feels alone. And each one of us is struggling, in his own way, to get past a great big hurt."

She looked at each of them. "I'm trying to bury my loneliness in a sandwich shop."

She looked at her hands again. "I hurt because my little boy, Charlie was killed by a drunk driver just when he was in his teens and was beginning to turn into a fine young man."

"Then the mourning of his son's death and dealing with the conflicts of divided loyalty weakened Charles. You see, one of his men had caused the accident. Charles felt both the parental need to punish and the duty to protect one of his men. The emotional struggle fueled the stroke which actually killed my Charles."

She focused on Ted. "Ted is trying to bury his loneliness by teaching, and coaching, and guiding, and volunteering; anything to keep too busy to have much time to think about the past."

She turned. "Laura, you are a strong woman, a good woman, so much like Sam in some ways. But you're mostly too strong for your own good. You aren't just trying to bury your loneliness; you're actually walling it in, refusing to acknowledge it. You keep everyone and all memories at a safe distance, trying to protect yourself from past, present, and future pain."

Sally Ann took time to wipe her eyes and her nose with a flowered handkerchief from her apron pocket. "You used alcohol as a kind of filter to keep your emotions dull enough that you could handle them. You weren't really living, at least not fully; you even kept a certain distance from Erin. I've seen it with my own eyes."

Sally Ann shifted her eye contact to Erin and Maria who were sharing the love seat. Maria's arm was around Erin's shoulders, hugging her in an easy closeness. "You two are the healthiest ones here."

She wiped her eyes again and bit her lip. "You two and Max."

She sniffed. "The three of you aren't afraid to love fully and to show that love."

She paused to frame her thoughts. "It's obvious to me that Maria loves Erin with her whole heart."

"And Erin. Erin cherishes the memory of her Daddy, no matter how much it hurts sometimes. She loves you, Laura, and Maria. She gives of herself to everyone she comes in contact with; look how she tried to protect her cab driver."

Sally Ann looked directly at Erin. "'A little child shall lead them.'" She shook her head. "You're the bravest among us, Erin; you really are."

Sally Ann stood up and moved behind her wingback chair, placing her hands on its back for some support. "Now it's time for us to quit this shit."

Each of their faces immediately mirrored Erin's in

showing shock at hearing Miss Sally say a bad word.

"It's getting us nowhere. We're all alone, and we're all lonely because we've been hurt so much that we're afraid to trust, to let ourselves get really close to anyone again."

She drew a deep breath and continued. "We need to form a family."

She allowed time for the idea to register, then continued, "Now don't laugh. I'm not talking about adoption or marriage or anything like that. I'm talking about becoming an informal family of five people who will dare to open their hearts to each other, five people who know that they each can trust and depend on the other four for anything which we can offer. Like Dr. Bratten said, 'unconditional love.'"

She looked at her hands for a moment. "All good psychiatrists talk a lot about unconditional love."

She focused on Laura. "Oh, yes, Laura; I know what you're going through; I've done my time on the couch too."

She drew a deep breath and looked off above their heads, out the large picture window. "Well, here goes, Sam. You laid this on me. Now help me find the right words."

. . .

"Laura, in my heart, I think you need to quit hiding from your memories and move here to Wellsboro where Erin obviously feels safe. Use Sam's house until you find the perfect place. Do what Ted is doing, take a sabbatical so you aren't afraid of burning your bridges. But commit to moving here for a year, so none of us will have to go through this again with Erin."

"I know this closeness thing will take time. And it wouldn't be good for you to just sit in Sam's house all of the time, but I also happen to know that our high school is desperate to fill the art teacher's position. Fill it. Get back in the classroom where you have to deal with people. Don't stay locked away in an office somewhere."

"Maria, you're in this country all alone. I would love for you to come into the shop with me. I'll give you half of it, legally. I'll still help, but I won't live there all hours of the day and night keeping myself too busy to think about things. And I certainly don't expect you to live there either. We'll hire more help, so we can develop sensible lives here."

She turned to Ted. "Ted, don't think I'm working up to trying to talk you into staying. It's no secret that you need a sabbatical. Follow your plan. Leave. Spend time alone, not surrounded by teenage boys. . . . Find a good counselor. Don't try to heal yourself. As it is you spend all of your time trying to take care of everyone but yourself. . . . You're important too, you know."

She took another pause, then looked off into space. "I remember once when a man who is both generous and wise told me that Max's primary purpose in life was to stay alive and healthy so he would be available to help when asked. . . . Well, it's that way with people too, Ted Weaver."

She looked back toward Laura. "I was talking to Jim Pierson at the board office the other day; Jim's school board president, Laura. I came right out and asked him about the art teacher's job; he's in a time crunch this year trying to find a qualified teacher before school starts."

She stopped for breath and, again, looked toward the ceiling. "There, now, Sam; I'm running everyone's business."

She brought her eyes back down to the group. "I am dead serious. Erin has given each of us one chance to see how sick we each are."

"We're not living; we're going through the motions, so afraid of getting hurt again that we refuse to grab life."

She looked fiercely at each of them. "Do it. We all need to remember our loved ones, but we have to begin living in the present."

She turned from the group. "Now I'm going to make a fresh pot of coffee and cut the pie."

She stopped and looked back. "I want us to talk about things, important things, before you leave here tonight."

She turned and started for her kitchen, then paused at the door. "Erin, dear, would you come help me a little? I've had a pretty big day for an old lady."

. . .

Sally Ann took her time making coffee, noting that it

was quiet in the living room. Finally, she returned with a tray filled with apple pie and fresh drinks for everyone.

"How about it, Maria? Will you come be a partner with an old know-it-all like me?"

"Oh, Miss Sally. You are not a know-it-all. You are an angel."

Maria looked at Laura, then back toward Sally Ann. "I will not leave Laura if she needs me in Danbury, but if Laura moves here, I would love to work with you and make friends in this town."

Maria smiled at Sally Ann. "Maybe someday I could have a house of my own, and my family could come visit me here in America instead of my always going to Spain to visit them."

Maria looked thoughtfully around the room. "America is my home now."

Sally Ann took courage where she had found it. "So, Ted, are you sure you can make it without kids for an entire school year?"

Ted swallowed hard. He took a bite of pie before answering. "I have a job waiting for me in a fly shop in West Yellowstone starting December first. Max and I plan to take our time driving out."

Max thumped his tail.

Laura swallowed some coffee. "Sally Ann. Where in the world is all of this coming from? Do you really think we should all just drop our lives and start again from scratch?"

Sally Ann smiled and, surprisingly, nodded in agreement. "Yes. Something like that, Laura."

She looked at Erin. "When that little girl is smart enough to know things have to change, and she has enough gumption to strike off on her own, I think we'd all better listen up."

She cleared her throat. "You know I listen to a man called Imus on the radio in the mornings while I'm making desserts for the shop. He has that ranch for kids with cancer that your dad left money to. Well, he has a saying, 'How's that workin' for you?' . . . Maybe it's time we all took a look at our lives and answered that question. Are you living each day of your life the way you would want to if it were your last?"

She looked at each of them.

After a pause during which Sally Ann tried to gauge Laura's feelings, she plowed on. "And, Erin, I want you to promise that, if all of this happens, we won't *ever again* have to be scared half to death wondering where you are. Will you stay here and not pull any more runaways no matter what?"

"It's what I want. I don't want to be afraid any more." Erin swallowed and looked at her mother. "It's why I came here, mommy. ... I wasn't mad at you. ... I just don't want to be afraid every day."

"I know we have to be strong and brave, but I'm tired, and almost everyone in the City is nervous and scared too. Look how they first thought the blackout was the terrorists again."

She twisted her little hands. "Planes, blackouts, alerts. When will they hit us next?"

Once started, Sally Ann was not going to back off, "So, Laura, I know this would be a big step for you. Do you think you can do it? ... Do you even want to try? ... Or are things working out fine for you just as they are?"

Laura looked at Erin. "Erin are you sure? You'll be giving up a whole lot to move to a small town."

Erin came to Laura and climbed up on her lap, something she hadn't done for a long time. She turned and put her arms around Laura's neck. "Hold me, Mommy. ... Mommy, I love you. I just want us to be safe." She hesitated for a minute. "But not if it means you have to drink again."

Laura returned the hug. "No, honey, that's over. I will never drink again. I almost did when I was frantic with hunting for you, but I didn't."

She sighed at the memory. "If I could make it through that, when I thought the most precious thing in my life had been taken from me, I can stay sober through anything." She tightened her arms around Erin and kissed her cheek. "Anything but losing you."

. . .

Laura turned and smiled at Sally Ann, a warm, open smile, covering a bit of fear, but tinged with more than the beginning of love and admiration.

"Whew, Sally Ann, I can see why you and dad got along so well. You're what he would have called 'hell on wheels' when you're worked up." Her smile deepened as did the warmth in her eyes. "You sure it was your husband who was the decorated war hero?"

Ted agreed. "I've only seen you like this two other times. One was when you were sure Sam and I were going to get Max hurt."

"Well, when you're in the Army, and, don't ever be fooled; the whole family is in the Army. When you're in the Army, you learn to stand your ground and get it off your chest while you can still do something about it."

Ted looked at Laura. "Max and I have planned to be here through the Memorial Service; then we'll load up and head on out."

He was quiet for a while. "What would you do about your home and apartment?"

"I'll keep them during the sabbatical, just in case. But I will try it here for a year for Erin's sake."

"You sure you can get one? A sabbatical?"

Laura nodded. "My superintendent urged me to take one two years ago and again last year."

She paused. "Not to come here, of course, but to take time off and go somewhere where the memories weren't so strong. Erin's counselor recommended it then too, and she talked with me about it again this past summer."

She looked at her hands for a while, then raised her head. "Sally Ann is probably right. Dr. Bratten has suggested the same things. Everyone can't be wrong."

Laura turned to look at Maria. "Are you sure this will work for you, Maria? Have you ever lived in a small town?"

"Oh, Laura, I think it will be fine for each of us; I grew up in a small village. My family moved to the city when all of us were out of high school. My parents were very protective."

"Well, then, we'll just lock up and set the alarms. We'll bring only our clothing and a few personal items. Dad's place isn't as big as we're used to, but we'll come see if things are better for us here."

Laura drew a long breath. "I feel so tired; I don't think I could face sorting, selling, moving, and worrying that I had made the wrong decision. But if this is really a trial and we can run back next year if we want to, I'll do my best."

Maria patted Laura's arm. "It will be good, Laura. I know it will. We can move here with little effort if we do as you suggested. We will not decide in haste. We will evaluate when school is out next summer."

Maria then turned to Sally Ann and searched her face for understanding. "I will work at the sandwich shop with you, Sally Ann, but I will sleep at Laura's. This is not the time for promises or permanent decisions."

. . .

The most amazing thing about the evening was the amount of time it *didn't take* for each of them to make the decision to change their lives.

Once Sally Ann had laid out the facts, everyone seemed to realize she was right: health meant living in the present.

. . .

School would open soon.

The move was a whirlwind.

Laura, Maria, and Erin went home to Danbury.

Each of them packed what she wanted to bring.

Erin included Nick's sweaters.

Laura requested and received a year's sabbatical.

. . .

Laura interviewed and was hired to teach high school art and photography.

. . .

A surprisingly small moving van brought their things to Wellsboro.

They were "home" within nine days.

Thankfully, Sam's house had three bedrooms, a den, a library, and the big playroom upstairs.

Laura contracted with Bud Johnson to turn the second floor into a suite for her. She wanted a bedroom, a bath with a whirlpool, two walk-in closets, and a darkroom.

Bud would do it first thing during his off season.

Maria began a routine of cooking breakfast for all of them each day; then she left for Sally Ann's.

Understanding that Laura had to become more responsible for herself and Erin, Maria allowed Laura to be in charge of their evening meal while Maria tidied the house and took care of laundry.

Laura began looking for easy recipes in her mother's old cookbook and asking for suggestions in the teacher's lounge. She called Sally Ann when she needed help.

Sally Ann promised to come by each Friday night for supper before the ball game.

. . .

Erin saw Matt Thornton the first day of school.

He assured her that he would keep an eye out for her. "If anyone gives you any guff, you just tell me about it. They sometimes like to test the new kids. We'll show 'em you're no wimp."

. . .

Dr. Bratten was delighted. He recommended an excellent semi-retired psychiatrist who taught in the neighboring town at Mansfield University.

Dr. James Turner agreed to begin seeing two private patients: Laura and Sally Ann.

Jamie found a good child psychologist who had just moved to Wellsboro and was working out of her home.

Erin could walk there after school.

. . .

Erin unexpectedly volunteered not only to attend the second anniversary ceremonies but also to participate.

52

Thursday, September 11, 2003, was a beautiful, but solemn day in the City. A bright blue sky, clear of clouds, blanketed the area that had become known as the Pit.

Thousands of mourners encircled it for the second Memorial Service.

Vice President Cheney had planned to be there.

City officials had respectfully asked that he not come; they didn't want the thousands of others to have to pass through the extra-tight security which his visit would mandate; they didn't want people to have to begin arriving at 5:00 a.m. as they had the previous year.

The names of all those who were thought to have perished in the Towers were to be read at the hallowed ground that had become the final resting place for so many.

Erin stood quietly in the line.

Watch now, Daddy. This is for you and your buddies. I won't cry; 'cause I know you're in heaven.

. . .

I wore this green dress just for you, Daddy; I know it was your favorite color. . . . See, I wore my fishing vest too. Mommy said I could if I really wanted to.

. . .

She's getting a lot better, Daddy.

A sigh escaped. *We're gonna make it.*

Happy tears stung her eyes, but Erin blinked them back.

You'll be proud when you hear me. The city sent me an audio tape to practice with so I'd say each of the names just right for the families.

And, Daddy, after the ceremonies, we're going back to our new home at grandpa Sam's in Wellsboro.

I won't come here to visit you much, but we'll still talk every night right after my prayers.

. . .

Erin began walking toward the lectern with her partner.

She stood straight and found Laura, Maria, Ted, Sally Ann, and Matt Thornton in the audience.

She pronounced every name clearly and perfectly.

. . .

"And last, my Daddy, Francis Nicholas McCort. I'll always love you, Daddy."

As she turned to leave the lectern, Erin noticed a single male hummingbird come over her right shoulder close enough that she heard it. The hummer landed on one of the roses fastened to the fence surrounding the Pit.

Her serene little face broke into a warm smile.

I knew you'd come if you could.

Discussion Topics

1. Describe Erin's former relationship with her Daddy.
How does she attempt to maintain their relationship?

2. How have Laura's actions, Rowdy's death, and Sam's death compounded Erin's sense of loss?

3. Why does Laura surround herself with a wall which "even little Erin cannot fully penetrate"?
What does this wall provide for Laura?
What does this wall steal from Laura?

4. What restrictions does Laura place on the relationship between Jamie, Erin's counselor, and Erin?
Evaluate such restrictions.

5. Why does Ted begin a relationship with Erin?
With Laura?

6. What is Ted's approach to empowering Erin?
Is this a reasonable approach? Explain.

7. Is Ted overstepping his bounds when he tells Erin that she should talk openly with her counselor?

8. Does Ted's desire to nurture kids mask an opportunity to manipulate them?
Is his approach healthy for the kids? For him?

9. Why does this man stay so busy? What are his own conclusions regarding this?

10. What do the welcome sign and decorations
in Sally Ann's sandwich shop reveal about Sally Ann?

11. Why did Sam and Sally Ann decide that Ted
should have Max?

12. What were the unusual provisions in Sam's will?
Was he trying to control from the grave?
What were his motivations?

13. Why did Lindy come to Teddy's grave that night?
What did the encounter do for Lindy?
In the long run, did this encounter help or hurt Ted?

14. Describe incidents of Erin's anger--with Ted,
with Max, with the terrorists, with Maria.
In each case how did she attempt to defuse her anger?
Why does she use each method?

15. After Matt 'rats' on Judd, Ted tells Matt that he
did the right thing by placing more "value on a friend than he
does on friendship." p. 218
What does he mean? Can the distinction be made?

16. On p. 232, Dr. Shonk says he will run the war or
he won't treat Judd.
Is such arrogance justified?
Do you think he meant what he said?

17. On page 307, Ted tells Erin that Judd needed a
break from 'the pressure to get well.'
Explain and discuss this phrase.
What are the benefits of 'living in the present' for one who is
trying to heal?

18. What do the contents of Ted's treasure chest, "nothing of value; just things that are priceless," tell you about Ted? p. 274

What "priceless" possession of yours comes to mind?

19. Why did Ted leave this with Erin?

20. Analyze Erin's decision to run away.

Is she just 'acting out'? Does she want to cause pain? Does she act in haste? To what degree is she reasonable?

21. Have you faced a major loss in your life?

Did it have 'carry-over' effects?

What factors determine how one best copes with a major loss?

Is there a formula?

22. Laura agrees to try completely changing her life.

Is this dramatic change better or worse than 'sticking it out?'

What less dramatic changes do regular people make in their lives when things don't seem to be working well?

23. On page 282, recalling Laura's justification for making Erin attend the first Memorial, Erin decides *Respect is remembering, not forgetting.* Is remembering, and thus acknowledging, necessary for sound mental health?

How important is 'a willing vulnerability' to the quality of humanity?

24. How do we rear our children to be more resilient, to resist seeing themselves as victims without inadvertently encouraging them to develop either walls of protection or agressive behavior?

Order Form

**Sigurd Press; 12652 Maysville-Williams Rd.;
Logan, Ohio 43138   (740) 385-3963**
*The Author will pay shipping on single orders from
this page.*
Phone regarding bookstore/book club discounts.

PLEASE PRINT!   Date _____

Please send _____ copies of *The Green Drake :*

Name _____

Street _____

City _____, State _____

Zip _____ Phone (____) _____ - _____.

Cost per book $16.02 ($15.00 cover price plus and $1.02,
Ohio Sales Tax @ 6.75%

# of copies _____ times $16.02 = $_____
Total enclosed. **Checks only.** $ _____

Check # _____

Thank you very much for wanting to share *The
Green Drake.*
**I will visit book clubs on a cost-sharing basis.
Carolyn Johnson**